PENNSYLVANIA COUNTRY STREAM
by Nita Engle

BEST
SELLERS

BEST SELLERS

**FROM READER'S DIGEST
CONDENSED BOOKS**

THE READER'S DIGEST ASSOCIATION
Pleasantville, New York

READER'S DIGEST CONDENSED BOOKS
Editor: John T. Beaudouin
Executive Editor: Joseph W. Hotchkiss
Managing Editor: Anthony Wethered
Senior Staff Editors: Ann Berryman, Noel Rae, John S. Zinsser, Jr.
Senior Editors: Anne H. Atwater, Doris E. Dewey, Tanis H. Erdmann, Fredrica S. Friedman,
Sigrid MacRae, Barbara J. Morgan, Marjorie Palmer, Robert L. Reynolds, Margery D. Thorndike,
Frances C. Travis, Angela Weldon
Associate Editors: Barbara Bradshaw, Catherine T. Brown, Linn Carl, Istar H. Dole,
Olive Farmer, Thomas Froncek, Virginia Rice, John R. Roberson,
Patricia Nell Warren, Angela C. Woods
Assistant Editor: Thea R. Crouch
Art Editor: William Gregory
Senior Art Editors: Marion Davis, Soren Noring, Thomas Von Der Linn
Associate Art Editor: Angelo Perrone
Art Research: George Calas, Jr., Katherine Kelleher
Senior Copy Editors: Jean E. Aptakin, Estelle T. Dashman, Alice Murtha
Associate Copy Editors: Claire A. Bedolis, Dorothy G. Flynn, Jean S. Friedman, Jeane Garment
Assistant Copy Editors: Jean G. Cornell, Clara E. Serton

CB PROJECTS
Executive Editor: Herbert H. Lieberman
Senior Editors: Marion C. Conger, Sherwood Harris, Ray Sipherd, John E. Walsh
Associate Editor: Carol Tarlow

Reader's Digest Condensed Books are published every two to three months at Pleasantville, N.Y.

The condensations in this volume have been created by The Reader's Digest
Association, Inc., and are used by permission of and special arrangement with
the publishers and the holders of the respective copyrights.

With the exception of actual personages identified as such, the characters and
incidents in the fictional selections in this volume are entirely the products of the
authors' imaginations and have no relation to any person or event in real life.

The original editions of the books in this volume are published and copyrighted as follows:
The Key to Rebecca, published at $12.95 by William Morrow and Company, Inc.
© 1980 by Fineblend N. V.

The Aviator, published at $10.95 by Arbor House Publishing Company
© 1981 by Ernest K. Gann

© 1981 by The Reader's Digest Association, Inc.
All rights reserved, including the right to reproduce this book or parts thereof in any form.
Printed in the United States of America.

CONTENTS

7
THE KEY TO REBECCA
by Ken Follett
PUBLISHED BY WILLIAM MORROW & COMPANY

157
THE AVIATOR
by Ernest K. Gann
PUBLISHED BY ARBOR HOUSE PUBLISHING COMPANY

The Key to Rebecca

Cairo, 1942.
The hunter: a British major. His quarry: a Nazi spy.
At stake: the outcome of the desert war.

A condensation of the novel by
Ken Follett

Illustrated by Kevin Tweddell

Midsummer. A hot, dusty wind is blowing in from the desert. And Major William Vandam is no closer to catching the German spy than when he started.

He has frighteningly little to go on: a bloody corpse, a name, a vague description—nothing more. Meanwhile, Rommel's armies are pushing closer to Cairo every day, and there seems to be no way to stop them.

Because Rommel knows in advance every move the British are planning.

Because Major Vandam has failed to unlock the German code.

And because, in this deadly game of hide-and-seek, the spy keeps wriggling out of Vandam's grasp. . . .

"The action is fast, furious, the plotting clever and devious, the excitement mounts and even the minor characters come alive." —*Publishers Weekly*

"Our spy in Cairo is the greatest hero of them all."
—Field Marshal Erwin Rommel, September 1942

Chapter 1

THE last camel collapsed at noon.

It was the five-year-old white bull he had bought in Jalo, the youngest and strongest of the three beasts, and the least ill tempered; he liked the animal as much as a man could like a camel, which is to say that he hated it only a little.

They climbed the leeward side of a small hill, man and camel planting big clumsy feet in the inconstant sand, and at the top they stopped. They looked ahead, seeing nothing but another hillock to climb, and after that a thousand more, and it was as if the camel despaired at the thought. Its forelegs folded, then its rear went down, and it couched on top of the hill like a monument, staring across the empty desert with the indifference of the dying.

The man hauled on its nose rope, but it would not get up. The man went behind and kicked its hindquarters. Finally he took out a razor-sharp curved bedouin knife with a narrow point and stabbed the camel's rump. Blood flowed, but the camel did not even look around.

The man understood what was happening. The animal's body, starved of nourishment, had simply stopped working, like a machine that has run out of fuel. He had seen camels collapse like this on the outskirts of an oasis, surrounded by life-giving foliage which they ignored, lacking the energy to eat.

It was time to stop, anyway. The sun was high and fierce. The long Saharan summer was beginning, and the midday temperature would reach 110 degrees in the shade. Without unloading the camel, the man opened one of the saddlebags and took out his tent. He pitched it beside the dying camel, there on top of the hillock.

He sat cross-legged in the open end of the tent, gnawed at some dates, and watched the camel die while he waited for the sun to pass overhead. His tranquillity was practiced. He had come more than a thousand miles in this desert. Two months earlier he had left El Agheila, on the Mediterranean coast of Libya, and traveled due south for five hundred miles, via Jalo and Kufra, into the empty heart of the Sahara. There he had turned east and crossed the border into Egypt unobserved by man or beast. He had turned north near Kharga; now he was not far from his destination. He knew the desert and was afraid of it—all intelligent men were. But he never allowed that fear to panic him. There were always catastrophes: mistakes in navigation that made you miss a well by a couple of miles; water bags that leaked or burst; apparently healthy camels that got sick. The only response was to say *Inshallah*—it is the will of God.

Eventually the sun began to dip toward the west. He looked at the camel's load, wondering how much of it he could carry. There were three small European suitcases, leather, two heavy and one light, all of them important. There was a little bag of clothes, a sextant, maps, food, a goatskin water bag. It was already too much; he would have to abandon the tent, the blanket, the cooking pot.

He made the three suitcases into a bundle and tied the clothes, the food and the sextant on top, strapping everything together with a length of cloth. He could put his arms through the cloth straps and carry the whole lot like a rucksack on his back. He slung the water bag around his neck. It was a heavy load.

Three months earlier he would have been able to carry it all day, then play tennis in the evening, but the desert had weakened him. His bowels were water, his skin was a mass of sores, and he had lost twenty pounds. Without the camel he could not go far.

He started walking. He followed his compass wherever it led, resisting the temptation to divert around the hills, for he was navigating by dead reckoning over the final miles, and a fractional error could take him a fatal few hundred yards astray.

The day cooled into evening. The water bag became lighter around his neck as he consumed its contents. He knew there was not enough for another day. Behind him, the sun sank lower and turned into a big yellow balloon. A little later a white moon appeared in a purple sky. He thought about stopping. Nobody could walk all night. But he had no tent, no blanket. And he was sure he was close to the well: by his reckoning he should have been there.

He walked on. His calm was deserting him now. He had set his strength and his expertise against the ruthless desert, and it began to look as if the desert would win. He could no longer repress the fear. When death became inevitable he would rush to meet it. Not for him the hours of agony and encroaching madness. He had his knife. He seemed to see his mother in the distance, hear a railway train that chugged along with his heartbeat, slowly. Small rocks moved in his path like scampering rats. He smelled roast lamb. He breasted a rise and saw the fire over which the meat had been roasted, and a small boy beside it gnawing the bones. There were the tents around the fire, the hobbled camels and the wellhead beyond. He walked into the hallucination. The people in the dream looked up at him, startled. A tall man stood up and spoke. The traveler pulled at his *howli*, partially unwinding the cloth to reveal his face.

The tall man stepped forward, shocked, and said, "My cousin!"

The traveler understood that this was not, after all, an illusion; and he smiled faintly and collapsed.

When he awoke at dawn he thought for a moment that he was a boy again, and that his adult life had been a dream.

Someone was touching his shoulder and saying, "Wake up, Achmed," in the language of the desert. Nobody had called him Achmed for years. He realized he was wrapped in a coarse blanket and lying on the cold sand, his head swathed in a *howli*. He opened his eyes to see the gorgeous sunrise like a straight rainbow against the flat black horizon. The icy morning wind blew into his face. In that instant he experienced again all the confusion and anxiety of his fifteenth year.

He had felt utterly lost, that first time he woke up in the desert. He had thought, *My father is dead,* and then, *I have a new father.*

Snatches of the Koran had run through his head, mixed with bits of the Christian creed which his mother still taught him secretly, in German, which was also the language of his dead father. He remembered the long train journey, wondering what his new desert cousins would be like, and whether they would despise his pale body and his city ways. He had walked out of the railway station and seen the two Arabs, sitting beside their camels in the dust of the station yard, covered in robes from head to foot except for the slit in the *howli* which revealed their dark, unreadable eyes. They had taken him to the well. It had been terrifying; nobody had spoken to him except in gestures. But although these were hard men they were not unkind. They had believed he could not speak their language, which was why they had tried to communicate with him in signs.

All these thoughts had run through his mind as he looked at his first desert sunrise, and they came back again now, twenty years later, with the words, "Wake up, Achmed," spoken by his boyhood companion.

He sat up abruptly, his head clearing. He had crossed the desert on a vitally important mission. He had found the well, and it had not been a hallucination: his cousins were here, as they always were at this time of the year. He suffered a sudden sharp panic as he thought of his precious baggage—had he still been carrying it when he arrived?—then he saw it, piled neatly at his feet.

Ishmael, squatting beside him, said, "Heavy worries, Cousin."

Achmed nodded. "There is a war."

Ishmael went away. One of the women subserviently brought Achmed tea. He took it without thanking her and drank it quickly. He ate some cold boiled rice while the unhurried work of the encampment went on around him. It seemed that this nomad branch of the family was still wealthy: there were several servants, many children, many sheep and more than twenty camels.

Achmed finished his breakfast and checked his baggage. He opened one of the heavy suitcases, and when he looked in at the switches and dials of the compact radio he had a sudden vivid memory like a movie: the frantic city of Berlin; a tree-lined street called the Tirpitzufer; a four-story sandstone building; a maze of hallways; an office; a prematurely white-haired admiral who said, "Rommel wants me to put an agent into Cairo."

The case also contained a book, a novel in English. Idly Achmed read the first line: "Last night I dreamt I went to Manderley again." A folded sheet of paper fell out from between the leaves of the novel. Carefully Achmed picked it up and put it back. He closed the book, replaced it in the case and closed the case.

Ishmael was standing at his shoulder. "Was it a long journey?" Achmed nodded. "I came from Libya. From the sea."

"From the sea!" Ishmael was awestruck: he had never seen the sea. He said, "But why?"

"It is to do with this war."

"One gang of Europeans fighting with another over who shall sit in Cairo— What does this matter to the sons of the desert?"

"My mother's people are in the war," Achmed said.

"A man should follow his father."

"And if he has two fathers?"

Ishmael shrugged. He understood dilemmas.

Achmed lifted the suitcase. "Will you keep this for me?"

"Yes." Ishmael took it. "Who is winning the war?"

"My mother's people. They are like the nomads—they are proud and cruel and strong. They are going to rule the world."

The two cousins looked at one another. It was five years since they had met. The world had changed. Achmed thought of the things he could tell: the crucial meeting in Beirut in 1938, his trip to Berlin, his great coup in Istanbul. . . . None of it would mean anything to his cousin—and Ishmael was probably thinking the same about events of *his* last five years. As boys they had loved each other fiercely, but they had never had anything to talk about.

After a moment Ishmael turned away and took the suitcase to his tent. Achmed fetched a little water in a bowl. He opened the bag of clothes and took out a small piece of soap, a brush, a mirror and a razor. He stuck the mirror in the sand, adjusted it, and began to unwind the *howli* from around his head.

The sight of his face in the mirror shocked him.

His strong, normally clear forehead was covered with sores. His dark beard grew matted and unkempt on his fine-boned cheeks, and the skin of his large hooked nose was red and split. He parted his blistered lips and saw that his small, even teeth were filthy.

He brushed the soap on his beard and began to shave. Gradually his old face emerged. It was strong rather than handsome, and normally wore a look which he recognized—in his more detached moments—to be faintly dissolute; but now it was simply ravaged.

He carried the bag into Ishmael's tent. He took off his desert robes and donned a white English shirt, a striped tie, gray socks and a brown checkered suit. When he tried to put on the shoes he discovered that his feet had swollen; it was agonizing to attempt to force them into the hard new leather. In the end, he slit the shoes with his curved knife and wore them loose.

He wanted more: a hot bath, a haircut, cool soothing cream for his sores, a silk shirt, a gold bracelet, a cold bottle of champagne and a warm soft woman. For those he would have to wait.

When he emerged from the tent the nomads looked at him as if he were a stranger. Ishmael came to him. The cousins embraced.

Achmed took a wallet from the pocket of his jacket to check his papers. Looking at the identity card, he realized that once again he was Alexander Wolff, age thirty-four, of Villa les Oliviers, Garden City, Cairo; a businessman; ancestry—European.

He put on his hat, picked up the two remaining cases—one heavy, one light—and set off to walk across the last few miles of desert to the town.

THE ancient caravan route, which Wolff had followed from oasis to oasis across the vast empty desert, led through a mountain pass and at last merged with a modern road. On one side were the yellow, dusty, barren hills; on the other were lush fields of cotton squared off with irrigation ditches, where the peasants bent over their crops. Walking north on the road, smelling the cool damp breeze off the nearby Nile, observing the increasing signs of urban civilization, Wolff began to feel human again. Finally he heard the engine of a car, and he knew he had made it.

The vehicle was approaching him from the direction of Asyut, the town. It was a military jeep. As it came closer he saw the British army uniforms of the men in it, and he realized he had left behind one danger only to face another.

Deliberately he made himself calm. I have every right to be here, he thought. I was born in Alexandria. I am Egyptian by nationality. I own a house in Cairo. My papers are genuine. I am a wealthy man, a European and a German spy behind enemy lines.

The jeep screeched to a halt in a cloud of dust. One of the men jumped out. He had three cloth pips on each shoulder of his uniform shirt: a captain. He walked with a limp.

The captain said, "Where the devil have you come from?"

Wolff put down his cases and jerked a thumb back over his shoulder. "My car broke down on the desert road."

"I'd better see your papers, please."

Wolff handed them over. The captain examined them, then looked up. "You seem all in, Mr. Wolff. How long have you been walking?"

"Since yesterday afternoon," he said with a weariness that was not entirely faked. "I got a bit lost."

"You've been out here all *night*? Good Lord, you'd better have a lift with us." The captain turned to the jeep. "Corporal, take the gentleman's cases."

Wolff opened his mouth to protest, then shut it again abruptly. A man who had been walking all night would be only too glad to have someone take his luggage. As the corporal hefted the bags into the back of the jeep, Wolff realized with a sinking feeling that he had not even bothered to lock them. How could I be so stupid? he thought. He knew the answer. He was still in tune with the desert, where the last thing anyone wanted to steal was a radio transmitter that had to be plugged in to a power outlet. Now he had to think of policemen and papers and locks and lies. He resolved to take more care, and climbed into the jeep.

The captain got in beside him and said to the driver, "Back into town." To Wolff he said, "By the way, I'm Captain Newman." He stuck out his hand.

Wolff shook it and looked closely at the man. He was young—early twenties, at a guess—with a boyish forelock and a ready smile; but there was in his demeanor the weary maturity that comes early to fighting men. Wolff asked him, "Seen any action?"

"Some." Captain Newman touched his lame leg. "Did this in the Libyan Desert at Cyrenaica. That's why they sent me to this one-horse town." He grinned. "Where does your accent come from?"

The sudden question took Wolff by surprise. It had been intended to, he thought; Captain Newman was sharp-witted. Fortunately Wolff had a prepared answer. "My parents were Boers who came from South Africa to Egypt. I grew up speaking Afrikaans and Arabic." He hesitated, nervous of seeming too eager to explain. "The name Wolff is Dutch, originally."

Newman seemed politely interested. "What brings you here?"

"I have business interests in several towns up the river." He smiled. "I like to pay them surprise visits."

They were entering Asyut. By Egyptian standards it was a large town, with factories, hospitals, a Moslem university and some sixty thousand inhabitants. Wolff nearly asked to be dropped at the railway station when Newman saved him from that error. "We'll take you to Nasif's garage," the captain said. "He has a tow truck."

Wolff forced himself to say, "Thank you." He swallowed dryly. He was still not thinking fast enough. It's the desert, he thought; it's slowed me down. He looked at his watch. He had time to go through a charade at the garage and still catch the daily train three hundred miles north to Cairo. He would have to go into the place until the soldiers drove away. He would make inquiries about car parts or something, then walk to the station. With luck, the garageman and Newman might never compare notes on the subject of Alex Wolff.

The jeep drove through the busy, narrow streets. The familiar sights of an Egyptian town pleased Wolff: the women carrying bundles on their heads, the sharp characters in sunglasses, the tiny shops spilling out into the rutted streets, the battered cars and the overloaded asses. They stopped in front of a row of low mud brick buildings. The road was half blocked by an ancient truck and the remains of a cannibalized Fiat.

Newman said, "I'll have to leave you here. Duty calls."

Wolff shook his hand. "You've been very kind."

"I don't like to dump you this way," Newman continued. "Tell you what— I'll leave Corporal Cox to look after you."

Wolff said, "It's kind, but really—"

Newman was not listening. "Get the man's bags, Cox. I want you to take care of him—understand?"

"Yes, sir!" said Cox.

Wolff groaned inwardly. Captain Newman's kindness was becoming a nuisance—could that possibly be intentional? Wolff realized that his plan of slipping unobserved into Egypt might well fail. He and Cox got out, and the jeep pulled away.

Wolff walked into Nasif's garage, and Cox followed, carrying the cases. Nasif, a smiling young man, was working on a car by the light of an oil lamp. Wolff spoke to him in rapid Egyptian Arabic. "My car has broken down. They say you have a tow truck."

"Yes. We can leave right away. Where is the car?"

"On the desert road, forty or fifty miles out. It's a Ford. But we're not coming with you." He took out his wallet and gave Nasif an English pound note. "You'll find me at the Grand Hotel by the railway station."

Nasif took the money with alacrity. "Very good!"

Wolff nodded curtly and turned around. Walking out of the garage with Cox behind him, he looked at his watch. He still had time to catch the train. He would get rid of Cox in the lobby of the hotel, then get something to eat while he was waiting.

Cox was a short, dark man with some kind of British regional accent which Wolff could not identify. He looked about Wolff's age, and as he was still a corporal he was probably not too bright.

They entered the hotel. Wolff turned to Cox. "Thank you, Corporal, I think you could get back to work now."

"No hurry, sir," Cox said cheerfully. "I'll carry your bags up."

"I'm sure they have porters here—"

"Wouldn't trust 'em, sir, if I were you."

The situation was becoming more and more like a nightmare or a farce, in which well-intentioned people pushed him into increasingly senseless behavior in consequence of one small lie. It crossed his mind with terrifying absurdity that perhaps they knew everything and were toying with him.

He pushed the thought aside. To Cox he said, "Thank you."

He turned to the desk and asked for a room. He looked at his watch: he had fifteen minutes before the train left. A Nubian porter led them upstairs to the room. Wolff tipped him at the door. Cox put the cases on the bed.

"Well, Corporal," Wolff began, "you've been very helpful—"

"Let me unpack for you, sir," Cox said.

"No, thank you," Wolff said firmly. "I want to lie down."

"You lie down," Cox persisted generously. "It won't take me—"

"Don't open that!"

Cox was lifting the lid of the light case. Wolff reached inside his jacket, thinking, *Damn the man, now I'm blown,* and *Can I do this quietly?* The little corporal stared at the neat stacks of new

English pound notes which filled the case. He said, "My God, you're loaded!" Cox began to turn, saying, "What do you want with all that—" Wolff pulled out the wicked curved bedouin knife, and it glinted in his hand as his eyes met Cox's, and Cox flinched and opened his mouth to shout; then the razor-sharp blade sliced into his throat, and his shout of fear came as a bloody gurgle and he died; and Wolff felt nothing but disappointment.

Chapter 2

IT WAS May, and the khamsin was blowing, a hot dusty wind from the south. Standing under the shower, William Vandam had the depressing thought that this would be the only time he would feel cool all day. He turned off the water and dried himself rapidly. His body was full of small aches. He had played cricket the day before, for the first time in years. General Staff intelligence had gotten up a team to play the doctors from the field hospital—spies versus quacks, they had called it—and Vandam, fielding on the boundary, had been run ragged. He had to admit he was not in good condition. Cigarettes had shortened his wind, and he had too many worries to concentrate on the game.

He lit a cigarette, coughed and started to shave. He always smoked while he was shaving—it was the only way he knew to relieve the boredom of the inevitable daily task. Fifteen years ago he had sworn he would grow a beard as soon as he got out of the army, but it was now 1942 and he was still in the army.

He dressed in the everyday uniform: heavy sandals, socks, bush shirt and khaki shorts. Then he went downstairs. Gaafar was in the kitchen, making tea. Vandam's servant was an elderly Copt with a bald head and a shuffling walk, and pretensions to be an English butler. That he would never be, but he had a little dignity and he was honest. Vandam said, "Is Billy up?"

"Yes, sir, he's coming down directly."

Vandam nodded. A small pan of water was bubbling on the stove. He put an egg in to boil and set the timer. He made toast, buttered it, then took the egg out of the water and decapitated it. Billy came into the kitchen and said, "Good morning, Dad."

Vandam smiled at his ten-year-old son. "Breakfast is ready."

The boy sat down and began to eat. Vandam sat opposite him

with a cup of tea, watching. People said Billy was like his father; Vandam could not see the resemblance. But he could see traces of Billy's mother: the gray eyes, the delicate skin and the faintly supercilious expression he wore when someone crossed him.

Vandam always prepared his son's breakfast. Most of the time the servant looked after the boy, but Vandam liked to keep this little ritual for himself. Often it was the only time he was with Billy all day.

After breakfast Billy brushed his teeth while Gaafar got out Vandam's motorcycle, a fast BSA 350, very practical for snaking through Cairo's traffic jams. Billy came back wearing his school cap, and Vandam put on his uniform cap. As they did every day, they saluted each other. Billy said, "Right, sir—let's go and win the war." Then they went out.

MAJOR Vandam's office was in a group of buildings surrounded by barbed wire which made up General Headquarters Middle East. There was an incident report on his desk when he arrived. He sat down, lit a cigarette and began to read.

The report came from Asyut, and at first Vandam could not see why it had been marked for intelligence. A patrol had picked up a hitchhiking European who had subsequently murdered a corporal with a knife. The body had been discovered last night, several hours after the death. A man answering the hitchhiker's description had bought a ticket to Cairo at the railway station. There was no indication of motive.

The Egyptian police force and the British military police would be investigating already, in Asyut and in Cairo. What reason was there for intelligence to get involved? Vandam frowned and thought again. Then it came to him. He called Asyut and reached Captain Newman.

Vandam said, "This knife murder looks like a blown cover."

"That occurred to me, sir," said Newman. He sounded like a young man. "That's why I marked the report for intelligence."

"Good thinking. What was your impression of the man? I've got your description here—six feet, one hundred seventy pounds, dark hair and eyes—but that doesn't tell me what he was *like*."

"Well, to be candid," Newman said, "at first I wasn't suspicious of him. He seemed an upright citizen: decently dressed, well spoken, with an accent he said was Dutch, or rather Afrikaans. His papers were genuine."

"But . . . ?"

"He told me he was checking on his business interests in Upper Egypt. But he didn't strike me as the kind of man to spend his life investing in a few shops and cotton farms. He was much more the assured cosmopolitan type. If he had money to invest, it would probably be with a London stockbroker or a Swiss bank. Then it occurred to me that he had, as it were, just appeared in the desert, and I didn't really know where he might have come from. . . . So I told poor old Cox to stay with him, on the pretense of helping him, until we had a chance to check his story. I should have arrested the man, of course, but I had only the most slender suspicion—"

"I don't think anyone's blaming you, Captain," said Vandam. "You did well to remember the name and address from the papers. Alexander Wolff, Villa les Oliviers, Garden City, right?"

"Yes, sir."

"All right, keep me in touch with any developments at your end." Vandam hung up. Newman's suspicions chimed with his own instincts about the killing. He decided to speak to his superior. He left his office, carrying the incident report.

Vandam's boss, Lieutenant Colonel Bogge, was a deputy director of military intelligence. Bogge was responsible for personnel security, and most of his time was spent administering the censorship apparatus. Vandam's concern was security leaks by means other than letters. He and his men had several hundred agents in Cairo and Alexandria; he had informants in most clubs and bars and among the domestic staffs of the more important Arab politicians. King Faruk's valet worked for Vandam, and so, on occasion, did Abdullah, Cairo's wealthiest thief, whose services were for sale to any and all sides. Vandam was interested in who was talking too much, and who was listening; and among the listeners, Arab nationalists were his main target. However, the mystery man from Asyut seemed to be a different kind of threat.

Vandam's wartime career had so far been distinguished by one spectacular success and one great failure. The failure took place in Turkey, where Rashid Ali, Iraq's nationalist prime minister, had escaped into exile. The Germans wanted to get him out and use him for propaganda. Vandam's job had been to make sure Ali stayed in Istanbul, but Ali had switched clothes with a German agent and slipped out of the country under Vandam's nose. A few days later Ali was making propaganda speeches to the Middle East on Nazi radio. Vandam had redeemed himself in Cairo, where he uncovered a major security leak: a senior American diplomat reporting to Washington in an insecure code. The code had been changed, the leak stopped up and Vandam promoted to major.

Had he been a peacetime soldier, he would have been proud of his triumph and reconciled to his defeat: "You win some, you lose some." But in war an officer's mistakes killed people. In the aftermath of the Rashid Ali affair an agent had been murdered, a young woman, and Vandam had not been able to forgive himself.

He knocked on Lieutenant Colonel Bogge's door and walked in. Reggie Bogge was a short, square man in his fifties, with an immaculate uniform and brilliantined black hair. He had a nervous cough which he used when he did not know quite what to say, which was often. He sat behind a huge curved desk, going through his in tray. As Vandam took a chair, Bogge said, "More bloody bad news. We expected Rommel to attack the Gazala line head-on. Should have known better. He went around our southern flank and took the Seventh Armored's headquarters."

"When are we going to *stop* him?" Vandam said wearily.

"He won't get much farther." Bogge did not want to criticize the generals. "What have you there?"

Vandam gave him the incident report. "It looks like a blown cover."

Bogge read the report. "You mean he was a spy?" He laughed contemptuously. "How d'you suppose he got to Asyut—by parachute? Or did he walk?"

That was the trouble with Bogge, thought Vandam: he had to ridicule the idea, as an excuse for not thinking of it himself. "It's not impossible for a small plane to sneak through. It's not impossible to cross the desert, either."

Bogge sailed the report through the air across the desk. "Not very likely," he said. "Don't waste any time on that one."

"Very good, sir." Vandam picked up the report from the floor, suppressing the familiar anger. "I'll ask the police to keep us informed of their progress, just for the file."

On the way back to his own office, a woman in a white hospital coat saluted him. He returned the salute absentmindedly. The woman said, "Major Vandam, isn't it?"

He stopped and looked at her. She had been a spectator at the cricket match, and now he remembered her name. "Dr. Abuthnot," he said. "Good morning." She was a tall, cool woman of about his age. He recalled that she was a surgeon with the rank of captain.

She said, "You played hard yesterday."

Vandam smiled. "I enjoyed myself, though."

"So did I." She had a low, precise voice and a great deal of confidence. "Shall we see you on Friday?"

"Where?"

"The reception at the Union."

"Ah." The Anglo-Egyptian Union, a club for bored Europeans, made occasional attempts to justify its name by holding a reception for Egyptian guests. "I'd like that." Vandam was professionally interested: it was an occasion at which Egyptians might pick up service gossip, and service gossip sometimes included information useful to the enemy. "I'll come."

"Splendid. I'll see you there." She turned away.

Vandam watched her go down the hall. She was trim, elegant and self-possessed: she reminded him of Angela, his wife.

He entered his office, his mind once more on Captain Newman's report. He had no intention of forgetting about the Asyut murder. Bogge could go to hell. Vandam would go to work.

First he called the Egyptian police and confirmed that they would be checking the hotels and flophouses of Cairo today. He contacted British field security and asked them to step up their spot checks on identity papers. He told the paymaster general to keep a special watch for forged currency. He advised the wireless listening service to be alert for a new, local transmitter; and he detailed a sergeant to visit every radio shop in the area and ask them to report any sales of parts and equipment which might be used to make or repair a transmitter.

Then he went to the address given on Alex Wolff's papers.

The Villa les Oliviers got its name from a small public garden across the street, where a grove of olive trees was now in bloom, shedding white petals like dust onto the dry, brown grass.

The house had a high wall broken by a heavy, carved wooden gate. Using the ornamentation for footholds, Vandam climbed over the gate and found himself in a large courtyard. The whitewashed walls were grubby, their windows blinded by closed, peeling shutters. The place had not been lived in for at least a year. He opened a shutter, broke a pane of glass, reached through to unfasten the window, and climbed over the sill into the house.

It did not look like the home of a European, Vandam thought as he walked through the dark, cool rooms. There were no hunting prints on the walls, no rows of bright-jacketed novels, no furniture imported from Harrods, in London. Instead, the place was furnished with large cushions, low tables, handwoven rugs and hanging tapestries.

Upstairs, behind a locked door which he kicked open, he found a clean and tidy study, with a few pieces of rather luxurious furniture: a wide, low divan covered in velvet, a hand-carved coffee table, a beautifully inlaid desk and a leather chair. In the desk drawer he found company reports from Switzerland, Germany and the United States. Gathering dust on a shelf behind the desk were books in several languages: nineteenth-century French novels; the *Shorter Oxford English Dictionary;* a volume of Arabic poetry, with erotic illustrations; and the Bible in German. There were no personal documents, no letters, not a single photograph.

Vandam sat in the soft leather chair behind the desk and looked around the room. It was a masculine room, the home of a cosmopolitan intellectual, a man who was on the one hand careful, precise and tidy and on the other hand sensitive and sensual.

Vandam was intrigued. A European name, a totally Arabic house. A wealth of information about a character, but not a single clue which might help find the man. There should have been bank statements, bills, a birth certificate, a will, photographs of parents or children. The man had left no trace of his identity, as if he knew that one day someone would come looking for him.

Vandam said aloud, "Alex Wolff, who are you?"

He got up from the chair and left the house. He climbed back over the gate and dropped into the street. Across the road an Arab in a plain white galabia—as the natives' loose robes are called—sat cross-legged on the ground in the shade of the olive trees, watching Vandam incuriously. Vandam thought of other sources from which he could seek information about the owner of this house: municipal records, local tradesmen, neighbors. He

would put two of his men on it, and tell Bogge some cover story. He climbed onto his motorcycle and kicked it into life. The engine roared, and Vandam drove away.

FULL of anger and despair, Wolff sat outside his home and watched the British officer ride off. The officer was arrogant and prying; he had broken in and violated Wolff's domain. Wolff wished he could have seen the man's face; he would like to kill him one day.

He had thought of this place all through his journey. In Berlin and Tripoli, in the desert crossing, in his hasty flight from Asyut, the villa had represented a haven, a place to rest and get clean and whole again. Now he would have to go away and stay away.

He had remained outside all morning, wearing the galabia he had bought in the native market, just in case Captain Newman should have remembered the address and sent somebody to search the house. It had been a mistake to show genuine papers. He could see that, with hindsight. The trouble was, he mistrusted forgeries made by German intelligence. Meeting other spies, he had heard horror stories about obvious errors in their documents: botched printing, misspellings of common English words. Wolff had weighed the alternatives and picked what seemed the least risky. He had been wrong, and now he had no place to go.

Wolff stood, picked up his two cases and began to walk.

He thought of his family. His mother and his Egyptian stepfather were dead, but he had three stepbrothers and a stepsister in Cairo. It would be hard for them to hide him. They would be questioned when the British realized their connection to him; they might lie for his sake, but their servants would surely talk.

He left Garden City and headed downtown. The streets were even busier than they had been when he left Cairo. There were countless uniforms—not just British, but Australian, New Zealand, Polish, Yugoslav, Palestinian, Indian and Greek. The beggars and peddlers were out in force, taking advantage of the influx of naïve foreigners.

The traffic was worse, too. The slow, verminous trams were more crowded than ever, with passengers perched on the running boards and sitting cross-legged on the roofs. The buses and taxis were no better: there seemed to be a shortage of vehicle parts, for many of the cars had broken windows, flat tires and ailing engines. The only decent cars were the monstrous American limousines of the wealthy pashas. Mixing with the motor vehicles were the horse-drawn gharries, the mule carts of the peasants, and the livestock—camels, sheep and goats.

And the noise— Wolff had forgotten the noise. Tram bells rang, cars hooted, drivers of carts and camels yelled at the tops of their voices. Shops and cafés blared Arab music from cheap radios turned to full volume. Street vendors called, dogs barked. From time to time all would be swamped by the roar of a plane.

This is my town, Wolff thought; they can't catch me here.

He remembered a cheap lodging house run by nuns at Bulaq, the port district. It catered mainly to the sailors who came down the Nile in steam tugs and feluccas laden with cotton, coal, paper and stone. Nobody would think to look for him there.

The hostel was a large, decaying building which had once been the villa of some pasha. Through the front arch Wolff could see a cool, quiet hall. He had walked miles today, with his cases; he looked forward to a rest.

Two Egyptian policemen came out of the hostel.

Wolff's heart sank. He turned away and walked on. It was worse than he had imagined. The police must be checking *everywhere*. He was beginning to feel as he had in the desert, as if he had been walking forever without getting anywhere.

He saw a taxi, a big old Ford with steam hissing out from under its hood. He jumped in and had himself driven to Coptic Cairo, the ancient Christian quarter. He paid the driver and went down the steps to the entrance.

The quarter was an island of darkness and quiet in the stormy sea of Cairo. Wolff walked its narrow passages and went into the smallest of the five ancient churches. The service was about to begin. He put his precious cases beside a pew and sat down.

The choir began to chant a passage of Scripture. Wolff settled into his seat. He would be safe here until darkness fell. Then he would take off the galabia and try his last shot.

THE Cha-Cha was a large nightclub in a garden beside the river. It was packed, as usual, but Wolff managed to get a table and ordered a bottle of champagne. The evening was warm and the stage lights made it worse. The rowdy audience began shouting for the star of the show, Sonja el-Aram. Finally there was a roll of drums, the lights went off and silence descended.

When the spotlight came on, Sonja stood still in the center of the stage with her arms stretched skyward. She wore diaphanous trousers and a sequined halter. The music began—drums and a pipe—and she started to move. Wolff sipped champagne and watched, smiling. She was still the best.

She jerked her hips slowly, stamping one foot and then the other. Her arms began to tremble, then her shoulders moved and her breasts shook; and then her famous belly rolled hypnotically. The rhythm quickened. She closed her eyes. Each part of her body seemed to move independently of the rest. The audience was silent, mesmerized. She went faster and faster, seeming to be transported. The music climaxed with a bang. In the instant of silence that followed, Sonja uttered a short, sharp cry; then she fell backward, her legs folded beneath her, until her head touched the boards of the stage. She held the position for a moment, then the spotlight went out. The audience rose to its feet with a roar of applause. The lights came up, and she was gone.

Sonja never gave encores.

Wolff offered the waiter a pound—three months' wages for most Egyptians—to lead him backstage. The waiter showed him the door to Sonja's dressing room and went away. Wolff walked in.

She was sitting on a stool, wearing a silk robe, taking off her makeup. She saw him in the mirror and spun around. Wolff said, "Hello, Sonja."

Her eyes flashed with anger. "What are you doing here?"

She had not changed. She was a handsome woman. She had long, glossy black hair; large brown eyes with lush eyelashes; high cheekbones and an arched nose, gracefully arrogant; a full mouth with even white teeth. Her body was all smooth curves, but because she was taller than average she did not look plump.

Wolff put down his cases and sat on the divan. She rose and stood with her hands on her hips, her chin thrust forward, her breasts outlined in green silk. "You're beautiful," he said.

"Get out of here."

He studied her carefully. She appeared angry and scornful, but did she mean it? "I need help," he said levelly. "The British are after me. They're watching my house. I want to move in with you."

"Go to hell," she said.

"Give me a minute. Let me tell you why I walked out on you."

"After two years no excuse is good enough." She glared at him a moment, then opened the door. He thought she was going to throw him out. Instead she put her head outside and yelled, "Somebody get me a drink!" Wolff relaxed a little.

Sonja closed the door. "A minute," she said. She went back to her stool and resumed working on her face.

He hesitated. How would he explain why he had left her without saying good-by and never contacted her since? Reluctant as he was to share his secret, he had to tell her the truth, for he was desperate and she was his only hope.

He said, "You remember I went to Beirut in 1938. I went there to see a German army officer. He asked me to work for Germany in the coming war. I agreed."

She turned from her mirror and faced him. He saw in her eyes something like hope.

"They told me to come back to Cairo and wait. Two years ago they told me to go to Berlin. I went. I took a training course, then I worked in the Levant. I went back to Berlin in February for briefing on a new assignment. They sent me here—"

"You're a *spy?*" she said incredulously. "I don't believe it."

"Look." He picked up a suitcase and opened it. "This is a radio, for sending messages to Rommel." He closed it and opened the other. "This is my financing."

She stared at the neat stacks of notes. "It's a *fortune.*"

There was a knock at the door. Wolff shut the case. A waiter came in with a bottle of champagne in a bucket of ice. Seeing Wolff, he said, "Shall I bring another glass?"

"No," Sonja said impatiently. "Go away."

The waiter left. Wolff uncorked the wine, filled the glass, gave it to Sonja, then took a long drink from the bottle.

"Listen," he said. "Our army needs to know about British strength—numbers of men, which divisions are in the field, names of commanders, quality of weapons and equipment, battle plans. We can find these things out. Then when the Germans take Cairo we will be heroes."

"We?"

"You can help, first by giving me a place to live. You hate the British, don't you? You want to see them thrown out?"

"I would do it for anyone but you."

"Sonja. If I had sent you so much as a postcard from Berlin, the British would have thrown you in jail. You must not be angry." He lowered his voice. "We can bring those old times back. We'll have good food, the best champagne and new clothes. We'll go to Berlin, you've always wanted to dance there, you'll be a star. We—" He paused. None of this was getting through to her. It was time to play his last card. "How is your friend Fawzi?"

Sonja lowered her eyes. "She left."

Wolff put both hands to Sonja's neck. With his thumbs under her chin he forced her to stand. "I'll find another Fawzi for you," he said softly. He saw that her eyes were suddenly moist. "I'm the only one who understands what you need." He lowered his mouth to hers.

Sonja closed her eyes. "I hate you," she moaned.

IN THE cool of the evening Wolff walked along the towpath beside the Nile toward Sonja's houseboat, the *Jihan*. The sores had gone from his face. He wore a new white suit, and he carried two bags full of his favorite groceries.

The island suburb of Zamalek was peaceful. The raucous noise of central Cairo could be heard only faintly across a wide stretch of water. The calm, muddy river lapped gently against the houseboats lined along the bank.

Sonja's was smaller and more richly furnished than most. A gangplank led from the path to the top deck. Wolff boarded the boat and went down the ladder to the interior. It was crowded with chairs, divans, tables, cabinets full of knickknacks. There was a tiny kitchen in the prow. Floor-to-ceiling curtains of velvet divided the rest of the interior in two, closing off the bedroom. Beyond the bedroom, in the stern, was a bathroom.

Sonja was sitting on a cushion painting her toenails before going to the Cha-Cha Club. Wolff put his grocery bags on a table and began to take things out. "French champagne . . . English marmalade . . . German sausage . . . Scotch salmon."

Sonja looked up, astonished. "Nobody has things like that—there's a war on."

Wolff smiled. "There's a little Greek grocer in Qulali. His shop is the only place in North Africa where you can get caviar."

She dipped into a bag. "Caviar!" She took the lid off the jar and began to eat with her fingers.

Wolff put a bottle of champagne in the icebox. He took a newspaper out of one of the bags and began to look through it. "Still nothing about me." He had told Sonja of the events in Asyut.

"They're always late with the news," she said through a mouthful of caviar.

"It's not that. The British don't want people to suspect that the Germans have spies in Egypt. It looks bad."

She went into the bedroom to change. She called through the curtain, "Does that mean they've stopped looking for you?"

"No. I saw Abdullah in the marketplace. He says there's a Major Vandam who's keeping the pressure on."

Sonja said, "How does Abdullah know?"

"He's a thief, he hears things." Wolff went to the icebox and took out the champagne. It was not really cold enough, but he poured two glasses. Sonja came out, her face lightly made up, wearing a sheer cherry-red dress and matching shoes. A couple of minutes later her taxi arrived. She drained her glass and left.

Wolff went to the cupboard where he had put the radio. He took out the English novel and the sheet of paper bearing the key to the code. He studied the key. Today was May 28. He had to add 42—the year—to 28 to arrive at the page number in the novel which he must use to encode his message. May was the fifth month, so every fifth letter on the page would be discounted.

He decided to send: "Have arrived. Acknowledge." Beginning at the top of page 70 of the book, he looked along the line of print for the letter *h*. It was the tenth character, discounting every fifth letter. In his code it would therefore be represented by the tenth letter of the alphabet, *j*. Next he needed an *a*. In the book, the third letter after the *h* was an *a*. The *a* of "have" would therefore be represented by the third letter of the alphabet, *c*. There were special ways of dealing with rare letters like *x*. To decode the message a listener had to have both the book and the key, making it unbreakable in theory and in practice.

When he had encoded his message he looked at his watch. He was to transmit at 2400 hours—midnight. He still had time. He poured another glass of champagne and decided to finish the caviar. He found a spoon and picked up the jar. It was empty. Sonja had eaten it all.

THE runway was a strip of desert hastily cleared of camel thorn and large rocks. Erwin Rommel looked down as the ground came up to meet him. The Storch, a light aircraft he used for short trips around the battlefield, came down like a fly and stopped. Rommel jumped out.

The heat hit him first, then the dust. It had been relatively cool up in the sky; now he felt as if he had stepped into a furnace. He began to perspire immediately. As soon as he breathed in, a thin layer of sand coated his lips.

Friedrich von Mellenthin, his intelligence officer, ran toward him across the sand. "Kesselring's here," he said.

"*Auch das noch,*" said Rommel. "That's all I need."

Albert Kesselring, the smiling field marshal, represented everything Rommel disliked in the German armed forces. He was a General Staff officer, and Rommel hated the General Staff; he was a founder of the Luftwaffe, which had let Rommel down so often in the desert war; and he was a snob.

Rommel stumped across the sand toward the command vehicle, with von Mellenthin in tow. They entered the back of the huge truck. Kesselring was bent over a map. He looked up. "My dear Rommel, thank heaven you're back," he said silkily.

Rommel took off his cap. "I've been fighting a battle."

"So I gather. What happened?"

Rommel pointed to the map. "This is the Gazala line." It was a string of fortified "boxes" linked by minefields which ran from the coast at El Gazala due south into the Libyan Desert for fifty miles. "We made a dogleg around the southern end and hit them from behind. Then we ran out of gasoline and ammunition." He sat down heavily, suddenly very tired. "Again," he added pointedly. Kesselring, as commander in chief (South), was responsible for Rommel's supplies. "But I'm winning," Rommel went on. "If I'd had my supplies, I'd be in Cairo now."

"You're not going to Cairo," Kesselring said sharply. "You're going to Tobruk. There you'll stay until I've taken Malta. Such are the Führer's orders."

"Of course." Rommel was not going to reopen that argument; not yet. The immediate objective was Tobruk, the fortified British port near the Egyptian border. Once that was taken, the convoys from Europe could come directly to the front line, cutting out the long journey across the desert. "And to reach Tobruk we have to break the Gazala line."

"What's your next step?"

"I'm going to fall back and regroup," replied Rommel.

"The British will chase us, but not immediately," added von Mellenthin. "They are always slow to press an advantage. But sooner or later they will try a breakout."

Rommel said, "The question is, when and where?"

"Indeed," von Mellenthin said. "There is a little item in today's summaries which will interest you. The spy checked in."

"The spy?" Then Rommel remembered. He had flown to the Jalo Oasis, deep in the Libyan Desert, to brief the man before the spy began a long marathon walk eastward. Wolff, that was his name. Rommel had been impressed by his courage. "Where was he calling from?"

"Cairo."

"So he got there. If he's capable of that, he's capable of anything. Perhaps he can foretell the breakout."

Kesselring broke in, "My God, you're not relying on spies now, are you? Intelligence from spies is the worst kind."

"I agree," Rommel said calmly. "But I have a feeling this one could be different."

Chapter 3

ELENE Fontana looked at her face in the mirror and thought, I'm twenty-three. I must be losing my looks.

She leaned closer to the glass and examined herself carefully, searching for signs of deterioration. Her complexion was perfect. Her round brown eyes were as clear as a mountain pool. There were no wrinkles. It was a childish face, delicately modeled, with a look of waiflike innocence. She smiled. It was a small, intimate smile, with a hint of mischief about it; she knew it could make a man break out into a cold sweat.

She picked up the note and read it again.

My dear Elene,

  I'm afraid it is all over. My wife has found out. Of course you can stay in the flat, but I can't pay the rent anymore. I'm so sorry it happened this way—but I suppose we both knew it could not last forever. Good luck—

Your Claud

Just like that, she thought. She tore up the note. Claud was a fat, half-French and half-Greek businessman. He was cultured and kind, but he cared nothing for Elene. He was the third in six years. It was her fault as much as the men's that the affairs broke up. The real cause was always the same: Elene was unhappy.

She contemplated the prospect of another affair. Perhaps he would be an Italian, with flashing eyes and glossy hair. She might meet him in the bar of the Metropolitan Hotel, where the reporters drank. He would speak to her, then offer her a drink. She would smile at him, and he would be lost. They would make a date, then another. He would spend more and more time at the flat, and he would begin to pay the rent and the bills. Elene would then have everything she wanted: a home, money and affection. She would begin to wonder why she was so miserable. There would be rows. She would throw a tantrum if he arrived half an hour late. Finally the crisis would come. His wife would get suspicious, or a child would fall ill, or he would run short of money. And Elene would be back where she was now: drifting, alone, disreputable—and a year older.

She looked again at her face in the mirror. Her face was the cause of all this. Had she been ugly, she would always have yearned to live like this, and would never have discovered its hollowness. You led me astray, she thought; you pretended I was somebody else. You're not my face, you're a mask. I'm not a beautiful Cairo socialite, I'm a slum girl from Alexandria. I'm not Egyptian, I'm Jewish. My name is not Elene Fontana. It's Abigail Asnani. And I want to go home.

THE young man behind the desk at the Jewish Agency in Cairo wore a yarmulke. Apart from a wisp of beard, his cheeks were smooth. He seemed confused. Elene was used to this; most men got a little flustered when she smiled at them. He said, "But why do you want to go to Palestine?"

"I'm Jewish," she said abruptly. She could not explain her life to this boy. "All my family are dead. I'm wasting my life." The first part was not true; the second part was.

"What work would you do in Palestine? It's mostly agricultural."

"That's fine."

He smiled gently. He was recovering his composure. "I mean no offense, but you don't look like a farmhand. What work do you do now?"

"I sing, and when I can't get singing I dance, and when I can't get dancing I wait on tables." She had done all three at one time or another. "Why all the questions? Is Palestine accepting only college graduates now?"

"It's very tough to get in. The British have imposed a quota, and all the places are taken by refugees from the Nazis."

"Why didn't you tell me that before?" she said angrily.

"Two reasons. One is that we can get people in illegally. The other . . . Would you wait a minute? I must telephone someone."

He went into a back room to phone. Elene waited impatiently. She felt a little foolish. She might have guessed they would ask her questions; she could have prepared her answers. She could have come dressed in something a little less glamorous.

The young man came back. "It's so warm," he said. "Shall we go across the street for a cold drink?"

So that was the game. "No," she said. "You're too young for me."

He was terribly embarrassed. "Oh, please don't misunderstand me. There's someone I want you to meet, that's all."

She had nothing to lose, she thought. "All right."

He held the door for her. They crossed the street and stepped into a café. The young man ordered lemon juice; Elene had gin and tonic. She said, "You can get people in illegally."

"Sometimes." He took half his drink in one gulp. "One reason we do it is if people have done a lot for the cause."

"You mean I have to earn the right to go to Palestine?"

"Look, maybe one day all Jews will have the right to go there. But while there are quotas there have to be criteria."

Elene asked, "What do I have to do?"

"We don't like the British much, but any enemy of the Nazis is a friend of ours, so at the moment we're working with British intelligence. I think you could help them."

"For God's sake! How?"

A shadow fell across the table, and the young man looked up. "Ah!" he said. He looked back at Elene. "I want you to meet my friend Major William Vandam."

He was a tall man, with wide shoulders. Elene guessed he was close to forty and beginning to go a little soft. He had a round, open face topped by wiry brown hair. He shook her hand, sat down, lit a cigarette and ordered gin. He wore a stern expression, as if he thought life was a very serious business.

The young man from the Agency asked him, "What's the news?"

"The Gazala line is holding, but it's fierce out there."

Vandam's voice was a surprise. He spoke precisely but softly, with a slight burr on the *r*.

"Where do you come from, Major?" she asked him.

"Dorset. Southwest England. Why do you ask?"

"I was wondering about your accent."

"You're observant. I thought I had no accent."

"Just a trace."

The young man rose to leave. To Elene he said, "I'll let Major Vandam explain everything. I hope you will work with him. It's very important."

Vandam shook his hand, thanked him, and the young man went out. Vandam said to Elene, "Tell me about yourself."

"No," she said. "You tell me about *your*self."

He raised an eyebrow at her, faintly startled, a little amused. "All right," he said. "Cairo is full of men who know secrets: our strengths, our weaknesses and our plans. The Germans have people in Cairo trying to get those secrets. It's my job to stop them."

"That simple."

He considered. "It's simple, but it's not easy."

He took everything she said seriously. She rather liked it; men generally treated her conversation like background music.

He was waiting. "It's your turn," he said.

She wanted to tell him the truth. "I'm a lousy singer and a mediocre dancer, but sometimes I find a rich man to pay my bills."

He said nothing, but he looked taken aback.

The imp of mischief seized her. "Isn't that what most women do when they get married—find a man to pay the bills? I just turn them around a little faster than the average housewife."

Vandam burst out laughing. Suddenly he looked a different man. He threw back his head and all the tension went out of his body. When the laugh subsided they grinned at one another. Then he was serious again. "My problem is information. Nobody tells an Englishman anything. That's where you come in. Because you're Egyptian, you hear the kind of gossip that never comes my way. Because you're Jewish, you'll pass it to me. I hope."

"What kind of gossip?"

"I'm interested in anyone who's curious about the British army. In particular, I'm looking for a man called Alex Wolff. He used to live in Cairo and he has recently returned via Asyut. He is certainly making inquiries about British forces."

Elene shrugged. "After all that buildup I was expecting to be asked to do something much more dramatic—like waltz with Rommel and pick his pockets."

Vandam laughed again. Elene thought, I could get fond of that laugh.

He said, "Well, mundane though it is, will you do it? I need people like you, Miss Fontana. You're observant, you have a perfect cover, and you're obviously intelligent. Please excuse me for being so direct—"

"Don't apologize, I love it," she said. "Keep talking."

"Most of my people are not very reliable. They do it for the money, whereas you have a better motive—"

"Wait a minute," she interrupted. "I want money, too. What does the job pay?"

"How much do you want?"

"Enough to pay the rent of my flat. Seventy-five a month."

"You'd have to be awfully useful to justify seventy-five a month. But all right, a month's trial."

Elene tried not to look triumphant. "How do I contact you?"

"Send me a message." He took out a pencil and a scrap of paper. "I'll give you my address and phone number, at GHQ and at home. As soon as I hear from you, I'll come to your place."

She wrote down her address. "If I'm asked who you are, I'll say you're my lover."

He looked away. "Very well."

"But you'd better act the part." She kept a straight face. "You must bring armfuls of flowers and boxes of chocolates."

"I don't know. . . ."

"Don't Englishmen give mistresses flowers and chocolates?"

He looked at her unblinkingly. "I've never had a mistress."

Elene thought, I stand corrected. She said, "Then you've got a lot to learn."

They rose. "I'll look forward to hearing from you," he said. She shook his hand and walked away. Somehow she had the feeling he was not watching her go.

VANDAM changed into a civilian suit for the reception at the Anglo-Egyptian Union. He would never have gone to the Union while his wife was alive: she said it was "plebeian." He told her not to sound like a snob. She said she was a snob.

Vandam had loved her then and he did now.

Her father was a fairly wealthy diplomat who had not been pleased at the prospect of his daughter marrying a postman's son. He was not much mollified to learn that Vandam was considered one of the most promising of junior army officers, but in the end he had accepted the match with good grace.

None of it mattered to Vandam; nor did the fact that his wife had a short temper and an imperious manner. Angela was graceful and dignified, the epitome of womanhood. The contrast with Elene Fontana could not have been more striking.

The day was cooling when Vandam parked his motorcycle at the Union and walked to the lawn. He accepted a glass of Cyprus sherry and moved into the crowd, exchanging pleasantries with people he knew. Someone spoke his name. He turned. "Dr. Abuthnot."

"We might be informal here," she said. "My name is Joan."

"Mine's William. Is your husband here?"

"I'm not married."

"Pardon me." Now he saw her in a new light. She was single and he was a widower, and they had been seen talking together three times in a week; by now the English colony in Cairo would have them practically engaged. "You're a surgeon?" he said.

She smiled. "All I do these days is sew people up and patch them—but yes, before the war I was a surgeon."

"How did you manage that? It's not easy for a woman."

"I fought tooth and nail." She was still smiling, but Vandam detected an undertone of remembered resentment. "You're a little unconventional, too, I'm told, bringing up your child yourself."

"No choice. If I had wanted to send him back to England, I wouldn't have been able to: you can't get a passage unless you're disabled or a general."

"But you didn't want to."

"He's my son. I don't want anyone else to bring him up—nor does he."

"I understand. Sorry, I've been prying. Another drink?"

Vandam looked into his sherry glass. "I think I shall have to go inside in search of a real drink."

"I wish you luck." She smiled and turned away.

Vandam walked across the lawn to the clubhouse. She was an attractive woman, courageous and intelligent, and she had made it clear she wanted to know him better. He thought, Why the devil do I feel so indifferent toward her?

ALEX Wolff wore his galabia and a fez and stood thirty yards from the gate of GHQ—British headquarters—selling paper fans. The hue and cry had died down. He had not seen the British conducting a spot check on identity papers for a week. As soon as he had felt reasonably safe he had gone to GHQ. Getting into Cairo had been a triumph, but it was useless unless he could get the information Rommel wanted—and quickly.

Somewhere inside GHQ there were pieces of paper which gave numbers of troops, names of divisions, numbers of tanks in the field and in reserve, quantities of ammunition, food and gasoline, the strategic and tactical intentions of the British High Command. It was those pieces of paper Wolff wanted.

For their headquarters the British had taken over a number of the large houses—most of them owned by pashas—in Garden City. The commandeered homes were surrounded by a barbed-wire fence. People in uniform were passed quickly through the gate, but civilians were stopped and questioned at length while the sentries made phone calls to verify credentials.

Wolff had spent a lot of time, back in the Abwehr spy school, learning to recognize uniforms, regimental identification marks and the faces of literally hundreds of senior British officers. Here, several mornings running, he had peeked through the windows of the arriving staff cars and seen colonels, generals, admirals, squadron leaders and the commander in chief of the Middle East, Sir Claude Auchinleck, himself.

The General Staff traveled by car, but their aides walked. Each morning the captains and majors arrived on foot, carrying briefcases. Toward noon some of them left, still carrying their cases, and each day Wolff followed one of them.

Most of the aides worked at GHQ, and their secret papers would be locked up inside. But a few of them had offices in other parts of the city; and they had to carry their briefing papers with them between GHQ and those offices. One of them went to the Semiramis Hotel, which housed something called British Troops in Egypt. Two went to the barracks in the Kasr-el-Nil. A fourth went to an unmarked building in the Shari Suleiman Pasha. Wolff wanted to get into those briefcases. Today he would do a dry run.

When the aides came out Wolff followed the pair that went to the barracks. A minute later Abdullah emerged from a café and fell into step beside him. "Those two?" Abdullah said.

"Those two."

Abdullah was a fat man with a steel tooth. He was one of the richest men in Cairo, but unlike most rich Arabs he did not ape the Europeans. He wore sandals, a dirty robe and a fez. His greasy hair curled around his ears and his fingernails were black. His wealth came from crime. Abdullah was a thief.

Wolff liked him. He was sly, deceitful, cruel, generous, and always laughing; for Wolff he embodied the age-old vices and virtues of the Middle East. His army of children, grandchildren, nephews and nieces had been burgling houses and picking pockets in Cairo for thirty years. He had tentacles everywhere.

They followed the two officers into the modern city center. Abdullah said, "Do you want one briefcase, or both?"

Wolff considered. One was a casual theft; two looked organized. "One," he said. "It doesn't matter which."

Wolff had considered going to Abdullah for help after the discovery that the Villa les Oliviers was no longer safe. He had decided not to. Abdullah could certainly have hidden him away somewhere, but as soon as he had Wolff concealed, he would have opened negotiations to sell him to the British. Abdullah divided the world in two: his family and the rest. He was utterly loyal to his family and trusted them completely; he would cheat everyone else and expected them to try to cheat him.

They came to a busy corner. The two officers crossed the road, dodging the traffic. Wolff was about to follow when Abdullah put a hand on his arm. "We'll do it here," Abdullah said.

Wolff looked around, observing the buildings, the road junction and the street vendors. He smiled. "It's perfect," he said.

THEY did it the next day. Abdullah had indeed chosen the perfect spot for the snatch. It was where a busy side street joined a main road. On the corner was a café with tables outdoors, reducing the pavement to half its width. Outside the café, on the main road, was a bus stop, and those waiting for the bus simply milled about on the already crowded pavement. The side street was a little clearer, but Abdullah had remedied this shortcoming by detailing two acrobats to perform there.

Wolff sat at the corner table and worried that things might go wrong. He was terrified of going to prison. He could live without good food and wine and girls if he had the vast wild emptiness of the desert to console him; and he could forgo the freedom of the desert to live in a crowded city if he had the urban luxuries to console him; but he could not lose both. The idea of living in a tiny, colorless cell, among the scum of the earth, eating bad food, never seeing the blue sky or the open plains . . . panic touched him. He pushed it out of his mind.

At eleven forty-five the large, grubby form of Abdullah waddled past the café. His expression was vacant, but his small black eyes looked around sharply, checking his arrangements. He crossed the road and disappeared from view.

At five past twelve Wolff spotted two military caps among the massed heads in the distance. He sat on the edge of his chair. The officers came nearer. They were carrying their briefcases.

Across the street a parked car revved its idling engine. A bus drew up to the stop, and Wolff thought, Abdullah can't possibly have arranged *that*: it's a piece of luck, a bonus.

The officers were five yards from Wolff.

The car across the street, a big black Packard, pulled out suddenly. It came across the road like a charging elephant, motor screaming in low gear, heading for the side street, its horn blaring.

On the corner, a few feet from where Wolff sat, it plowed into the front of an old Fiat taxi.

The two officers stopped beside Wolff's table and stared at the crash. The taxi driver, a young Arab in a Western shirt and a fez, leaped out of his car. A young Greek in a mohair suit jumped out of the Packard. The Arab slapped the Greek and the Greek punched the Arab. The people getting off the bus, and those who had been intending to get on it, came closer.

Around the corner the acrobat who was standing on his colleague's head turned to look at the fight, seemed to lose his balance and fell into his audience. A small boy darted past Wolff's table. Wolff stood up, pointed at the boy and shouted at the top of his voice, "Stop, thief!"

The boy dashed off, running between the two officers. Wolff went after him, and four people sitting near Wolff jumped up and tried to grab the boy. Together they cannoned into the officers, knocking both of them to the ground. Several people began to shout, "Stop, thief!" Some newcomers thought the thief must be one of the fighting drivers. The crowd from the bus stop, the acrobats' audience, and most of the people in the café surged forward and began to attack one or the other of the drivers. Someone picked up a chair from the café and hurled it through the windshield of the Packard. The waiters, the kitchen staff and the proprietor of the café rushed out and began to attack everyone who swayed against, stumbled into or sat on their furniture. Everyone yelled at everyone else in five languages. Passing cars halted to watch the melee, the traffic backed up in three directions, and every stopped car sounded its horn. A dog struggled free of its leash and started biting people's legs in a frenzy of excitement. Everyone got off the bus. Drivers who had stopped to watch the fun regretted it when the fight engulfed their cars. Men, women and children jumped on the car roofs, fought on the hoods, fell on the running boards. A frightened goat ran into the souvenir shop next to the café and began to knock down all the tables laden with china and pottery and glass. A baboon came from somewhere—it had probably been riding the goat, in a common form of street entertainment—and ran across the heads in the crowd. From a window above the café a woman emptied a bucket of dirty water into the melee. Nobody noticed.

At last the police arrived.

When people heard the whistles there was a sudden scramble to get away before the arrests began. Wolff, who had fallen over early in the proceedings, picked himself up and strolled across the road to watch the denouement. By the time six people had been handcuffed there was no one left fighting except an old woman in black and a one-legged beggar, feebly shoving each other in the gutter. The café proprietor and the owner of the souvenir shop were berating the police for not coming sooner.

When the police tried to move the two crashed cars they discovered that during the fight the street urchins had jacked up the rear ends of both vehicles and stolen the tires. Every single light bulb in the bus had also disappeared.

And so had one British army briefcase.

Not long afterward Wolff sat in Abdullah's living room. Like its owner, it was dirty, comfortable and rich. Three small children and a puppy chased each other around the expensive sofas and inlaid tables. Abdullah sat cross-legged on an embroidered cushion with a baby in his lap. He smiled at Wolff. "My friend, what a success we have had!"

Wolff, sitting opposite him, said, "It was wonderful."

"Such a riot! And the bus arriving at just the right moment."

Wolff looked more closely at what Abdullah was doing. On the floor beside him was a pile of wallets, handbags and watches. As they spoke, Abdullah began to rifle a wallet. "You old rogue," Wolff said. "You had your boys in the crowd picking pockets."

Abdullah grinned, showing his steel tooth. "To go to all that trouble and then steal only one briefcase . . ."

"But you have got the briefcase."

"Of course." Abdullah made no move to produce the case. "You were to pay me fifty pounds on delivery."

Wolff counted out the notes and handed them over. Abdullah reached under the cushion he was sitting on and pulled out the briefcase.

Wolff took it from him and pried open the lock. Inside were ten sheets of paper closely typewritten in English. He read the first, then with growing incredulity leafed through the rest. "Dear God," he said softly. He started to laugh. He had stolen a complete set of barracks canteen menus for the month of June.

Vandam said to Colonel Bogge, "I've issued a notice reminding officers that General Staff papers are not to be carried about the town. One of my informants, the new girl I told you about, heard a rumor that the riot had been organized by Abdullah. He's a kind of Egyptian fagin. He also happens to be an informant."

"For what purpose was the riot supposedly organized?"

"Theft. A lot of stuff was stolen, but we have to consider the possibility that the main object was the briefcase. Abdullah may have been put up to it by Alex Wolff. The Asyut knife man."

"Oh, now really, I thought we had finished with all that."

"The Asyut murderer is still at large," Vandam said. "It may be significant that soon after his arrival in Cairo a General Staff officer is robbed of his briefcase. I've talked to Abdullah. He denies all knowledge of Alex Wolff, but I think he's lying. We could have field security pull him in and sweat him a little."

Bogge smiled. "If I went to field security with this story of stolen canteen menus, I'd be laughed out of the office. We've discussed this enough, Major. I don't believe the riot was organized, I don't believe Abdullah intended to steal the briefcase, and I don't believe Wolff is a Nazi spy. Is that clear?"

"Yes, sir."

"Good. Dismissed."

Chapter 4

Anwar el-Sadat fingered his mustache. He was rather pleased with it. He was only twenty-three years old, and in his Egyptian captain's uniform he looked a bit like a boy soldier; the mustache made him seem older. He needed all the authority he could get, for what he was about to propose was—as usual—faintly ludicrous. At these little meetings he was at pains to talk and act as if the handful of hotheads in the room really were going to throw the British out of Egypt any day now.

He deliberately made his voice a little deeper as he began to speak. "We have all been hoping that Rommel would defeat the British in the desert and so liberate our country. Now we have very bad news. Hitler has agreed to give Egypt to the Italians."

Sadat was exaggerating; this was not news, it was a rumor. The audience, however, responded with angry murmurs.

Sadat continued. "I propose that the Free Officers' Movement should negotiate a treaty with Germany, under which we would organize an uprising against the British in Cairo, and the Germans would guarantee the independence of Egypt after the defeat of the British." As he spoke, the irony of the situation struck him afresh: here he was, a peasant boy just off the farm, talking to half a dozen discontented Egyptian subalterns about negotiations with the German Reich. And yet, who else would represent the Egyptian people? The British were conquerors, the parliament was a puppet and King Faruk was of foreign descent: a fat, licentious Turk.

There was another reason for the proposal: Gamal Abdel Nasser had been posted to the Sudan; his absence gave Sadat a chance to become the leader of the rebel movement. He pushed the thought out of his mind, for it was ignoble. He had to get the others to agree to the proposal, then to agree to the means of carrying it out.

It was Kemel who spoke first. "But will the Germans take us seriously?" The others began to talk about whether it would work. Sadat made no contribution to the discussion. Let them talk, he thought; it's what they really like to do. In fact, he and Kemel had agreed beforehand that Kemel should ask this question, for it was a red herring. The real question was whether the Germans could be trusted to keep any agreement they made with a group of rebels; Sadat did *not* want the meeting to discuss that. If the Egyptians did rise up against the British, and if they were then betrayed by the Germans, they would see that nothing but independence was good enough—and perhaps turn for leadership to the man who had organized the uprising. Such hard political realities were not for meetings such as this. Kemel was the only person with whom Sadat could discuss tactics. Kemel was a policeman, a detective superintendent with the Cairo force, a shrewd, careful man.

"But we haven't any means of contacting the Germans." It was Imam speaking, one of the pilots. Sadat was pleased that they were already discussing *how to* do it rather than *whether to*.

Kemel had the answer. "We might send the message by plane."

"Yes!" Imam was young and fiery. "One of us could go up on patrol, divert from the course and land behind German lines."

One of the older pilots said, "On his return he would have to account for his diversion."

"He could not come back at all," Imam said forlornly.

Sadat said quietly, "He could come back with Rommel."

Imam's eyes lit up, and Sadat knew that the young pilot was seeing himself marching into Cairo at the head of an army of liberation. Sadat decided that Imam should take the message.

"Let us agree on the text of the message," Sadat said democratically. "I think we should make four points. One: We are honest Egyptians who have an organization within the army. Two: Like you, we are fighting the British. Three: We are able to recruit a rebel army to fight on your side. Four: We will organize an uprising in Cairo if you will guarantee the independence of Egypt after the British defeat. That leaves only the question of which of us will fly the plane." Sadat looked around the room, letting his gaze rest finally on Imam. After a moment's hesitation, Imam stood up. Sadat's eyes blazed with triumph.

Two days later Kemel walked the three miles from central Cairo to the suburb where Sadat lived. As a detective superintendent, Kemel had the use of an official car, but he rarely used it to go to rebel meetings, for security reasons.

Kemel was fifteen years older than Sadat, yet his attitude toward the younger man was one almost of hero worship. Kemel shared Sadat's cynicism, his realistic understanding of the levers of political power; but Sadat had something more, and that was a burning idealism which gave him unlimited energy.

Kemel wondered how to tell him the news.

The message to Rommel had been typed out and signed by Sadat and all the leading Free Officers except the absent Nasser. Imam had taken off in his Gladiator, with a compatriot, Baghdadi, following in a second plane. They had touched down at a prearranged spot in the desert to pick up Kemel, who gave the message to Imam and then climbed into Baghdadi's plane.

It was the first time Kemel had flown. The desert, so featureless from ground level, had been a mosaic of shapes and patterns: the patches of gravel, the carved volcanic hills. After a while both planes had turned due east, and Baghdadi spoke into his radio, telling base that Imam had veered off course and was not replying to radio calls. As expected, base told Baghdadi to follow

Imam. This little charade was necessary so that Baghdadi, who was to return, should not fall under suspicion.

They flew over a British army encampment. Both planes climbed. Directly ahead they saw signs of battle: great clouds of dust, explosions and gunfire. They turned to pass south of the battlefield. Kemel thought, Next we should come to a German base. Imam's plane lost height. Instead of following, Baghdadi climbed a little more and peeled off farther to the south. Then Kemel saw what the pilots had seen: a camp and a runway.

Now, approaching Sadat's house, Kemel recalled how elated he had felt, up there in the sky, when he realized the treaty was almost in Rommel's hands.

He knocked on the door. It was an ordinary family house, rather poorer than Kemel's home. In a moment Sadat came to the door, wearing a galabia and smoking a pipe. He saw Kemel's face and said immediately, "It went wrong."

"Yes." Kemel stepped inside. They went into the little room Sadat used as a study. There were a desk, a shelf of books, some cushions on the bare floor. They sat down. Kemel said, "We found a German runway. Imam descended. Then the Germans started to fire on him. It was an English plane, you see—we never considered that. He waggled his wings, and I suppose he tried to radio; anyway, they kept firing. The tail of the plane took a hit."

"Oh, God."

"He seemed to be going down very fast. Somehow he managed to land on his wheels, but he went off the hard surface and into a patch of sand; then his plane blew up."

"And Imam?"

"He could not possibly live through such a fire."

"We must find another way to get a message through," Sadat said. Kemel stared at him, and realized that his brisk tone was phony. Sadat tried to light his pipe, but his hand was shaking too much, and he had tears in his eyes. "The poor boy," he whispered.

WOLFF was back at square one; he knew where the secrets were, but he could not get at them. He might steal another briefcase, but that would begin to look, to the British, like a conspiracy. Besides, he needed regular, unimpeded access to secret papers. That was where Sonja came in.

She was lying on the bed, eating chocolates. Wolff came out of the bathroom wrapped in a big towel. "I've thought of another way to get into those briefcases," he said. "I'm going to make friends with a British officer. Then I'll bring him to the boat and go through his briefcase while he's in here with you."

Sonja said, "Oh, no."

He said, "Yes."

She sulked. "You promised to find me another Fawzi."

"All right. I'm still looking."

"You didn't promise to *look*, you promised to *find*."

Wolff went into the other room and got a bottle of champagne out of the icebox. He picked up two glasses, took them back into the bedroom. He poured and handed her a glass. "To the unknown British officer who is about to get the nicest surprise of his life."

"I won't have anything to do with an Englishman," Sonja said. "I hate them."

"That's why you'll do it—because you hate them. Just imagine it: while he's in here with you and thinking how lucky he is, I'll be reading his secret papers."

Wolff began to dress for the evening. He put on a shirt which had been made for him in a tiny tailor shop in the Old City—a British uniform shirt with a captain's pips on the shoulders.

Sonja said, "You're going to pretend to be British?"

"South African, I think. If I find a likely one, I'll take him to the Cha-Cha." He reached into his shirt and drew his knife from its underarm sheath. He went close to her and touched her naked shoulder with its point. "If you let me down, I'll use this."

She did not speak, but there was fear in her eyes.

SHEPHEARD's Hotel, as always, was packed with people: Levantine merchants holding noisy business meetings, Egyptian girls in their cheap gowns, and British officers—the hotel was out-of-bounds to other ranks. Wolff made his way through the crowded lounge to the long bar at the far end. Here it was a little quieter. Women were banned, and serious drinking was the order of the day. It was here that a lonely officer would come.

Wolff sat at the bar. He was about to order champagne, but then remembered his disguise and asked for whiskey and water. He had given careful thought to his clothes. The brown shoes were highly polished; the baggy brown shorts had a sharp crease; the bush shirt was worn outside the shorts; the flat cap was just slightly raked. He had also grown a mustache to complete the disguise. Since he was looking for an officer from GHQ, he would say that he himself was with BTE—British Troops in Egypt—a separate outfit.

There were fifteen or twenty officers in the bar, but he recognized none of them. He was looking specifically for any one of the aides who left GHQ each midday with their briefcases. He had memorized their faces and would recognize them instantly. He hoped it would not take long.

It took five minutes.

The major who walked in was a small man, thin, and probably in his mid-forties. His cheeks had the broken veins of a hard drinker. He had bulbous blue eyes and thin sandy hair. Every day he left GHQ at noon and walked to an unmarked building in the Shari Suleiman Pasha—carrying his briefcase.

Wolff's heart missed a beat.

The major came up to the bar, took off his cap and said, "Scotch. No ice. Make it snappy." He turned to Wolff. "Bloody weather," he said conversationally.

"Isn't it always, sir?" Wolff said.

"Bloody right. I'm Smith, GHQ."

"How do you do, sir," Wolff said. He knew that since Smith went from GHQ to another building every day, the major could not really be at GHQ; and he wondered briefly why the man should lie about it. He said, "I'm Slavenburg, BTE."

"Jolly good. Get you another?"

"Very kind of you, sir," Wolff said.

"Ease up on the sirs. No bull in the bar. What'll it be?"

"Whiskey and water, please."

"Shouldn't take water with it if I were you. Comes straight out of the Nile, they say."

"I'm used to it. Born in Africa, been in Cairo ten years." Wolff was slipping into Smith's abbreviated style of speech. I should have been an actor, he thought.

"Africa, eh? I thought you had a bit of an accent."

"Dutch father, English mother," Wolff explained. He raised his glass. "Cheers."

They drank. Smith said, "You know this place. What's a chap to do in the evening, other than drink in Shepheard's bar?"

Wolff pretended to consider. "Seen any belly dancing?"

Smith snorted in disgust. "Once. Fat woman wiggling her hips."

"Ah. Then you ought to see the real thing. Real belly dancing is the most erotic thing you've ever seen."

There was an odd light in Smith's eyes. "Is that so?"

Wolff thought, Major Smith, you are just what I need. He said, "Sonja is the best. Matter of fact, I was toying with the idea of going on to see her act myself. Care to join me?"

"Let's have another drink first," said Smith.

Watching Smith put away the liquor, Wolff reflected that the major seemed bored, weak-willed and alcoholic. Sonja should be able to seduce him easily.

They finished their drinks and took a taxi to the Cha-Cha Club. The place was crowded and hot, again. Wolff had to bribe a waiter to get a table. Sonja's act began moments after they sat down. Smith watched Sonja while Wolff watched Smith.

Wolff said, "Good, isn't she?"

"Fantastic," Smith replied without looking around.

"Matter of fact, I know her slightly," Wolff said. "Shall I ask her to join us afterward?"

This time Smith did look around. "Good Lord! Would you?"

In the storm of applause following her act, Sonja crossed the darkened stage to the wings. She walked quickly to her dressing room, where she took off her filmy pantaloons and sequined halter and put on a silk robe. She sat in front of the mirror to remove her makeup. There was a knock on the door. She called, "Come in."

One of the waiters entered with a note. The message said: "Table 41. Alex."

She crumpled the paper. So he had found one. That was quick. His instinct for weakness was working again.

She understood him because she was like him. She, too, used people. She even used him. He had style, taste, high-class friends and money; and one day he would take her to Berlin. It was one thing to be a star in Egypt, and quite another in Europe. She wanted to be queen of the cabaret in the most decadent city in the world. Wolff would be her passport. It must be unusual,

she thought, for two people to be so close and yet to love each other so little. He *would* use his knife on her if she did not do what he wanted.

She shuddered, stopped thinking about it. She put on a white gown with a low neck, stepped into white high-heeled sandals and fastened a heavy gold bracelet around each wrist. Around her neck she hung a gold chain with a teardrop pendant.

As she went out into the club, people fell quiet. Onstage she was separated from them by an invisible wall. Down here they could touch her, and they all wanted to. The danger thrilled her. She reached table 41 and both men stood up.

Wolff said, "Sonja, my dear, you were magnificent, as always. Allow me to introduce Major Smith."

Sonja shook his hand. He was a thin, chinless man with a fair mustache and ugly, bony hands. He looked at her as if she were an extravagant dessert. He said, "Enchanted, absolutely."

They sat down. Wolff poured champagne. Smith said, "Your dancing was splendid, mademoiselle. Very . . . artistic."

"You're too kind, Major."

Wolff was nervous, she could tell. He was not sure whether she would do what he wanted. In truth, she had not yet decided.

Wolff said to Smith, "I knew Sonja's late father."

It was a lie. Sonja knew why he had said it: to remind her. Her father had been a part-time thief. When there was work he worked, and when there was none he stole. One day he had tried to snatch the handbag of a European woman. In the scuffle the woman had been knocked down. She was an important woman, and Sonja's father had been flogged for the offense. He had died during the flogging.

Since then Sonja had hated the British with all her being. She wanted Hitler to humiliate them. She would do anything she could to help. She would even seduce an Englishman.

"Major Smith," she said, "you're a *very* attractive man." Wolff relaxed visibly.

Smith was startled. "Good Lord! Do you think so?"

"Yes, I do, Major."

"I say, I wish you'd call me Sandy."

Wolff stood up. "I'm afraid I've got to leave. Sonja, may I escort you home?"

Smith said, "You can leave that to me. That is, if Sonja..."

Sonja batted her eyelids. "Of course, Sandy."

Wolff excused himself. A waiter brought dinner. Sonja picked at it while Smith related his successes on the school cricket team. He was boring. Sonja kept remembering the flogging.

He drank steadily through dinner. When they left he was weaving slightly. She gave him her arm, more for his benefit than hers. They walked to the houseboat in the cool night air. "Would you like to see inside?" Sonja asked.

"Rather," Smith said. She led him over the gangplank and down the ladder. He looked around, wide-eyed. "I must say, it's very luxurious."

She gave him a drink and sat close to him. He touched her shoulder, kissed her cheek, roughly grabbed her. She shuddered but pulled him to her. She said, "Oh, Sandy, you're so strong."

She looked over his shoulder and saw Wolff watching through the hatch, laughing soundlessly.

Chapter 5

WILLIAM Vandam was beginning to despair of ever finding Alex Wolff. The Asyut murder was almost two weeks in the past, and Vandam was no closer to his quarry. He knew he was becoming a little obsessed with the man. What fascinated him had something to do with Wolff's *style:* the sideways manner in which he had slipped into Egypt, the sudden murder of Corporal Cox, the ease with which Wolff had melted into the city.

Vandam had made no real progress, but he had gathered some information, and the information had fed his obsession. The Villa les Oliviers was owned by someone called Achmed Rahmha. Achmed had inherited the house from his stepfather, Gamal Rahmha, a wealthy Cairo lawyer. Gamal had married one Eva Wolff, widow of Hans Wolff, both German nationals; he'd then adopted Hans and Eva's son, Alex, which explained how Achmed Rahmha got legitimate Egyptian papers in the name of Alexander Wolff.

Interviews with all surviving Rahmhas had produced nothing. Achmed, or Alex, had disappeared two years ago and had not been heard from since. Vandam was convinced that he had been in Germany. There was another branch of the Rahmha family, but they were nomads, and no one knew where they could be found. No doubt, Vandam thought, they had helped Wolff somehow with his reentry into Egypt.

Vandam sat in his office, smoking one cigarette after another, worrying about Wolff. The man was no low-grade collector of gossip. The briefcase theft proved he was after top-level stuff. But the spy had his problems, too. He had to explain himself to inquisitive neighbors, conceal his radio somewhere, find informants. One way or another, traces had to appear.

Vandam was convinced that Abdullah the thief was involved with Wolff. Vandam had offered him a large sum of money for information. Abdullah claimed to know nothing of anyone called Wolff, but the light of greed had flickered in his eyes.

Vandam paced the room. Something to do with *style*. Wolff might almost have been a man Vandam had known long ago but could no longer bring to mind. Style.

The phone rang. He picked it up. "Major Vandam."

"This is Major Calder in the paymaster's office. You sent us a note to look out for forged sterling. We've found some."

That was it—that was the trace. "Good!" Vandam said. "I need to see it as soon as possible."

"It's on its way, along with a list of people who paid it in."

"Marvelous." Vandam hung up. Forged sterling—it fitted. Sterling was no longer legal tender in Egypt. Officially Egypt was a sovereign country. However, people who did business with foreigners usually accepted sterling, then exchanged it for Egyptian money at the office of the paymaster general. Vandam opened his door and shouted along the hall. "Jakes! Bring me the file on forged bank notes."

"Yes, sir!" came a return shout.

Captain Jakes, an eager, reliable young man, was the most senior of Vandam's team. He appeared a moment later with a file.

Vandam switched on his desk light and said, "Right. Show me a picture of Nazi-style funny money."

Jakes flicked through the forgery file. He extracted a sheaf of glossy photographs. Each print showed the front and the back of a forged bank note—money taken from German spies captured in England. Black arrows indicated the errors by which the forgeries might be identified. Jakes said, "You'd think they'd know better than to give their spies funny money."

"Espionage is an expensive business," Vandam replied. "Why should they buy English currency in Switzerland when they can make it themselves? A spy has forged papers, he might as well have forged money."

Vandam's secretary came in. "Package from the paymaster, sir." Vandam signed the receipt and tore open the envelope. It contained several hundred pound notes. He put a pound note next to one of the photographs. "Look, Jakes."

The note bore the same error as the one in the photograph. "That's it, sir," said Jakes.

"Nazi money, made in Germany," said Vandam. "*Now* we're on his trail."

A short while later Vandam walked into the Cha-Cha Club. The manager said that since more than half his customers settled their bills in sterling, he could not possibly identify who paid in which currency. The chief cashier of Shepheard's Hotel told him something similar.

Vandam was expecting much the same story from the next location on his list, a small grocery store owned by one Mikis Aristopoulos. The store smelled of spices and coffee, but there was not much on the shelves. Aristopoulos himself was a short Greek of about twenty-five, with a wide, white-toothed smile. He said, "Good morning, sir. How can I help you?"

"You don't seem to have much to sell," Vandam remarked.

Aristopoulos smiled. "If you're looking for something particular, I may have it in stock. Have you shopped here before?"

So that was the system: scarce delicacies in the back room for regular customers only. Vandam said, "I'm not here to buy. Two days ago you exchanged one hundred and forty-seven English pounds at the office of the British paymaster general. Most of that was counterfeit."

Aristopoulos spread his arms in a huge shrug. "I take the money from English, I give it back to English. What can I do?"

"You can go to jail for passing counterfeit notes."

Aristopoulos stopped smiling. "Please. How could I know?"

"Was all that money paid to you by one person?"

"I don't know—"

"Think! Did anyone pay for a large order with English pounds?"

"Ah, yes! One hundred and twenty-six pounds ten shillings."

"His name?" Vandam held his breath.

"Wolff. I am shocked. He has been a good customer for years."

"Listen," Vandam said. "Did you deliver the groceries?"

"We offered to deliver, as usual, to his home, Villa les Oliviers, but this time Mr. Wolff took them with him."

"You haven't delivered there recently?"

"Not since Mr. Wolff came back. Sir, I am very sorry about this bad money. Perhaps something can be arranged . . . ?"

"Perhaps," Vandam replied thoughtfully.

Aristopoulos led him into the back room. The shelves here were well laden. Vandam noticed Russian caviar, American canned ham and English jam. Aristopoulos poured thick strong coffee into tiny cups. They drank. Aristopoulos said, "Perhaps, as a gesture of friendship, I could offer you something from my store. Some Scotch whisky?"

"I'm not interested in *that* kind of arrangement. I want to find Wolff. You said he was a regular customer. What does he buy?"

"Much champagne. Caviar. Coffee. Foreign liquor."

Style, Vandam thought. It was a question of style. "When he comes back I must find out where he lives. I'm going to give you an assistant."

"I want to help you, sir, but my business is private—"

"You've got no choice. It's help me, or go to jail." Vandam smiled. "I think I know the ideal person."

That evening after dinner Vandam called on Elene, carrying a huge bunch of flowers, feeling foolish. She lived in a spacious old apartment house near the Place de l'Opéra. The concierge directed him to the third floor. He climbed the curving marble staircase and knocked at 3A.

The door opened. She was wearing a simple yellow cotton dress with a full skirt; the color looked very pretty against her tan skin. She gazed at him blankly for a moment, then gave her impish smile. "Well, hello!" She stepped forward and kissed his cheek. "Come in."

He went inside and she closed the door. "I wasn't expecting the kiss," he said.

"All part of the act. Let me relieve you of your disguise."

He gave her the flowers. He felt he was being teased.

"Go in there while I put these in water," she said.

He followed her pointing finger into the living room. The room was comfortable, decorated in pink and gold and furnished with deep soft seats and a table of pale oak. It was a corner room, with windows on two sides, and now the evening sun shone in and made everything glow. On a couch was a book which she had, presumably, been reading when he knocked. He picked it up and sat down. The book was called *Stamboul Train*. It looked like cloak-and-dagger stuff.

She came in with the flowers in a vase, and the smell of wisteria filled the room. "Would you like a drink?"

"Can you make martinis?"

"Yes. Smoke if you want to."

"Thank you." She knew how to be hospitable, Vandam thought. He supposed she had to, given the way she earned her living.

"Do you like this stuff?" He indicated the book.

"I've been trying to find out how a spy should behave."

He saw her smiling, and realized he was being teased again. "I never know whether you're serious."

"Very rarely." She handed him a drink, sat down on the couch and looked at him over the rim of her glass. "To espionage."

He sipped his martini. It was perfect. So was she. The mellow sunshine burnished her skin. Her arms and legs looked smooth and soft. Damn. She had had this effect on him last time.

"What are you thinking about?" she said.

"Espionage."

She laughed. "You must love it," she said, knowing he was lying.

Vandam thought, How does she do this to me? She kept him always off-balance with her teasing and her insight, her innocent face and her long brown limbs. He said, "Catching spies can be satisfying work, but I don't love it."

"Why—because they hang when you catch them?"

"No. Because I don't always catch them."

"Are you proud of being so hardhearted?"

"I don't think I'm hardhearted. We're trying to kill more of them than they can kill of us." He thought, Why am I defending myself? Quickly he changed the subject. "Are your parents alive?"

She looked away from him, and then, seeming to yield to an

impulse, began to tell him of her background. She had been the eldest of five children in a desperately poor Jewish family in Alexandria. Her parents were cultured and loving people. "My father taught me English and my mother taught me to wear clean clothes," she said. When Elene was fifteen years old her father, a tailor, began to go blind. He could no longer work. Elene went to a British home as a live-in maid and sent her wages to her family. She fell in love with the son of the house and he seduced her. They had been found out, the son was sent away to the university, and Elene was paid off. She was terrified to return home and tell her ultra-orthodox father why she had been fired. She had lived on her payoff until a businessman set her up in a flat. Soon afterward her father was told how she was living, and he made the family sit *shibah* for her.

"What is *shibah?*" Vandam asked.

"Mourning."

Since then she had not heard from them, except for a message from a friend to tell her that her mother had died.

Vandam said, "Do you hate your father?"

She shrugged. "I think it turned out rather well." She spread her arms to indicate the apartment.

"But are you happy?"

She looked at him. Twice she seemed about to speak. Then she looked away. It was her turn to change the subject. "What brings you here tonight, Major?"

Vandam collected his thoughts. "I'm still looking for Alex Wolff," he began. "I haven't found him, but I've found his grocer. I want to put someone inside the shop in case he comes back."

"Me."

"That's what I had in mind."

"Then when he comes in I hit him over the head with a bag of sugar and guard the unconscious body until you come along."

Vandam laughed. "I believe you would." He realized how much he was relaxing, and resolved to pull himself together before he made a fool of himself. "Seriously, you have to discover where he lives. I thought perhaps you might befriend him."

"What do you mean by 'befriend'?"

"That's up to you. Just as long as you get his address."

"I see." Suddenly her mood had changed, and there was bitterness in her voice. The switch astonished Vandam. Surely a woman like Elene would not be offended by this suggestion? She said, "Why don't you have one of your soldiers follow him home?"

"He might realize he was being followed and shake off the tail—then he would never go back to the grocer's. But if you can persuade him, say, to invite you to his house for dinner, then we'll get the information we need without tipping our hand."

"I suppose it's no worse than what I've been doing."

"That's what I thought," said Vandam with relief.

She gave him a very black look.

"You start tomorrow," he said. He gave her the address. "I'll get in touch with you every few days, to make sure everything's all right. By the way, the shopkeeper thinks we're after Wolff for forgery. Don't talk to him about espionage."

"I won't." The change in her mood was permanent. They were no longer enjoying each other's company.

Vandam said, "I'll leave you to your thriller."

She stood up. "I'll see you out."

They went to the door. As Vandam stepped out, the tenant of the neighboring flat approached along the corridor. Vandam did what he had been determined not to do. He took Elene's arm, bent his head and kissed her mouth. Her lips moved briefly in response. The neighbor passed by, entered his flat and closed the door. Vandam pulled away. She said, "You're a good actor."

"Yes," he said. "Good-by." He turned and walked briskly down the corridor. He should have felt pleased with his evening's work, but instead he felt as if he had done something shameful. He heard her apartment door bang shut behind him.

ELENE leaned back against the closed door and cursed William Vandam. He had come into her life, full of English courtesy, asking her to do a new kind of work and help win the war. She had really thought he was going to change her life, give her a worthwhile job, something that mattered. Now it turned out to be the same old game—the one she wanted to stop.

She had been curiously happy to have him in her home, sitting on her couch, smoking and talking. He treated her as a person. She knew he would never pat her and say, "Don't you worry your pretty head."

And he had spoiled it all. He had revealed that he regarded her as nothing but a woman who sold herself.

She thought, But why do I mind so much?

IN THE early morning the tiled floor of the mosque was cold to Alex Wolff's bare feet. In the vastness of the pillared hall there was a silence, a sense of peace. A shaft of sunlight pierced one of the high narrow slits in the wall, and at that moment the muezzin began to cry, *"Allahu akbar! Allahu akbar!"*

Wolff turned to face Mecca.

He was wearing a long robe and a turban, and the shoes in his hand were simple Arab sandals. He was never quite sure why he did this. He was a true believer only in theory. He had been circumcised according to Islamic doctrine, and he had completed the pilgrimage to Mecca; but he drank alcohol and ate pork and he did not pray every day—let alone five times a day. Nevertheless, every so often he felt the need to immerse himself, just for a few minutes, in the familiar rituals.

He touched his ears with his hands, then clasped his hands in front of him, the left within the right. He bowed, then knelt down. Touching his forehead to the floor at appropriate moments, he recited the *el-fatha:* "In the name of God the merciful and compassionate. Praise be to God, the lord of the worlds, the merciful and compassionate, the Prince of the day of judgment; Thee we serve, and to Thee we pray for help . . ."

He looked over his right shoulder, then his left, to greet the two recording angels who wrote down his good and bad acts.

As he looked over his left shoulder he saw Abdullah. The thief smiled broadly, showing his steel tooth. Wolff got up and went out. He stopped outside to put on his sandals, and Abdullah came waddling after him.

"You are a devout man, like myself," Abdullah said. "I knew you would come, sooner or later, to your father's mosque."

Together they walked away from the mosque. Wolff said, "You've been looking for me?"

"Many people are looking for you. Knowing you to be a true believer, I could not betray you to the British; so I told Major Vandam that I knew nobody by the name of Alex Wolff, or Achmed Rahmha."

Wolff stopped abruptly. He steered Abdullah into an Arab café. They sat down. Wolff said, "He knows my Arab name."

"He knows all about you—except where to find you. He is patient and determined. If I were you, I should be afraid of him."

Suddenly Wolff *was* afraid.

"He has talked to your brothers. They said they knew nothing."

The café proprietor brought each of them a dish of mashed fava beans and a loaf of coarse bread. Abdullah spoke with his mouth full. "Vandam is offering one hundred pounds for your address. Ha! As if we would betray one of our own for money."

Wolff swallowed. "Even if you knew my address."

Abdullah shrugged. "It would be a small thing to find out."

"I know," Wolff said. "So I am going to tell you, as a sign of my faith in your friendship. I work in the kitchens at Shepheard's Hotel, cleaning pots. I sleep there on the floor."

"So cunning! You hide under their noses!"

"I know you will keep this secret," Wolff said. "And as a sign of my gratitude for your friendship, I hope you will accept from me a gift of one hundred pounds."

"But this is not necessary—"

"I insist. I will have the money sent to your house."

"Very well." Abdullah wiped his empty bowl with the last of his bread. "I must leave you now. *Allah yisallimak*—may God protect thee." He went out.

Wolff called for coffee and thought about Abdullah. The thief would betray him for a lot less than a hundred pounds, of course. The story about living in the kitchens was no more than a delaying tactic; so was the bribe. However, when at last Abdullah found out that Wolff was living on Sonja's houseboat in Zamalek, he would probably come to Wolff for more money instead of going to Vandam. The situation was under control—for the moment.

Wolff left the café and made his way to the central post office to use a telephone. He called GHQ and asked the operator for Major Sandy Smith.

"He's not here at the moment. May I take a message?"

Wolff had known the major would not be in—it was too early. "Tell him: Twelve noon today at Zamalek. Sign it: S." Wolff hung up and headed for the boat.

Since Sonja had seduced Smith, the major had sent her a dozen roses, a box of chocolates and two hand-delivered messages asking for another date. Wolff had forbidden her to reply. After a couple of days of suspense Smith would jump at any chance to see her again.

When Wolff got to the houseboat Sonja was just waking up. He prowled around the living room. At the far end, in the tiny open kitchen, there was a large broom closet. Wolff could just get inside if he bent his knees and ducked his head. However, he needed a peephole in the door.

He took a nail and with a flatiron banged it through the thin wood of the door at eye level. He used a kitchen fork to enlarge the opening. He got inside the closet again, shut the door and put his eye to the hole. He saw the bedroom curtains part. Sonja came into the living room. She looked around, surprised that he was not there. She shrugged, came across to the kitchen, picked up the kettle and turned on the tap.

Wolff opened the door and stepped out. "Good morning."

Sonja screamed.

Wolff laughed. "It's a good hiding place, isn't it?"

"What do you need a hiding place for?"

"To watch you and Major Smith. He's coming at noon today."

"Oh, no. Why so early?"

"Listen. If he's got anything worthwhile in that briefcase, he certainly isn't allowed to go wandering around the city with it. We mustn't give him time to take it to his office and lock it in the safe. What we want is for him to come rushing here straight from GHQ. You'd better start getting ready. I want you to look irresistible."

"I'm always irresistible." She went back to the bedroom.

Wolff took out a bottle of champagne, put it in a bucket of ice and placed it beside the bed with two glasses. Then he sat on a divan by a porthole to watch the towpath.

A few minutes after noon Major Smith appeared. He was hurrying, as if afraid to be late. He was carrying his briefcase.

Wolff grinned with satisfaction. "Here he comes," he called. He got into the closet and shut the door.

He heard Smith's footsteps on the gangplank and then on the deck. Looking through the peephole, he saw Smith come down the ladder into the boat. "Is anybody there?" Smith's voice was full of the expectation of disappointment. "Sonja?"

The Key to Rebecca

The bedroom curtains parted. Sonja stood there, her arms lifted to hold the curtains apart. She had put her hair up in a complex pyramid as she did sometimes for her act. She wore the baggy trousers of filmy gauze and a jeweled collar around her neck.

Smith dropped his briefcase and went to her. Quickly she undid the buttons on his bush shirt, slipped it off his shoulders and let it drop to the floor. As he embraced her, she drew him into the bedroom and closed the curtains behind them.

Wolff opened the closet door and stepped out. The briefcase lay on the floor just this side of the curtains. He knelt down and tried the catches. The case was locked. His eyes fell on Smith's bush shirt, lying in a heap where Sonja had dropped it.

With any luck the key to the briefcase would be in one of the breast or side pockets of the shirt. Wolff put his hand into the first pocket he came to and felt for a key. The pocket was empty. He turned the shirt over until he found another pocket. He felt in it. There was a bunch of keys inside. He breathed a silent sigh of relief. He tried the smallest key in the lock. It worked.

He opened the catch and lifted the flap. Inside was a sheaf of papers in a stiff cardboard folder. Wolff thought, No more menus, please. He opened the folder. The top sheet read:

OPERATION ABERDEEN

1. Allied forces will mount a major counterattack at dawn on June 5.

2. The attack will be two-pronged. . . .

"My God," Wolff whispered. "This is it!"

He listened to the noises of lovemaking in the bedroom. They were quite loud now. There might not be much time. The report was detailed. Wolff was not sure exactly how the British chain of command worked, but presumably the battles were planned at desert headquarters, then sent to GHQ in Cairo for approval. Plans for important battles would be discussed at the morning conferences, which Smith obviously attended. Wolff wondered again what department was housed in the unmarked building in the Shari Suleiman Pasha where Smith went each afternoon.

Wolff found a writing pad and a red pencil in a drawer, and began to make notes. The main Allied forces were besieged in an area they called the Cauldron. The June 5 counterattack was intended to be a breakout. It would begin at 0250 hours with the bombardment, by four regiments of artillery, of the Aslagh Ridge, on Rommel's eastern flank. The spearhead attack by the infantry of the 10th Indian Brigade would follow. When the Indians had breached the line the tanks of the 22nd Armored Brigade would rush through the gap. Meanwhile the 32nd Army Tank Brigade, with infantry support, would attack Rommel's northern flank at Sidra Ridge.

When he came to the end of the report Wolff realized he had been so absorbed that he had not noticed that the sounds of lovemaking had ceased. Now the bed creaked and a pair of feet hit the floor. Wolff tensed. He heard Sonja say, "Darling, drink a glass of champagne with me before you go."

"Your wish is my command."

Wolff relaxed. She may complain, he thought, but she does what I want! He looked quickly through the rest of the papers, making more notes. He was determined that he would not be caught now; Smith was a wonderful find, and it would be a tragedy to kill the goose the first time it laid a golden egg.

A cork popped loudly as he was writing. He wondered how quickly Smith could drink a glass of champagne, and decided to take no chances. He put the papers back in the folder and the folder back in the case. He closed the case and locked it. He put the keys back in the pocket of the bush shirt, got into the closet and shut the door. He was jubilant. He had struck gold.

It was half an hour before he saw, through the peephole, Smith come into the living room and reach for his shirt. Wolff was feeling very cramped. Sonja said, "Must you go so soon?"

"I'm afraid so," Smith said. "To be perfectly frank, I'm not actually supposed to carry this briefcase around with me. I had the very devil of a job to come here at noon. You see, I have to go from GHQ straight to my office. Well, I didn't do that today. I told my office I was lunching at GHQ, and told the chaps at GHQ I was lunching at my office. However, next time I'll go to my office, dump the briefcase and come on here."

Wolff thought, For God's sake, Sonja, say something!

She said, "Oh, but, Sandy, my housekeeper comes every afternoon to clean—we wouldn't be alone."

Smith frowned. "Then we'll have to meet in the evenings."

"But I have to work—and after my act I have to stay in the club and talk to the customers." She took Smith's hands and placed them on her hips. "Oh, Sandy, say you'll come at noon."

It was more than Smith could withstand. "Of course."

They kissed, and Smith picked up his case and left. Wolff listened to the footsteps crossing the deck and the gangplank. He stepped out of the closet. Sonja watched with malicious glee as he stretched his aching limbs. "Did you get what you wanted?"

"Better than I could have dreamed."

Wolff cut up bread and sausages for lunch while Sonja took a bath. After lunch he took out the English novel and the key to the code, and drafted his signal to Rommel. That evening when Sonja had gone to the Cha-Cha Club he set up the radio.

At exactly 2400 hours he tapped out his call sign, Sphinx. A few seconds later Rommel's desert listening post, or Horch Company, answered. Wolff sent a series of v's to enable them to tune in exactly; then, in code, he began: "Operation Aberdeen."

THE signal from the spy was only one of twenty or thirty reports on the desk of von Mellenthin, Rommel's intelligence officer, early on the morning of June 4. Von Mellenthin despised spy reports. Based on gossip and sheer guesswork, they were wrong as often as they were right. But this one *looked* different.

The spy, whose call sign was Sphinx, began his message: "Operation Aberdeen." He gave the date of the attack, the brigades involved and their specific roles, the places they would pounce, and the tactical thinking of the planners.

Von Mellenthin was not convinced, but he was interested. As the thermometer in his tent passed the 100-degree mark he began his routine round of morning discussions. In person and by field telephone he talked to the divisional intelligence officers and the Luftwaffe liaison officer for aerial reconnaissance. He told them to look out for the brigades mentioned in the spy's report. He also told them to watch for battle preparations in the areas from which the counterthrust would supposedly come. Von Mellenthin then went to the command vehicle.

The morning discussion there was brief, for Rommel had already made his major decisions and given his orders for the day during the previous evening. Besides, Rommel was not in a reflective mood in the mornings; he wanted action. He tore around the desert, going from one front-line position to another in his staff car or his Storch aircraft, giving new orders, joking with the men and taking charge of skirmishes. Von Mellenthin went with him today to make his own assessment of the intelligence reports.

In the evening the Italian division on the Aslagh Ridge reported signs of increased enemy air reconnaissance. The Luftwaffe reported activity in no-man's-land which might have been an advance party marking out an assembly point. There was a garbled radio intercept in which an Indian brigade requested urgent clarification of the morning's orders with reference to the timing of artillery bombardment. The evidence was building.

Von Mellenthin checked his card index for the 32nd Army Tank Brigade and discovered that they had recently been sighted at Rigel Ridge—a logical position from which to attack Sidra Ridge. He decided to gamble on Sphinx.

At 1830 hours he took his report to the command vehicle. Rommel was there with his chief of staff, Colonel Fritz Bayerlein, and Field Marshal Kesselring. They stood around a camp table, looking at the operations map. Rommel's large, balding head appeared too big for his small body. He looked tired and thin. But his slitted dark eyes were bright with enthusiasm.

Von Mellenthin clicked his heels and handed over the report, then he explained his conclusions on the map. When he was done, Kesselring said, "And all this is based on the report of a spy?"

"No, Field Marshal," von Mellenthin said firmly. "There are confirming indications."

Kesselring said, "We really can't plan battles on the basis of information from some grubby little secret agent in Cairo."

Rommel said crossly, "I am inclined to believe this report."

Von Mellenthin watched the two men. They were curiously balanced in terms of power. Kesselring outranked Rommel, but Rommel did not take orders from him, by some whim of Hitler's. Both men had patrons in Berlin. Although Rommel had the last word here in the desert, back in Europe—von Mellenthin knew—Kesselring was maneuvering to get rid of him.

Rommel looked at the map again. "Let us be ready, then, for a two-pronged attack."

SIXTEEN DAYS LATER VON MELLENTHIN and Rommel watched the sun rise over Tobruk.

They knelt together near an escarpment, waiting for the start of the battle. Rommel was wearing the goggles which had become his trademark. He was in top form: bright-eyed, lively and confident. You could almost hear his brain tick as he scanned the landscape and computed how the battle might go.

Von Mellenthin said, "The spy was right."

Rommel smiled. "That's exactly what I was thinking."

The Allied counterattack of June 5 had come precisely as forecast, and Rommel's defense had worked so well that three of the Allied brigades involved had been wiped out. Rommel had pressed his advantage remorselessly. On June 14 the Gazala line had been broken and today, June 20, they were to besiege the vital British coastal garrison of Tobruk, with its supplies of fuel, explosives, vehicles.

At twenty minutes past five the attack began.

A sound like distant thunder swelled to a deafening roar as the Stukas approached. The first formation flew over, dived toward the British positions and dropped their bombs. A great cloud of dust and smoke arose, and with that, Rommel's entire artillery forces opened fire with an earsplitting crash.

AT TEN thirty that morning Lieutenant Colonel Bogge poked his head into Vandam's office and said, "Tobruk is under siege."

It seemed pointless to work then. Vandam went on mechanically, trying to think of a fresh approach to the Alex Wolff case, but everything seemed hopelessly trivial. The news became more depressing as the day wore on. The Germans breached the thirty-five-mile perimeter wire around Tobruk; they bridged the anti-tank ditch; they crossed the inner minefield; they reached the strategic road junction known as King's Cross. By evening the 21st Panzers had entered Tobruk and fired from the quay on several British ships which were trying, belatedly, to escape to the open sea. A number of vessels had been sunk.

Vandam spent the night in the officers' mess, waiting for news. The sun rose. A cook came in with coffee. As Vandam was drinking his, a captain came down with a bulletin. "General Klopper surrendered the garrison of Tobruk to Rommel at dawn today."

Vandam, overwhelmed with despair, left the mess and walked home. He felt impotent and useless, sitting in Cairo hunting spies while out in the desert his country was losing the war. It crossed his mind that Alex Wolff might have had something to do with Rommel's latest victories; but he dismissed the thought as farfetched. He felt so depressed that he wondered if things could possibly get any worse, and he realized that of course they could.

Chapter 6

AFTER two weeks in the shop Elene was ready to strangle Mikis Aristopoulos. The shop itself was fine. She liked the spicy smells and the rows of gaily colored boxes and cans on the shelves in the back room. The work was easy, the time passed quickly. But the boss was a pain, always making passes. Every chance he got he would touch her arm or her shoulder; each time he went by her he would brush against her.

She did not need this. Her emotions were too confused already. She both liked and loathed William Vandam, who talked to her as an equal, then treated her like a kept woman; she was supposed to entice Alex Wolff, whom she had never met; and she was being harassed by Mikis Aristopoulos. They all use me, she thought; it's the story of my life.

She wondered what Wolff would be like. It was easy for Vandam to tell her to befriend him. But a lot depended on the man. Some men liked her immediately. With others it was impossible. Half of her hoped it would be impossible with Wolff. The other half remembered that he was a German spy, and Rommel was coming closer every day, and if the Nazis ever got to Cairo . . .

Aristopoulos brought a box of pasta out from the storeroom. On the way he stroked her hip. She moved aside. She heard someone come into the shop. She thought, I'll teach the Greek a lesson. As he went into the storeroom, she shouted after him in Arabic, "If you touch me again, I'll cut your hand off!"

There was a burst of laughter from the customer. She turned and looked at him. He was a European, but he understood Arabic. He called toward the back room, "What have you been doing, Aristopoulos, you young goat?"

Aristopoulos poked his head around the door. "Good day, sir.

This is my niece, Elene." His face showed embarrassment and something else which Elene could not read. He ducked back into the storeroom.

"Niece!" The customer looked at Elene. "A likely tale."

He was a big man in his thirties with dark hair, dark skin and dark eyes. He had a large hooked nose. When he smiled he showed small even teeth—like a cat's. Elene knew the signs of wealth and she saw them here: a silk shirt, a gold wristwatch, tailored cotton trousers with a crocodile belt, handmade shoes.

Elene said, "How can I help you?"

He looked at her, contemplating several possible answers, then said, "Let's start with some English marmalade."

"Yes." She went to the storeroom to get a jar.

"It's him!" Aristopoulos hissed. "The bad-money man—Wolff!"

"Oh, God!" Her mind went blank. "What shall I say to him?"

"I don't know—give him the marmalade— I don't know—"

"The marmalade, right." She got a jar and returned to the shop. She forced herself to smile at Wolff. "What else?"

"Two pounds of the dark coffee, ground fine."

He was watching her while she weighed the coffee and put it through the grinder. Suddenly she was afraid of him. He seemed poised and confident: it would be hard to deceive him. "Something else?" she asked.

"A tin of ham."

She moved around the shop, finding what he wanted and putting the goods on the counter. She thought, I must talk to him, I can't keep saying "Something else?" I'm supposed to befriend him. "Something else?" she said.

"A half case of champagne. I think that's all."

The cardboard box containing six full bottles was heavy. She dragged it out of the back room. "I expect you'd like us to deliver this order," she said. She tried to make it sound casual.

He seemed to look through her with his dark eyes. "No delivery," he said firmly.

She nodded. "As you wish." She had not really expected it to work, but she was disappointed all the same.

She began to add up the bill. Wolff said, "Aristopoulos must be doing well, to employ an assistant."

"You wouldn't say that if you knew what he pays me."

"Don't you like the job?"

She looked at him. "I'd do *anything* to get out of here."

"What did you have in mind?" He was very quick.

She shrugged, and went back to her addition. Eventually she said, "Thirteen pounds ten shillings and fourpence."

"How did you know I'd pay in sterling?"

He was *quick*. She was afraid she had given herself away. She had an inspiration. "You're a British officer, aren't you?"

He laughed loudly at that. He took out a roll of pound notes and gave her fourteen. She gave him his change in Egyptian coins. She was thinking, What else can I do? What else can I say? She began to pack his purchases in a brown paper shopping bag. She said, "Are you having a party? I love parties."

"What makes you ask?"

"The champagne."

"Ah. Well, life is one long party."

She thought, I've failed. He will go away now, and perhaps he won't come back for weeks, perhaps never.

He lifted the case of champagne to his left shoulder, and picked up the shopping bag with his right hand. "Good-by," he said. But he turned around at the door. "Meet me at the Oasis Restaurant on Wednesday night at seven thirty. The name is Alex Wolff."

"All right!" she said jubilantly. Then he was gone.

IT WAS a long drive out into the desert. Jakes sat next to the driver; Vandam and Bogge sat in back. Vandam was exultant. An Australian company had captured a German wireless listening post. It was the first good news Vandam had heard for months.

They arrived at midday. Field intelligence men were already at work. Prisoners were being interrogated in a small tent. Enemy-ordnance experts were examining weapons and vehicles. It was the task of Bogge's squad to go through the material in the captured radio trucks to determine how much the Germans had been learning in advance about Allied movements.

They each took a truck. Vandam's was a mess. The Germans had begun to destroy their papers when they realized the battle was lost. Boxes had been emptied and a small fire started, but it had been put out quickly. There was blood on a cardboard folder: someone had died defending his secrets.

Vandam went to work. They would have tried to destroy the important papers first, so he began with the half-burned pile. There were many Allied radio signals, intercepted and in some cases decoded. As he worked, Vandam began to realize that German intelligence's wireless interception was picking up an awful lot of useful information.

At the bottom of the half-burned pile was a novel in English. Vandam read the first line: "Last night I dreamt I went to Manderley again." The title was familiar: *Rebecca* by Daphne du Maurier. Vandam thought his wife might have read it. It seemed to be about a young woman living in an English country house.

It was peculiar reading for the Afrika Korps. And why in English? It might have been taken from a captured British soldier, but Vandam was doubtful; in his experience, soldiers read hard-boiled private-eye stories and the Bible. He could think of only one possibility: the book was the basis of a code.

A book code was a variation on the one-time pad, which had letters and numbers randomly printed in five-character groups. Only two copies of each pad were made: one for the sender, one for the recipient. Each sheet was used for one message, then destroyed. Because each sheet was used only once, the code could not be broken. A book code worked the same way, except that the pages were not necessarily destroyed after use.

A book had one big advantage over a pad. A pad was unmistakably intended for ciphering, but a book looked quite innocent. This would be important to an agent behind enemy lines. This might also explain why the book was in English. A spy in British territory would need to carry a book in English.

Vandam examined the book closely. The price had been written in pencil on the endpaper, then erased. Trying to read the impression left by the pencil, Vandam made out the number 50, followed by *esc*—fifty escudos. The book had probably been bought in neutral Portugal, a hive of low-level espionage.

As soon as he got back to Cairo he would send a message to the Lisbon intelligence station to check the English-language bookshops in Portugal—there could not be many. At least two copies would have been bought, and a bookseller might remember such a sale. Vandam was pretty sure the other copy was in Cairo, and he thought he knew who was using it.

He picked up the book and stepped out of the truck. Bogge, white-faced and angry to the point of hysteria, was stomping across the dusty sand. He handed Vandam a sheet of paper.

It was a decoded radio signal, timed at midnight on June 3, call sign, Sphinx. The message bore the heading Operation Aberdeen.

Vandam was thunderstruck. Operation Aberdeen had taken place on June 5, and the Germans had received a signal about it over twenty-four hours earlier. "My God, this is a disaster."

"Of course it's a disaster!" Bogge yelled. "It means Rommel is getting full details of our attacks before they begin!"

Jakes appeared. "Excuse me, sir—"

Vandam said abruptly, "Not now, Jakes."

"Stay here, Jakes," Bogge said. "This concerns you, too." Then the enraged Bogge turned back to Vandam. "They must be getting this stuff from an English officer. Your job is security leaks—this is your bloody responsibility!" He stumped off in a fury.

Vandam sat down on the step of the truck and lit a cigarette with a shaking hand. He thought, Who is this man Wolff? Not only had he penetrated Cairo and evaded Vandam's net, he had gained access to high-level secrets. Of course it was possible that Wolff had nothing to do with the radio signal—but it was hard to believe there might be two like him in Cairo.

Jakes was standing beside Vandam, staring at the decoded signal. Vandam said, "Not only is this information getting through, but Rommel is using it. If you recall the fighting on June fifth—"

"It was a massacre," Jakes said.

And it was my fault, Vandam thought. Bogge had been right about that. One man could not win the war, but one man could lose it. Vandam did not want to be that man.

Jakes snapped his fingers. "I forgot what I came to tell you: you're wanted on the field telephone. It's GHQ. There's an Egyptian woman in your office, asking for you, refusing to leave. She says she has an urgent message."

Vandam thought, Elene! She must have made contact with Wolff. He ran to the command vehicle and grabbed the phone. "Yes?"

"William?"

"Elene!" He wanted to tell her how good it was to hear her voice, but instead he said, "What happened?"

"He came into the shop. I've got a date with him."

"Well done! Where and when?"

"Tomorrow night, seven thirty, at the Oasis Restaurant."

"I'll be there. Elene, I can't tell you how grateful I am." Vandam put down the phone.

Bogge was standing behind him. "What the devil do you mean by using the field telephone to make dates with your girl friends?"

Vandam gave him a sunny smile. "That wasn't a girl friend, it was an informant," he said. "She's made contact with the spy. I expect to arrest him tomorrow night."

WOLFF watched Sonja eat. The liver was underdone, pink and soft, just as she liked it. She ate with relish, as usual. They both knew that Wolff was taking a small but unnecessary risk by bringing her to a restaurant, and they both felt the risk was worth it. The most important thing in life for both of them was the indulgence of their appetites, and life would hardly be worth living without good food.

Sonja finished her liver and the waiter brought an ice-cream dessert. When finally she quit dancing she would grow fat. Wolff imagined her in twenty years' time: she would have three chins and a vast bosom.

"What are you smiling at?" Sonja said.

"You as an old woman, in a shapeless black dress and a veil."

"I won't be like that. I shall live in a palace surrounded by attractive young men and women eager to gratify my slightest whim. What about you?"

Wolff laughed. He called the waiter and asked for coffee, brandy and the bill. He said to Sonja, "There's some news. You were so good with Major Smith, you deserve a treat. I think I've found another Fawzi."

She was suddenly very still. "Who is she?"

"The grocer's niece. She's a beauty. And she's dying to get away from Aristopoulos. I'm taking her to dinner tomorrow night."

"Will you bring her home?"

"Maybe. I don't want to spoil everything by rushing her." Wolff sipped his brandy. He felt good: full of food and wine, his mission going remarkably well and a new adventure in view. When the bill came he paid it with English pound notes.

As they were about to leave, Ibrahim, the proprietor, came over with the brandy bottle. "Monsieur, madame, I hope you will accept a glass of brandy with the compliments of the house."

"Very kind," said Wolff.

Ibrahim poured them more brandy and bowed away. That should keep them sitting still for a while longer, he thought. Two days earlier a friend who was a cashier at the Metropolitan Hotel had told him how the British paymaster general had refused to exchange some English pound notes which had been passed in the hotel bar. The notes were counterfeit. What was so unfair was that the British had confiscated the money.

This was not going to happen to Ibrahim. His friend from the Metropolitan had told him how to spot the forgeries, and since then he had checked every pound note before putting it in the till. When he received the counterfeit notes from the tall European who had bought the most expensive dishes for the famous belly dancer, he decided to call the British military police. They would prevent the customer from running off and perhaps help persuade him to pay by check or with an IOU. Ibrahim left by the back door and went to use a neighbor's telephone.

He returned in a few minutes, and Wolff saw him whispering to a waiter. He guessed they were talking about the famous Sonja.

She yawned. It was time to put her to bed. Wolff waved to the waiter and said, "Please fetch Madame's wrap." The man went off, paused to mutter something to the proprietor, then continued toward the cloakroom. An alarm sounded in Wolff's mind.

He toyed with a spoon as he waited for Sonja's wrap. The proprietor went out the front door and came back in again. He approached their table. "May I get you a taxi?"

Wolff said, "I'd like a breath of air. We'll walk a little."

The waiter brought Sonja's wrap. The proprietor kept looking at the door. Wolff heard another alarm, this one louder. He said to the proprietor, "Is something the matter?"

The man looked very worried. "I must mention a delicate problem, sir." There was the sound of a vehicle noisily drawing up outside. "The money with which you paid me. It's counterfeit."

The restaurant door burst open and three military policemen marched in. Wolff stared at them openmouthed. It was all happening so quickly. Military police. Counterfeit money. He was suddenly afraid. He might go to jail. Those imbeciles in Berlin must have given him forged notes.

The MPs marched up to the table. Two were British and the third was Australian. Each of them had a small gun in a belt holster. The senior British MP said, "Is this the man?"

"Just a moment," Wolff said, and was astonished at how cool his voice sounded. "The proprietor has, this very minute, told me that my money is no good. I don't believe this, but I'm prepared to humor him. I'm sure we can make some arrangement. It really wasn't necessary to call the police."

The senior MP said, "It's an offense to pass forged money."

"It is an offense *knowingly* to pass forged money." As Wolff listened to his own voice, quiet and persuasive, his confidence grew. "Well then, I will write a check to cover my bill, and use Egyptian money for the tip. Tomorrow I will take the allegedly counterfeit notes to the British paymaster general for examination, and if they really are forgeries I will surrender them. That should satisfy everyone."

The MP replied, "All the same, sir, you'll have to come with me. We need to ask you some questions. Those are my orders."

"Very well then," said Wolff. He could feel the fear pumping desperate strength into his arms. As he stood up, he picked up the table and threw it at the senior MP. Its edge struck him on the bridge of the nose. He fell back and the table landed on top of him.

Wolff grabbed the proprietor and pushed him at the second British MP. Then he jumped the third MP, the Australian, and punched his face. The Australian took the punch, but did not fall. The British MP pushed the proprietor out of the way and kicked Wolff's feet from under him.

Wolff landed heavily, his back hitting the tiled floor. The Englishman jumped on his chest, beating him about the head. The Australian sat on Wolff's feet. Then Wolff saw above him Sonja's face, twisted with rage. The thought flashed through his mind that she was remembering another beating that had been administered by British soldiers. She raised a heavy chair high in the air, and brought it down with all her might. A corner struck the British MP's mouth, and he gave a shout of pain.

The Australian stood up and grabbed Sonja from behind. Wolff threw off the wounded Englishman, then scrambled to his feet.

He reached inside his shirt and whipped out his knife.

The Australian pushed Sonja aside, took a pace forward, spotted the knife and stopped. Wolff saw the man's eyes flicker to one side, then the other, where his partners lay on the floor. The Australian's hand went to his holster.

As Sonja threw herself at the MP, Wolff turned and dashed for the door. He flung it open with a crash. A shot rang out.

VANDAM raced the motorcycle through the streets at a dangerous speed. He had ripped the blackout mask off the headlight and was driving with his thumb on the horn, weaving through the traffic, ignoring the outraged hooting of the cars, the raised fists.

The assistant provost marshal had called him at home. "Vandam, we've just had a call from a restaurant where a European is trying to pass some of that funny money."

"*Where?*" The APM told him, and Vandam ran out of the house. He wanted desperately to get his hands on Alex Wolff.

He swerved to avoid a pothole, then opened the throttle and roared down a quiet street. The address was near the Old City. He turned two more corners and was there. The street was narrow and dark. He was halfway down it when he heard the *crack!* of a small firearm and the sound of glass shattering. A tall man ran out of a door. It had to be Wolff.

Vandam felt a surge of savagery. He twisted the throttle and roared after the man, catching him in the beam of the headlight. The fugitive was running strongly, legs pumping. When the light hit him he glanced back over his shoulder. Vandam glimpsed a hawk nose, a mustache, a mouth open and panting. Vandam would have shot him, but GHQ officers did not carry guns.

The motorcycle gained fast. When they were almost level Wolff suddenly turned a corner. Vandam braked and went into a back-wheel skid, came to a stop and then raced forward again.

He saw Wolff disappear into a narrow alleyway. Without slowing down, Vandam turned the corner and drove into the alley. The bike plunged out into empty space. Vandam's stomach turned over. The white cone of his headlight illuminated nothing. He thought he was falling into a pit. The back wheel hit something. The front wheel went down, then hit. The headlight showed a flight of steps. The bike bounced, landed again, descended the steps in a series of spine-jarring bumps. With each bump Vandam was sure he would lose control and crash. He reached the foot of the staircase. He saw Wolff turn another corner, and followed. They were in a maze of alleys. Wolff ran up a short flight of steps.

Vandam accelerated. A moment before hitting the bottom of the stairs he jerked the handlebars. The front wheel lifted. The bike bumped crazily up. Vandam reached the top.

He found himself in a long passage with high, blank walls on either side. Wolff was still in front of him, still running. Vandam put on a burst of speed, drew level, eased ahead, then braked sharply. The back wheel skidded and the front wheel hit a wall. He leaped off as the bike fell over, and landed on his feet, facing Wolff. The smashed headlight threw a shaft of light into the darkness of the passage. Without pausing in his stride, Wolff jumped over the bike and crashed into Vandam. Vandam, still unsteady, stumbled backward and fell. He reached out blindly in the dark, found Wolff's ankle, gripped and yanked. Wolff crashed to the ground.

The engine of the bike had cut out, and in the silence Vandam could hear Wolff's breathing, ragged and hoarse. He could smell him, too: a smell of booze and perspiration and fear. But he could not see his face. For a split second the two of them lay on the ground, one exhausted, the other momentarily stunned. Then they both scrambled to their feet. Vandam jumped at Wolff. He tried to pin his arms, but he could not hold on to him. Suddenly Vandam let go and threw a punch. It landed somewhere soft, and Wolff said, "*Ooff.*" Vandam punched again, aiming for the face, but Wolff dodged. Something in his hand glinted in the dim light. Vandam thought, A knife!

The blade flashed toward his throat. He jerked back reflexively. There was a searing pain all across his cheek. His hand flew to his face. He felt a gush of hot blood. Then he felt himself falling, and he heard Wolff running away, and everything turned black.

IN THE hospital a nurse froze half of Vandam's face with anesthetic, then Dr. Abuthnot stitched up his cheek. She put on a dressing and secured it by tying a bandage around his head. "I must look like a toothache cartoon," he said.

She looked grave. She did not have a big sense of humor. "You won't be so chirpy when the anesthetic wears off. Your face is going to hurt. I'll give you a painkiller."

"No, thanks," said Vandam.

"Don't be a tough guy, Major," she said. "You'll regret it."

He looked at her, in her white hospital coat and her sensible flat-heeled shoes, and wondered how he had ever found her even faintly desirable. She was pleasant enough, but she was also cold, superior and antiseptic. Not like Elene.

"A painkiller will send me to sleep," he told her. "I have some important work that won't wait."

"You can't *work*. You're weak from loss of blood. In a few hours you'll feel dizzy and exhausted."

"I'll feel worse if the Germans take Cairo." He stood up, shook her hand and left.

Jakes was waiting outside with a car. "I knew they wouldn't be able to keep you long, sir. Shall I drive you home?"

"No." Vandam's watch had stopped. "What's the time?"

"Five past two."

"I presume Wolff wasn't dining alone."

"No, sir. His companion is under arrest at GHQ. A real dish. Name of Sonja."

"The dancer?"

"No less."

"Drive me there." The car pulled away.

Wolff was a cool customer, Vandam thought, to go out with the most famous belly dancer in Egypt in between stealing British military secrets. Well, he would not be so cool now. That was unfortunate in a way: having been warned by this incident that the British were on to him, he would be more careful from now on.

They arrived at GHQ and got out of the car. Vandam said, "What's been done with her since she arrived?"

"The no-treatment treatment," Jakes said. "A bare room, no food, no drink, no questions."

"Good." It was a pity, all the same, that she had been given time to collect her thoughts.

Jakes led the way to the interview room. Vandam looked in through the peephole. It was a square room, without windows but bright with electric light. There were a table and two chairs.

Jakes was right, Vandam thought; Sonja was a dish. However, she was by no means *pretty*. She was something of an amazon, with her ripe, voluptuous body and strong features. She wore a long gown of garish yellow. She was pacing back and forth.

Vandam opened the door and went in. He sat down at the table without speaking. This left her standing, which was a psychological disadvantage for a woman. Score the first point to me, he thought. He heard Jakes come in behind him. He looked up at Sonja. "Sit down."

She stood gazing at him, and a slow smile spread across her face. She pointed at his bandage. "Did he do that to you?"

Score the second point to her.

"Sit down." She sat. "Who is 'he'?"

"Alex Wolff, the man you *tried* to beat up tonight."

"And who is Alex Wolff?"

"A wealthy patron of the Cha-Cha Club."

"How long have you known him?"

She looked at her watch. "Five hours."

"What is your relationship with him?"

She shrugged. "He was a date."

"How did you meet?"

"The usual way. Mr. Wolff invited me to his table, gave me a glass of champagne and asked me to have dinner. I accepted."

"Why?"

"Mr. Wolff seemed like an unusual sort of man." She looked at Vandam's face again, and grinned. "He *was* an unusual man."

"What is your address?"

"*Jihan*, Zamalek. It's a houseboat."

"Age?"

"How discourteous. I refuse to answer."

"You're on dangerous ground—"

"No, *you* are on dangerous ground." Her sudden fury startled Vandam. "At least ten people saw your uniformed bullies arrest me. By midday half of Cairo will know that the British have put Sonja in jail. If I don't appear at the Cha-Cha, there will be a riot. No, mister, it isn't me who's on dangerous ground."

Vandam remained expressionless. He had to ignore what she said, because she was right. "Let's go over this again," he said mildly. "You say you met Wolff at the Cha-Cha—"

"No," she interrupted. "I won't go over it again. I'll answer questions, but I will not be interrogated." She stood up, turned her chair around and sat down with her back to Vandam.

Vandam stared at the back of her head. He was angry with himself for letting her outmaneuver him, but his anger was mixed with a sneaking admiration for the way she had done it. Abruptly he got up and left the room. Jakes followed. In the corridor Vandam told him, "We'll have to let her go."

Jakes went to give instructions. While he waited, Vandam thought about Sonja. He wondered from what source she had been drawing the strength to defy him. It was true that her fame gave her some protection, but in threatening him with it she ought to have been blustering and a little desperate.

He ran over the conversation in his mind. She had been calm, expressionless, except when she had smiled at his wound. Then at the end, as she raged at him, what had he seen there in her face? Not just anger. Not fear. Then he had it: hatred. She hated him. But he was nothing to her, except a British officer. Therefore she hated the British. And her hatred had given her strength.

Suddenly Vandam was tired. He sat down heavily on a bench in the corridor. From where was *he* to draw strength? He imagined the Nazis marching into Cairo. People like Sonja looked at Egypt under British rule and felt that the Nazis had already arrived. And seeing the British through her eyes, it had a certain plausibility: the Nazis said that Jews were subhuman, and the British said that blacks were like children; there was no freedom of the press in Germany, and there was none in Egypt, either; and the British, like the Germans, had their political prisoners.

The anesthetic in his face was wearing off. He could feel a sharp line of pain across his cheek. He thought of Billy. He did not want the boy to miss him at breakfast. Perhaps I'll stay awake, take him to school, then go home and sleep. What would Billy's life be like under the Nazis? They would teach him to despise the Arabs. His present teachers were no great admirers of African culture, but at least Vandam could do a little to make his son realize that people who were different were not necessarily stupid.

He thought of Elene in a concentration camp. He shuddered.
We're not very admirable, especially in our colonies, he thought.

But the Nazis are worse. Think about the people you love, and the issues become clearer. Draw strength from that.

Jakes came back. Vandam said, "She's an Anglophobe—she hates the British. I don't believe Wolff was a casual pickup. Now take me to the main police station."

When Jakes stopped the car outside police headquarters Vandam said, "We want the chief of detectives."

"I shouldn't think he'll be here at this hour—"

"No. Get his address. We'll wake him up."

Jakes went into the building. Vandam stared ahead through the windshield. Dawn was on its way. The stars had winked out, and now the sky was gray rather than black.

Jakes came back. "Gezira," he said. They drove across the bridge to the island. Jakes stopped the car outside a small, pretty single-story house with a garden. Vandam guessed that the chief of detectives was doing well enough out of his bribes, but not too well. A cautious man, perhaps; it was a good sign.

They walked up the path and hammered on the door. Jakes put on his drill sergeant's voice. "Military intelligence—open up!"

A minute later a small, handsome Arab opened the door, still belting his trousers. He said in English, "What's going on?"

Vandam took charge. "An emergency. Let us in, will you?"

"Of course." The detective led them into a small living room. "What has happened?" He seemed frightened.

Vandam said, "There's nothing to panic about. We want you to set up a surveillance, and we need it right away."

"Certainly. Please sit down." The detective found a notebook and pencil. "Who is the subject?"

"Sonja el-Aram, the dancer. I want you to put a twenty-four-hour watch on her home, a houseboat called *Jihan* in Zamalek."

As the detective wrote, Vandam wished he did not have to use the Egyptian police for this work. But it was impossible, in an African country, to use conspicuous, white-skinned people for surveillance. The detective said, "And what is the nature of the crime?"

I'm not telling *you*, Vandam thought. "We believe she is an associate of whoever is passing counterfeit sterling."

"So you want to know who comes and goes. . . ."

"Yes. And there is a particular man that we're interested in: Alex Wolff, the man suspected of the Asyut knife murder; you

81

have his description already. If Wolff is seen, I want to know immediately. You can reach Captain Jakes or me at GHQ during the day. Give him our home phone numbers, Jakes."

Vandam stood up. Suddenly he could not see straight. He felt himself losing his balance. Then Jakes was beside him, holding his arm. "All right, sir?"

Vandam's vision returned slowly. "I'm all right now," he said.

"You've had a nasty injury," the detective said sympathetically. At the door he added, "Gentlemen, be assured that I will handle this surveillance personally. I know the area. The towpath will be a good place for a beggar to sit. Nobody ever sees a beggar. They won't get a mouse aboard that houseboat without your knowing it."

Vandam shook hands. "By the way, I'm Major Vandam."

The detective gave a little bow. "Superintendent Kemel, at your service, sir."

Chapter 7

SONJA had half expected Wolff to be at the houseboat when she returned near dawn, but she had found the place empty. At first when she had been arrested, she had felt nothing but rage toward Wolff for leaving her at the mercy of the British thugs. Being an accomplice in Wolff's spying, she was terrified of what they might do to her. Then she had realized that Wolff had been smart. By abandoning her he had diverted suspicion away from her. It was for the best. Sitting alone in the bare little room at GHQ, she had turned her anger toward the British. She had defied them, and they had backed down.

At the time she had not been sure that the man who interrogated her was Major Vandam, but when she was being released the clerk had let the name slip. The confirmation had delighted her. She smiled again when she thought of the grotesque bandage on Vandam's face. Wolff must have cut him. What a glorious night! She wondered where Wolff was now. She would have liked him here, to share the triumph.

She put on her nightdress, poured herself a whiskey. As she was tasting it she heard footsteps on the gangplank. She called, "Achmed?" Then she realized the step was not his.

The hatch was lifted and an Arab face looked in. "Sonja?"

"Yes—"

"You were expecting someone else, I think." The man climbed down the ladder. Sonja watched him, wondering, What now? He was a small man with a handsome face and quick, neat movements. He wore European clothes: dark trousers, black shoes and a short-sleeved white shirt. "I am Detective Superintendent Kemel, and I am honored to meet you." He held out his hand.

Sonja turned and sat down on the divan. "What do you want?"

"I am interested in your friend Alex Wolff."

"He's not my friend."

Kemel ignored that. "The British have told me two things about Mr. Wolff: one, that he knifed a soldier in Asyut; two, that he tried to pass counterfeit English bank notes. Why was he in Asyut? Where did he get the forged money?"

"I don't know anything about the man," said Sonja.

"I do, though," said Kemel. "I know who Alex Wolff is. His stepfather was a lawyer, here in Cairo. His mother was German. I know, too, that Wolff is a nationalist. I know that he used to be your lover. And I know that you are a nationalist."

Sonja had gone cold. She sat still, her drink untouched.

Kemel went on. "Where did he get the forged money? I don't think there is a printer in Egypt capable of doing the work. Therefore the money came from Europe. Now Wolff, also known as Achmed Rahmha, quietly disappeared a couple of years ago. Where did he go? Europe? He came back—via Asyut. Why? Did he want to sneak into the country unnoticed? Perhaps he teamed up with a counterfeiting gang. But I don't think so, for he is not a poor man. Thus there is a mystery."

He knows, Sonja thought. Dear God, he knows.

"Now the British have asked me to put a watch on this houseboat. Wolff will come here, they hope; and then they will arrest him; and then they will have the answers."

A watch on the boat! Why, she thought, is Kemel telling me?

"The key, I think, lies in Wolff's nature: he is both a German and an Egyptian." Kemel crossed the floor to sit beside Sonja. "I think he is fighting for Germany and Egypt. I think the forged money comes from the Germans. I think Wolff is a spy. If he is, I can save him."

Sonja looked at him. "What does that mean?"

"I want to meet him, secretly, along with Captain Anwar el-Sadat, a leader of the Free Officers' Movement. You are not the only one who wants Egypt to be free. There are many of us. We want to see the British defeated, and we are not fastidious about who does the defeating. We want to talk to Rommel. If Achmed is a spy, he must have a way of getting messages to the Germans."

Sonja's mind was in a turmoil. From being her accuser, Kemel had turned into a co-conspirator—unless this was a trap.

Kemel persisted gently. "Can you arrange a meeting?"

She could not possibly decide so quickly. "No," she said.

"Remember the watch on the houseboat. The surveillance reports will come to me before being passed on to Major Vandam. If you can arrange a meeting, I in turn can make sure that the reports are edited so as to contain nothing ... embarrassing."

Sonja had no choice. "I'll arrange a meeting."

"Good." He stood up. "Call the main police station and leave a message saying that Sirhan wants to see me. When I get that message I'll contact you to arrange date and time."

Sonja said, "I'll get in touch just as soon as I can."

"Thank you." He held out his hand. This time she shook it. He went up the ladder and out, closing the hatch behind him.

Sonja felt tired. She finished the whiskey in the glass, then went through the curtains into the bedroom. She heard a tapping sound. She whirled around to the porthole on the side of the boat that faced across the river. There was a head behind the glass. She screamed. The head disappeared.

She realized it had been Wolff.

She ran up onto the deck. Looking over the side, she saw him in the water. He appeared to be naked. He clambered up the side of the little boat, using the portholes for handholds. She reached for his arm and pulled him aboard. He scampered down the ladder. She followed him.

He stood on the carpet, dripping and shivering. She said, "What happened?"

"Run me a bath," he said.

She went through to the bathroom and turned the taps on. Wolff got into the tub and let the water rise around him. "I didn't want to risk coming down the towpath, so I took off my clothes on the opposite bank and swam across. I looked in and saw that man with you. Another policeman?"

"Yes."

"So I had to wait in the water until he went away. My God, I'm cold. The damned Abwehr gave me dud money. Turn off the water, will you?" He began to wash the river mud off his legs.

"You'll have to use your own money," she said.

"I can't get at it. You can be sure the bank has instructions to call the police the moment I show my face."

Therefore you will have to use my money, Sonja thought. You won't ask, though; you'll just take it. "That detective is putting a watch on the boat—on Vandam's instructions."

Wolff grinned. "So it was Vandam."

"Did you cut him?"

"Yes, but I wasn't sure where. It was dark."

"The face. He had a huge bandage."

Wolff laughed. "I wish I could see him. Did he question you?"

"Yes. I told him that I hardly knew you."

"Good girl." He looked at her appraisingly, and she knew that he was pleased. "Did he believe you?"

"Presumably not, since he ordered this surveillance. But don't worry. The detective is one of us."

"A nationalist?"

"Yes. He wants to use your radio."

"How does he know I've got one?" Wolff said.

"He doesn't. He deduces that you're a spy; and he presumes a spy has a means of communicating with the Germans. The nationalists want to send a message to Rommel."

Wolff shook his head. "I'd rather not get involved."

"You've got to," she said sharply.

"I suppose I do," he said wearily. "They're closing in. I'd like to leave this boat, but I don't know where to go. Damn."

She sat on the edge of the tub, looking at him. He seemed . . . not defeated, but at least cornered. For the first time he was dependent on her. He needed her money, he needed her home; a few hours earlier he had depended on her silence under interrogation, and just now he had been saved by her deal with the nationalist detective. She felt an odd sense of power. It was as if she were taking control. She found it exhilarating.

Wolff said, "I wonder if I should keep my date with that girl, Elene, tonight. It might be safer to lie low."

"No," said Sonja firmly. "I want her."

He looked up at her through narrowed eyes. She wondered if he recognized her newfound strength. "All right," he said finally. "I'll just have to take precautions."

He had given in. She had tested her strength against his, and she had won. It gave her a kind of thrill.

VANDAM was in high spirits as he sat in the Oasis Restaurant, sipping a cold martini, with Jakes beside him. He had slept all day and had waked up feeling battered but ready to fight back. He had gone to the hospital, where Dr. Abuthnot had changed his dressing for a smaller one that did not have to be secured by a bandage around his head. Now, in a few minutes, he would catch Alex Wolff.

Vandam and Jakes were at the back of the restaurant, able to see the whole place. The table nearest to the entrance was occupied by two hefty sergeants eating fried chicken. Outside, in an unmarked car, were two MPs in civilian clothes, with handguns in their jacket pockets. The trap was set: all that was missing was the bait. Elene would arrive at any minute.

Billy had been shocked by the bandage at breakfast that morning. Vandam had sworn the boy to secrecy, then told him the truth. "I had a fight with a German spy. He had a knife. He got away, but I think I may catch him tonight." It was a breach of security, but the boy needed to know why his father was wounded. Billy was thrilled.

Vandam looked at his watch. It was seven thirty. At any moment Alex Wolff would walk through the door. Vandam felt sure he would recognize him—a tall, hawk-nosed European with brown hair and brown eyes; a strong, fit man—but he would make no move until Elene came in and sat by Wolff. Then Vandam and Jakes would close in. If Wolff fled, the two sergeants would block the door. The MPs outside would provide backup.

Seven thirty-five. The restaurant door opened and Elene walked in. She looked stunning. She wore a cream-colored silk dress. Its simple lines drew attention to her slender figure, and its color and texture flattered her tan skin.

She looked around the restaurant, searching for Wolff and not finding him. Her eyes met Vandam's and moved on without hesitating. The headwaiter seated her at a table close to the door.

Where was Wolff? Vandam lit a cigarette and began to worry. Suppose that after last night's scare Wolff had decided to lie low for a while? Somehow Vandam felt that lying low was not Wolff's style. He hoped not.

A waiter brought Elene a drink. It was seven forty-five. The door of the restaurant opened. Vandam froze, then relaxed again, disappointed: it was only a small boy. The boy handed a piece of paper to a waiter, then went out.

Vandam saw the waiter go to Elene's table and give her the paper. He frowned. What was this? An apology from Wolff, saying he could not keep the date? Elene looked at Vandam and gave a small, dainty shrug. She took her clutch bag from the chair beside her and stood up. Vandam thought she was going to the ladies' room. Instead, she went to the door and opened it.

Vandam and Jakes got to their feet together. As they hurried across the restaurant to the exit, Vandam said to the sergeants, "Follow me."

They went out into the street. A few yards away Elene was getting into a taxi. Vandam broke into a run. The door of the taxi slammed and it pulled away.

Across the street the MPs' car roared, shot forward and collided with a bus. Vandam caught up with the taxi and leaped onto the running board. The car swerved suddenly. Vandam lost his grip, hit the road running and fell. He got to his feet. His face blazed with pain: his wound was bleeding again. Jakes and the two sergeants gathered around him. Across the road the MPs were arguing with the bus driver.

The taxi had disappeared.

ELENE was terrified. It had all gone wrong. Wolff was supposed to have been arrested, and now he was here, in a taxi with her, smiling a feral smile. She sat still, her mind a blank.

"Who was he?" Wolff said. "That man who ran after us. I couldn't see him properly, but I thought he was a European."

Elene fought down her fear. "I don't know." Suddenly she was inspired. "He was bothering me. It's your fault, you were late."

"I'm so sorry," he said quickly. "But I had a wonderful idea. We're going to have a picnic. There's a basket in the trunk."

She did not know whether to believe him. Why had he sent a boy in with the message "Come outside.—A.W." unless he suspected a trap? What would he do now, take her into the desert and knife her? She had a sudden urge to leap out of the car. She forced herself to think calmly. If he suspected a trap, why did he come at all? No, it had to be more complex than that. She said, "Where are we going?"

"A few miles out of town, to a little spot by the river where we can watch the sun go down."

"I don't want to go. I hardly know you."

"Please." He touched her arm lightly. "I have some smoked salmon and a cold chicken and a bottle of champagne. I get so bored with restaurants."

Elene considered. She could leave him now, and she would be safe. But I'm Vandam's only hope, she thought. She *had* to stay with Wolff, try to find out where he lived. She gave him a weak smile. "Okay."

He turned his attention to the driver. They were out of the city, and Wolff began to give directions. They passed through a series of villages, then followed a winding track up a small hill and emerged on a little plateau atop a bluff. The river was immediately below them, and on its far side Elene could see the neat patchwork of cultivated fields stretching to the edge of the desert. Wolff said, "Isn't this a lovely spot?"

Elene had to agree. A flight of swifts rising from the far bank of the river drew her eye upward, and she saw that the evening clouds were already edged in pink. A lone felucca sailed upstream, propelled by a light breeze.

The driver got out of the car and walked fifty yards away. He sat down, turned his back on them and unfolded a newspaper. Wolff fetched a picnic hamper from the trunk and set it on the floor of the car between them. Elene asked him, "How did you discover this place?"

"My mother and I came here when I was a boy." He handed her a glass of wine. "After my father died, my mother married an Egyptian. From time to time she would find the Moslem household oppressive, so we would come here."

"Did you enjoy it?"

"At that age I preferred my Arab family. My stepbrothers were wicked, and nobody tried to control them. We used to steal oranges, puncture bicycle tires. Only my mother minded. She was always saying, 'They'll catch you one day, Alex!'"

The mother was right, Elene thought. She said, "Where do you live now?"

"My house has been . . . commandeered by the British. I'm living with friends." He handed her a slice of smoked salmon on a china plate, then sliced a lemon in half. Elene wondered what *he* wanted from *her*, that he should work so hard to please her.

VANDAM's face hurt, and so did his pride. The great arrest had been a fiasco. He had failed professionally—he had been outwitted by Alex Wolff and he had sent Elene into danger.

He sat at home, his cheek newly bandaged, drinking gin to ease the pain. They had the license number of the taxi. Every policeman and MP in the city had orders to stop the car and arrest the occupants. They would find it, sooner or later, and Vandam felt sure it would be too late. Nevertheless, he was sitting by the phone.

What was Elene doing now? Perhaps she was in a candlelit restaurant, drinking wine and laughing at Wolff's jokes. What would they do later? If they went to his place, Elene would report in the morning, and Vandam would be able to arrest Wolff, with his radio and his code book. Professionally that would be better—but it would also mean that Elene would have spent a night with Wolff, and that thought made Vandam more angry than it should have. Alternatively, if they went to her place, where Jakes was waiting with ten men, Wolff would be grabbed before he had a chance to . . .

Vandam got up and paced the room. He had sent a young woman into danger once before. It had happened after his other great fiasco, when Rashid Ali, the Iraqi nationalist, had slipped out of Turkey under Vandam's nose. Vandam had sent a woman to pick up the German agent who had helped Ali to escape. He had hoped to salvage something from the shambles by learning all about the man. But next day the woman had been found dead in a hotel bed. It was a chilling parallel.

There was no point in trying to sleep. He would join Jakes at Elene's apartment, despite Dr. Abuthnot's orders. He put on a coat, went to the garage and wheeled out his motorcycle.

ELENE and Wolff stood together close to the edge of the bluff, looking at the distant lights of Cairo. Elene was thinking that it was time for Wolff to make his pass. They had finished the meal, emptied the champagne bottle, picked clean the bunch of grapes. Now he would expect his reward. Without speaking she turned away from the view and walked back to the car. He stayed a moment longer on the edge of the bluff, then walked toward her, calling to the driver. He got in beside her. "Did you enjoy the picnic?"

She made an effort to be bright. "Yes, it was lovely."

The car pulled away. Either he would invite her to his place or he would take her to her flat and ask for a nightcap. She would have to find a way to refuse him.

They reached the outskirts of the city. It was after midnight, and the streets were quiet. Wolff said, "Where do you live?"

She told him. So it was to be her place.

Several miles from her home, he told the driver to stop. He turned to her. "Thank you for a lovely evening. I'll see you soon." He got out of the car.

She stared in astonishment. He bent down by the driver's window, gave the man some money and told him Elene's address. The driver nodded and pulled away. Elene looked back and saw Wolff start walking toward the river.

She thought, What do you make of that? No pass, no invitation to his place, not even a good-night kiss—what game was he playing? Whatever it was, she was grateful he had left.

The taxi drew up outside her building. Suddenly, from nowhere, three cars roared up. Men materialized out of the shadows. All four doors of the taxi were flung open, and four guns pointed in. Elene screamed.

Then a head was poked into the car, and she recognized Vandam. "Gone?" he said. "How long ago did you leave him?"

"Five or ten minutes. May I get out of the car?"

He gave her a hand, and she stepped onto the pavement. He said, "I'm sorry we scared you." He looked utterly defeated.

She felt a surge of affection for him. She touched his arm. "Why don't you send your men home and come and talk inside?"

He hesitated, then turned to one of his men. "Jakes, see what you can get out of the driver. I'll see you at GHQ."

Elene led the way inside. It was so good to enter her own apartment and slump on the sofa. The trial was over, Wolff had gone and Vandam was here. She said, "What went wrong?"

Vandam sat down opposite her. "We expected him to walk into the trap all unawares—but he was suspicious, or at least cautious, and we missed him. What happened then?"

She told him about the picnic. She spoke abruptly; she wanted to forget, not remember. When she finished she said, "Make me a drink, and have one yourself."

He went to the liquor cabinet. Elene could see that he was angry. For the first time she wondered about the bandage he wore. She said, "What happened to your face?"

"We almost caught Wolff last night."

"Oh, no." So he had failed twice in twenty-four hours; no wonder he looked defeated. She wanted to console him, to put her arms around him, to lay his head in her lap and stroke his hair.

He gave her a drink. As he stooped to hand her the glass she reached up and turned his chin with her fingertips so that she could look at his cheek. He let her look, just for a second, then moved his head away.

She had not seen him this tense before. He crossed the room and sat opposite her again, holding himself upright on the edge of the chair. He was full of a suppressed emotion, something like rage, but when she looked into his eyes she saw not anger but pain.

He said, "How did Wolff strike you?"

"Charming. Intelligent. Dangerous. What are you fishing for?"

He shook his head irritably. "Nothing. Everything."

What was the matter with him? There was something familiar in his anger. It was not just that he felt he had failed. It was his attitude toward her.

"Wolff said he would see you again?" Vandam asked.

"He said, 'We must do this again'—something like that."

"What do you think he had in mind, exactly?"

She shrugged. "Another date. William, what has got into you?"

"I'm just curious," he said. His face wore a twisted grin. "I'd like to know what the two of you did, other than eat and drink; all that time together, in the dark, a man and a woman—"

"Shut up." She closed her eyes. Now she understood. Without opening her eyes she said, "I'm going to bed. You can see yourself out." A few seconds later the front door slammed.

She went to the window and looked down at the street. She saw him leave the building and get on his motorcycle. He kicked the engine into life and roared off down the road at breakneck speed. Elene was very tired, but she was not unhappy, for she knew the cause of his anger, and that gave her hope. She smiled faintly and said, "William Vandam, I do believe you're jealous."

Chapter 8

BY THE time Major Smith made his third lunch-hour visit to the houseboat, Wolff and Sonja had gotten into a routine. Wolff hid in the closet when the major approached. Sonja met him in the living room with a drink. She made him sit there, ensuring that his briefcase was put down. After a minute or two she began kissing him, contrived to get his bush shirt off, then soon afterward took him into the bedroom. As soon as Wolff heard the bed creak, he emerged from the closet. He took the key out of the shirt pocket and opened the case, his notebook and pencil ready.

Smith's second visit had been disappointing; however, this time Wolff struck gold again. He discovered that General Sir Claude Auchinleck, the Middle East commander in chief, had taken over direct control of the British Eighth Army. That fact alone, as a sign of Allied panic, would be welcome news to Rommel. It might also help Wolff, for it meant that battle plans were now being drawn up in Cairo rather than in the desert, in which case Smith was more likely to get copies.

The most important paper in Smith's briefcase was a summary of the Allies' new defense line at Mersa Matruh. The new line began at the coastal village of Matruh and stretched south into the desert as far as an escarpment called Sidi Hamza. The 10th Corps was at Matruh; then there was a heavy minefield fifteen miles long; then a lighter minefield for ten miles; then the escarpment; then, south of the escarpment, the 13th Corps.

The picture was fairly clear: the Allied line was strong at either end and weak in the middle. Armed with this information, Rommel could hit the soft center and pour his forces through the gap, like a stream bursting a dam. Wolff smiled to himself. He felt he was playing a major role in the struggle for German domination of North Africa; he found it enormously satisfying.

In the bedroom a cork popped—the sign that it was all over. Wolff put the papers back in the case, locked it and put the key back in the pocket. He no longer hid in the closet afterward—once had been enough. He tiptoed soundlessly up the ladder, across the deck and down the gangplank to the towpath. Then he went to lunch.

THE day after the picnic Elene went shopping in the late afternoon. Her apartment had come to seem claustrophobic. She had spent most of the day pacing around, unable to concentrate on anything, alternately miserable and happy; so she put on a cheerful striped dress and went out.

She liked the fruit and vegetable market. It was a lively place, especially at the end of the day, when the tradesmen were trying to get rid of the last of their produce. She bought tomatoes and eggs, having decided to make an omelet for supper. It was good to be carrying a basket of food, more food than she could eat at one meal; it made her feel safe. She could remember days when there had been no supper, when as a ten-year-old she had wondered, secretly, how long people took to starve to death.

She left the market and went window-shopping for dresses. She wanted one day to have her own dressmaker. Could William Vandam afford that for a wife?

When she thought of Vandam she was happy, until she thought of Wolff. She knew she could escape simply by refusing to make another date with Wolff. She was under no obligation to act as the bait in a trap for a knife murderer. She kept returning to this idea, worrying at it like a loose tooth: I don't have to.

She suddenly lost interest in dresses, and headed for home. When she turned into the entrance to her apartment house a voice said, "Abigail." She froze with shock. It was the voice of a ghost. She made herself turn around. A figure came out of the shadows: an old Jew, shabbily dressed, with a matted beard, veined feet in rubber-tire sandals.

The Key to Rebecca

Elene said, "Father."

He stood in front of her, as if afraid to touch her, just looking. He said, "So beautiful still, and not poor."

Impulsively she stepped forward and kissed his cheek. Then she took his arm and led him up the stairs. It was all unreal, like a dream.

Inside the apartment she said, "You should eat," and took him into the kitchen. She put a pan on to heat and began to beat the eggs. She said, "How did you find me?"

"I've always known where you were," he said. "Your friend Esme writes to her father, who sometimes I see."

Elene said, "I didn't want you to ask me to come back."

"And what would I have said to you? Come home, it is your duty to starve with your family. No. But I knew where you were."

She sliced tomatoes into the omelet. "You would have said it was better to starve than to live immorally."

"Yes, I would have said that. And would I have been wrong?"

She turned to look at him. The glaucoma which had taken the sight of his left eye years ago was now spreading to the right. He was fifty-five, she calculated; he looked seventy. "Yes, you would have been wrong. It is always better to live."

"Perhaps. I'm not as certain of these things as I used to be."

Elene served the omelet and put bread on the table. Her father blessed the bread. "Blessed art thou, O Lord our God . . ." Elene was surprised that the prayer did not drive her into a fury. In the blackest moments of her lonely life she had cursed her father and his religion for what it had condemned her to.

Her father was very hungry and gulped his food. Elene wondered why he had come. She asked about her sisters. After the death of their mother all four of them, in their different ways, had broken with their father. Two had gone to America, one had married the son of her father's greatest enemy, the youngest had died. It dawned on Elene that her father was destroyed.

He asked her what she was doing. She decided to tell him. "The British are trying to catch a German spy. It's my job to befriend him. But I think I may not help them anymore."

He had stopped eating. "Are you afraid?"

She nodded. "He's very dangerous."

They finished their meal, and Elene got up to make him a glass

of tea. He said, "The Germans are coming. It will be very bad for Jews. I'm going to Jerusalem."

"How? The trains are full, there's a quota for Jews—"

"I am going to walk." He smiled. "It's been done before."

"As I recall, Moses never made it," she said angrily. "You're crazy!"

"Haven't I always been a little crazy?"

"Yes!" she shouted. Suddenly her anger collapsed. "Yes, and I should know better than to try to change your mind."

"I will pray to God to preserve you. You will have a chance here—you're young and beautiful, and maybe they won't know you're Jewish. But me, a useless old man . . . me they would send to a camp to die. It is always better to live. You said that."

She tried to persuade him to stay with her, for one night at least, but he would not. She gave him a sweater and a scarf and all the cash she had in the house. She cried and dried her eyes and cried again. When he left she looked out her window and saw him walking along the street, an old man going up out of Egypt and into the wilderness, following in the footsteps of the children of Israel. When she thought of his courage she knew she could not run out on Vandam.

"SHE's an intriguing girl," Wolff said. "I can't quite figure her out." He was sitting on the bed as Sonja dressed. "She's a little jumpy. When I told her we were going on a picnic she acted quite scared. Yet she can be very earthy and direct."

"Just bring her home to me. I'll figure her out."

"It bothers me." Wolff frowned. He was thinking aloud. "Somebody tried to jump into the taxi with us."

"This town is full of crazy people, you know that." Sonja was brushing her hair. "When am I going to tell Kemel you'll meet him? He must know by now that you're living here."

Wolff sighed. Another claim on him; another danger. "Call him tonight from the club. I'm not in a rush for this meeting, but we've got to keep him sweet."

"Okay." She was ready, and her taxi was waiting. "And you make a date with Elene." She went out.

She was not in his power the way she had once been, Wolff realized. The walls you build to protect you also close you in.

And Sonja might be crazy enough to betray him, if she really got angry. He got up from the bed, found paper and pen and sat down to write a note to Elene.

The message arrived a few days after Elene's father had left for Jerusalem. A small boy came to the door with an envelope. Elene tipped him and read the letter. "My dear Elene, let us meet at the Oasis Restaurant at eight o'clock Thursday. I eagerly look forward to it. Fondly, Alex Wolff." Thursday—the day after tomorrow. She did not know whether to be elated or scared. Her first thought was to telephone Vandam; then she hesitated.

She had become intensely curious about Vandam. She knew so little about him. What did he do when he was not chasing spies? What was his home like? With whom did he live? She wanted to patch up their quarrel, and she had an excuse to contact him now, but instead of telephoning she would go to his home.

She decided to wear her pale pink dress, the one with puffed sleeves and buttons down the front. She put on a little perfume, then sat in front of the mirror to comb her short hair. The dark, fine locks gleamed. I look ravishing, she thought.

She left the apartment and headed for his house in Garden City. She felt gay and reckless. What a good idea it was to go there—so much better than sitting alone at home. She found the house easily. It was a small French colonial villa, all pillars and high windows, its white stone reflecting the evening sun with painful brilliance. She walked up the short drive and rang the bell. An elderly, bald Egyptian came to the door. "Good evening, madam," he said, speaking like an English butler.

"I'd like to see Major Vandam. My name is Elene Fontana."

"The major has not yet returned, madam."

"Perhaps I could wait," Elene said.

"Of course, madam." He led her into a drawing room. "My name is Gaafar. Please call me if there is anything you require."

Elene was delighted to be left alone to look around. The drawing room had a large marble fireplace and very English furniture. Everything was clean and tidy and not very lived in.

The door opened and a boy walked in. He was good-looking, with curly brown hair and smooth skin. He seemed about ten years old. He looked familiar. He said, "Hello, I'm Billy Vandam."

Elene stared in horror. A son—Vandam had a son! She knew now why he seemed familiar: he was a miniature of his father. Why had it never occurred to her that Vandam might be married? A man like that—charming, handsome, clever—was unlikely to have reached his late thirties without getting hooked.

She shook Billy's hand. "How do you do. I'm Elene Fontana."

"We never know what time Dad's coming home," Billy said. "I hope you won't have to wait long. Would you like a drink?"

He was very polite, like his father, with a formality that was somehow disarming. Elene said, "No, thank you."

"Well, I've got to have my supper. Sorry to leave you alone."

The boy went out, and Elene sat down heavily. She was disoriented, as if in her own home she had found a door to a room she had not known was there. She noticed a photograph on the marble mantelpiece and got up to look at it. It was of a beautiful woman in her early twenties: cool, aristocratic-looking, with a faintly supercilious smile. The woman's eyes were clear and perceptive and light in color; Elene realized that Billy had eyes like that. This, then, was Billy's mother—Vandam's wife: a classic English beauty with a superior air.

Elene wandered around the room, wondering if it held any more shocks. Against one wall was a small upright piano. Perhaps Mrs. Vandam played in the evenings, filling the air with Chopin while Vandam sat in the armchair watching her fondly. Elene picked up a novel which was lying on the top of the piano and read the first line: "Last night I dreamt I went to Manderley again." The opening sentence intrigued her. She read on, wondering whether the book belonged to Vandam's wife.

In a while Billy came back. Elene put the book down, feeling as if she had been prying. "That one's no good," Billy said. "It's about some silly girl who's afraid of her husband's housekeeper. There's no action."

Elene sat down, and Billy sat opposite her. Obviously he was going to entertain her. She said, "You've read it, then?"

"*Rebecca?* Yes. I didn't like it. I like tecs—detective stories—best. I've read all of Agatha Christie's. I like the American ones most of all—S. S. Van Dine and Raymond Chandler."

"Really? I read detective stories all the time."

"Oh! Who's your favorite author?"

Elene considered. "Georges Simenon. He writes in French, but some of the books have been translated into English."

"Would you lend me one? It's so hard to get new books. I've read all the ones in this house, and in the school library."

"All right. Let's swap. What have you got to lend me?"

"I'll lend you a Chandler. The American ones are much more true to life. I've gone off those stories about English country houses and people who probably couldn't murder a fly."

It was odd, Elene thought, that a boy for whom the English country house might be part of everyday life should find stories about American private eyes more true to life. She hesitated, then asked, "Does your mother read detective stories?"

Billy said briskly, "My mother died last year in Crete."

"Oh!" Elene put her hand to her mouth. So Vandam was *not* married! She said, "Billy, how awful for you. I'm so sorry."

"It's all right," Billy said. "It's the war, you see."

And now he was like his father again. The mask was on: the mask of courtesy, formality. *It's the war, you see.* He had heard someone else say that, and had adopted it as his own defense. She decided to talk of other things.

She said awkwardly, "I suppose, with your father working at GHQ, you get more news of the war than the rest of us."

"I suppose I do, but usually I don't really understand it. When he comes home in a bad mood I know we've lost another battle." He started to bite a fingernail, then stuffed his hands into his shorts pockets. "I wish I was older."

"You want to fight?"

He looked at her fiercely, as if he thought she was mocking him. "It's just that I'm afraid the Germans will win. Then it would all have been for nothing." He bit his nail again, and this time he did not stop himself. Elene wondered *what* would have been for nothing: the death of his mother? His own struggle to be brave?

Billy looked at the clock on the mantelpiece. "I'm supposed to go to bed at nine." Suddenly he was a child again. He stood up.

"May I come and say good night to you in a few minutes?"

"If you like." He went out.

What kind of life did they lead in this house? Elene wondered. The man, the boy and the old servant lived here together, each with his own concerns. Billy's young-old wisdom was charming, but he seemed like a child who did not have much fun. She experienced a rush of compassion for him, a motherless child in an alien country besieged by foreign armies.

She left the drawing room and went upstairs. One of the bedroom doors was open, and she went in, expecting to see model planes, sport gear, clothes on the floor. But the place might almost have been the bedroom of an adult. The clothes were folded neatly on a chair, schoolbooks were stacked tidily on the desk, and the only toy in evidence was a cardboard model of a tank. Billy was in bed, his striped pajama top buttoned to the neck, a book on the blanket beside him.

"What are you reading?" Elene said.

"*The Greek Coffin Mystery.*"

She sat on the edge of the bed. "Don't stay awake too late."

"I have to put out the light at nine thirty."

She leaned forward suddenly and kissed his cheek.

At that moment the door opened and Vandam walked in.

The familiarity of the scene shocked him: the boy in bed with his book, the woman leaning forward to kiss the boy good-night. Vandam stood and stared, feeling like one who knows he is in a dream but cannot wake up.

"Good night, Billy." Elene stood up. "Hello, William."

"Hello, Elene."

She moved past Vandam and left the room. Vandam came in and sat by Billy. "Been entertaining our guest?"

"Yes. I like her—she reads tecs. We're going to swap books. She's ever so pretty, isn't she?"

"Yes. She's working for me—it's a bit hush-hush, so . . ."

Billy lowered his voice. "Is she, you know, a secret agent?"

Vandam put a finger to his lips. "Walls have ears."

The boy looked suspicious. "You're having me on."

Vandam shook his head silently.

Billy said, "Gosh!"

Vandam said good night and went out. As he closed the door it occurred to him that Elene's good-night kiss had probably done Billy a lot of good.

He found Elene in the drawing room, stirring martinis. He felt he should have resented more than he did the way she had made herself at home in his house, but he was too tired to strike attitudes. He sank gratefully into a chair and accepted a drink. He said, "What made you come here?"

"I've got a date with Wolff."

"Wonderful! When?"

"Thursday." She handed him the letter.

He studied the message. "How did this come?"

"A boy brought it to my door. What will we do?"

"The same as last time, only better." Vandam tried to sound more confident than he felt. Wolff was unpredictable. He might try another trick.

As if reading his mind, Elene said, "I don't want to spend another evening with him. He frightens me. If he tries to seduce me, I'm afraid he won't take no for an answer."

Vandam felt guilty—*remember Istanbul*—but suppressed his sympathy. "We've learned our lesson," he said with false assurance. "There'll be no mistakes this time." Secretly he was surprised by her simple determination not to go to bed with Wolff. He had assumed that such things did not matter much one way or the other to her. He had misjudged her, then. Seeing her in this new light somehow made him very cheerful.

Gaafar came in and said, "Dinner is served, sir." Vandam smiled. Gaafar was doing his English butler act.

"What have we got, Gaafar?"

"For you, sir, clear soup, scrambled eggs and yogurt. But I took the liberty of grilling a chop for Miss Fontana."

Elene said to Vandam, "Do you always eat like that?"

"No, it's because of my cheek; I can't chew."

They went into the dining room and sat down. Gaafar served the dinner.

Elene said, "Your son is old beyond his years."

"He's been through a couple of things that ought to be reserved for adults."

"Yes." Elene hesitated. "When did your wife die?"

"May the twenty-eighth, nineteen forty-one, in the evening."

"Billy told me it happened in Crete."

"Yes. She worked on cryptanalysis for the air force. She was on a temporary posting to Crete at the time the Germans invaded the island. The British lost and decided to get out. Apparently she was hit by a stray shell and killed instantly. Of course, we were trying to get live people away then, not bodies, so... There's no grave, you see. No memorial. Nothing left."

Elene said quietly, "Do you still love her?"

"I think I always will. It's like that with people you really love. If they go away, or die, it makes no difference."

"Were you very happy?"

"We..." He hesitated, thinking of the diplomat's daughter, graceful, imperious, who had married an unknown junior army officer. "Ours wasn't an idyllic marriage. It was *I* who was devoted. Angela was fond of me."

"Do you think you will marry again?"

He shrugged. He did not know the answer. Elene seemed to understand, for she fell silent and began to eat her dessert.

Afterward Gaafar brought them coffee in the drawing room. Vandam sent Gaafar to bed, and as they drank, Vandam smoked a cigarette.

He felt the desire for music. He had loved music at one time, although lately it had gone out of his life. Now, with the mild night air coming in through the open windows, he wanted to hear clear, delightful notes and sweet harmonies. He went to the piano and began to play Beethoven's "Für Elise." The ability to play came back to him instantly, almost as if he had never stopped. His hands knew what to do in a way he always felt was miraculous.

When the song was over he went to Elene, sat next to her and kissed her cheek. Her face was wet with tears. She said, "William, I love you with all my heart."

Chapter 9

ROMMEL could smell the sea. At Tobruk the heat and the dust and the flies were as bad as they had been in the desert, but it was all made bearable by that occasional whiff of dampness in the faint breeze.

Von Mellenthin came into the command vehicle with his intelligence report. "Good evening, Field Marshal."

Rommel smiled. He had been promoted after the victory at Tobruk, and he was not yet used to the title. "Anything new?"

"A signal from the spy in Cairo. He says the Mersa Matruh line is weak in the middle."

Rommel took the report and glanced over it. "If this is correct, we can burst through the line as soon as we get there."

"I'll be doing my best to check the spy's report, of course," said von Mellenthin. "But he was right last time."

The door to the vehicle flew open and Kesselring came in.

"Field Marshal!" Rommel said. "I thought you were in Sicily."

"I was," Kesselring said. He stamped the dust off his handmade boots. "I've flown here to see you. Damn it, Rommel, this has got to stop. Your orders were to advance to Tobruk and no farther."

Rommel sat back in his canvas chair. He had hoped to keep Kesselring out of this argument. "Circumstances have changed."

"But your original orders have been confirmed by the Italian Supreme Command," said Kesselring. "Your air and sea support are needed for the attack on Malta. After we have taken Malta your communications will be secure for the advance to Egypt."

"You people have learned nothing!" Rommel said. "While we are digging in, the enemy, too, will be digging in. I did not get this far by playing the old game of advance, consolidate, then advance again. They are running now, and now is the time to take Egypt."

Kesselring turned to von Mellenthin. "How many tanks and men do we have?"

Rommel suppressed the urge to tell von Mellenthin not to answer; he knew this was a weak point.

"Sixty tanks, Field Marshal. Two thousand five hundred men. The Italians have six thousand men and fourteen tanks."

Kesselring turned back to Rommel. "And you're going to take Egypt with a total of seventy-four tanks? Von Mellenthin, what is our estimate of the enemy's strength?"

"Allied forces are three times as numerous as ours, but we are well supplied and the men are in tremendous spirits."

Rommel said, "Von Mellenthin, go to the communications truck and see what has arrived."

Von Mellenthin went out. Rommel said, "The Allies are regrouping at Mersa Matruh. They expect us to move around the southern end of their line. Instead, we will hit the middle, where they are weakest—"

"How do you know all this?" Kesselring interrupted.

"Our intelligence assessment, based on a spy report—"

"My God! You've no tanks, but you have your spy!"

"He was right last time."

Von Mellenthin came back.

Kesselring said, "All this makes no difference. I am here to confirm the Führer's orders: you are to advance no farther."

Rommel smiled. "I have sent a personal envoy to the Führer. I think von Mellenthin may have the reply."

Von Mellenthin read the message. "It is only once in a lifetime that the goddess of victory smiles. On to Cairo. Adolf Hitler."

WHEN Vandam got to his office on Wednesday morning he learned that the previous evening Rommel had advanced to within sixty miles of Alexandria. Rommel seemed unstoppable. The Mersa Matruh line had broken in half like a matchstick. The Allies had fallen back once again. The new line of defense stretched across a thirty-mile gap between the sea and the impassable Qattara Depression, and if that line fell, there would be no more defenses. Egypt would be Rommel's.

The news was not enough to dampen Vandam's elation. Since that dawn, when he had awakened on the sofa in his drawing room with Elene in his arms, he had been suffused with a kind of adolescent glee.

In the office he was visited early by a Captain Brown from the special liaison unit of military intelligence. Brown leaned on the edge of the table and spoke around the stem of his pipe. "Are you being evacuated, sir?"

Vandam said, "What? Evacuated? Why?"

"Our lot's off to Jerusalem. So's everyone who knows too much. Keep people out of enemy hands. Now then, I've got a little snippet for you. Rommel's got a spy in Cairo."

"How did you know?" Vandam said.

"Stuff comes from London, sir." The special liaison unit had an ultrasecret source of intelligence. "The chap has been identified as 'the hero of the Rashid Ali affair.' Mean anything to you?"

Vandam was thunderstruck. "It does!" he said.

"Well, that's all, sir," Brown said. "Good luck. I may not see you for a while."

"Thanks," Vandam muttered distractedly as Brown went out.

The hero of the Rashid Ali affair. It was incredible that Wolff should have been the man who outwitted Vandam in Istanbul. Yet it made sense: Vandam recalled the odd feeling he had had about Wolff's *style*, as if it were familiar. The girl Vandam had sent to pick up the mystery man had had her throat cut.

And now Vandam was sending Elene against the same man.

A corporal came in with an order. Vandam read it with mounting horror. All departments were to extract from their files those papers which might be dangerous in enemy hands, and burn them. Clearly the brass thought the Germans might soon be taking Egypt. It's going to pieces, Vandam thought; it's falling apart.

He called Jakes in and watched him read the order. Jakes nodded, as if he had been expecting it. "We'll have the bonfire in the yard at the back, sir.".

After Jakes went out, Vandam opened his file drawer and began to sort through his papers: names and addresses, security reports on individuals, details of codes, a little file on Alex Wolff. Jakes brought him a big cardboard box, and Vandam began to dump papers into it, thinking, This is what it is like to be the losers.

The box was half full when Vandam's corporal sent in a Major Smith, a small man with bulbous blue eyes and an air of being rather pleased with himself. He shook hands and said, "Sandy Smith, SIS."

"What can I do for the Secret Intelligence Service?"

"I'm the liaison man between SIS and the General Staff," Smith explained. "Your inquiry about a book called *Rebecca* got routed through us." Smith produced a piece of paper with a flourish.

Vandam read the message. The SIS head of station in Portugal had sent one of his men to visit all the English-language bookshops in the country. In the holiday area of Estoril he had found a bookseller who recalled that he had sold six copies of *Rebecca* to one woman—the wife of the German military attaché in Lisbon.

Vandam said, "This confirms something I suspected. Thank you for taking the trouble to bring it over."

"No trouble," Smith said. "I'm over here every morning, anyway. Glad to help." He left.

Vandam reflected on the news while he went on with his work. There was only one plausible explanation for the fact that the book had found its way from Estoril to the Sahara. Undoubtedly it was the basis of a code. It was a pity the key to the code had not been captured along with the book.

The Key to Rebecca

When the cardboard box was full Vandam hefted it onto his shoulder and went outside. Jakes had the fire going in a rusty steel water tank propped up on bricks. A corporal was feeding papers to the flames. Charred scraps floated up on a pillar of hot air. Vandam dumped his box and turned away.

He wanted to think, to walk. He left GHQ and headed downtown. His cheek was hurting. He thought he should welcome the pain, for it was supposed to be a sign of healing. He was growing a beard to cover the wound so that he would look a little less unsightly when the dressing came off.

He thought of Elene. It was, of course, a disaster that the two of them had fallen so joyfully in love. His parents, his friends and the army would be aghast at the idea of his marrying an Egyptian and a Jew. But Vandam decided not to worry about all that. He and Elene might be dead within a few days. We'll bask in the sunshine while it lasts, he thought.

He kept remembering the girl whose throat had been cut, apparently by Wolff, in Istanbul. He was terrified that Elene might find herself alone with Wolff again tomorrow evening.

Looking around him, he observed that there was a festive feeling in the air. He passed a hairdresser's salon and noticed that it was packed, with women standing and waiting. The dress shops seemed to be doing a good business, too. Vandam realized that the Egyptians were looking forward to being liberated.

He could not escape a sense of impending doom. Even the sky seemed dark. He looked up; the sky *was* dark. There seemed to be a gray swirling mist, dotted with particles, over the city: smoke mixed with charred paper. All across Cairo the British were burning their files, and the soot had darkened the sun.

Vandam was suddenly furious with himself and with the Allied armies for preparing so equally for defeat. What had happened to that famous mixture of obstinacy, ingenuity and courage which was supposed to characterize the British nation? What, Vandam asked himself, are *you* planning to do about it?

He turned around and walked back toward GHQ. He visualized the map of the El Alamein line, where the Allies would make their last stand. This was one line Rommel could not circumvent, for below it was the vast impassable Qattara Depression. Rommel would have to break the line. But where? Immediately behind the line was the heavily fortified Alam Halfa Ridge. Clearly it would benefit the Allies if Rommel spent his strength attacking Alam Halfa. Furthermore, the southern approach to the ridge was through treacherous soft sand. It was unlikely that Rommel knew about the quicksand, for he had never penetrated this far east before, and only the Allies had good maps of the desert.

So, Vandam thought, my duty is to prevent Alex Wolff from telling Rommel that Alam Halfa is well defended and cannot be attacked from the south. Then it hit him. Suppose I capture Wolff, get his radio, find the key to his code. Then I could impersonate Wolff, get a message to Rommel saying the El Alamein line was weak at the southern end and that Alam Halfa itself was poorly defended.

The temptation would be too much for Rommel to resist. He would break through the line at the southern end and swing north toward Alam Halfa. Then he would hit the quicksand. While he was struggling through it, our artillery would decimate his forces. When he reached Alam Halfa he would find it heavily defended. At that point we would bring in more forces from the front line and squeeze the enemy like a nutcracker.

If the ambush worked well, it might not only save Egypt but annihilate the Afrika Korps.

Vandam began to feel elated. He thought, I've got to put this idea up to the brass. I'll write a memo to Bogge, who of course will block it. But I'll send a copy straight to the director of military intelligence. There would be time to get it to him before tomorrow's staff conference. He hurried to his office. Suddenly the future looked different. Perhaps the jackboot would not ring out on the tiled floors of the mosques. Perhaps Billy would not have to live under Hitler. Perhaps Elene would not be sent to Dachau.

We could all be saved, he thought. If I catch Wolff.

ON THURSDAY, Major Smith came to the houseboat at noon, straight from the morning conference at GHQ, at which Auchinleck and his staff discussed Allied strategy.

He and Sonja went through their now familiar routine, beginning on the couch and moving into the bedroom. When Wolff emerged from the closet, there on the floor were Smith's briefcase and his bush shirt, with the key ring poking out of the pocket.

Wolff opened the briefcase and began to read.

After a few minutes Wolff realized that what he held in his hand was a complete rundown of the Allies' last-ditch defense on the El Alamein line: artillery on the ridges, tanks on the level ground and minefields all along. The Alam Halfa Ridge, five miles behind the center of the line, was heavily fortified. The southern end of the line was weaker, both in troops and mines.

Smith's briefcase also contained a paper assessing the enemy position. Allied intelligence thought Rommel would probably try to break through at the southern end. Beneath this, written in pencil, in what was presumably Smith's handwriting, was a note which Wolff found more exciting than all the rest: "Major Vandam proposes deception plan. Encourage Rommel to break through at southern end, lure him toward Alam Halfa, catch him in quicksand, then nutcracker. Plan accepted by Auchinleck."

What a discovery! Not only did Wolff hold in his hand the details of the Allies' defense line—he also knew their deception plan. This was the greatest espionage coup of the century. Wolff himself would be responsible for Rommel's victory in North Africa. They should make me king of Egypt for this, he thought.

He looked up and saw Smith holding aside the curtains, staring down at him. Smith roared, "Who the devil are you?"

Wolff realized angrily that he had not been paying attention to the noises from the bedroom. Something had gone wrong; there had been no champagne-cork warning.

Smith said, "That's my briefcase!" He took a step forward. Wolff reached out, caught Smith's foot and heaved sideways. The major toppled over and hit the floor with a thud. Both men scrambled to their feet.

Smith was a small man, ten years older than Wolff and in poor shape. He stepped backward, fear showing in his face. He bumped into a shelf, glanced sideways, saw a glass fruit bowl on the shelf, picked it up and hurled it at Wolff. It missed, fell into the kitchen sink and shattered loudly. The noise, Wolff thought; if he makes any more noise, people will come to investigate. He moved toward Smith.

Smith, with his back to the wall, yelled, "Help!"

Wolff hit him on the point of the jaw and he collapsed, sliding down the wall to sit, unconscious, on the floor.

Sonja came out and stared at Smith. "What are we going to do about him?"

"I don't know." To kill Smith would be dangerous. The death of an officer—and the disappearance of his briefcase—would cause a terrific rumpus throughout the city.

Smith groaned and opened his eyes. "You. You're Slavenburg," he said. He looked at Sonja, then back at Wolff. "It was you who introduced . . . in the Cha-Cha . . . this was all planned. . . ."

"Shut up," Wolff said mildly. Only one option: keep him here, bound and gagged, until Rommel reached Cairo.

"You're damned spies," Smith said. His face was white.

Sonja said nastily, "And you thought I was crazy about you."

"Stop it!" Wolff said. "Got any rope to tie him with?"

Sonja thought for a moment. "Up on deck, in the locker."

Wolff took from the kitchen drawer the heavy steel he used for sharpening the carving knife. He gave it to Sonja. "If he moves, hit him with that," he said.

He went up the ladder and onto the deck, opened the locker and took out a coil of rope. Then he heard Sonja's voice raised in a shout. There was a clatter of feet on the ladder. Wolff whirled around. Smith came up through the hatch at a run. Sonja must have missed him with the steel.

Wolff dashed across the deck to the gangplank to head him off. Smith turned, ran to the other side of the boat and jumped into the water. Wolff looked around quickly. There was no one on the decks of the other houseboats—it was the hour of the siesta. The towpath was deserted except for the "beggar" he presumed Kemel had stationed there. Kemel would have to deal with him. On the river there were a couple of feluccas, at least a quarter of a mile away.

Wolff ran to the rail. Smith surfaced, gasping for air, and began to swim, inexpertly, away from the houseboat. Wolff stepped back several paces and took a running jump into the river. He landed, feetfirst, on Smith's head.

For several seconds all was confusion. Wolff went under in a tangle of arms and legs and struggled to push Smith down. When Wolff could hold his breath no longer he wriggled away from Smith and came up.

He sucked air and wiped his eyes. Smith bobbed up in front of him, coughing and spluttering. Wolff got behind him and crooked one arm around his throat while he used the other to push down on the top of his head. Smith continued to thrash around underwater, jerking, flailing his arms, kicking his legs.

This was no good, it was taking too long. Wolff let Smith go and pulled out his knife. Grabbing Smith by the hair, he stabbed him repeatedly. The river water turned muddy red all around him.

Sheathing the knife, Wolff pulled the body over to the houseboat. Sonja, wearing a robe, stared over the side. "Is he dead?"

"Yes. We have to sink the body. Get that rope!"

She disappeared for a moment, and returned with the rope. "Now get Smith's briefcase and put something heavy in it. I know, bottles. Fill his briefcase with full bottles of champagne."

She went away again. Through the porthole he could see her going down the ladder into the living room. She picked up the briefcase, then walked to the kitchen area and opened the icebox. She took out four champagne bottles and, laying them head to toe, managed to get all four into the case. She added the sharpening steel and a glass paperweight and fastened the briefcase. Then she came up on deck. "What now?" she said.

"Tie the end of the rope around the handle of the briefcase." Her fingers moved quickly.

"Now throw me the rope," Wolff said.

She threw down the free end of the rope. Treading water, he threaded the rope under the dead man's armpits, wound it around the torso twice, then tied a knot.

"Throw the briefcase into the water," he told Sonja.

She heaved the briefcase over the side. It splashed a couple of yards away from the houseboat and went down. The rope became taut, then the body went under. Wolff kicked his legs underwater where the body had gone down: they did not make contact with anything. The body had sunk deep.

Wolff climbed on deck. Looking back, he saw that the pink tinge was rapidly disappearing from the water.

Down below, Sonja slumped on the couch and closed her eyes. Wolff stripped off his wet clothes.

Sonja said, "It's the worst thing that's ever happened to me."

"You'll survive," Wolff said.

"At least it was an Englishman."

Wolff went into the bathroom and turned on the taps of the tub. When he came back Sonja said, "Was it worth it?"

"Yes." Wolff pointed to the military papers, which were still on the floor where he had dropped them when Smith surprised him. "That stuff is red-hot. With that, Rommel can win the war."

"When will you send it?"

"Tonight, at midnight."

"Tonight you're going to bring Elene here."

Wolff hesitated. "I'd have to broadcast while she's here."

"I'll keep her busy. Damn it, Alex, you *owe* me!"

"All right." Wolff went into the bathroom. Sonja was unbelievable, he thought. He got into the hot water.

"But now Smith won't be bringing you any more secrets," she called to him.

"I don't think we'll need them after the next battle," Wolff replied. "He's served his purpose."

Chapter 10

VANDAM knocked at the door of Elene's flat an hour before she was due to meet Alex Wolff. She came to the door wearing a black cocktail dress and high-heeled black shoes with silk stockings. Her face was made up, and her hair gleamed. She had been expecting Vandam.

He smiled at her. She looked astonishingly beautiful. "Hello."

"Come in." She led him into the living room. "Sit down."

He wanted to kiss her, but she did not give him a chance. He sat on the couch. "I want to tell you the details for tonight."

"Okay." She sat down on a chair. "If you want a drink, help yourself."

He stared at her. "Is something wrong?"

"Nothing. Get yourself a drink, then brief me."

Vandam frowned. He stood up, went across to her and knelt in front of her chair. "Elene, what is it?"

She glared at him. She seemed close to tears. She said loudly, "Where have you been for the last two days?"

"I've been at work."

"And where do you think I've been?"

"Here, I suppose."

"Exactly!"

He did not understand what that meant. He said, "I've been working, and you've been here, and so you're mad at me?"

"Yes! You could have sent me a note or a bunch of flowers!"

"Flowers? What do you want with flowers? We don't need to play that game anymore."

"Oh, really? We made love the night before last, in case you've forgotten. You brought me home and kissed me good-by. Then—nothing."

He sat on the floor and looked away from her. "In case *you* have forgotten, a certain Erwin Rommel is knocking at the gates with a bunch of Nazis in tow, and I'm one of the people who's trying to keep him out."

"You could have taken five minutes to send me a note."

It still made no sense, but now he could hear the pain in her voice. He turned to face her. "You're the most wonderful thing that's happened to me for a long time, perhaps ever. Please forgive me. I've been a fool." He took her hand in his own.

She bit her lip, fighting back tears. "Yes, you have," she said. She looked down at him and touched his hair. "A bloody fool," she whispered, stroking his head.

"I've such a lot to learn about you," he said.

"And I about you."

He tried to be honest. "Look, I'm not good at symbolic gestures. Either we love each other or we don't, and all the flowers in the world won't make any difference. But my work could affect whether we live or die. I *did* think of you, all the time; but I don't worry about you when I know you're okay. Can you imagine yourself getting used to that?"

She gave him a watery smile. "I'll try."

"What I want to say, after all that, is, Forget about tonight, don't go. But I can't. We need you, and it's terribly important."

"That's okay, I understand."

"But first of all, may I kiss you hello?"

Kneeling beside the arm of her chair, he took her face in his big hand and kissed her. Her mouth was soft and yielding. He felt he could go on kissing her forever.

Eventually she drew back, took a deep breath and said, "My, my, I do believe you mean it."

"You may be sure of that."

She laughed. "When you said that, you were the old Major Vandam for a moment. Brief me, Major."

"I'll have to get out of kissing distance."

Vandam crossed the room to the liquor cabinet and found the gin. "A major in intelligence vanished today—along with a briefcase full of secrets. It turns out he has been disappearing at lunchtime a couple of times a week, and nobody knows where he's been going. I've a hunch that he might have been meeting Wolff."

"What was in his briefcase?"

"A rundown of our defenses which was so complete that we think it could alter the result of the next battle. So we'd better catch Wolff tonight."

"But it might be too late already!"

"No. We found the decrypt of one of Wolff's signals a while back. It was timed at midnight. Spies generally report at the same time every day; at other times their masters won't be listening. I think Wolff will send this information tonight at midnight unless I catch him first." He hesitated, then decided she ought to know the full importance of what she was doing. "There's something else. He's using a code based on a novel called *Rebecca*. I've got a copy of the book. If I can get the key to the code—"

"What's that?"

"A piece of paper telling him how to encode signals. If I can get the key to the *Rebecca* code, I can impersonate Wolff over the radio and send false information to Rommel. It could save Egypt. But I must have the key."

"All right. What's tonight's plan?"

"It's the same as before, only more so. I'll be in the restaurant with Jakes, and we'll both have pistols."

Her eyes widened. "You've got a gun?"

"I haven't got it now, but I will have. There will be two other men in the restaurant, six more outside, and civilian cars ready to block all exits from the street at the sound of a whistle. No matter what Wolff does tonight, if he wants to see you, he's going to be caught."

There was a knock at the apartment door.

Vandam said, "What's that? Are you expecting someone?"

"No, of course not. It's almost time for me to leave."

Vandam frowned. "I don't like this. Don't answer."

"I have to. It might be my father. Or news of him."

Elene went out of the living room. Vandam sat listening as she opened the door. He heard her say, "Alex!"

He heard Wolff's voice. "You're all ready. How delightful." It was a deep, confident voice, with only a trace of an accent.

Elene said, "But we were to meet in the restaurant—"

"I know. May I come in?"

Vandam leaped over the sofa and lay on the floor behind it.

Wolff's voice came closer. "This way?"

"Um . . . yes. . . ."

Vandam heard the two of them enter the room. Wolff said, "What a lovely apartment. Mikis Aristopoulos must pay you well."

"Oh, I don't work there regularly. It's family; I help out."

"Well. These are for you."

"Oh, flowers. Thank you."

Vandam thought, Damn you.

Wolff said, "May I sit down?"

Vandam felt the sofa shift as Wolff lowered his weight onto it. He thought, I could jump him now. They were about the same weight, and evenly matched—except for the knife. If they fought, and Wolff had the knife, Wolff would win. It had happened before, when they had grappled in the alley. Vandam thought, Why didn't I bring the gun?

If they fought, and Wolff won, then what? Wolff would know Elene had been trying to trap him. In Istanbul, in a similar situation, he had slit the girl's throat.

Wolff said, "I see you were having a drink before I arrived. May I join you?"

"Of course," Elene said. "What would you like?"

"What's that?" Wolff sniffed. "A little gin would be nice."

Vandam thought, That was my drink. Thank God Elene didn't have one as well—two glasses would have given the game away.

He heard ice clink. "Cheers!" Wolff said.

"Cheers."

She was coping so well, Vandam thought. What does she think I'm planning to do? She must have guessed by now where I'm hiding. Poor Elene! Once again she had gotten more than she bargained for. Vandam hoped she would be passive and trust him.

Wolff said, "You seem nervous, Elene. I hope I didn't confuse you by coming here. To be truthful, I'm bored with restaurants. I arrange to have dinner with people, then when the time comes I can't face it, and I think of something else to do."

So they're not going to the Oasis, Vandam thought. Damn. That means no help from Jakes and the others.

Elene said, "What do you want to do?"

"May I surprise you again?"

Vandam thought, Make him tell you!

Elene said, "All right."

Vandam groaned inwardly. If Wolff would reveal where they were going, Vandam could contact Jakes and move the ambush.

Wolff said, "Shall we go?" The sofa creaked as he got up. Vandam thought, I could go for him now! Too risky.

He heard them leave the room. Wolff, in the hallway, said, "After you." Then the front door was slammed shut.

Vandam stood up. He would have to follow them, and take the first available opportunity to contact Jakes. He went to the front door and listened. He heard nothing. He opened it a fraction; they had gone. He hurried along the corridor and down the stairs.

As he stepped outside, he saw them across the road. Wolff was holding open a car door for Elene. It was not a taxi; Wolff must have rented, borrowed or stolen a car for the evening. Wolff closed Elene's door and walked around to the driver's side. Vandam climbed on his motorcycle.

The car pulled away, and Vandam followed.

The city traffic was heavy. Vandam was able to keep five or six cars behind without losing his quarry. If only Wolff would stop someplace where there was a telephone. . . .

They headed out of the city, toward Giza. Darkness fell and Wolff turned on the car lights. Vandam left his lights off so that Wolff would not see that he was being followed. The desert road was strewn with potholes, and several times Vandam almost came off the bike.

The pyramids loomed ahead. Wolff slowed down and then stopped. They were going to picnic by the pyramids. Vandam cut the motorcycle engine and wheeled his bike onto the sand. He hid the bike behind a rocky hump and lay down beside it.

The car stayed still, its engine off, its interior dark. What were they doing in there? Vandam was seized by jealousy. He told himself not to be stupid—they were eating, that was all. He decided to risk a cigarette.

Five cigarettes later the desert silence was broken by the roar of Wolff's car. Vandam watched it turn and take the road toward Cairo. He jumped up, wheeled his cycle onto the road and followed. He wondered where Wolff was going next.

He began to suspect the answer when, at the outskirts of the city, they crossed the bridge to Zamalek, where the dancer Sonja had her houseboat. It was surely not possible that Wolff was living there. The place had been under surveillance for days, and Kemel had reported nothing unusual.

Wolff parked and got out. Vandam stood his motorcycle against a wall and followed Wolff and Elene to the towpath. From behind a bush he watched as they walked to one of the boats and Wolff helped Elene onto the gangplank. Wolff followed her onto the deck. Then they disappeared below.

This was his chance to send for help, Vandam thought. There must be a policeman around here. "Hey!" he said in a stage whisper. "Is anybody there? Police?"

A dark figure materialized from behind a tree. A voice with an Arab accent said, "Yes?"

"Hello. I'm Major Vandam. Are you the police officer watching the houseboat?"

"Yes, sir."

"The man we're chasing is on board now. Do you have a gun?"

"No, sir."

"Hell." Vandam considered whether he and the Arab could raid the boat on their own, and decided they could not: in that confined space Wolff's knife could wreak havoc. "I want you to go to the nearest telephone, ring GHQ and get a message through to Captain Jakes or Colonel Bogge: they are to raid the houseboat immediately. Is that clear?"

"Captain Jakes or Colonel Bogge, GHQ. Yes, sir."

The Arab left at a trot. He had been instructed to report to his superior officer and no one else on this case. He would go to the station house and call Superintendent Kemel at home. Kemel would know what to do.

Vandam found a position in which he was concealed from view

but could still watch the houseboat and the towpath. A while later the figure of a woman came along the path. She looked familiar. She boarded the houseboat, and Vandam realized she was Sonja.

He was relieved; at least Wolff could not molest Elene while there was another woman on the boat. He settled down to wait.

ELENE stepped off the ladder and looked nervously around the interior of the houseboat. She had expected the decor to be sparse and nautical. In fact, it was luxurious, if a little overripe. There were thick rugs, low divans, occasional tables, and rich velvet floor-to-ceiling curtains which divided this area from what was presumably the bedroom.

"Is this yours?" she asked Wolff.

"It belongs to a friend," he said. "Do sit down."

Elene felt trapped. Where was William Vandam? Several times she had thought there was a motorcycle behind the car, but she had been unable to look carefully for fear of alerting Wolff. Now he was going to the icebox, taking out a bottle of champagne, finding two glasses, pulling the cork with a loud pop and pouring the champagne. She was terrified of Wolff. What kind of game was he playing? She shuddered.

"Are you cold?" Wolff said as he handed her a glass.

"No, I wasn't shivering."

He raised his glass. "Your health."

Her mouth was dry. She sipped the cold wine, then took a gulp. It made her feel a little better.

He sat beside her on the divan. "I enjoy your company so much," he said. "You're an enchantress." He put his hand on her knee.

She froze. Here it comes, she thought.

"You're enigmatic," he said. "Desirable, rather aloof, very beautiful, sometimes naïve and sometimes so knowing." With his fingertip he traced the silhouette of her face: forehead, nose, lips, chin. He said, "Why do you go out with me?"

What did he mean? Was it possible he suspected what she was really doing? Or was this just the next move in the game?

She looked at him and said, "You're a very attractive man."

"I'm glad you think so." He leaned forward to kiss her. She offered him her cheek. His lips brushed her skin, then he whispered, "Why are you frightened of me?"

There was a noise up on deck—quick, light footsteps—and then the hatch opened. Elene thought, William!

A high-heeled shoe and a woman's foot appeared. The woman came down, and Elene recognized her as Sonja the belly dancer.

She thought, What on earth is going on?

"ALL right, Sergeant," Kemel said into the telephone by his bed. "You did exactly the right thing in contacting me. I'll deal with everything myself. In fact, you may go off duty now."

"Thank you, sir," said the sergeant. "Good night."

Kemel hung up. This was a catastrophe. The British had followed Alex Wolff to the houseboat, and Vandam was trying to organize a raid. The consequences would be twofold. First, the prospect of the Free Officers using Wolff's radio to contact Rommel would vanish. Second, once the British discovered that the houseboat was a nest of spies, they would realize that Kemel had been protecting the agents. What was he going to do?

He dressed quickly. From the bed his wife said, "What is it?"

"Work," he whispered.

"Oh, no." She turned over.

He took his pistol from the locked drawer in the desk and put it in his jacket pocket, then he kissed his wife and left the house quietly. He got into his car and started the engine. He had to consult Sadat about this, but meanwhile Vandam might grow impatient, waiting at the houseboat, and do something precipitate. Vandam would have to be dealt with first.

Kemel drove to Zamalek and parked near the towpath. From the trunk of the car he took a length of rope. He carried his gun in his right hand, holding it reversed, for clubbing.

He reached the riverbank. He looked at the silver Nile, the black shapes of the houseboats. Vandam would be in the bushes somewhere. Kemel stepped forward, walking softly.

In front of him a voice hissed, "Who is it? Jakes?"

Kemel raised his arm and brought it sweeping down. The blow landed squarely on Vandam's head, knocking him unconscious.

Kemel knelt beside the supine figure. Working quickly, he took off Vandam's sandals, removed his socks and stuffed them into his mouth. That should stop him from calling out. Next he rolled Vandam over, crossed his wrists behind his back and tied them together with the rope. Then he bound Vandam's ankles. Finally he tied the rope to a tree.

Vandam would come around in a few minutes, but he would find it impossible to move or cry out. Kemel decided to take a quick look at the houseboat. He walked along the towpath to the *Jihan*. There were lights on inside, but curtains were drawn across the portholes. He was tempted to go aboard, but he wanted to consult with Sadat first, for he was not sure what should be done. He turned around and headed back to his car.

SONJA smiled. "Alex has told me all about you, Elene."

Elene smiled back. Was this the friend of Wolff's who owned the houseboat? Had he not expected her back so early? Why was neither of them angry or embarrassed?

Wolff handed Sonja a glass of champagne. She took it without looking at him, and said to Elene, "So you work in Mikis' shop?"

"No, I don't," Elene said. "I helped him for a few days, that's all. We're related."

"So you're Greek?"

"That's right." The small talk was giving Elene confidence. Her fear receded. Whatever happened, Wolff was not likely to rape her at knife point in front of one of the most famous women in Egypt. Sonja gave her a breathing space, at least. William was determined to capture Wolff before midnight— Midnight!

She had almost forgotten. At midnight Wolff was to contact the enemy by wireless, and hand over the details of the defense line. But where was the radio? Was it here on the boat? Would he send his message in front of Elene and Sonja?

Wolff sat down beside Elene. She felt vaguely threatened, with one of them on either side of her. He said, "What a lucky man I am, to be sitting here with two such beautiful women."

Elene looked straight ahead, not knowing what to say.

Wolff said, "Isn't she beautiful, Sonja?"

"Oh, yes." Sonja touched Elene's face, then took her chin and turned her head. "Do you think I'm beautiful, Elene?"

"Of course." Elene frowned. This was getting weird.

"I'm so glad," Sonja said. She put her hand on Elene's knee.

And then Elene understood.

Everything fell into place: Wolff's phony courtliness, the houseboat, the unexpected appearance of Sonja. Elene realized she was not safe at all. The pair of them wanted to use her in some way. Her fear of Wolff came back, stronger than before.

Stop it. I won't be afraid. I can stand being mauled by two depraved fools. There's more at stake here. Forget about yourself, think about the radio and how to stop Wolff from contacting Rommel. She looked furtively at her wristwatch: it was a quarter to midnight.

IT WAS almost dawn. In the houseboat's bedroom Wolff and Sonja lay fast asleep. The game they had made Elene play had been for Sonja's benefit: it was clearly her fantasy, her kink. The more Wolff turned his attention to Elene, the harder Sonja tried to get between them, until in the denouement Wolff rejected Elene and made love to Sonja. It was so silly, so farcical that Elene had almost found it comic. But by not resisting she had succeeded in making Wolff forget all about his midnight transmission to Rommel.

Now, waking on the living-room divan, she wondered what had happened to Vandam. Had he lost sight of Wolff's car in the traffic or had an accident? Whatever the reason, Vandam was no longer watching over her. She was on her own. What was to stop Wolff from sending his message another night? If his radio was here on the houseboat, that might make all the difference. She remembered something Vandam had said: "If I can get the key to the *Rebecca* code, I can impersonate Wolff over the radio. . . . It could save Egypt."

Elene thought, Perhaps I can find the key. Vandam had said it was a sheet of paper explaining how to use the book to encode messages. She decided to search the houseboat, beginning at the stern and working forward.

She tiptoed into the bedroom. Wolff's breathing was quiet and even. Sonja did not stir. Elene went into the tiny bathroom. There were a basin, a small tub, and a cupboard that contained shaving gear and pills. The radio was not in the bathroom.

She passed back through the bedroom into the living room. The divan was screwed to the floor. The radio would not be there. She moved into the kitchen. There was a tall closet. She opened it gently. There were a broom and some cleaning materials. No radio. She opened six small cupboards. They contained crockery, canned food, saucepans, glasses. There were several drawers. She opened one. The rattle of cutlery shredded her nerves. Another held bottled spices and flavorings. Another, kitchen knives.

Next to the kitchen was a small desk with a fold-down top. Beside it was yet another cupboard. Elene opened it. There was a suitcase. Her heart skipped. Elene pulled the case onto the floor. It was heavy.

The radio fitted inside the suitcase exactly, as if it had been designed that way. On top of the radio was a book. Elene lifted it out. It was *Rebecca*. In the middle there was something between the pages. She let the book fall open and a sheet of paper dropped to the floor. She picked it up. It was a list of numbers and dates, with some words in German. This was surely the key to the code.

She held in her hand what Vandam needed to turn the tide of the war. She had to run away, now, with the book and the key.

The bed creaked. From behind the curtains came the unmistakable sound of someone getting up. Elene went to the ladder and ran up the narrow wooden steps. Glancing down, she saw Wolff appear between the curtains and look up at her in astonishment. His eyes went to the open suitcase on the floor. Elene turned to the hatch. It was secured on the inside with two bolts. She slid them back. From the corner of her eye she saw Wolff dash to the ladder. She pushed open the hatch and climbed out onto the deck. Wolff was scrambling up the ladder. As he grasped the rim of the opening, Elene slammed the hatch down on his hand with all her might. There was a roar of pain. Elene ran across the deck and down the gangplank. Once on the riverbank she stooped, lifted the end of the plank and threw it into the river.

Wolff came up through the hatch, his face a mask of pain and fury. Elene panicked as she saw him come across the deck at a run. She thought, He's naked, he can't chase me! He took a flying jump over the rail of the boat and landed on the edge of the riverbank, arms windmilling for balance. With a sudden burst of courage Elene ran at him and pushed him backward into the water. She turned and fled along the towpath.

When she reached the lower end of the pathway that led to the street she stopped and looked back. Her heart was pounding. She

felt elated when she saw Wolff, dripping wet and naked, climbing out of the water up the muddy riverbank. It was getting light; he could not chase her far in that state. She spun around toward the street, broke into a run and crashed into someone.

Strong arms caught her in a tight grip. She struggled desperately. The man holding her got an arm around her throat before she could scream.

Wolff came up and said, "Who are you?"

"I'm Kemel. You must be Wolff."

"Thank God you were there. You'd better come aboard." Wolff led the way to the boat, retrieved the floating plank from the river and laid it across the gap between the houseboat and the bank. "This way," he said.

Kemel marched Elene across the deck and down the ladder. He pushed her over to the divan and made her sit down.

Wolff went through the curtains and came back a moment later with a big towel wrapped around his waist. He sat down and examined his hand. "She nearly broke my fingers," he said. He looked at Elene with a mixture of anger and amusement.

Kemel said, "Where's Sonja?"

"In bed," Wolff said, jerking his head toward the curtains. "She sleeps through earthquakes."

"You're in trouble," Kemel said.

"I know. I suppose this woman's working for Vandam."

"I don't know about that. I got a call from my man on the towpath. Vandam had come along and sent my man for help."

Wolff was shocked. "That was close!" He looked worried. "Where's Vandam now?"

"Out there still. I knocked him on the head and tied him up."

Elene's heart sank. Vandam was incapacitated—and nobody else knew where she was. It had all been for nothing.

Wolff nodded. "Vandam must have followed her. That's two people who know about this place. If I stay here, I'll have to kill them both."

"Not good enough," Kemel said. "If you kill Vandam, the murder will eventually be blamed on me." He paused, watching Wolff with narrowed eyes. "And if you were to kill me, that would still leave the man who called me last night."

"So . . ." Wolff frowned. "I have to go. Damn."

Kemel nodded. "If you disappear, I think I can cover up. But I want something from you. Remember the reason we've been helping you. We want to talk to Rommel."

"I'll be sending tonight. Tell me what to say, and I'll—"

"No. We want to do it ourselves. We want your radio." Sadat's instructions had been clear on that point.

Wolff frowned. Elene realized that Kemel was a nationalist rebel, trying to cooperate with the Germans.

Kemel added, "We could send your message for you."

"Not necessary," Wolff said. He seemed to have reached a decision. "I have another radio."

"It's agreed, then."

"There's the radio." Wolff pointed to the case, still open on the floor. "It's already tuned to the correct wavelength. All you have to do is broadcast at midnight, any night."

Kemel went over to the radio and examined it. Elene wondered why Wolff had said nothing about the *Rebecca* code. Wolff was playing safe, she decided: to give Kemel the code would be to risk that he might give it to someone else.

Wolff said, "Where does Vandam live?"

Kemel had done some checking. He told Wolff the address.

Elene thought, *Now* what is he after?

Wolff said, "He's married, I suppose."

"A widower. His wife was killed in Crete last year."

"Any children?"

"Yes," Kemel said. "A small boy called Billy. Why?"

Wolff shrugged. "I'm a little obsessed with the man who's come so close to catching me." Elene was sure he was lying.

Kemel closed the suitcase, apparently satisfied. Wolff said, "Keep an eye on her for a minute, would you?"

"Of course."

Wolff had noticed that Elene still had *Rebecca* in her hand. He reached down and took it from her, then disappeared through the curtains. In a few minutes he came back without the book, wearing his clothes.

Kemel said to him, "Do you have a call sign?"

"Sphinx," Wolff said shortly.

"A code?"

"No code."

"What was in that book?"

Wolff looked angry. "A code. But you can't have it. You'll have to take your chances and broadcast in the clear." Suddenly Wolff's knife was in his hand. "Don't argue," he said. "I know you've got a gun. But if you shoot, you'll have to explain the bullet to the British. You'd better go."

Without speaking, Kemel picked up the suitcase and went out through the hatch. Wolff put his knife away in the sheath under his shirt. He got the book from the next room, extracted the paper bearing the key, crumpled it, dropped it into a glass ashtray and set fire to it with a kitchen match.

He must have another key with the other radio, Elene thought.

Wolff made sure the paper was entirely burned. Then he opened a porthole and dropped the book into the river.

He took a small suitcase from a cupboard and began to pack a few things.

"Where are you going?" Elene said.

"You'll find out—you're coming."

"Oh, no." What would he do with her? He had caught her deceiving him—had he dreamed up some appropriate punishment? She felt very afraid. Nothing she had done had turned out well.

Wolff continued packing his case. When he was ready he took a last look around. He said, "I hate to disturb Sonja's beauty sleep." He grinned. "Let's go."

They walked along the towpath, Wolff carrying his case in one hand and gripping Elene's arm with the other. Why was he leaving Sonja behind? she wondered. Wolff was completely unscrupulous, she decided; and the thought made her shudder.

They turned onto the footpath, walked to the street and went to Wolff's car. He made her climb in on the driver's side and over the gearshift to the passenger's side. He got in beside her and they drove away.

Elene thought, Where are we going? Wherever it was, Wolff's second radio was there, along with another copy of *Rebecca* and another key to the code. When we get there I'll have to try again. Now that Wolff had left the houseboat there was nothing Vandam could do, even after somebody untied him. Elene, on her own, had to try to stop Wolff from contacting Rommel, and if possible steal the key to the code. The idea was ridiculous. All she really wanted was to get away from this evil, dangerous man, to go home, to feel safe again. But she thought of her father, walking to Jerusalem, and she knew she had to try.

Wolff stopped the car. Elene said, "This is Vandam's house!" She gazed at Wolff. "But Vandam isn't here."

"No." Wolff smiled bleakly. "But Billy is."

Chapter 11

ANWAR el-Sadat was delighted with the radio. He plugged it in to test it, and told Kemel it was very powerful. They hid it in the oven in Sadat's kitchen. Then Kemel drove back to Zamalek, rehearsing the story he had prepared to cover up his role in the events of the night.

He parked his car, went cautiously down to the towpath and slipped into the bushes thirty or forty yards from where he had left Vandam. He rolled on the ground to make his clothes dirty, smeared some of the sandy soil on his face and ran his fingers through his hair. Then, rubbing his wrists to make them look sore, he went in search of Vandam.

He found him exactly where he had left him. The bonds were still tight and the gag still in place. Vandam looked at Kemel with wide, staring eyes. Kemel said, "My God, they got you, too!"

He bent down, removed the gag and began to untie Vandam. "The sergeant contacted me," he explained. "I came down here looking for you, and the next thing I knew, I woke up bound and gagged, with a headache. I just got free." Kemel threw the rope aside. Vandam stood up stiffly. Kemel said, "How do you feel?"

"I'm all right."

"Let's board the houseboat and see what we can find."

As soon as Kemel turned, Vandam stepped forward and hit him as hard as he could with an edge-of-the-hand blow to the back of the neck. It might have killed Kemel, but Vandam did not care. He knew that Kemel had betrayed him. He had been bound and gagged, but he had been able to hear, "I'm Kemel. You must be Wolff." Since then, Vandam had been seething, and all his pent-up anger had gone into the blow.

Kemel lay on the ground, stunned. Vandam rolled him over, searched him and found the gun. He used the rope that had bound his own hands to tie Kemel's hands behind his back. Then he slapped Kemel's face until he came around.

"Get up," Vandam said.

Fear showed in Kemel's eyes. He struggled to his feet. Vandam took hold of Kemel's collar with his left hand, keeping the gun in his right. "Move."

They walked to the houseboat. Vandam pushed Kemel ahead, up the gangplank and across the deck. Awkwardly, with his hands tied, Kemel descended the ladder. Vandam bent down to look inside. There was nobody there. He went quickly down the ladder. Pushing Kemel to one side, he pulled back the curtains. He saw Sonja in bed, sleeping. "Get in there."

Kemel went through and stood beside the head of the bed.

"Wake her."

Kemel shouted at Sonja. She opened her eyes and sat up. She recognized Kemel, then saw Vandam with the gun. She and Vandam said simultaneously, "Where's Wolff?"

Vandam was sure she was not dissembling. It was clear now that Kemel had warned Wolff, and Wolff had fled without waking Sonja. Presumably he had taken Elene with him for some reason.

Vandam said, "Did Wolff send a radio message last night?"

"No," Sonja replied. "No, he didn't."

"What *did* happen here?" Vandam asked, dreading the answer.

"We went to bed."

"Who did?"

"Wolff and me."

Was that all? Was Sonja telling the truth—had Wolff failed to radio Rommel last night? Vandam could only hope it was true. "Get dressed," he told Sonja.

She got off the bed and hurriedly put on a dress. Then Vandam ordered Kemel and Sonja inside the tiny bathroom, closed the door on them and began to search the houseboat. He found a glass ashtray full of charred paper, but it was completely burned up. After half an hour he was sure that the houseboat contained no radio, no copy of *Rebecca* and no code key.

He found some rope. He got the two prisoners from the bathroom, bound Sonja's hands, then tied Sonja and Kemel together. He marched them off the boat and up to the street, where he hailed a taxi. He put Sonja and Kemel in the back. Keeping the gun pointed at them, he climbed in the front. "GHQ," he told the wide-eyed, frightened Arab driver.

The two prisoners would be interrogated, but really there were only two questions: Where was Wolff? And where was Elene?

SITTING in the car, Wolff took hold of Elene's wrist. He drew out his knife and ran its blade lightly across the back of her hand. The knife was very sharp. Elene stared at her hand in horror. At first there was just a line like a pencil mark. Then blood welled up and there was a sharp pain. She gasped.

Wolff said, "You're to stay very close to me and say nothing."

"Otherwise you'll cut me?" Elene said with scorn.

"No," he said. "Otherwise I'll cut Billy."

He got out of the car. Elene sat still, feeling helpless. What could she do against this ruthless man? She took a handkerchief from her bag and wrapped it around her bleeding hand. Wolff came around to her side and, taking her arm, made her get out.

They walked up the drive to Vandam's house and rang the bell. Gaafar opened the door. He said, "Good morning, Miss Fontana," and looked briefly at her hand.

Wolff said, "Good morning. I'm Captain Alexander. The major asked me to come round. Let us in, would you?"

"Of course, sir." Gaafar stood aside. Wolff, still gripping Elene's arm, stepped into the tiled hall. Gaafar said, "I hope the major is all right."

"Yes, he's fine. But he can't get home this morning, so he asked me to drive Billy to school, since I'm off duty."

Elene was aghast. Wolff was going to kidnap Billy. She must not let it happen! She wanted to shout, No, Gaafar, he's lying, take Billy and get away, run, run! But Wolff had the knife, and Gaafar was old, and Wolff would get Billy anyway.

Gaafar seemed to hesitate. Wolff said, "All right, Gaafar, snap it up. We haven't got all day."

"Yes, sir," Gaafar said. "Billy is just finishing his breakfast. Would you wait in here for a moment?" He opened the drawing-room door for them.

Wolff propelled Elene into the room and at last let go of her arm. He sat down at the desk, found paper and a pencil and began to write. "Why did you bring me here?" Elene cried.

Wolff looked up from his writing. "To keep the boy quiet. We've got a long way to go."

"Leave Billy here," she pleaded. "He's a child."

"Vandam's child," Wolff said with a smile. "Vandam may be able to guess where I'm going. I want to make sure he doesn't come after me." He continued to write.

Elene forced herself to concentrate. They were going on a long journey. At the end, surely, was the spare radio, with a copy of *Rebecca* and a copy of the key to the code. Somehow she had to help Vandam follow them. Where would Wolff have kept a spare radio? He might have hidden it somewhere in the desert, or somewhere between Cairo and Asyut. Maybe . . .

Billy came in. "Hello," he said to Elene. "Did you bring me that book?"

"Book?" She stared at him, thinking that he was still a child, despite his grown-up ways. He wore gray flannel shorts, a white shirt and a school tie. He was carrying a school satchel.

"You were going to lend me a detective story by Simenon."

"I forgot. I'm sorry."

Wolff had been staring at Billy, like a miser looking into his treasure chest. Now he stood up. "Hello, Billy," he said with a smile. "I'm Captain Alexander."

Billy shook hands and said, "How do you do, sir."

"Your father asked me to tell you that he's pretty busy coping with old Rommel and I'm to take you to school."

"Has he been in another fight?"

Wolff hesitated. "Matter of fact he has, but he's okay. He got a bump on the head." Billy seemed more proud than worried.

Wolff spoke to Elene in rapid Arabic. "Keep the boy quiet for a minute." He turned back to the desk.

Elene looked at Billy's satchel and had an idea. "Show me your schoolbooks," she said. The satchel was open, and an atlas stuck out. She reached for it. "What are you doing in geography?"

"The Norwegian fjords."

Elene saw Wolff finish writing and put the sheet of paper in an envelope. He sealed the envelope and slipped it in his pocket.

"Let's find Norway." Elene flipped the pages of the atlas.

Wolff picked up the telephone and dialed. He looked at Elene, then looked away, out the window.

Elene found the map of Egypt. Billy said, "But that's—"

Quickly Elene touched his lips with her finger. He stopped speaking and frowned at her. She said, "That's Scandinavia, yes, but Norway is in Scandinavia. Look." She unwrapped the handkerchief from around her hand. With her fingernail she opened the cut and made it bleed. Billy turned white.

Elene was now almost sure Wolff was going to Asyut. He had said he was afraid Vandam would guess their destination, and it was likely Vandam would associate that town with Wolff. Just then she heard Wolff say into the phone, "Hello? Give me the time of the train to Asyut."

I was right! she thought. She dipped her finger in the blood from her hand. With three strokes, she drew an arrow in blood, pointing to the town of Asyut, three hundred miles south of Cairo. She closed the atlas. She used her handkerchief to smear blood on the cover, then pushed the book behind her. Billy seemed dumbstruck. He was staring at Elene's hand.

Wolff put down the phone. "Let's go. You don't want to be late for school, Billy." He went to the door and opened it.

Billy, frowning, picked up his satchel and went out. Elene followed. There was a little pile of letters on a table in the hall. Wolff dropped his envelope on top of the pile and they left the house. Wolff asked Elene, "Can you drive?"

"Yes," she answered, then realized she should have said no.

"You two get in the front." Wolff got in the back.

As she pulled away, Wolff leaned forward. He said, "See this?" He was showing the knife to Billy.

"Yes," Billy said in an unsteady voice.

Wolff said, "If you make trouble, I'll use it on you."

Billy began to cry.

THE interrogation room was bare except for a table and chair. Vandam followed Jakes and Kemel in and sat down. Vandam said, "Where is Alex Wolff?"

"I don't know," said Kemel.

Vandam said, "Listen, Kemel. As things stand, you're going to be shot for spying. If you tell us all you know, you could get off with a prison sentence. Be sensible. Now, you came to the towpath and knocked me out, didn't you?"

"No, sir."

Vandam sighed. Kemel had his story and he was sticking to it. Vandam said, "What is your wife's involvement in all this?"

Kemel said nothing, but he looked scared.

"If you won't answer my questions, I'll have to ask her."

Kemel's lips were pressed together in a hard line.

Vandam stood up. "All right, Jakes," he said. "Bring in the wife on suspicion of spying."

Kemel said, "Typical British justice."

Vandam looked at him. "Where is Wolff?"

"I don't know."

Vandam went out. Jakes followed. Vandam said, "He's a policeman, he knows the techniques. He'll break, but not today." And Vandam had to find Wolff and Elene today.

They walked to another room and went in. Sonja sat on a chair, wearing a gray prison dress. Beside her stood a woman army officer who would have scared Vandam, had he been her prisoner. She was short and stout, with a hard face and short gray hair.

Vandam and Jakes sat down. Vandam had interrogated Sonja here before, and she had been stronger than he. This time Elene's safety was in the balance, and Vandam had few scruples left. He said, "Where is Alex Wolff?"

"I don't know."

"Wolff is a German spy, and you have been helping him."

"Ridiculous."

Vandam watched her face. She was proud, confident, unafraid. "Wolff betrayed you," he said. "Kemel the policeman warned Wolff of the danger, but Wolff left you sleeping and went off with another woman. Are you going to protect him after that?"

She said nothing.

"Wolff kept his radio on your boat. He sent messages to Rommel. You knew this, so you are an accessory. You're going to be shot for spying."

"All Cairo will riot! You wouldn't dare!"

"You think so? What do we care if Cairo riots now? The Germans are at the gates—let them put down the rebellion."

"You can't touch me."

"I think I'd better prove to you that I can." Vandam nodded to the woman officer.

The woman held Sonja still while Jakes tied her to the chair. She struggled for a moment, but it was hopeless. For the first time there was a hint of fear in her eyes. The woman officer took a large pair of scissors from her bag. She lifted a hank of Sonja's long, thick hair and cut it off.

"You can't do this!" Sonja shrieked.

The officer continued to cut. As the heavy locks fell away, she dropped them in Sonja's lap. Sonja's screams subsided into tears.

Vandam said, "You see, we don't care much about Egyptian public opinion anymore. We've got our backs to the wall."

The officer took soap and a shaving brush and lathered Sonja's head, then began to shave her scalp. Finally the officer took a mirror from her bag and held it in front of Sonja. She gasped when she saw the reflection of her totally bald head. "No," she said. "It's not me." She burst out into wilder crying.

All the hatred was gone now; she was completely demoralized. Vandam said softly, "Where was Wolff getting his information?"

"From Major Smith," Sonja replied. "Sandy Smith."

Vandam glanced at Jakes. That was the name of the major from SIS who had disappeared—it was as they had feared. "How did he get the information?"

"Sandy came to the houseboat on his lunch break to visit me. While we were together Alex went through his briefcase."

As simple as that, Vandam thought. God, I feel tired. Smith was liaison man between the Secret Intelligence Service and GHQ. He had been privy to all strategic planning. He had been going straight from the morning conferences at GHQ to the houseboat, with a briefcase full of secrets.

Vandam said, "Where is Smith now?"

"He caught Alex going through his briefcase. Alex killed him. He's in the river by the houseboat."

Vandam nodded to Jakes, and Jakes went out.

Vandam said to Sonja, "Tell me about Kemel."

She was in full flood now, eager to tell all she knew, her resistance quite crushed. "He came and told me you had asked to have the houseboat watched. He said he would censor his surveillance reports if I would arrange a meeting between Alex and Anwar el-Sadat. He's a captain in the army."

"Why did Sadat want to meet Wolff?"

"So the Free Officers' Movement could send a message to Rommel."

Vandam said to the woman officer, "Go and find the address of Captain Anwar el-Sadat."

"Yes, sir." The woman left.

Vandam said, "Do you know where Wolff might have gone?"

"The thief Abdullah. He might have gone to Abdullah."

"Good idea. Any other suggestions?"

"His cousins in the desert."

"And where would they be found?"

"No one knows. They're nomads."

"Might Wolff know their movements?"

"I suppose he might."

"I'll see you again," Vandam said, and went out.

The woman officer handed him a slip of paper with Sadat's address on it. Jakes was waiting in the muster room. "The navy is lending us a couple of divers," Jakes said. "They're on their way."

"Good. I'm going to arrest Sadat. Has everyone been briefed?"

Jakes nodded. "They know we're looking for a wireless transmitter, a copy of *Rebecca* and a set of coding instructions."

"I want you to raid Abdullah's place. Then meet me at the houseboat."

SADAT lived in a suburb three miles out of Cairo in the direction of Heliopolis. Four jeeps roared up to his house, and the soldiers immediately surrounded it and began to search the garden. Vandam rapped on the front door. It was opened. "Captain Anwar el-Sadat?"

"Yes." Sadat was a thin, serious young man of medium height. His curly brown hair was already receding. He wore his uniform and fez, as if he were about to go out.

"You're under arrest," Vandam said, and pushed past him into the house. "Which is your bedroom, Captain?"

Sadat pointed. He was calm and dignified, but hiding some tension. He's afraid, Vandam thought, but not of going to prison; he's afraid of something else.

They went into the room together. It was a simple bedroom with a mattress on the floor and a galabia hanging from a hook. Two soldiers began to search.

"You know Alex Wolff," Vandam said to Sadat. "He also calls himself Achmed Rahmha, but he's a European."

"I've never heard of him."

Clearly Sadat was a fairly tough personality, not the kind to break down and confess everything just because a few burly soldiers started messing up his home.

A shout came from another part of the house. "Major Vandam!"

Vandam followed the sound into the kitchen. A sergeant MP was opening a suitcase that had been hidden in the oven. Inside was a radio. Vandam looked at Sadat, who had followed him into the kitchen. The Arab's face was twisted with bitterness and disappointment. So the rebels had warned Wolff, and in exchange they had gotten his radio. Did that mean he had another?

"Well done, Sergeant. Finish searching the house. Then take Captain Sadat to GHQ."

"I protest," Sadat said. "The law states that officers in the Egyptian army may be detained only in the officers' mess and must be guarded by a fellow officer."

"The law also states that spies are to be shot," Vandam said. He turned back to the sergeant. "Have the captain charged with espionage."

He looked again at Sadat. The bitterness and disappointment had gone from his face, to be replaced by a calculating look. He's going to make the most of all this, Vandam thought; he's preparing to play martyr. Very adaptable—he should be a politician.

Vandam went out to his jeep. "To Zamalek," he told the driver.

When Vandam reached the houseboat the divers had done their work. Two soldiers were hauling the body out of the Nile. Jakes came over. "Look at this, sir." He handed Vandam a waterlogged book. It was *Rebecca*.

The radio went to Sadat; the code book went into the river. Vandam remembered the ashtray full of charred paper. Had Wolff burned the key to the code? But why, when he had a vital message to send to Rommel? The conclusion was inescapable: Wolff had *another* radio, book and key hidden somewhere.

The soldiers got the body onto the bank. Vandam stood over it. "Ugly, isn't it?" he said to Jakes. "Stabbed to death, then dumped in the river. Wolff's damn quick with that knife." Vandam touched his own cheek: the dressing had been taken off, and several days' growth of beard hid the wound. *But not Elene, not with the knife, please.* "I gather you haven't found Wolff."

"There was no sign of him at Abdullah's house."

"Nor at Captain Sadat's." Suddenly Vandam felt utterly drained. It seemed that Wolff outwitted him at every turn. He rubbed his face. He had not slept in the past twenty-four hours. "I think I'll go home and get some rest," he said. "It might help me think more clearly. This afternoon we'll interrogate all the prisoners again."

On the way home, Vandam recalled that Sonja had mentioned another possibility: Wolff's nomad cousins. But who could tell where they would be, except Wolff himself? The jeep stopped outside Vandam's house. He got out and dismissed the driver.

There was mail on the hall table. The top envelope had no stamp, and was addressed to Vandam in a vaguely familiar hand. It had "Urgent" scribbled on it. Vandam picked it up.

He went into the drawing room, looking for a letter opener. Somehow the search for Wolff had to be narrowed down. He remembered where all this had started: Asyut. That seemed to be where Wolff had come in from the desert, so maybe he would go out that way. Maybe his cousins were in that vicinity.

There was more he should do, Vandam realized. Wolff could well be heading south now. Roadblocks should be set up on the route. There should be someone at every stop on the railway line, looking for him. Vandam was finding it hard to concentrate.

Where was that damned letter opener? He went to the door and called, "Gaafar!" He came back into the room, and saw Billy's school atlas on a chair. It looked mucky. The boy had dropped it in a puddle, or something. Vandam picked it up. It was sticky. He realized there was blood on it. He felt as if he were in a nightmare. What was going on?

Gaafar came in. Vandam said, "What's this mess?"

Gaafar looked. "I'm sorry, sir, I don't know. They were looking at it while Captain Alexander was here—"

"Who's they? Who's Captain Alexander?"

"The officer you sent to take Billy to school, sir."

A terrible fear cleared Vandam's brain in an instant. "A British army captain came here this morning and took Billy away?"

"Yes, sir, he took him to school. He said you sent him—"

"Gaafar, *I sent nobody.*"

The servant's brown face turned gray.

Vandam said, "Didn't you check that he was genuine?"

"But, sir, Miss Fontana was with him, so it seemed all right."

"Oh, my God." Now he knew why the handwriting on the envelope was familiar: it was the same as that on the note Wolff had sent Elene. He ripped open the envelope. Inside was a message in the same writing.

> Dear Major Vandam,
>
> Billy is with me. Elene is taking care of him. He will be quite all right as long as I am safe. I advise you to stay where you are and do nothing. I have no wish to harm the boy. All the same, the life of one child is as nothing beside the future of my two nations, Egypt and Germany; so be assured that if it suits my purpose I will kill Billy.
>
> Alex Wolff

It was a letter from a madman: the polite salutation, the correct English, the attempt to justify the kidnapping of an innocent child. Wolff was insane. And he had Billy.

Vandam handed the note to Gaafar, who put on his spectacles with a shaky hand. What was the point of the kidnapping? Where had they gone? And why the blood? Gaafar was weeping openly. Vandam said, "Who was hurt? Who was bleeding?"

"There was no violence. Miss Fontana had a cut on her hand."

And she had smeared blood on Billy's atlas and left it on the chair. It was a sign, a message. Vandam held the book and let it fall open. Immediately he saw the map of Egypt with a blotted red arrow pointing to Asyut.

If I report this to GHQ, he thought, Bogge will order Wolff arrested at Asyut. There will be a fight. Wolff will know he has lost. What will he do then? He will kill my son.

He felt paralyzed by fear. Of course that was Wolff's aim in taking Billy, to paralyze Vandam. That was how kidnapping worked. There was only one option. Vandam had to go after them alone. Wolff had come from Asyut by train. Vandam had to gamble that he would return there by train.

Vandam went into the hall, put on his motorcycle goggles, then found a scarf and wound it around his mouth and neck. He left the house, climbed onto his motorcycle and kicked the bike into life. The fuel tank was full. Gaafar had followed him, still weeping. Vandam touched the old man's shoulder. "I'll bring them back," he said. He rocked the bike off its stand, drove into the street and turned south.

Chapter 12

BILLY is so pale, Elene thought. He's trying to be brave. They were riding in a first-class coach with Wolff toward Asyut. What am I going to do? she wondered. She got a chill every time she glanced at Wolff. The way he stared at Billy. The gleam in his eye, the look of triumph. Perhaps she could take Billy's mind off things by playing a game. What a ridiculous idea. Perhaps not so ridiculous. Here was his school satchel. Here was an exercise book. He watched her curiously. What game? Ticktacktoe. Four lines for the grid; her cross in the center. He took the pencil and put a zero in the corner. I believe he's going along with this idea in order to comfort me! she thought. Wolff snatched the book, looked at it, shrugged and gave it back. Her cross, Billy's zero . . . the game was a draw.

I have to get Billy away from that knife, thought Elene. Billy made a cross in the center of a new grid. She made a zero, then scribbled hastily: "We must escape—be ready." Billy made another cross, and: "OK." Her zero. "Next station." Billy's third cross made a line. He smiled up at her jubilantly. He had won. The train slowed down. The thing to do was to give Billy a chance to run, then try to prevent Wolff from giving chase.

Elene looked around her. Think quickly! They were in a car with fifteen or twenty rows of seats. She and Billy sat side by side, facing forward. Wolff was opposite them, his suitcase at his feet. Beside him was an empty seat. Behind him was the door to the coach platform. The other passengers were a mixture of Europeans and wealthy Egyptians, all of them in Western clothing. Everyone was hot and weary. Several people were asleep.

The train stopped in the station.

Not yet, Elene thought; not yet. The time to move would be when the train was about to pull out again—that would give Wolff less time to catch them. She sat feverishly still.

A priest in Coptic robes boarded the train and took the seat next to Wolff. Elene murmured to Billy, "When the whistle blows, run for the door and get off the train."

Wolff said, "What was that?"

The whistle blew. Billy looked at Elene, hesitating.

Wolff frowned.

Elene threw herself at Wolff, reaching for his face. He put up his arms protectively, but they did not stop her furious rush. She raked his face with her fingernails, and saw blood spurt. The priest gave a shout of surprise. Over the back of Wolff's seat she saw Billy run to the door and struggle to open it. She collapsed on Wolff and tried to scratch his eyes.

At last he found his voice, and roared with anger. He pushed himself out of his seat, driving Elene backward. She caught hold of his shirtfront. His fist came up and struck the side of her jaw. She fell back into her seat. When her vision cleared she saw Wolff heading for the boy. She stood up. Billy was going through the doorway, Wolff close behind. Elene followed them.

Billy was racing along the station platform. Wolff was charging after him. The few Egyptians standing around were looking on, mildly astonished, and doing nothing. Elene ran after Wolff. The train shuddered, about to move. Wolff put on a burst of speed. Elene yelled, "Run, Billy, run!" Billy was almost at the station exit. The train was inching forward, and Wolff had to get back on it. Elene thought, We did it!

Then Billy slipped and fell, hitting the ground hard. Wolff was on him in a flash, bending to lift him. Elene caught up with them and jumped on Wolff's back. Wolff stumbled, losing his grip on Billy. Elene clung to Wolff. The train was moving slowly but steadily. Wolff broke Elene's hold and threw her to the ground. Then he lifted Billy across his shoulder. The boy was yelling and hammering on his back. Wolff ran alongside the train for a few paces, then leaped on.

Elene struggled to her feet. She could not leave Billy. She ran, stumbling, to the train. Someone reached out a hand to her. She took it, and jumped. She was aboard, back where she had started. Crushed, she followed Wolff to their seats. She did not look at the faces of the people she passed. She saw Wolff give Billy one sharp smack on the bottom and dump him into his seat. The boy was crying silently.

Wolff turned to Elene. "You're a crazy girl," he said loudly, for the benefit of the other passengers. He grabbed her arm and slapped her face. The priest stood up, touched Wolff's shoulder and said something.

Wolff let her go and they sat down. She looked around. The other passengers were all staring at her. None of them would help her, for she was an Egyptian woman, and women, like camels, had to be beaten from time to time. Useless, impotent rage boiled within her. They had almost escaped. She put her arm around the child and pulled him close. She began to stroke his hair. After a while he fell asleep.

VANDAM knew that he was—by now—well ahead of the train. He had stopped at four stations to ask if the train had passed through yet. It had not. He drove very fast, his goggles and the scarf around his mouth and neck protecting him from the worst of the dust. He knew what he had to do, but he needed time. He would stop at the next station and put his plan into effect.

Somewhere along the road he had made a decision. He had set out from Cairo to rescue Billy and Elene; but then he had realized that that was not his only duty. There was still the war.

Vandam was certain that Wolff had another radio, another copy of *Rebecca* and another key to the code, and that they were all hidden at Asyut. To implement the plan for deceiving Rommel, Vandam had to have the radio and the key—and that meant he had to let Wolff get to Asyut and retrieve his spare set. Only then could he rescue Billy and Elene. It would be tough on them, savagely tough, but living under Nazi rule would also be savagely tough.

Having made the decision, Vandam now needed to be certain that Wolff was on that train. At the same time he might just be able to make things a little easier for Billy and Elene.

When Vandam reached the next town he pulled up outside the police station. It was in a central square, opposite the railway station. He gave a series of peremptory blasts on the horn of his bike. Two Arab policemen came out of the building: a gray-haired man in a white uniform and a boy of eighteen or twenty. Vandam got off the bike and bawled, "Attention!" Both men stood straight and saluted. Vandam returned the salute. "I'm chasing a

dangerous criminal, and I need your help," he said dramatically. "Let's go inside."

Vandam led the way. He said to the older man, "Call British headquarters in Cairo for me." He gave him the number and the man picked up the phone from a table. Vandam turned to the younger policeman. "Could you ride my motorcycle?"

The boy was thrilled by the idea. "I ride very well."

"Go out and try it."

The older man, who had been shouting into the telephone, held it out to Vandam. "This is GHQ."

Vandam spoke into the phone. "Connect me with Captain Jakes." Jakes's voice came on the line. "Hello?"

"This is Vandam. I'm in the south, following a hunch. In order to assure the maximal support of the indigenous constabulary"—he spoke like this so that the policeman would not understand—"I want you to do your Dutch uncle act."

Vandam gave the phone to the gray-haired man. He unconsciously stood straighter as Jakes instructed him, in no uncertain terms, to do everything Vandam wanted and do it fast. "Yes, sir!" the policeman said several times. Finally he said, "Be assured, sir and gentleman, that we will do all in our power."

Vandam went to the window. The young policeman was driving around the square on the motorcycle, tooting the horn and over-revving the engine. A small crowd had gathered to watch. The boy was grinning from ear to ear. He'll do, Vandam thought.

"Make arrangements for me to get on the Asyut train when it stops here," he said to the older man. "And have your boy drive my bike to the next station and meet me there."

"Yes, sir!" He went out at a run.

Vandam could not hear the train yet. He had time for one more phone call. He picked up the receiver and asked the operator for Captain Newman at the army base in Asyut. After a long wait Newman came on the line.

"This is Vandam. I think I'm on the trail of your knife man."

"Jolly good show, sir!" said Newman. "Anything I can do?"

"I'll be arriving in Asyut by road in a few hours. I need a taxi, a large galabia and a small boy. Will you meet me?"

"I'll be at the city limits, how's that?"

"Fine." Vandam heard a distant *chuff-chuff-chuff*. "I have to go." He hung up. He put a five-pound note on the table beside the telephone; a little baksheesh never hurt. He went out into the square. Away to the north he could see the approaching smoke of the train. The younger policeman drove up to him on the bike. Vandam said, "I'm getting on the train. You drive the motorcycle to the next station and meet me there. Okay?"

"Okay, okay!" He was delighted.

Vandam took out a pound note, tore it in half, and gave him half the note. "You get the other half when you meet me."

The train was almost in the station. Vandam crossed the square, and ran along the platform so that he could board at the front without being seen by the passengers. The train came in, billowing smoke. When it stopped, Vandam climbed aboard.

He found himself in an economy coach. Wolff would surely travel first-class. Vandam began to walk through the cars, picking his way over the people sitting on the floor with their boxes and crates and animals. He passed through three economy coaches, then he was at the door to a first-class car. Suddenly he was not sure that he had the nerve to go through with this. Wolff had never gotten a good look at him—they had fought in the dark in the alley—and the gash on his cheek was almost completely covered now by his beard. Billy was the real problem. Vandam had to warn his son, somehow, to pretend not to recognize his father. He took a deep breath and opened the door.

Stepping through, he glanced quickly and nervously at the first few rows of seats; no Billy. He spoke to the passengers nearest him. "Your papers, please."

"What's this, Major?" said an Egyptian army colonel.

"Routine check, sir," Vandam replied. He moved along the aisle, checking people's papers. By the time he was halfway down the car he was sure that Wolff, Elene and Billy were not there. He began to wonder if he had guessed wrong.

He reached the end and passed through the door into the space between the coaches. Ahead was the last car. If they are on the train, I'll know now, he thought.

He opened the door and saw Billy immediately. He felt a pang of distress, like a wound. The boy was asleep in his seat, his feet only just reaching the floor, his body slumped sideways, his hair falling over his forehead. Elene had her arm around him. She looked up. Her eyes widened. Vandam quickly raised a finger to his lips. She dropped her eyes, but Wolff had caught her look, and he was turning his head to find out what she had seen. Vandam stepped up to Wolff. "Papers, please."

It was the first time Vandam had seen his enemy face to face. Wolff was a handsome fellow, with strong features. Only around the eyes and the corners of the mouth was there a hint of weakness, of depravity. And there were fresh scratches on his cheek; perhaps Elene had put up some resistance. He handed over his papers, then looked out the window, bored. The papers identified him as Alexander Wolff, Villa les Oliviers, Garden City. Vandam said, "Where are you going, sir?"

"Asyut. To visit relations."

"Are you people together?"

"That's my son and his nanny," Wolff said.

Vandam took Elene's papers and glanced at them. He wanted to take Wolff by the throat. *My son and his nanny.* You bastard.

He gave Elene her papers. "No need to wake the child," he said. He looked at the priest sitting next to Wolff, and took the proffered wallet. The priest said, "I'm going to Asyut, too."

"I see," said Vandam. He returned the papers. "Thank you." He went to the next row of seats and continued to examine papers. When he looked back, Wolff was staring out the window again.

Vandam reached the end of the coach. He was returning the last of the papers when he heard a cry that pierced his heart: *"That's my dad!"*

He looked up. Billy was running along the aisle toward him, stumbling, bumping against the seats, his arms outstretched. *Oh, God.* Beyond Billy, Vandam could see Wolff and Elene standing up, watching—Wolff with intensity, Elene with fear. Vandam opened the door behind him, pretending not to notice the boy, and walked onto the coach platform. Billy came flying through. Vandam slammed the door. He took Billy in his arms.

"It's all right," Vandam said. "It's all right."

Wolff would be coming to investigate.

"They took me away!" Billy said. "I missed school and I was really really scared!"

"It's all right now." Vandam felt he could not leave Billy; he would have to kill Wolff, to abandon his deception plan and the search for the radio and the code. No, it *had* to be done. He fought down his instincts. "Listen," he said. "I have to catch that man, and I don't want him to know who I am. He's the German spy I'm after, do you understand?"

"Yes, yes. . . ."

"Can you pretend I'm not your father? And go back to him?"

Billy stared, openmouthed. His whole expression said, *No, no!*

"This is a real-life tec story, Billy, and we're in it, you and I. You have to pretend you made a mistake. But remember, I'll be nearby, and together we'll catch the spy."

The door opened. Wolff came through. "What's all this?"

Vandam made his face bland. "He seems to have woken up from a dream and mistaken me for his father. We're the same build. You did say you were his father, didn't you?"

"What nonsense, Billy!" Wolff said. "Come back to your seat."

Billy stood still.

"Come on, young man," Vandam said, putting a hand on Billy's shoulder. "Let's go and win the war."

The old catchphrase did the trick. Billy gave a brave grin. "I'm sorry, sir," he said. "I must have been dreaming."

Vandam felt as though his heart would break.

Billy turned away and went back inside the coach. Wolff and Vandam followed. As they walked along the aisle, the train slowed down. They were approaching the next station, where Vandam's motorcycle would be waiting. Billy reached his seat and sat down. Elene was staring at Vandam uncomprehendingly. Billy touched her arm and said, "It's okay, I made a mistake." A strange light came into her eyes; she seemed on the point of tears.

Vandam paused at the coach door. "Have a good trip," he said to Billy.

"Thank you, sir."

The train pulled into the station and stopped. Vandam got off and walked forward along the platform a little way. He stood in the shade of an awning and waited. There was a whistle, and the train began to move. His eyes were fixed on the window which he knew to be next to Billy's seat. As the window passed him, he saw Billy's face. Billy raised his hand in a little wave. Vandam waved back, and the face was gone.

Vandam realized he was trembling all over.

When the train was almost out of sight he left the station. Outside was the young policeman from the last town, sitting astride the motorcycle. Vandam gave him the other half of the pound note, climbed on the motorcycle and took the road south. He would reach Asyut thirty or forty minutes ahead of the train, he calculated. Captain Newman would be there to meet him.

He pulled ahead of the train which carried Billy and Elene, the only people he loved. He explained to himself again that he had done the best thing for everyone, the best thing for Billy; but in the back of his mind a voice said, Cruel, cruel, cruel.

The train entered the station and stopped. Elene saw a sign which said, in Arabic and English: Asyut. They had arrived.

What game was Vandam playing? She realized he must have some scheme to rescue her and Billy and also get the key to the code. She wished she knew what it was. Fortunately Billy did not seem to be troubled by such thoughts. He had perked up, taking an interest in the countryside through which they were passing, and had even asked Wolff where he had bought his knife.

She glanced at Wolff. He seemed full of nervous excitement. Some kind of change had occurred in him in the last twenty-four hours, she thought. When she first met him he had been a poised, suave man. Now all that had gone. He fidgeted, he looked about him restlessly, and every few seconds a corner of his mouth twitched almost imperceptibly. It was curious that Wolff, the ruthless one, was getting desperate while Vandam just got cooler.

Elene and Billy followed Wolff from the train and onto the crowded platform. Suddenly a dirty boy in green striped pajamas snatched Wolff's case, shouting, "I get taxi!" Wolff gave a good-humored shrug and let the boy lead him to the gate.

They went out into the square. Elene looked around for a sign of Vandam. Wolff told the Arab boy, "I want a motor taxi." There was one behind the horse-drawn cabs. The boy led them to it.

"Get in the front," Wolff told Elene. He gave the boy a coin and got into the back with Billy. The driver wore dark glasses and a kaffiyeh—an Arab headdress. "Go south," Wolff told him in Arabic.

"Okay," the driver said.

Elene's heart missed a beat. She knew that voice. She stared at the driver. It was Vandam.

VANDAM DROVE AWAY FROM THE station, thinking, So far, so good. His knowledge of Arabic was rudimentary, but he was able to give—and therefore to understand—directions. He would be all right as long as Wolff did not want to discuss the weather and the crops.

Captain Newman had come through with everything Vandam had asked for, even adding a six-shot Enfield .38 revolver. Having studied Newman's map of the Asyut area, Vandam knew how to find the southbound road out of the city. He drove through the marketplace, honking his horn continually in Egyptian fashion, steering dangerously close to the great wooden wheels of the carts, nudging sheep out of the way with his fenders.

Pretending to adjust his rearview mirror, he stole a glance at Billy, wondering if he had recognized his father. Billy was staring at the back of Vandam's head with an expression of delight. Vandam thought, Don't give the game away!

They left the town behind and headed south on a straight desert road. On their left were irrigated fields and groves of trees; on their right, a wall of granite cliffs, colored beige by a layer of dusty sand. Wolff said, *"Rûh yameen."*

Vandam knew this meant "Go right." Up ahead he saw a turnoff which seemed to lead straight to the cliff. He took the turn, then saw that he was headed for a pass through the hills. The road began to climb, and the old car struggled to take the grade, finally making the summit in second gear. Vandam looked out across the apparently endless Western Desert.

The road became a track. Directly ahead the sun rolled down the edge of the sky. Wolff sat up in his seat and began to look about him. Soon afterward the road intersected a wadi. Cautiously Vandam let the car roll down the bank of the dried-up river. Wolff said, *"Rûh shemal."*

Vandam turned left. The going was firm. He was astonished to see groups of people, tents and animals in the wadi. It was like a secret community. A mile farther on they saw the explanation: a wellhead, marked by a low circular wall of mud brick. Beyond it was a large encampment where Wolff made Vandam stop. There were tents in a cluster, hobbled camels and cooking fires. Wolff reached into the front of the car, switched off the engine and pulled out the key. Without a word he got out.

The Key to Rebecca

ISHMAEL WAS SITTING BY THE fire, making tea. He looked up and said, "Peace be with you," as casually as if Wolff had dropped in from the tent next door.

"And with you be health and God's mercy and blessing," Wolff replied formally.

Ishmael handed him a cup. Wolff drank. The tea was sweet and very strong. Ishmael said, "What of your friends?" He looked toward the taxi.

"They are not friends," Wolff said.

Ishmael nodded. He was incurious. "You will join us in eating?"

"Alas, no. Already the sun is low, and I must be back in the city before night falls."

Ishmael shook his head sadly. "You have come for your box."

"Yes. Please fetch it, my cousin."

Ishmael spoke to a man standing behind him, who brought the case. Wolff opened it. A great sense of euphoria flooded over him as he looked at the radio, the book and the key to the code. He felt intoxicated with a sense of power and imminent victory. He stood up. "I thank you, my cousin. May God protect thee."

"Go in safety."

Wolff turned and walked toward the taxi.

ELENE saw Wolff walk away from the fire with the suitcase in his hand. "He's coming," she said. "What now?"

"He'll want to go back to Asyut," Vandam said, not looking at her or Billy. "Those radios have no batteries, they have to be plugged in. He has to go someplace where there's electricity."

Wolff got into the car. "Asyut," he said. He handed Vandam the key. Vandam started the car and turned it around. They went along the wadi and then onto the road. The sun was low behind them now. Evening clouds were gathering over the hills ahead.

"Go faster," Wolff said in Arabic. "It's getting dark."

Vandam increased speed. The car bounced and swayed on the dirt road. Billy said, "I feel sick."

Elene turned around to look at him. His face was pale and he was sitting bolt upright. "Go slower," she said in Arabic.

Vandam slowed down for a moment, but Wolff said, "Go faster." He said to Elene, "Forget about the child."

Vandam went faster.

Elene looked at Billy again. He was as white as a sheet and on the brink of tears. "Damn you," she said to Wolff.

"Stop the car," Billy said.

Wolff ignored him, and Vandam had to pretend not to understand English.

The car hit a bump in the road, rose into the air and came down hard. Billy yelled, "Dad, stop the car! Dad!"

Vandam slammed on the brakes. The gearshift bent in his hand. Elene braced herself against the dashboard and glanced at Wolff. For a split second he was stunned with shock. His eyes went to Vandam, then to Billy, then back to Vandam. She knew he was thinking about the incident on the train, and the Arab boy at the railway station, and the kaffiyeh that covered the taxi driver's face; and then she saw that he understood it all.

The car was grinding to a halt. Wolff threw his arm around Billy and pulled the boy to him. Then he pulled out the knife.

The car stopped. Elene saw Vandam's hand go to the side slit of his galabia—and freeze there as he looked into the back seat.

Wolff was holding the knife an inch from Billy's throat. Billy was wild-eyed with fear. Vandam looked stricken. At the corners of Wolff's mouth there was the hint of a mad smile.

"You almost had me," he said. Then he added, "Take off that foolish hat." Vandam removed the kaffiyeh. They all stared at Wolff in silence.

"Let me guess," said Wolff. "Major Vandam." He was enjoying the moment. "What a good thing I took your son for insurance." Then he said to Elene, "Underneath the galabia, Major Vandam is wearing khaki trousers. In one of the pockets or possibly in the waistband, you will find a gun. Take it out."

Elene found the gun and took it out.

Wolff said, "Break the back of the gun, remove the cartridges and drop them outside the car." She did. "Put the gun on the floor." She put it down. Now, once again, Wolff held the only weapon—his knife. He spoke to Vandam. "Get out of the car."

Vandam sat motionless.

"Get out," Wolff repeated. With a sudden precise movement he nicked the lobe of Billy's ear with the knife. A drop of blood welled out. Vandam got out of the car.

Wolff said to Elene, "Get into the driver's seat."

She climbed over the wobbly gearshift. Vandam stood beside the car, staring in. "Drive," Wolff said.

Elene started the car and pulled away. Looking in the mirror, she saw Wolff put the knife away and release Billy. Behind the car, already fifty yards away, Vandam stood on the desert road, his silhouette black against the sunset. He was quite still. Elene said, "He's got no water!"

"No," Wolff replied.

Then Billy went berserk.

Elene heard him scream, "You can't leave him behind!" She turned around, forgetting about her driving. Billy had leaped on Wolff like an enraged wildcat, punching and scratching and kicking. Wolff, who had relaxed, thinking the crisis was over, was momentarily powerless to resist. He raised his arms to protect himself.

Elene looked back to the road. The car had gone off course, and the left front wheel was plowing through some sandy scrub. She swung the steering wheel around and stamped on the brake. The rear of the car began to slide sideways. Too late, she saw a deep rut running across the road immediately in front. The car hit the rut with an impact that jarred her bones, and skidded off the far side of the road into soft sand. Then it tilted and began to roll. Elene wrestled with the wheel and the gearshift. The car came to rest on its left side, like a coin dropped edgeways into the sand. The gearshift came off in her hand. She fell against the door, banging her head.

She got to her hands and knees, holding the broken-off gearshift. She had one knee on the car door and the other on the window. She looked into the back seat. Wolff and Billy had fallen in a heap, with Wolff on top. Wolff got to his feet. Billy seemed to be unconscious.

Standing on the left rear door, Wolff threw his weight against the floor of the car. The car rocked. He did it again; the car rocked more. On his third try the car tilted and fell on all four wheels with a crash. Wolff opened the door and got out. He crouched and drew his knife.

Elene saw Vandam approaching. He crouched, like Wolff, ready to spring, his hands raised protectively. He was red-faced and panting: he had run after the car. They circled. Wolff was limping slightly. The sun was a huge orange globe behind them.

Vandam moved forward, then hesitated. Wolff lashed out with the knife, but he had been surprised by Vandam's hesitation, and his thrust missed. Vandam's fist shot out. Wolff jerked back. His nose was bleeding. They faced each other again.

Vandam jumped forward. Wolff dodged, the knife striking Vandam's shoulder. Vandam kicked out. Wolff jabbed again with the knife. It ripped through Vandam's galabia. A dark stain appeared on his trouser leg. Vandam stepped away slowly, then went down on one knee. His left arm hung limply from a shoulder covered with blood. He held his right arm up defensively. Wolff approached him.

Elene jumped out of the car. She still had the broken-off gearshift in her hand. She saw Wolff bring back his arm, ready to slash at Vandam once more. She rushed up behind Wolff, raised the gearshift high in the air and brought it down with all her might on the back of his head. Wolff seemed to stand still for a moment.

She hit him again. He fell. She dropped the gearshift and knelt beside Vandam.

"Well done," he said weakly. He put a hand on her shoulder and struggled to his feet. "It's not as bad as it looks. Help me with this." Using his good arm, he took hold of Wolff's leg and pulled him toward the car. Elene grabbed the unconscious man's arm and heaved, until Wolff was lying beside the car.

Vandam leaned into the back of the car and put a hand on Billy's chest. "Alive," he said. "Thank God." Billy's eyes opened. "It's all over," Vandam said. Billy closed his eyes.

Vandam got into the front seat. "Where's the gearshift?"

"It broke off. That's what I hit him with."

Vandam started the car. The engine fired. "Good—it's still in gear. We're mobile," he said.

"What will we do with Wolff?"

"Lock him in the trunk."

Vandam took another look at Billy. He was conscious now, his eyes wide open. "How are you, son?" said Vandam.

"I'm sorry," Billy said, "but I couldn't help feeling sick."

Vandam looked at Elene. "You'll have to drive," he said. There were tears in his eyes.

Chapter 13

THERE was the sudden, terrifying roar of nearby aircraft. Rommel saw the British bombers approaching from behind the nearest line of hills. "Take cover!" he yelled. He dived into a slit trench.

The noise was so loud it was like silence. Rommel lay with his eyes closed. He had a pain in his stomach. They had sent him a doctor from Germany, but Rommel knew that the only medicine he needed was victory.

Today was September 1, and everything had gone terribly wrong. What had seemed to be the weak point in the Allied defense line was looking more and more like an ambush. The minefields were heavy where they should have been light, the ground beneath had been quicksand where a hard surface was expected, and the Alam Halfa Ridge, which should have been taken easily, was being mightily defended. Rommel's strategy was wrong; his intelligence had been wrong; his spy had been wrong.

The bombers passed overhead. Rommel got out of the trench. His aides and officers emerged from cover and gathered around him again. He raised his field glasses and looked out over the desert. Scores of tanks stood still in the sand, many of them blazing furiously. The Allies, well dug in, were picking off the panzers like fish in a barrel.

It was no good. His forward units were fifteen miles from Alexandria, but they were stuck. Another fifteen miles, he thought, and Egypt would have been mine. He looked at the officers around him. He saw in their faces what they saw in his: defeat.

HE KNEW it was a nightmare, but he could not wake up.
The cell was six feet long by four feet wide, and half of it was taken up by a bed. The walls were of smooth gray stone. A light bulb hung from the ceiling by a cord. In one end of the cell was a door. In the other end was a small square window, set just above eye level; through it he could see the bright blue sky.

In his dream he thought, I'll wake up soon, and there will be a beautiful woman beside me, and she will kiss me, and we will drink champagne.... But the dream of the prison cell came back and he was so horrified that he forced his eyes open.

He looked around him. He was wide awake and the dream was over; yet he was still in a prison cell. It was six feet long by four feet wide, and half of it was taken up by a bed. He stood upright. Quietly and calmly he began to bang his head against the wall.

JERUSALEM, 24 September 42
My dear Elene,
   Today I went to the Wailing Wall. I stood before it with many other Jews, and I prayed. I wrote a *kvitel* and put it into a crack in the wall. May God grant my petition.
   This is the most beautiful place in the world, Jerusalem. I crossed the desert in a British army truck. I sleep on a mattress on the floor in a little room with five other men. I am very poor, like always, but now I am poor in Jerusalem, which is better than rich in Egypt.
   I must tell you that I am dying. My illness is quite incurable, and I have only weeks left. Don't be sad. I have never been happier in my life.
   I should tell you what I wrote in my *kvitel*. I asked God to grant happiness to my daughter Elene. I believe he will. Farewell.
                                             Your Father

THE smoked ham was sliced thin. The rolls were fresh that morning. There was potato salad made with real mayonnaise, a bottle of wine, a bottle of soda and a bag of oranges. Elene began to pack the food into the picnic basket. She had just closed the lid when she heard the knock at the door. She went to open it. Vandam stepped inside, closed the door and put his arms around her painfully tight. He always did this, but she never complained, for they had almost lost each other, and now when they were together they were enormously grateful.
   They went into the kitchen. "What's the news?" Elene asked.
   "Axis forces in full retreat, and I quote." She thought how relaxed he was these days. A little gray was appearing in his hair, but he laughed a lot.
   They went out. The afternoon sky was curiously dark, and Elene said in surprise, "I've never seen it like this."
   They got on the motorcycle and headed for Billy's school. The sky became even darker. The first rain fell as they were passing

Shepheard's Hotel. The raindrops were enormous; each one soaked right through her dress to the skin. Vandam turned the bike around and parked in front of the hotel. As they dismounted, the clouds burst.

They stood under the hotel canopy and watched the storm. The sheer quantity of water was incredible. Within minutes the gutters overflowed and the pavements were awash. Opposite the hotel the shopkeepers waded through the flood to put up shutters. Cars had to stop where they were. Elene said, "What about Billy?"

"They'll keep the kids at school until the rain stops."

At last the storm ended and the sun came out. As they drove up to the school, they saw Billy waiting outside. "What a storm!" he said excitedly. He climbed onto the bike and sat between them.

They drove out into the desert. Holding on, eyes half closed, Elene did not see the miracle until Vandam stopped the bike. The three of them got off and looked around, speechless.

The desert was carpeted with flowers.

"It's the rain, obviously," said Vandam. "But . . ."

Millions of flying insects had also appeared from nowhere, and now butterflies and bees dashed frantically from bloom to bloom, reaping the sudden harvest.

Billy said, "The seeds must have been in the sand, waiting."

"That's it," Vandam said. "The seeds have been there for years, just waiting for this."

The flowers were all tiny, like miniatures, but brightly colored. Billy walked a few paces from the road and bent down to examine one. Vandam put his arms around Elene and kissed her. It started as a peck on the cheek, but turned into a long, loving embrace. Eventually she broke away from him, laughing. "You'll embarrass Billy," she said.

"He's going to have to get used to it," Vandam said.

Elene stopped laughing. "Is he?" she said. "Is he, really?"

Vandam smiled, and kissed her again.

The Key to Success

Several years ago Ken Follett, an obscure young reporter on the London *Evening News*, needed two hundred pounds to have his car repaired. A friend of his had earned that exact sum by writing a mystery novel. So Follett sat down at his typewriter, knocked out a mystery in six weeks, and made the two hundred pounds. Not only did he get his car back on the road but he was on his way as a writer.

In 1978 he published his first best seller, *Eye of the Needle* (a Condensed Books selection). At the time, the Welsh-born Follett and his wife, Mary, were living comfortably

Ken Follett

in a neo-Georgian house in Surrey with their two children. Shortly thereafter, to avoid prohibitive British income taxes, they moved to the picturesque town of Grasse, in southern France. They enjoy their new life—the food, the weather, the swimming. "We've made delightful friends, of various nationalities," reports Follett, "and, most important of all, I've continued to work steadily."

Follett is a history buff, and like his previous thrillers, *The Key to Rebecca* had its genesis in fact. "I got the idea reading Anthony Cave Brown's *Bodyguard of Lies*," explains Follett. "Later I followed it up in other history books. There was a German spy ring in 1942 in Cairo; they did use a belly dancer to seduce an English major so that they could go through his briefcase; the belly dancer did live on a houseboat on the Nile; Anwar el-Sadat did borrow the spies' radio and attempt to negotiate with Rommel; and they were all caught as a result of using forged currency. Subsequently the British did use the *Rebecca* code as part of a deception plan for the battle of Alam Halfa." To add to the authenticity, Follett visited Cairo, where he soaked up atmospheric details.

His next thriller, he says, will be set in Edwardian London, with a suffragette as heroine and an anarchist as villain.

The Aviator

A CONDENSATION OF THE NOVEL BY

ERNEST K. GANN

He already knew about loneliness.
A frightening ordeal
would teach him about love.

ILLUSTRATED BY
NITA ENGLE AND PAUL GRANT

December, 1928. A Stearman biplane is flying
the mails from Elko, Nevada, to Pasco, Washington.
The weather is uncertain, the terrain below
perilous, but for the veteran pilot it is a joy to be
aloft. Here, at eight thousand feet, no one can see
the sadly scarred face that makes his life on the
ground a lonely torment. No one, that is, except his
eleven-year-old passenger, and she—surprisingly—
seems not to notice it.

Then, without warning, the plane runs into
trouble. The two are marooned on a snowy
mountainside. With almost no food and small hope
of rescue, their situation is desperate indeed.
All the pilot has going for him is a little girl's trust...
and a strangely haunting message from a
letter in a mailbag.

Against a background of personal experience,
Ernest Gann has fashioned a moving and suspenseful
story that vividly brings to life the pioneering
days of flight.

PREFACE

Nineteen twenty-eight, like 1914, was a last year of innocence for much of the world. Only a very few foresaw the catastrophic financial events that began in North America the following year and soon affected all nations. Then innocence died once more, as it had when the cannons were silenced in 1918.

In 1928 the overwhelming majority of young Americans believed fervently in God, honor, duty, and country. They were proud of themselves and usually of their lifework. This was particularly true of airmen, many of whom first ventured aloft during the great war that ended in 1918. They were often men of dash and predilection for hazard. They were instinctively obliged to continue in a profession that was opening new frontiers almost daily. Practicing it was still an art. It paid them modestly in money but lavishly in broken bones and death. Many of their kind died with their boots on while flying the mails.

Airmail pilots were not considered solid citizens but bad insurance risks. Most did not really care, because they were enamored of flight. They lost themselves in it as a man may sometimes utterly abandon himself to an enchanting woman.

The vehicles that bore these men through the lower altitudes were fragile creations of elementary design. Their engines were temperamental and sometimes betrayed their trust. Navigational aids were nonexistent along many airmail routes, and the airmen found their way in good weather and bad by employing a combination of experience, daring, and cunning. They found in themselves a sort of sixth sense of chance and direction because they had to, and as a consequence many developed the fierce independence known to old sailors and desert Tuaregs.

This loyalty to and reliance upon self was true among airmen of all countries, although the more technically advanced Europeans did enjoy primitive radio communication with earthlings. Except in the eastern United States, American airmen did not, and thus once launched into the sky they simply disappeared. After a certain amount of time they reappeared—without ceremony and without anyone on earth being aware of their interim whereabouts.

Sometimes they did not reappear. . . .

CHAPTER ONE

Now the pilot glanced down at the terrain and knew again a momentary sense of foreboding. Unless the weather was very fine it was always the same through here. The mountain plateau was high and devoid of human trespass. The surface of the earth seemed to be made of rough cast iron. Bold and barren escarpments served the pilots who flew this way as recognizable markers in a rumpled ocean of rock and desert. It was wild country, and there had been times when the pilot wondered if it were possible to fear land itself.

He glanced down at the gray scud that was unquestionably congealing into a solid overcast. There were still breaks here and there in the vapor, revealing gray rock teeth and scrubby black trees. Tendrils of soupy cloud hung from the peaks that towered in the distance, but they did not immediately concern him. He was preoccupied with studying the overcast above him. It could squash him.

Before he had taken off from Elko in Nevada and headed north, the pilot suspected the weather might be deteriorating. And he supposed it might not be the best of days. But then, he was flying the mails and was not expected to squat on the ground like a frightened canary every time there was a cloud in the sky. If a pilot showed an obvious preference for flying only in the best conditions, he soon found himself looking for work. This was his way of life, and he had always ascended even when others had found excuses to keep their feet on the ground.

He listened for a moment to the steady thunder of the Wright Whirlwind engine that gave his aircraft flight. He thought of it as a beautiful engine, and he was glad he was not sitting behind a Liberty—one of those leftovers from the war that had lasted long enough for him to learn to fly and finally to qualify as an instructor. He smiled. Now, still courtesy of the same generous United States government, he continued to be airborne. Because he had spent much of the past ten years aloft, he had come to accept the fact that here he was almost at home. To be totally at home in the air, he knew, a man must cease being mortal. Even so, he thought, here is the only place I am content.

Although the route was prescribed, every flight was different. There was the weather according to the seasons, which in this region of the North American continent presented violent contrasts. Flights also differed because of the time of day or the wind. During strong winds the flight became a wrestling match as he worked to keep the Stearman biplane on a reasonably straight and level course. The Stearman was a good airplane, fashioned of the finest wood, the best wire, and the stoutest fabric. While it was smaller than the old De Havillands and Pitcairns flown in the mail service across the eastern states, it was stronger, more maneuverable, and less likely to have ailments.

The pilot thought there was no more dependable aircraft engine in the world than the nine-cylinder Wright Whirlwind. He knew its heavy drumming would now be echoing over the plateau below, and he was easy about trusting his life to it. Thus far, my one and only life, he mused. Of course, many men ended their one life at this work—abruptly. Those who fancied they were unkillable often proved that their faith had been misplaced. It was the way of things aloft.

This flight was different from most, because he had a passenger. She was a little blond girl and he had guessed she must be about eleven or twelve, but then he knew little of such matters. Her parents had brought her to the airfield at Elko, and they had said her name was Heather.

The pilot had declared it was a pretty name, and the child's answer had come instantly. "It has rosy flowers and in Scotland sometimes they make brooms out of it." Her eyes sparkled as if she were challenging him, and he found her smile disconcerting.

When he had asked her parents why they were sending her to Pasco by airplane rather than by rail, Heather had not given them a chance to reply. "My grandfather has this disease and ever since he can't see very well. So my parents thought I would have much more to tell him if I saw like a bird."

"Have you ever flown before?" he asked the girl.

"No. But sometimes I act it out . . . like if I was a real bird."

"Good for you. If you're a good girl on the flight this morning, maybe I can teach you to see like a real bird."

The takeoff was more than an hour late because Probosky, the mechanic, had said he would feel better if he changed several plugs on the Whirlwind engine. Finally, when he was done and the pilot was heaving the mail sacks up to Probosky, who stowed them in the bin, the girl tapped his arm and asked, "When do I get my parachute?"

"You don't." He regretted the annoyance in his voice.

"Why not? Don't you have a parachute?"

"Yes. I'll be sitting on it. My seat was designed to fit around it and it's sort of a cushion. You ride up here in the mail bin right on top of the sacks, so you'll have plenty of cushions."

"Well, I want a parachute. Supposing I have to jump out?"

"Do you get everything you want?" Now he wondered why he had been compelled to taunt her. Even if she was spoiled rotten, it was not his obligation to reform little girls at eleven o'clock in the morning. At thirty-one, was he becoming crotchety?

"At school my English teacher, Miss Atcheson, told me I would have a parachute, so I know I'm supposed to have one."

"Miss Atcheson is wrong. We don't furnish parachutes to passengers, because jumping out of an airplane is a very dangerous business and you have to know exactly what you're doing. I've never jumped out of an airplane and I'm not going to today."

"You better not." The girl was pouting, and he decided what she really needed was a spanking. And yet . . . and yet there was something very special about her.

Now the time was nearly noon and he saw the sun appear momentarily through a break in the overcast, and he thought how often he had witnessed the same development. Standing at its zenith, the sun would be viewed through the most shallow part of a flat overcast. Seen obliquely at a different time of day, it seemed to dim or to be gone entirely. Or was it, he thought, as his passenger turned to glance at him, just being shy?

He would have liked to share his questioning with the little girl, but rendered aloud by a man of his age it might sound silly. And Heather did not seem in the least silly.

For protection against the cold he knew they would encounter, he had borrowed a flying suit for her like his own, a great "teddy bear," as the garment was known to the profession. Heather's parents and everyone around the Stearman had laughed hilariously while they tried to fit her into it. "We need six more of you to fill it up," the pilot had said.

Finally he carried her to the Stearman, because she could not walk in the teddy bear. Perhaps it was the way she clung to him with her arms around his neck and her blue-green eyes looking up at him that made him wonder at her magic. And perhaps his present fascination with her meant more than he realized. How long had he starved for the touch of another human being?

Now, remembering the wonderment of holding such a lovely little creature, he sighed. And he warned himself that such recollection was dangerous. It could lead to the self-pity he had long managed to avoid. It could lead to other memories.

He reached forward into the slipstream and tapped the girl

The Aviator

gently on top of the leather helmet he had loaned her. As was customary when carrying the occasional passenger, the metal cover of the mail bin had been removed. She resembled, it occurred to him, a little sparrow perched on the sacks.

She turned quickly to look back at him and he hoped he had not alarmed her. He held up his gloved hand and made the questioning sign with his fingers for "Okay?"

She smiled and nodded vigorously. The helmet was too large for her, and he saw how the slipstream lifted it from her forehead and teased a wisp of her blond hair. He thought the thin band of freckles across her nose added to her beauty, and he was pleased to see her eyes so full of excitement.

He formed the words "Are you cold?" with his lips, and he shivered to illustrate his question. She shook her head and laughed, although he could not hear her above the roar of the wind. At over one hundred miles an hour it was like trying to carry on a conversation in a hurricane.

It *was* cold. It was always cold in these mountains in December, and he supposed the temperature at this altitude was below the twenty degrees indicated by the new little dial on his instrument panel. Why did he mistrust it? Because it was new?

He did trust the other instruments arrayed before him. There was a gauge to show his speed, and the needle was now quivering slightly as if to prove its alertness. The altimeter announced that he was holding the aircraft steady at eight thousand feet. There was a rate-of-climb instrument with a needle hovering a hair below horizontal—an indication of descent. The instrument was lying, provoked by his habit of trimming the Stearman slightly nose-heavy and thus gaining a minute advantage in cruising speed.

There was a turn-and-bank instrument, consisting of a ball free to roam like a bubble in a carpenter's level and a pointer known as "the needle." A magnetic compass just under the windscreen gave him direction, and there was also a clock, which in this Stearman did not function. In addition, there were instruments to tell him of the health of his engine. They announced the oil pressure, temperature, and revolutions per minute.

These were the simple tools of his craft. Combined with the flight controls—a stick projecting between his knees for maneuvering about the vertical and horizontal axes, and two rudder pedals to control the lateral axis—he was able to pilot his airplane to any destination within range of its fuel. Like any experienced workman he trusted his tools, but most of all he trusted himself.

The girl looked back at him again. He saw her eyes questioning and her lips forming the words, "Where are we?"

He throttled back the engine momentarily and shouted, "You're still over Nevada. It will be an hour before we are over Idaho!"

She smiled and looked down. Then she looked back at him and he saw her smile fade. Her eyes were still questioning, but her lips did not move, and after an instant she turned her head away.

Angrily he shoved the throttle full forward, and some of his desolation was lost in the snarl of the engine. Why had he been so busy convincing himself that for some unique reason she seemed to be different? Why had she been so long in seeing what everyone else saw right away?

Instinctively he touched his glove to the side of his face he knew would never go away. The right side held a bare hint of the handsome youth he had been eight years ago, but the left? Beginning just below the scalp line was an ugly mass of tortured scar tissue, pitted and ravined and accented by a slackness in the corner of his mouth. It was the best job the doctors had been able to do to a face that had been smashed to a bloody pulp, then scorched by exploding gasoline. By some miracle the left eye had emerged unscathed, but no surgical miracle could replace what had been lost in the crash on that long-ago terrible morning.

Soon after the removal of the bandages he had learned to present the right side of his face to the world. The other side made people squirm, and it was even worse when they were overpolite. When this sort of thing happened the pilot found it convenient to think of Moravia—because Moravia understood. He had flown in the Great War and he had also been damaged. Yet Moravia only limped on an artificial leg, which was more easily acceptable. It was not like an affliction born out of an inferno.

The Aviator

Still, it was because of Moravia's understanding that the pilot had been hired. Moravia did not believe a pretty face or a formal education were necessary requirements for a man who flew the mails. He wanted men who could take care of themselves.

MORAVIA was superintendent of the line. The post office was very demanding of companies awarded mail contracts, and Moravia knew his airmail route—between Pasco, Washington, and Elko, Nevada—was the most difficult of all. It was Moravia's affair to keep the eight pilots who did the actual flying at their task and reasonably happy. In the air it was their business to keep themselves alive, yet he knew that he held the power of life and death over them. He had hired all eight, and each one was aware that if his flying were curtailed, he would wither and eventually die within. Moravia was reluctant to take advantage of his power, but he did not hesitate if a pilot erred.

"One thing. You fly for this company and you stay out of trouble both aloft and on the ground. Second thing. You carry on to your destination unless you are absolutely certain the weather is impossible. Otherwise you will be replaced."

Moravia was severe, but he was not unkind. He was sympathetic when a pilot was ill, clucking like a mother hen over his symptoms and admonishing him not to fly if he felt the least chill. "Flying is uncomfortable enough as it is," he often said. "If you're shivering with fever, then what will you have left to tell you it is time to be scared?"

Moravia loved his pilots and the aircraft in which they flew. Yet he was extraordinarily careful that his feelings would never be known.

Because of his handicap Moravia had become fat. Photographs taken when he was flying Nieuports in France and had two good legs testified that he had then been a dashing youth, if somewhat short and wild of eye, but now he supported a considerable paunch. He wore glasses, which he so hated he was constantly whipping them on and off, and he smoked Caporals continuously—black tobacco cigarettes, which he imported from

France at great trouble and considerable expense. Only his deep and vibrant voice suggested that he was still a young man.

While they were in flight Moravia did not think of or refer to his pilots by name; instead he employed the company number painted on the tail of the Stearman they were flying. In his mind there was no distinct separation between man and aircraft. "Seven should change to Nine when he lands. His oil pressure is acting up." When eventually Seven landed, Moravia's orderly mind would see to it that Seven would automatically become Nine.

Now Moravia studied the large wall map that portrayed the tortured and desolate terrain over which his pilots flew. There were great valleys where the flying was relatively easy, but the largest portion of the route was over mountains and high desert, both unforgiving. During the summer the desert was an oven, and the little mail planes were tossed about like thistles dancing on the wind. In winter cruel winds tore blizzards out of the western ranges and flayed them all along the route.

Moravia was vaguely displeased with what little information he had just received, and he tried to ease his suspicions by limping to the window of his simple office and regarding the view. Beyond was the airport, or "aerodrome," as he sometimes still referred to it. A wind sock topped the hangar adjacent to the small structure that housed both his office and a cramped waiting room for visitors who might have business with the line. The waiting room was also a place to stow the mail, and a changing room where pilots squirmed into their heavy flight suits if they were about to fly or removed them if they had just landed.

Moravia understood that when a pilot had just arrived he experienced a period of readjustment, a necessary and sometimes unhappy rejoining of himself with his earthly life. Depending on the man, it took as much as half an hour to shed the peculiar euphoria of flight and to substitute the cares of wife, money, and food for those of wind and cloud. To ease the transformation Moravia had purchased an electric coffee urn, and out of his own pocket bought sweet rolls to complement the refreshment. He cared little whether his pilots appreciated his gesture. Seeing to their well-being once

The Aviator

they had performed he considered a part of his duty. As he blew smoke at the window, Moravia looked across the field at the metal tower of a rotating beacon that had been recently installed by the government. It flashed a green and then a white light, marking the airport's location for those who sought it at night or in poor visibility. Otherwise there was nothing to see except the flat expanse of prairie now officially designated as the Pasco airport and the heavy, gray cloud ceiling above it. Moravia concentrated on the sky and how the present swift passage of clouds might influence further flight operations. And he regretted the limited intelligence that he had at hand.

One hour previously he had received a telegram advising that Fourteen had taken off from Elko with two hundred pounds of mail and one passenger. Female. The weather had been good with some high stuff. Thin sun visible through same. No problem. Twenty-five degrees. Too cold for snow. Good enough, he thought. But what of the weather situation along the route?

Between Elko and Pasco there was always a void. Boise, Idaho, was the halfway mark, and there Moravia's airplanes were refueled, the mails were re-sorted, and sometimes pilots were changed for either the north- or southbound flights. Boise weather could not be considered indicative of the entire route. Two hours ago Moravia had telephoned both Boise and Twin Falls airports for a synopsis of their weather. The ceiling was high and the visibility lower to the west. There were snow squalls on the horizon and the wind was variable. Nothing to provide a sense of certainty.

Better to consult a rancher at Rome, west of Boise, who had a good view of the surrounding mountains and, more important, a telephone. He was cooperative about giving local weather reports, and to express his gratitude Moravia occasionally sent him a bottle of whiskey smuggled down from Canada. But this morning there had been no answer to the ranch phone's persistent ringing.

So much for the weather in between, Moravia thought. He then reminded himself that Fourteen was a good and wise pilot. There was nothing to be concerned about.

Still, sucking on his cigarette, Moravia decided that he did not like the smell of things this morning. He should not have to send his pilots into uncertainties. That transferred the burden from them to him.

THE pilot eased his weight off the parachute seat momentarily and moved his gun holster farther forward on his belt. He considered the gun a nuisance, a hangover from pony express days, when bandits were supposedly always after the mail. The gun was a small .380 automatic that he had never fired. But carrying a gun to protect the mails was a post-office regulation, and Moravia saw that there were no infractions. He was deaf to entreaties that the gun would be almost useless should anyone go down; that a man needed a rifle to hit anything in the wilderness. "You will wear the gun because the post office says you will. I do not want inspectors sniffing around here and finding we fail to take them seriously."

Apparently every mail contractor in America felt the same way, for the ever present gun had become the badge of airmail pilots throughout the land. Most of them thought that wearing the gun in these tranquil times was ridiculous.

Moravia's pilots also had mixed feelings about the extra paraphernalia that he insisted be part of their personal gear. In addition to a knife, he decreed they must carry pliers, a crescent wrench, and a screwdriver. "And if I were you," he said in a voice that offered little option, "I would also carry pain pills. There was a time when I would have given my soul for just one."

Now somehow the gun had worked itself around until it prodded the pilot in the ribs. He thought that he would like to throw it over the side. Am I going to be held up? Up *here*?

When he was settled again he took off one of his gloves and reached into the knee pocket of his teddy bear. He found his knife and the chocolate bar he always carried should he feel the need of fresh energy. Then he remembered he was searching in the wrong pocket. The chewing gum was in the other knee pocket along with those items he thought might ease the stress of a forced landing: a box of matches, which he carried although he did not smoke; a small bottle of iodine; a roll of gauze; adhesive tape; and a bottle of pain-relieving pills.

Every airman had his own version of what might come in handy if a forced landing became necessary. A few carried a flask of whiskey, but the pilot preferred to hold his emergency items to a minimum. He used the extra pocket space for a thin leather notebook, which he updated with meticulous care. It contained diagrams of the most likely fields and pastures for emergency landings along the route. The altitudes, lengths, and surface characteristics were carefully recorded.

He had also drawn in the surrounding hazards: clumps of high trees, power lines, a water tower. Elsewhere in the notebook were listings of the few airports within the Stearman's limited range and arrowed lines illustrating the best approaches in bad weather. Fly up the canyon until passing over the pond with a beaver dam. Continue for one minute ten seconds. Make steep left turn and go back to canyon entrance. Turn right and fly ninety degrees for eighty seconds. Good meadow for landing. Ten-mile walk to telephone at Brogan.

The notebook listed many other items, and its compilation had won considerable respect for the pilot among his fellows. They knew it represented much work, and they made excuses for themselves, saying they carried all such information in their heads. A few had started their own notebooks, but most of these were incomplete, and the pilot thought he knew why. The other pilots were married or had many friends of both sexes. They would not understand why it was so necessary for a man who was rarely in the company of others to keep his evenings busy.

The pilot withdrew the packet of gum from his pocket and reached out again into the slipstream. He tapped his passenger's helmet. She turned and smiled as she saw the gum. She pulled out a piece and said "Thank you" with her lips, and the pilot marveled at his pleasure in such a simple exchange. He stuck a piece of gum in his mouth, and as he chewed he thought that his life aloft was very good. Here, at altitude, he knew a sense of well-being he would not have dared elsewhere.

Ever since the crash and the terrible flames he had been haunted by an insidious sense of failure. His student had died in the crash and there was no redemption. Early on, the student had displayed a lack of natural flying talent. He should have been washed out instead of being encouraged because he was a pleasant and eager young man. Lesson learned by his instructor. In the flying business, kindness could kill.

Now doubt was still the pilot's master. How many times had he reviewed every detail of the crash and always returned to the same ugly answer? He should have prevented the tragedy somehow. His guilt would not go away simply because a committee of men who were not present at the calamity later declared it was not his fault. The wind had been strong and perhaps the base commander should have canceled all training, but who was in charge of the only aircraft that crashed?

A gust of wind had caught the Jenny just as the student was flaring for his fifth landing of the day. A wing tip hit the ground and the Jenny cartwheeled and went to pieces. Then there was only the flame, dust in his mouth, and the confused vision of people in brown uniforms running.

It struck the pilot as odd that almost eight years later he still felt confident in the sky, but once he became an earthling he seemed to be a born loser.

This morning he decided to deviate from the usual route northward to Boise and fly a more westerly course. There were roads both to the east and west that were navigational references along the way. The mountains were highest to the east. Once he had passed over the mine at Tuscarora, the pilot saw that the whole range was shrouded in heavy cloud, and he knew there would be little chance of getting through. The Santa Rosa Mountains, which projected along the western side of the plateau, displayed an occasional break in the cloud, and he might work his way through the pass north of Winnemucca.

Directly ahead, above an enormous high plateau that covered a junction of the Oregon-Idaho-Nevada boundaries, the weather was relatively bright and the separation between earth and cloud more than adequate. The pilot was certain he would be able to get around the scattered snow squalls with only minor detours. Thus he carried on, passing two ranches he recognized.

Far ahead he could see a dark gash in the plateau, which he knew had been cut by the Owyhee River. If he held his present compass course, he must pass over the Little Owyhee and then he could start letting down around Rome, Oregon. Once past Rome, there was a road he could follow northeastward and eventually come out near Boise. The rest would be easy.

He rocked the Stearman's wings gently. Heather looked back at him, her blue-green eyes asking if something were wrong. He made a gesture with his right hand, pointing at a clearing below. She peered over the side of the cockpit and saw the herd of antelope he had wanted her to see. Her look of delight rewarded him beyond measure. Why am I so anxious to please her? he thought. If I could snap my fingers and call out a herd of elephants, I would. Anything to turn the warmth of that face back on me.

Suddenly, reflected in the glass covering the altimeter, he caught a glimpse of his own face. He looked away instantly and for several minutes sat immobilized, listening to the steady drumming of the engine. Soon his brooding was relieved by duty. An hour had passed since takeoff and now a low scum of cloud covered the terrain. He had watched it slip in gradually, a feathery mantle laced to numerous snow squalls.

The pilot became busy with choices. Fly around that squall to the northwest, say three miles, then turn back northeast on the back side for an equal amount of time. Then once again settle on course. That big hooligan, a grandfather of squalls, could be avoided by another westerly heading as long as it remained isolated. Be wary, though, if it joins too many of its neighbors now multiplying along the horizon. If they become a solid wall, then think about turning back to Elko.

Moravia would not like that. To his surprise the pilot now found that what his superior might think was not of primary importance. Would turning back disappoint his passenger? Come on! Since when did little girls decide the course of aircraft?

He was watching the parade of squalls dragging a white veil of snow along the surface of the plateau when he first smelled the musky odor of overheated oil. He sniffed at the slipstream. Was he imagining the smell? He tried to smile, reminding himself that engines had a habit of giving in to "automatic rough" when over hostile terrain. He thought this must be the very first aeronautical joke. Yet— He checked for oil along the fuselage and engine cowling. Nothing. He glanced at the oil-pressure gauge. He saw it had slipped down from normal, although only a few pounds. Perhaps the oil-cooling system was jammed.

He waited, uneasy with the moment. He looked back over the Stearman's tail. A few snow squalls were widely separated, with even a thin shaft of sunlight stabbing down through the overcast. A return to Elko would be easy. Have Probosky check the engine again. Maybe a valve sticking, a needed adjustment to the carburetor, water in the fuel . . . something.

Still, if Probosky found nothing wrong? He would hand down his supreme opinion as only Probosky could do. "You daydream up there? That engine runs like a sewing machine."

He glanced down at the control stick. He took off his right glove, the better to feel any unusual vibration. Yes, there was some, but had it not always been so? Why was he so convinced there was more vibration than normal? Moravia wanted solid thinkers in his cockpits, not fanciers.

He glanced at the instrument panel. The oil pressure seemed the same, but the glass covering the instrument was trembling enough to multiply a partial reflection of his helmet. He pushed up his goggles and studied the instruments one by one. He reached out and pressed his hand against the panel, trying to steady it. No question. The thunder of the engine remained steady, but the vibration was increasing. There was a roiling in his stomach. His whole body tensed. Here! Of all places.

He looked down and started a turn. He eased back slightly on the throttle. Perhaps if the engine were straining less, it would hold together until he could return to Elko or until they were near something, for below was only a vast wilderness.

The Aviator

Surprised at the steep banking of the Stearman, the girl turned to look back at him. "Don't worry!" he yelled, but his voice was lost in the roar of the slipstream and the engine.

Suddenly the Stearman shuddered mightily, as if fighting for its life. The pilot saw the instrument panel shake itself into a blur, and a fountain of black smoke enveloped the fuselage.

He cut the throttle, the fuel mixture, and the magneto switch immediately. He kicked hard right rudder, dipped the left wing, and eased the nose down. The roar of the slipstream diminished rapidly until there was only the low humming of the flying wires.

"We have to land. Don't worry!" he shouted.

The pilot was unbelieving. How could the finest engine in the flying world have packed up over one of the worst places in the world? Gliding down, holding the airspeed at a mere sixty miles per hour, he began to count those few weapons remaining to him. He estimated his height above the overcast at a thousand feet, which translated into a grace period of perhaps four minutes if he squeezed the maximum time from the glide. There was a hole in the overcast only a mile or so away. He had no idea of the actual height of the terrain, although judging from the fringes of the hole there was very little space between cloud and earth. If any. He eased up on the ailerons, keeping the bank as shallow as possible while turning for the hole. More time that way.

The smoke had disappeared soon after he had shut down the engine, and for a moment he considered trying to start it up again. Wishful thinking, he knew. And wrong. If he did succeed in starting the engine, then it might vibrate itself right off the mounts, and that would most certainly be the end of everything.

He saw the girl looking at him, and he managed a smile. He heard her call out, "I'm not afraid!" In that instant his resolve took command. Somehow he must bring his machine to earth so gently that Heather would not be harmed.

Now the Stearman was directly above the hole, circling, descending slowly at just above stalling speed. The more the pilot studied the hole, the more apprehensive he became. He saw nothing but rocks and trees projecting from patches of snow.

The Aviator

He thought, Welcome to the side of a mountain. He estimated the incline at the base of the hole to be as much as twenty degrees. He searched for another gap. Somewhere there must be one with a more inviting interior, but he saw nothing within range of his glide. How leisurely time passed when there was no choice.

Looking everywhere, his eyes finally met those of his passenger. He saw that she was waiting patiently for him to do something and that her confidence was total. Did you tell those eyes that no aviator could land down there without smashing something? Did you say, The purpose of this flight is to deliver the mail. Your pilot was not thinking of you when he flew this direct route over the plateau. It will do no good to complain to the Postmaster General, or even to a man named Moravia. He looked away from her eyes long enough to make one last search for another way to descend.

Suddenly he called out, "Get down as far as you can between the mail sacks!"

She smiled as if she knew exactly why he wanted her to comply, and after a moment only the top of her helmet was visible.

"Treat her easy, God," he murmured as the Stearman sank to the cloud level. Just as he slipped into the hole and began the final descent, the whole aircraft shuddered at the odd angle it was asked to fly. He remembered in a flash the standard objection most mail pilots had to flying passengers. Alone and in serious trouble, a pilot had only to bail out and float safely to earth. Now he was pleased that he had forgotten he was wearing a parachute.

Two minutes later the details of the mountainside were visible. As the rocks and trees and bushes rushed upward, the low vibrato of the flying wires seemed to climb higher in pitch. There was a clear space. It was not nearly long enough for a normal landing, but it was something to aim at. Two pines stood in the way. He must slip between them. Knocking the wings off might slow the Stearman's fuselage enough to survive.

He held the sideslip until he could see the cascades of shale mounded about the rocks. Then he brought the Stearman's nose up, kicked full right rudder to lift out of the slip, and waited. He pulled the control stick as far back as possible and braced one hand against the cockpit cowling. The flying wires sighed, and then there was only a stunning dissonance of metal against stone and the flat shriek of tearing wood. The pilot closed his eyes and almost immediately knew a tumbling sensation.

CHAPTER TWO

Moravia sucked deeply on his Caporal while he reviewed the flight operations report for the previous month. November invariably presented weather problems, but the report was not bad. The post office would be pleased and the company that employed him should be satisfied, along with the stockholders. There would be little profit, of course. No one who was realistic about the flying business dared to expect true profit. At least, Moravia thought, we are temporarily out of the red. Which was more than most companies doing the same thing could say. "A hand-to-mouth business," Moravia cautioned all investors who came to him with dreams of getting in on the ground floor of an industry that would soon be carrying tremendous loads of cargo. A few predicted airborne vehicles would even begin to carry such commodities as coal and iron ore.

Lovely, Moravia thought. Our present problem is to get a big enough mail load to make it worthwhile each way. Like other operators flying the mail under contract, Moravia sometimes found it necessary to mail a few telephone books back and forth. The post office paid by weight. Pilots and mechanics had to be paid, and there was his own modest salary to be remembered.

Moravia's mind drifted to more personal affairs. After ten years in the flying business, where did he stand? On one leg, of course, but he had yet to miss a meal. There had always been a comfortable roof over his head and his divine Marsha's. Not too bad, if certain inevitable cares were set aside.

He fell to thinking of number Fourteen, who was, he thought, in some ways a man to be envied, although he would certainly disagree if challenged. He lived alone, a man without apparent cares. When he descended from his daily work he could do as he pleased—go to the movies or a speakeasy, or he could just go back to his room and read.

Moravia grunted. Would he trade places with him? The answer, he decided, was yes and no. Fourteen was a free agent all right; he left his work behind him when he went home. But what waited for him when he went up those steps behind a hardware store and turned in to that single room? Moravia had been there once when Fourteen suffered a severe case of bronchitis. Moravia had brought him the newspapers and a copy of *Aero Digest* that carried an article on the new trimotor Fords. "Someday," he had told Fourteen, "we'll be flying them on the line, and I thought you'd like to learn something about them."

But Fourteen had turned his head to the wall, keeping the good side of his face toward Moravia, and he had said he hoped it would be a long time before carrying passengers would become a regular thing. Moravia was sure he was thinking about his face and how difficult it would be for him before any assembly of people. Fourteen's appearance was accepted here, Moravia was reminded, but among strangers he collided with an awkward problem. The bad side of his mouth offered a permanent snarl that was enough to discourage the friendliest overtures.

Moravia decided the man was almost completely isolated. His room was so barren it could have been a monk's cell. There was a bed that reminded Moravia of the cot he had been assigned when he had flown in France. There was a wooden bureau, and one drab brown suit hung on a rod that extended from the washbasin to the door. There was also one pair of slacks and the usual hard-worn leather jacket, which nearly all pilots wore like a second skin. There was a telephone on top of the bureau, and nothing more. The telephone was a company regulation, and Moravia found himself wondering if it ever rang except for a call from himself.

One of the few clues to the inner man that Moravia had been able to discover was something the local librarian had told him. "He treats books as if they were living creatures," she reported. "He reads everything from Henry James to Maugham."

Now, as Moravia glowered at the heavy sky through his office window, he knew he would not trade places with Fourteen. It could be no great pleasure to be a free agent when you limited your own freedom—or events had destroyed any hope of a woman's love. Indeed, what could Fourteen do but turn his face the other way, being careful to position himself so there was always something between the rest of the world and his misfortune. A man could do very well without a leg, Moravia reminded himself, as witness his own marriage. Yet even his wife, Marsha, whose tolerance and sympathies overflowed, found it difficult not to flinch when she encountered Fourteen.

Moravia turned his thoughts from the pilot and went to the phone. He hoped to reach the rancher who might give him the latest weather to the west of Boise. He listened to the ringing for a long time before he knew there would be no response.

THE pilot licked his lips and tasted oil. He opened his eyes and saw the familiar rim of the cockpit, but it did not look at all the same. The windscreen was opaque instead of transparent, and for a moment he studied the cobweb pattern of cracks in the glass. Then he realized what was wrong. He was lying with his head resting on a pile of shale. The entire fuselage lay on its side, and he was still strapped in his seat.

His thoughts were feathery. The leg straps of his parachute were pinching him, but the pain was insignificant compared with the realization that the bad side of his face, the same side that had been his curse for so long, was once again pressed hard against the planet Earth. His mind laughed. Some landing, old sport. Why don't you try the other side next time? Then suddenly he remembered he was not alone.

His thoughts congealed as a chill ran through his body. He quickly opened the clip of his safety belt. Then his fingers found the snaps to his parachute harness. He squirmed out of the cockpit and came to his knees. He waited a moment, trying to assure himself that what he saw was not real. The crumpled wings of the Stearman were embracing two trees more than fifty yards away. In between there were a wheel and a tire, a piece of propeller, and two bags of mail. One bag had burst, and its contents formed a path to the Stearman's tail, which was intact except for the crushed elevator and horizontal stabilizer on the down side. Between the cockpit and the tail, the fuselage was bent and wrinkled, but not badly damaged.

The pilot caught his breath as his eyes focused on the mail bin, which was normally sheltered beneath the upper wing. He could hardly recognize what he was looking at. The center-section struts were bent back and lay almost flat against some mail sacks. He noted some of the sacks were smeared with oil, and he thought the Post Office Department would be unhappy. He would tell them, Well, what can you expect when they've had a big fat thousand-pound engine lying right on top of them?

The engine was out of its mounts, twisted on its side at a crazy angle. Otherwise, he thought, it looked fine. Just wipe off a little oil and probably it could be sold almost as good as new—except for a rather poor behavior record.

A sound punctured his errant thought and left him gasping at his confusion. The girl! The faint little cry told him she was just a few feet from him, buried beneath the center section, somewhere under the sacks and the engine.

He rose, staggered a few feet, then lunged at the engine. He heard his own voice, but it seemed to be that of a ventriloquist calling from far away. "O God, *please* don't let her be hurt! I will give you my life if she is not hurt." Then he spoke to his passenger. "Don't worry, girl. I'll have you out of there in a jiffy. Just be patient." He was angry at his inability to remember her name.

His only answer was a faint cry, so small and fragile he thought she sounded like a just hatched bird.

Tearing at a mail sack with all his strength failed to move it from beneath the engine. He saw her foot extending from under another mail sack and he thought, O God, please.

"Listen, girl." What was her name? "I have to move the engine off the sacks. It's very heavy, and I have to find something to pry it with. Please, just wait, please."

He turned away from the wreckage, stumbling and slipping on the shale and trying to remember the little girl's name. He followed a straight and shallow trench, which he realized had been dug by the fuselage as it slid to a stop. He decided that he had done an acceptable job of hitting the two trees in such a way the wings were knocked off simultaneously. He had avoided a slew, which at that speed might have killed them both. They would have hit the mountain at an angle. As it was they had grafted onto it. The trench could have been drawn with a ruler, he thought. The Stearman had decelerated relatively smoothly, and while it was a hell of a mess, any landing you could walk away from was better than an uncontrolled crash. So they said. And right. The girl's name was Heather.

He found a broken branch hanging from one of the trees and yanked at it until it came away. With it fell soft loaves of snow, which struck him in the face and refreshed him. As he dragged the branch back across the shale, he avoided looking at the wreckage. If the truth were known, he thought unhappily, he had *not* done things right. If he had just flown the regular route instead of bearing off to the west and the same thing had happened, then he would have had much flatter terrain for an emergency landing. Probably Moravia's other pilots would have maintained the regular course, or they would have turned back, landed, and done their explaining. Maybe even the engine would have held up until they returned to Elko. Now Moravia was minus one whole airplane.

When he arrived back at the fuselage he paused and tried to recover from a wave of dizziness. He congratulated himself on doing something right. Telling the little girl to get down under the mail sacks had probably saved her life. Probably. He would point that out to her, because, he warned himself, this whole thing was going to be very difficult to explain to those eyes of hers, and he would need all the credit he could manage. God Almighty, weren't her parents aware that flying was not exactly safe and that maybe a thing like this *could* happen? God Almighty, please don't let her be hurt!

He fought off his vertigo and shoved one end of the branch between the shale and the bottom cylinder of the engine. He pried with all his strength, then rested while he tried to drive the confusion from his thoughts. This was obviously impossible. Four men might move the engine, but one tired aviator heaving on the end of a pine branch— Who are you? Samson?

He heaved on the branch once more and saw the engine tilt slightly. Or was it just his imagination? He moved around to the front of the fuselage, where the engine would normally be, and told himself to start using his brain instead of his back.

He fell to his knees and started pawing at the shale. Perhaps if he worked hard, he could dig out enough beneath the wreckage to pull the mail sacks away. The shale made a clicking sound as it slithered down the slope. Here I am, he thought, scratching away at a mountain like an animal. They should tell people who say they love to fly that someday, if they are stupid and have the talent for doing the wrong thing at the right time, they will wind up trying to dig a hole in the side of a mountain.

After removing only a few inches of shale, he halted his efforts. He had hit bedrock. When the chittering noise of the shale ceased somewhere far below, there was only the sound of his own heavy breathing. "Heather?" he asked softly. "Can you hear me?"

The silence shocked him. No, no. She was all right. She *must* be all right. He pushed himself to his feet and stepped cautiously around to the branch again, listening for the slightest sound from the mail bin. A wild thought occurred to him. Maybe she could dig herself out, kick the mail sacks away. Should he say, as if he really believed it, Listen, Heather. I need your help to get you out of there because we have a lot to do before it gets dark. We have to build some kind of shelter and wait for the weather to clear. Then we can just walk down the mountain.

He stood staring at the engine as if it were alive, and it was some time before he realized the faint pecking sound he heard was snowflakes touching the drum-tight fabric of the fuselage. He removed the belt that held his airmail gun. It had become surprisingly heavy, and he was about to toss it away when he decided the gun might prove useful after all. Maybe if it snowed too hard and they had to stay here a day or two, he could shoot something. Heather would be hungry, because kids always were.

As he placed the gun carefully on the top of the fuselage he heard a faint whimper. It was an almost inhuman sound, and he thought that if he heard it just once more, he would go insane.

Yet, hating the absolute quiet, he waited impatiently for it to end. And when he heard another faint cry from the wreckage, he instantly forgot the branch and his unsteady footing on the shale. Seething with fury, he threw himself at the engine. He seized it by two cylinders, and jamming his shoulder against the gear section, he pushed and shoved until his blood pounded against his temples and his sight became clouded.

He had no idea how long he had been wrestling with the monstrous mass of metal, when suddenly he sensed that it had shifted position. He fought still harder, lifting and pushing, intermittently gasping at the oil-smelling air. Every muscle and fiber in his body was fully committed to the attack. Then at last he heard a metallic tearing sound, and he knew something had given way. He shoved with his final strength, and the engine rolled away from the mail sacks. He fell upon it for support, still unbelieving of his victory, sobbing for wind.

Moments later he heaved the mail sacks aside and saw his passenger. She was sprawled on her back, strangely twisted, but her eyes were open. He knelt beside her and brushed the new flakes of snow from her forehead. "Are you all right now?"

He waited for tears, but there were none. Instead she stared up at him, her eyes uncertain. She said, "I don't think so."

"Can you get up if I help you?"

"I don't know. I think . . . my back maybe."

He slid one hand behind her neck, then eased the other beneath her legs. Maybe, if she were set on her feet? He had lifted her legs less than half an inch when she screamed in agony.

Just south of the Black Rock Desert near Winnemucca Lake, Nevada, the center of the low-pressure area tightened. It slowly moved northeast across the barren mountains and the desolate valleys where only a few ranchers had learned to exist with the environment. The low sent harbingers ahead of it in the form of snow squalls, which sifted downward in gray-white columns.

Behind the squalls came wind and much heavier snows, which rapidly enveloped the mountain peaks and transformed the adjacent valleys and canyons into an almost featureless landscape. The ravines were the first to disappear, then the outcroppings, and finally the smaller streams. Soon there remained only a vast white emptiness beneath which all of nature slept.

Four hundred miles to the north in Pasco, Moravia's ordered mind was uncomfortable with speculation. He detested not knowing what he thought he should know. It struck him as nearly incredible that in this day and age, in the December of 1928, indeed in the supposedly civilized United States of America, he could be held in such ignorance. The days of Lewis and Clark were long gone, and the few Indians who inhabited the land over which his mail planes flew were peaceable. There were railroads and a few good highways, and yet now, he thought, he might as well be a major of cavalry marooned within a log fort. In fact, he concluded, his boots-and-saddles counterpart might be better informed with a few galloping troopers to bring him news.

During the past hour Moravia had rung his favorite rancher again and again, always with the same negative result. He found the ringing discouraging, a repetitive monotone that seemed to mock his increasing anxiety. Fourteen was not due to land in Boise for over an hour, so there was nothing to worry about there, but the southbound mail, number Eight, was due to take off in twenty minutes. Eight was waiting for the arrival of the mail in the post-office truck, and was already in his teddy bear, although he had not yet buttoned up.

The question now was should Eight go at all? If it became necessary for him to turn around and bring the mail back, the postmaster would be extremely unhappy. If the airmail was delayed too many times during a year, there would be ugly hints of contract cancellation, which would mean the end for Moravia and the entire line. The alternative was to "train" the mail, an embarrassing con-

fession of incompetence that left the railroads laughing and the bureaucrats convinced they should have relied on the iron horse to begin with.

In good weather the morning plane took away the mail at eleven and that was that. The trouble was that when the train was on time it left the station at eleven forty. If the weather was uncertain and Moravia delayed his decision on the mail, it might miss the train. The result was an automatic uproar with accusations doing all the flying. The postmaster would be furious that his mail was a whole day late and would direct his wrath first at Moravia and then at the railroad. The railroad people would maintain their usual haughty attitude toward anything to do with flying machines, while at the same time berating the post office for not allowing more time between the arrival of the mail at the station and the departure of their precious choo-choo. A monumental pain, Moravia thought, as he lit another Caporal.

The heavy, lung-scratching smoke sent him off into a coughing fit, which was at least less annoying than his present and all too frequent dilemma. The flying conditions between Pasco and Elko were the real villain. His rancher, who must have gone to Florida for the winter, would know something of his local weather, but the true need was to know the weather along the entire route. When Fourteen landed he would give a full report, but whatever he might have to say would have to be classed as ancient history. It might have been fine for him in the south, but by the time Eight reached the same area things could be stinking. The solution, of course, was direct ground-to-air communication. Moravia understood there were some experimental installations being used back east, but successful two-way contacts were so rare it was not worth the cost. Maybe someday.

Maybe someday the gates of paradise would swing open and reveal at least one banker who thought making progress in the sky was more important than an immediate profit. That same intelligent, imaginative banker might have been to Europe, where airplanes were flying all over the place with mail, where between London and Paris and Berlin and Moscow they were carrying as many as fourteen passengers and serving them lunch on white linen tablecloths, with wine and all the fixings. No American line had even given serious thought to such things.

Moravia watched the mail truck pull up outside his office window. It was precisely ten forty. Decision time had come, and it was not made easier by the fact that the mail truck had an unusually heavy load. Money! Moravia thought. It was always a good payload that was the hardest to divert.

Moravia expected the knock on his door. His caller was number Eight, a slight, soft-spoken Carolinian named Manigault, who looked physically lost in his enormous teddy bear. He was a thorough gentleman, an attribute Moravia appreciated. He would want to know what decision Moravia had reached, although both men understood the decision was not Moravia's alone to make. If Manigault chose not to fly and his reasons were sound, his was the final word. The code was unwritten, as was the understanding that there would be no penalties or recriminations inflicted upon the reluctant pilot. The code did not apply to those who might repeatedly find reason not to fly. Moravia was well aware that there were a few who might employ dubious weather as an excuse to lie with their latest female conquest. To the best of Moravia's knowledge these rascals had never outwitted him.

Manigault asked, "Do I earn my keep today?"

"It's up to you. Elko is fine, two thousand and ten with snow squalls. Boise has a good ceiling and visibility between snow squalls, but I can't find out what you'll have en route."

Manigault bent slightly for a better view out the window. Then, as if he could actually see beyond the horizon, he said, "It looks okay. I'll sneak around things if there is anything."

"Keep your eye out for Fourteen. You should pass him on the route."

Manigault clapped his helmet and goggles on his head. As he buttoned up his teddy bear he said, "Sometimes I wish I were back in Carolina. You start out the day there and you know pretty well how the rest of the day will go. But in this country . . ."

Manigault left his sentence unfinished and Moravia knew why. He was intolerant of complaints and Manigault was aware of it, as were all the others. His pilots were *flying*, which to a certain breed of man was as necessary as breathing. They did not know what it was like to be denied the privilege, as Moravia had been, but by God if they grumbled about anything at all, they knew they could expect a stern lecture. They would be reminded that flying the mails was not for babies. They would also be reminded that more than forty pilots had been killed flying the mails and twenty-three seriously injured since the service began. Of course, if they preferred to lead the lives of butchers, bakers, or candlestick makers, Moravia would be glad to show them the door and offer them a souvenir hook on which to hang their helmet and goggles. Instead of wasting their wind complaining, he urged his men to expend the same effort in learning every stream, mountain, and glade along their route. Such knowledge just might prove beneficial when the sketchy road maps they used for navigation ran out of information.

This year for the first time private operators were flying the mails, and now that the job was no longer a government affair, Moravia intended to prove that the dubious safety record could be improved. "If you will give me your two legs, then I will tune my two ears to your complaints," he was fond of saying. "But my sympathies are hard to arouse if you kill yourself with some foolishment. Be assured my letter to your survivors will be truthful instead of laudatory. Do not oblige me to write that he was so busy finding fault with every little thing, he failed to perceive the faults within himself. So the dunce flew into a rock-lined cloud."

CHAPTER THREE

It was nearly dusk before the pilot had done all he thought he had to do. The terrible sound of Heather's screaming still echoed in his ears, and he had resolved not to move her out of the wreckage until help was available. As long as she remained still she seemed comfortable enough, but something was grievously wrong with her back, and the slightest movement was obvious torture.

He had decided he must build their shelter around Heather, and he had arranged the mailbags into a sort of foundation. Although they smelled of oil and gasoline, they provided a barrier against the drifting snow. All during the afternoon the snowfall had increased until now he was wading in it up to his knees.

He had cut large sections of fabric off the Stearman's broken wings, tied down the ends with shale and rocks, and stretched them over the twisted fuselage. He had opened his parachute and draped the silk over the tail and engine. The result was a tent, which he thought might even be considered cozy under different circumstances. It was almost dark when he surveyed his handiwork. For a moment the sight of such a flimsy structure nearly overwhelmed his resolve. He saw that a moderate wind would blow the whole crazy thing away, and he wondered how so little could have been accomplished after so much hard labor.

He had told himself it was certainly the altitude that had brought on his exhaustion. Now he thought he knew the truth. His weariness, this yearning just to lie down and sleep, was the sum of his fears. For now that the physical work was done he had at last made himself look at their true situation. And what he saw was dismaying.

He stood in snow that was rapidly becoming deeper. The snow blanketed a Nevada mountain, or was it actually in Nevada? Perhaps they had flown farther than he realized and crossed over the state line. He was aware that he was approximately one hour's flying time from Elko, a morsel of knowledge that was presently not of much value.

He was a stranger lost in hostile land. For company he had a helpless little girl whose eyes declared she trusted him with their future. There was no escaping those eyes; they said, I know we are in deep trouble, but you will find a way out of it.

At least, he thought, Moravia would now be certain that he was missing and would have already organized a search. But where would his searchers look except along the usual route, which would not bring them this way?

He looked up at the trees that clung to the side of the mountain and realized that they would render him nearly invisible from the air, unless a plane flew directly over the site and its pilot happened to be looking down at just the right instant. Even the wreckage would be hard to spot, scattered as it was beneath the snow.

The pilot paused to take stock of his assets. There was one bar of chocolate, which he would feed to Heather in small amounts. In the dark she would not know he was not consuming a like amount. A piece of gum would ease his appetite and there were four left in the pack. There was a full box of matches, but he had not gathered any wood. Tomorrow he hoped to explore.

He had given one of the pain pills to Heather, and there were nine left. He had used half the bottle of iodine swabbing at the cuts on her face and upon his own left arm, which bore an ugly gash. Somehow the sleeve of his teddy bear had been pushed up during impact, and the shale had cut into his flesh. The wound had stopped bleeding and was now wrapped in gauze.

He sank to his knees and crawled inside the shelter. The last of the daylight filtered through the parachute fabric, and he saw that Heather's eyes were open. "I expected you to be asleep."

She made no reply, and he thought that if she let one tear go, he would have to find some excuse to go outside for a while. "Do you realize that you are probably the only girl in the world with your very own silken tent?"

She looked at him steadily. Were those eyes accusing him? Or were they expressionless because of the pain pill?

"Do you hurt?" he asked.

She shook her head ever so slightly.

The Aviator

"Is there anything I can do to make you more comfortable?"

"I'm cold."

He took off his teddy bear and carefully tucked it around her. She protested, saying she did not want him to be cold.

"I'm really hot," he said. "I've been getting us organized."

"Could we have a fire if we're going to camp out all night?"

All night? They would be very lucky if help came within a week. He explained that he would not build a fire inside their tent, since the airplane's fuel tank was still in place and leaking slowly. Maybe in the morning he could separate the fuel tank from the center section somehow.

"Tomorrow I'll build a fire outside so we can melt some snow for water. And now for the menu. The entree is a special chocolate pudding, which you can wash down with snow champagne. Dessert, if you are good, might even be a piece of gum."

A silence fell between them. The pilot listened to the ticking of snow above his head and thought that it was going to be a very long night. It was dark inside the shelter. He pulled off his gloves, and feeling in the knee pocket of his teddy bear, he found the chocolate bar. He broke off a piece and reached out for Heather's hand. "Here's dinner. Eat slowly and it will last longer. And be sure to fold your napkin afterward."

He heard her chewing, and when she had finished she said, "You are a good cook."

"It may not be like your mother would make, but it will have to do for now."

"My mother will be worried. Will someone look for us?"

"Yes."

"Tonight? They can't find us at night, can they?"

"No. Tomorrow at first light they'll be looking." The pilot could see them—six airplanes of the line and some from the National Guard. Yet he saw them to the east, covering the regular route. They would not be looking in the right area. "Probably," he said, wondering how he could lie so easily. "Probably they will find us tomorrow."

"Then what?"

Indeed. Then what? "Someone will come after us."

"If I could move, we could go down the mountain by ourselves. I'm all right as long as I stay perfectly still, but when I move even a teensy bit . . . well . . ."

"You'll be much better tomorrow."

"I hope so. Can I tell you something? Sort of confidential?"

"I'm your best and only listener. And my lips are sealed."

"I have to—you know—go."

"Oh. Just a minute. I should have thought. . . ." He fumbled for his gloves, found them, and crawled outside. Somewhere in the wreckage, he remembered, there was a section of metal cowling. Normally it was fitted between the fuselage and the engine, but it had been separated and badly bent by the impact.

He waded through the snow toward the crumpled wings and was halfway there before his boot slid over something hard. He reached down and pulled up the piece of cowling. Laboring in the darkness, he placed the metal beneath one knee and forced his weight downward until he bent it more and managed to form a crude pan. He took it to the shelter and crawled inside. "Hello," he said. "It's me. The duty nurse. Now if you will just bite a bullet and let me ease this under you . . ."

Fumbling in the dark, he heard her gasp several times, but at last she lay quiet and he asked if he could remove the pan.

"Yes," she whispered. "I'm so embarrassed."

"Don't be. I'm your friend."

As he crawled toward the exit he heard her say very softly, "Thank you. You are a very beautiful person."

He was glad it was so dark.

Later he lay down beside her, sensing her closeness and trying not to think about their situation. Tomorrow his head might not ache. He would concentrate on getting off the mountain.

He could not sleep. Armies of thoughts marched across his mind. Why had he given so much of his life to flying? Very few businessmen died at their desks, and very few farmers were run over by their tractors. Flying paid well, but he could not think of a pilot who flew just for the money. Some of the pilots he knew were a little odd in their ways, but they were not daredevils, and if any of them thought they might die in an airplane, they never said so. Only Moravia mentioned the possibility once in a while, and he was just trying to do his job.

Now there was no sound of snow, and the pilot knew it must be very deep on the fuselage. There was only an almost suffocating silence. Still, that was healthy. He did not like to think what it would be like on the mountain if there were much wind. He was lying on a piece of fabric, with a mail sack for a pillow, and he shifted position slightly just to hear the familiar squeaking of his leather jacket. At least it was some sound. Moments later he heard Heather's muffled voice. "Are you awake?"

"Yes. Are you warm enough?" He didn't dare ask if she hurt.

"Oh, yes. I've been thinking. What's your name?"

"Jerry."

"*Mister* Jerry? My mom says I should call older people mister or missus."

"Just call me Jerry."

"I guess it won't hurt to pretend I'm a grown-up."

"Why not? I'm beginning to think you are."

They were silent for a long time, and he was hoping she had fallen asleep when he heard her voice again, somehow sounding even more frail. God Almighty, he thought, she can't be dying. It's just her back.

"I have all the clothes," she was saying. "You must be cold."

"No. I've slept in this jacket a hundred times."

"What's your wife's name?"

"I don't have one."

Another silence followed, then she asked, "Is she dead?"

"No. I've never had a wife."

"Why?"

Now there, he decided, was one question he did not feel obliged to answer. How could he say, Listen, little Heather. Maybe you failed to take a good look at me. How would you like to look at this face all day long? And anyway, to meet wives, you first have to meet girls, and they are not found in the sky. They are found in churches or speakeasies, depending on what sort they are, or some kind of place where people gather because they find each other's company makes them feel better. Well, I tried it a few times after the accident, and I saw what happened. People would shake my hand and even try to make conversation. All the time they would be looking anywhere except at me, and they would find someone else to be with as quickly as they could. And I couldn't blame them. So in the interest of the general public's comfort I just decided not to depress them any more than I could help.

He cleared his throat as if he were giving Heather's question serious consideration and said, "I don't know why I never got married. I guess I have just been too much in love with flying."

"At least it's good to be in love with *something*."

"You are very wise for your age."

"But have you ever been really, *really* in love with a girl?"

Now there again was something he did not care to discuss with a stranger, and for the past eight years, ever since the accident, it seemed everyone was in the stranger class. He had not been inclined to even think of Sally, much less discuss her. Yet, because a little girl had asked a question she thought was innocent, here was Sally imposing on his thoughts once more.

It was no use trying to deny that he had been totally in love with Sally, and regardless of the outcome, he would not allow anything to damage the memories of the joyous times they had known together. The pilot remembered one weekend in San Antonio, when Sally had said almost exactly the same words he had heard a few minutes ago. "You are a very beautiful man."

But now he knew the words were far from the same, because Sally had been looking directly in his face. That weekend they had decided to get married "sometime in October." Sally was still trying to choose a specific date when the accident occurred.

A month passed in the hospital before they told him the worst about the damages to his body and the ravages to his face. He was a tin-and-pin man, and when at last he forced himself to look in a mirror he failed to recognize the artificial man he saw.

Sally had not run away from the calamity. She suggested they be married right in the hospital. But her eyes said clearly, I am going through with this because it is the only decent thing to do. Sally deserved a whole man. One more long look in the mirror made his decision relatively easy. A sudden change of mind, he had explained. "Sorry, Sally. I've done a lot of thinking and I don't think it would work for the two of us now."

For Sally, running out on another's misfortunes was unthinkable. It had taken some extra doing to discourage her. For a while she came to the hospital regularly, but after two months she gave up and just disappeared. A buddy told him she had gone to Chicago and married a reporter for the *Tribune*.

Now he said to the darkness, "Heather, how come a girl your age asks such questions? How old are you, anyway?"

"Eleven going on twelve. You think I still play with dolls?"

"Well, I'm not much of an authority on the habits of young ladies, because my life just hasn't worked out like most people's."

"I wish you would tell me about your life."

"Why, for gosh sake?"

"If I can listen to you about anything, maybe my back won't hurt so much because my brain won't be able to worry about two things at the same time. That's what my teacher keeps saying in school. Don't be a flibbertigibbet. Don't try to think about a whole bunch of things at once. She says we have to learn to concentrate, and if I can concentrate on you, then I can't concentrate on my back, if you see what I mean."

"I wish I could help you more," he said. "Would it feel better if I rolled you over on your side? I would be very careful."

She hesitated. "I guess you'd better try, because it seems to be getting worse."

Moving with caution lest he bump her in the darkness, he reached out until he found her hip. "Let's just take it easy."

He eased his other hand slowly behind her neck and told her to take a deep breath and exhale. Then he rolled her very gently toward him. For an instant he thought all would be well. He felt her breath on his cheek, and he realized with sudden pleasure that at this moment he was closer to Heather than he had been to another human being in eight years. She caught her breath and a choked little cry escaped her. "Oh, no . . . *no!* Please let me down."

He eased her back into her original position and waited in despair for her sobs to diminish. "Just stay there. Try to relax for tonight. We'll think of something in the morning."

"It hurts so. Even if I move a teeny bit."

He reached out to her face and felt her tears. He wiped them away and continued to caress her cheeks. "I don't want to give you another pill if you can stand to be without it."

"Why not?"

As he heard her catching her breath in jerky whimpers, he wondered if he dared tell her she might need them even more tomorrow. If help failed to come, and if by some miraculous effort he could take her to help, then the pills might make it possible.

"Too many pills would not be good for you."

"I wish I could go to sleep."

"You will. Will it hurt if I rub the back of your neck?"

"I don't think so." Her voice sounded so feeble that even in the stillness he could hardly hear her.

His fingers found the warmth of her neck and moved very gently in small circles. "Okay, Heather?"

"Yes . . . okay."

As his fingers moved and she quieted, he began to talk to her, keeping his voice low and soothing. After a time he realized the tenseness was leaving her, and she was breathing regularly.

It had been so long since he had talked at length with anybody that he now found it awkward. There was so much he longed to share, his thoughts seemed to meet each other head-on.

"I guess there really isn't much to tell about my life, Heather. I was born and then I grew for a while and I made friends along the way. Some of them I still hear from, but people change and drift apart, and since I've been flying, the people I went to school with don't seem to talk the same language. I have one friend now who is very special, although I suppose he doesn't really consider me a friend. His name is Moravia and he is my boss, and it is very difficult to explain how I feel about him. He has only one leg, and maybe that made it easier for him to hire me. The day he said that I had the job—well, I just can't tell you what that did for me. I had been to every flying outfit in this country, and they all looked at me like I was a ghost and told me how lucky I was to be alive. They offered me ground jobs, but no one wanted me to fly for them. Moravia was not spooked by the way I looked, and when you meet people like that you just want to hold on to them and do your best for them. He is a strange man, Moravia. The more I know him, the less I know him."

The pilot had no conception of how long he talked. He slipped into a near trance as he spoke of his early flying days. He told her how his parents had taken him to the Nebraska State Fair, where he had seen a small yellow airplane fly. Looking up, his mouth wide in fascination, he could see the sunlight through the wings, and on the bottom wing and also on the top the pilot had had his name painted for everyone to see—BEECHY. He had thought the little flying machine was the most beautiful thing he had ever seen, and he vowed right then and there that he would one day fly himself. Later there was a man named Sloniger who had taught him to fly a Jenny he had bought right after the war. Sloniger flew the mails with Lindbergh before Lindbergh became so famous, and he was still flying somewhere back east.

"There was the usual barnstorming all over the country, north with the sun in the summer and south with the birds in winter ... a gypsy life, Heather, without much point to it. Then the army needed instructors in primary flight training, and the job was regular and paid well, and they employed civilians when they could find them reliable and sober during the day."

The pilot realized at last that he was talking to himself, for the girl's breathing had become regular and she had been silent for a long time. He withdrew his hand very slowly from the back of her neck and whispered, "Thank you, little girl."

He bent down until his twisted mouth almost touched her cheek, and all the yearning for affection he had known for eight long years rose to help him form his lips into a gentle kiss.

He retreated instantly, as if he had done something very wrong.

CHAPTER FOUR

Moravia was upset with himself because he had chosen to sleep in his office. What an unforgivable, sentimental gesture! There was nothing he could do during the night, and every available contact had reported to him before darkness fell.

They had all been discouraging. Elko: Fourteen had taken off over an hour behind schedule. He had not returned nor had Elko had any positive response from those few people they had managed to contact along the route. Boise, the same. Fourteen had never appeared there and so it was reasonable to assume that he had landed somewhere in between Elko and Boise. And Moravia's rancher near Rome, who had finally answered his telephone, had said that if Fourteen had landed right in his back pasture, he would not have been able to see him. It was snowing that heavily.

All sheriffs and forest rangers along the line had been alerted to the possibility of a downed aircraft, and Moravia had badgered the weather bureaus in both Salt Lake City and San Francisco trying to obtain a definite weather forecast. His dissatisfaction mounted as he listened to a long series of hems and haws and ifs and practiced equivocations.

Now, as he drank the stale coffee in the waiting room, Moravia sighed and repented his night on the couch. If he had gone home, Marsha would have soothed him and he might have had a good night's rest instead of fretting helplessly over Fourteen's fate.

Fourteen could have encountered ice and failed to get himself out of it immediately. He could have postponed his decision to follow the old airman's dictum that a hundred-eighty-degree turn is the safest maneuver in the business. As little as two minutes in clear ice and his airplane might have become uncontrollable.

Fourteen could have decided to climb on top of an overcast rather than hunt through the valleys like a ferret and, once above the clouds, found too late that the holes he expected were just not there. With nothing to guide him over a vast sea of white except his rather dicey magnetic compass, he could have become lost. As his fuel reserve slipped away he would have had to descend through the cloud into the unknown. Then Fourteen would sweat in spite of the cold, for he would know that within that cloud layer might be granite. Moravia could picture such a predicament all too easily. He had been there.

Moravia considered the possibility of engine failure in flight and dismissed it. Engines did sometimes fail under the pressure of full takeoff power, but trouble at cruise was extremely rare.

Long after dusk and well into the night, Moravia had told himself that soon his phone would ring, and it would be Fourteen reporting that he had set down in some field. Fourteen was a laconic man and would not elaborate except to say that the mail was safe and he would be off as soon as the local weather cleared. Yet as the hours passed, Moravia lost faith in this analysis.

Fourteen was no careless fool. He knew people would be concerned about him, and he was an extremely sensitive man. He was the only pilot Moravia knew who had three books of poetry in what passed for his home, and last October when a symphony played in Salt Lake he had asked for an extra day off so he could attend. Fourteen was not one to land in some farmer's field, accept a congratulatory series of drinks, and forget to telephone.

When midnight came with no report from anywhere or anyone, Moravia was certain that Fourteen must be in serious trouble—if indeed he was alive. The fact that he was carrying a passenger only made it more vexatious and complicated.

Moravia was haunted by the faces of the girl's grandparents. They had arrived to meet the airplane well ahead of the appointed time. Then, as the afternoon passed and nothing came out of the sky, he had at last told them that it was unlikely anything would be coming. They had collapsed on his office couch and refused to leave until long after dark.

Even more difficult was his obligatory call to the girl's parents, who lived near Elko. At least, he thought, he was spared the sight of their faces as he told them there was an excellent chance the pilot would be calling in soon. The parents remained calm, although they did say they hoped he was not lying. "I am not cruel," he had responded testily in his anxiety. "And I am an optimist."

Finally he had thought to call on Fourteen's behalf. But who? After some searching he found Fourteen's original job application in the office file. He had designated both parents as deceased. There was a box at the bottom of the page marked "Notify in case of accident. Next of kin or friends." The box was empty.

Empty like his life, Moravia thought.

Now with the dawn there was much to do. He could stop scratching at his stubble of beard and get on the telephone. By ten he would have three airplanes searching the northern section of the route where the weather was still passable. The National Guard had promised the assistance of all their available aircraft, but it would be afternoon before they arrived from Spokane. And at eleven, willy-nilly, there would be the southbound mail to be flown. Moravia was grateful there were still so many things to be done. They would ease the gradual decay in his belief that Fourteen would soon be found.

AT FIRST the pilot thought it was the wind that was causing the intermittent whistling noise somewhere along the side of the shelter. Then, as he awakened fully, he realized the faint keening came from the girl. It was a high-pitched, plaintive lament that followed the cadence of her breathing. The pilot wondered how long he could stand to hear it. "Are you awake?" he asked finally.

"Yes."

He hoped she would go back to sleep, but the sound persisted. He waited as long as he could, then he asked, "How goes it?"

He wondered if she had heard him, since she made no reply. "Today will be a big day," he said. "We'll get out of here somehow. What would you like for breakfast? The management regrets that we are out of bacon and eggs, and the cook burned the last piece of toast. Will you settle for a nice chunk of chocolate?"

"Yes." Her voice was very faint.

"How do you want it? Sunny-side up or over? If you can wait a little bit, I'll build a fire outside and make you some pine-needle tea. They say it will cure anything."

"My back. Could I have a pill now?"

"Sure." He shook one from the little bottle and crawled to the entrance. He reached outside, made a miniature snowball, and placed the pill in the center. "Here. Pretend it's ice cream." Still on his knees, he looked down at her as she swallowed. He saw her try to smile, but the expression was far different from the one he had seen before. "Did anyone ever tell you that you are a very pretty little girl?" he asked.

He saw a strange concern in her eyes. Suddenly he realized that because of the shelter's low ceiling he was bent over her, his face hardly a foot from hers. And now light was filtering through the parachute silk. He retreated instantly, backing away crab-fashion, horrified that the vision of his face might have shocked her. "I'll go make a fire. We'll have some good hot tea to cheer us up."

He crawled quickly out of the shelter and stood up. A bitter wind struck his cheeks, and the same wind picked up little plumes of snow and took them twirling down the mountain. He looked up at the clouds and saw they were moving rapidly. We are on the lee side and very lucky, he thought. And there will be sun today.

The balance of what he beheld depressed him. The knee-deep snow had obliterated the trench dug by the fuselage, and it was obvious that finding wood was going to take a long time. He had landed on a wide plateau that was littered with enormous boulders along the higher perimeter. The bottom edge was equally uninviting. There was an almost vertical drop-off into a frozen valley far below. Escape via that route appeared impossible.

He made himself count the good things. The plateau was sheltered from the present winds, and the trees offered some protection from a possible avalanche. He could walk in either direction as far as he could see as long as he stayed at approximately the same level as the shelter. He trudged off in search of wood.

The sun had risen by the time he had gathered an armful of broken branches from the area where the Stearman's wings had torn through the trees. The wood was green and heavy with sap, and he knew it would not make much of a fire. He worried about errant sparks setting fire to the shelter, so he dug a hole in the snow some distance from it. Then, remembering his days as a Boy Scout, he cut shavings from the branches and stacked them carefully in the hole. After using four of his precious matches, he finally had a fire that promised to keep burning. He decided that as soon as he had given Heather tea he would try to construct some kind of container, drain the oil from the engine, and soak the branches in it. Maybe then he would have a real fire.

He was proud of his two cooking utensils. They were the cone-like housings that contained the Stearman's landing lights. One was badly crumpled, but he used it to melt snow for water. He was shocked by how much snow he had to feed into his crude bucket to make even half an inch of water.

He blessed the tool kit, which had enabled him to remove two of the engine's rocker-arm covers. They would serve as shallow cups, and he had carefully scrubbed them with snow to remove the sludge of oil. And who knew? Perhaps the remaining aroma of oil might complement pine needles. Perhaps the engine, which had proved so false, might become their salvation.

The fire made snapping sounds, which he found reassuring, but continuous feeding of snow to make so little water was discouraging. Several times the capricious wind alternated between enveloping him in smoke and bringing to him the disturbing sounds from the shelter. He wondered how long he could bear Heather's moaning.

He looked at the sun, which slipped in and out of the clouds as if reflecting his spirits. He told the smoke and the mountain and the clouds that he was not a religious man and was not asking for help for himself, but would God, if He was awake, please help a nice little girl? "Something has to stop her from making those noises," he muttered aloud. "I can't stand it much longer and neither can she. Something has to be done to distract her."

Then he thought that if he was talking to himself after less than one day on the mountain, they were already slipping into worse trouble. He forced himself to think about what he must do. First keep the fire going. Take oil from the engine and put it in some kind of receptacle. Keep it handy to make black smoke in case he heard an airplane engine. Next, food. In another hour or two they were going to know what it was like to be really hungry.

Where had he put his mail gun, the silly blunderbuss with the holster so shiny from rubbing against his hip? He wondered if a man who had shot a pistol only once before in his life could hit anything more than a few feet away. But what have you done with the gun, fathead? It could make the difference between surviving and not surviving. His thoughts hammered at his inadequacies. Can't you ever do anything right? You land with a perfectly good gun and lose it first thing. It isn't the little girl who needs a nurse, it's you!

Then suddenly he hoped he knew where it was. He left the fire and ran to the shelter. He pushed his hand slowly through the snow along the top of the fuselage, exploring tenderly lest he push the gun off into deeper snow and maybe never find it again. It is here somewhere, he thought. His whole world seemed centered on this one object that he had treated with contempt for so long. The snow piled up to his elbow and slid away as his hand uncovered, inch after inch, the Stearman's pale gray fabric. Because the fuselage lay on its left side, his plowing revealed a part of the letters U.S. Soon he knew there would be the word MAIL. He was positive he had placed the gun somewhere along there. Well, fairly sure.

He stopped when he encountered something solid. He held his breath as he moved his cold fingers forward until his hand covered the object. Then suddenly he clutched it with all his strength, pulled his hand away in a flurry of snow, and said aloud, "There you are." He brought the gun to his lips and kissed it. And he thought, I am going mad. Kissing guns!

He heard her call his name from beneath the shelter. "Jerry?"

Still clutching the gun, he dropped to his knees and crawled inside. Although Heather's mouth was strained, he persuaded himself that some of the sparkle had returned to her eyes.

She said, "I heard you talking to someone. Have they come for us already?"

"No. I was just talking to myself. I hope it doesn't become a habit."

"I talk to myself all the time. All my friends do."

She watched him place the gun under the mail sack he had been using as a pillow. "What are you going to do with that gun?"

"Nothing, probably. I just had an idea it might come in handy in case I wanted to shoot something."

"Why would you want to shoot anything? You're such a nice person, and I can't imagine any animal not liking you a lot."

"Well, I like animals too, but..."

"If you're thinking of killing animals for food, I'm not hungry," she said.

He detected a note of peevishness in her voice. Somewhere he had heard, maybe his mother had told him when he was sick as a boy, that people always became peevish when they were on the way to recovery. He cautioned himself not to tell her there might soon come a time when she would be hungry.

"How does your back feel?" he asked.

"It still hurts. Can I have another pill?"

"No. It's too soon."

"But I hurt so much. When do you think they will come?"

If I begin to lie now, he thought, I'll have to start a whole series of lies. Then she won't believe whatever it is I might have to tell her when things get really tough.

"I'm not sure when they will come," he said as he adjusted the teddy bear around her legs. Trying to dismiss the doubts, he said that her tea was almost ready. Then he crawled out of the shelter and stood watching the vapor of his breath blow away on the wind. When he heard the whimpering start again he went down to the fire, where he could not hear it.

CHAPTER FIVE

STILLER, one of the oldest pilots of the line, was not happy with the morning, because the overcast was low and sliding across the dreary Nevada landscape at a pace that told him of strong winds aloft. For sure he would have a bumpy ride with the northbound mail out of Elko and probably a continuous wrestling match with

The Aviator

his airplane over the more mountainous areas. Worse, he would have to stay just under the overcast, thereby limiting his altitude and field of vision. He had been told to keep a sharp eye on the terrain on the flight north. One of the pilots was down somewhere along the route—that fellow Jerry, whom no one seemed to know very well. Stiller was not surprised that he could not even remember Jerry's last name.

Never mind. He *was* peculiar and certainly a loner, but he had twice volunteered to take Stiller's flight when Stiller had wanted to spend an extra day with the family. With five children you appreciated a man making gestures like that.

Probosky, the mechanic, held the straps as Stiller slipped into the parachute. Some pilots put it on in the airplane and saved an awkward walk with the chute banging against their thighs, but Stiller wanted to have a good look at the D ring assembly rather than just glance at it. With five kids you thought that way.

When he had clipped the shoulder straps together and then brought up the leg straps, he straightened and fastened the chin strap of his helmet. And he swore for the hundredth time that when he got to Pasco he was going to stop by the repair hangar, find a leather punch, and put a new hole in the chin strap. As it was, the holes were in the wrong place and had been for more than a year of his forgetting to make the alteration. Using hole number one made the helmet too loose, and the next one tightened it until it nearly choked him. You could ruin the whole helmet by cutting a new hole with a knife, and helmets were expensive.

If you were a family man, you counted your pennies. Caution

was the word at all times. Caution in flight led to long life. Stiller had convinced himself that his prudent philosophy was responsible for twelve years of flying without scratching an airplane or himself.

MORAVIA thought it had been one of the longest days he had ever known. He was slumped in the leather chair behind his desk, rubbing at his sore eyes. He was disgusted. A shaft of late afternoon sunlight illuminated Stiller, who sat opposite him. Stiller's teddy bear was unbuttoned and his white scarf hung loosely about his neck. Moravia watched him toy with the chin strap of his helmet and thought it was unforgivable for the man to seem so relaxed, considering the circumstances.

Moravia glared at him. "Do you mean to sit there and tell me that you actually saw a wing and what looked like pieces of a fuselage and you didn't go down to confirm it?"

"You don't understand. I just had a peek down through a hole. And not a very big hole."

"Well, why the hell didn't you dive down through the hole and have a better look?"

"The wind was rougher than a cob. Near the mountain I might have hit some heavy downdrafts and never been able to climb out. Then you would have had two airplanes to look for."

"That's a chance I might be willing to take in exchange for confirmation," Moravia muttered. Why, he asked himself, did it have to be this chickenhearted son of a gun who just thought he might have seen something? All the other pilots who had been aloft this day, and who would certainly have gone down through any hole if there had been one available, had reported no sightings of anything even remotely interesting. He studied Stiller and decided again that he had never liked the man's sanctimonious air.

"Let me get this straight," Moravia began as easily as he could manage. "You took off from Elko and ran into more wind than you expected. You were off course to the west maybe twenty or thirty miles and on top of a broken overcast. You were not exactly sure where you were until you realized by what you saw below that you were over more mountainous terrain than you should be. Is that essentially correct?"

"Essentially, yes."

"Okay. Now you just happened to be looking down when you saw a hole with a wing and a fuselage at the bottom of it—"

"I *think* that's what I saw."

"Well, was it a plane or wasn't it?"

"From that altitude it was hard to be sure. And the whole side of the mountain was covered with heavy snow. So was whatever it was I saw. You can't imagine how small it was."

"I can imagine." Moravia found it impossible to keep sarcasm from his voice. "I suppose it never occurred to you to descend?"

"Yes, it did. I even turned around and went back over the area, but the hole was gone. I circled around above the overcast for about five minutes before I gave up."

"Five minutes," Moravia said flatly.

"With the way the wind was blowing I had to think of my fuel. If the wind had swung to the north, I might not have made Boise."

And it could be, Moravia thought, that you left a buddy to die right under you. If you had just waited a little longer, there might have been another hole, and you could have dived down to have a look around and still have had more than enough fuel to get you to a nice flat field for an emergency landing.

Yet Moravia kept his recriminations to himself and laid his palm over the map beneath his desk glass. "Were you somewhere over the Santa Rosa Range in Nevada?"

Stiller leaned forward the better to view the map. "I'm quite sure I was more to the northeast. I'm reasonably sure I saw Capitol Peak sticking up through the overcast."

Moravia made no attempt to hide his bitterness. "That would put whatever you thought you saw somewhere up here in the wilderness, which only leaves us a mere few thousand square miles to search."

"If you're through with me," Stiller said anxiously, "I'd just as soon get on home." He tried to smile. "My wife has a lot of things she wants me to do."

Moravia lit a Caporal. "Sure," he said. "Just stay near the telephone. I may need you."

As Stiller shuffled through the door in his heavy boots, Moravia noted the special stoop in his posture. He could not decide whether Stiller was a man simply burdened with domestication or a man who knew he had failed not only a comrade but himself.

THE pilot could not believe the sun was already so low. All day he had reminded himself that if he lost his sense of humor entirely, then he must certainly lose the challenge which was becoming increasingly apparent. And he thought that he might die of many things on the mountain, but it would not be from boredom, for never had he been so busy.

The fire had gone out twice. Rekindling it and tending it, he now calculated, had taken him at least three hours. He had drained some oil from the engine, catching it in one of the wheel flanges. He had experimented by pouring a little on the fire and producing a black smoke.

Twice during the morning he had been convinced he heard a plane, but the wind was blowing hard enough to confuse all sounds. He decided it might have been just wishful thinking.

He had cut some fabric off the wings and the fuselage. He had laid the pieces on the snow in the form of a huge X and secured the edges with chunks of shale. If there was no more snow, then the X should be easily visible, although he wished the Stearmans had been painted any other color except neutral gray.

By the time he had finished his chores and had spent as much time as he could bear with Heather, it was midafternoon. It was not easy, he told himself, to maintain a sense of humor when a little girl was hurting. He called himself a coward for giving her another pill and sneaking off under the pretext of hunting.

Hail the mighty hunter! He had waded through the snow for two exhausting hours, skinned his knee on a rock when he had stepped into an invisible crevasse, and frightened himself badly when he had slipped and nearly gone over a high cliff.

When he first left the vicinity of the wreckage he found himself holding the gun at the ready, as if some rabbit or deer or antelope were determined to jump right out in front of him and commit suicide. But all that afternoon he had not seen a living creature, and worse, he had not even seen any tracks.

His shadow was very long when he returned to the shelter. There he broke the remainder of the chocolate bar into several pieces and gave Heather one. He took only pine-needle tea for himself. When she had finished the chocolate she began whimpering again, and he thought that he would have to start thinking of her as just "the girl." The name Heather was too personal and beautiful. It identified her as someone he might value. When he had lain so long in the hospital, his body so battered the nurses thought he could never be put back together again, they never referred to him by name. They spoke of him only as "the aviator," thereby avoiding any personal involvement with his dubious future. Now, he thought, "the girl" must be stripped of her exactness. She must become any little girl, and therefore her hurting might not find so much sympathy in his heart.

If I am to keep my sanity, he resolved, I cannot think of her as the dear friend she is becoming. I have to force her to keep her distance or we'll go down the drain together. I cannot function efficiently if I have to suffer right along with her.

Things had to change. Otherwise his tolerance was going to break down. He longed to shout, Will you please stop that whining? But he had to quell all traces of impatience.

She whimpered again, and he hoped he could keep his vow. "Is there anything I can do to make you more comfortable?"

There was not the honest solicitation in his voice he would have liked to hear. The tone reminded him somewhat of Sally's voice during her visits to the hospital in San Antonio. There were times when no matter what she said it sounded as if she were pleading with him to stop his loafing in bed and get going.

Now he noticed that Heather had not responded to his concern. "I asked you a question. Cat got your tongue?"

Still she said nothing. He waited, listening to the almost inaudible whirring of the wind through the treetops. "It's going to be dark pretty soon and if there's anything I can do for you then, it will be much easier to do it now."

At last he heard her whisper, "I hurt so...."

Was she blaming him for her pain? How many hundred times did she have to say she hurt? Look, you silly little girl, *I* did not make the damned engine. "If I give you another pill, we could run short just when we might need them more."

"I need a pill now."

"Well for God—" He caught himself. "Tell you what. We'll take a chance. I got the fuel out of the tank, so I'll bring the fire in here to cheer things up. How would that be?"

"That would be nice."

He scrambled out of the entrance. There were two good embers left in the fire, and he brought them into the shelter. Near the entrance he dug a shallow pit. He cut off some shavings from the best piece of wood he had and fed them carefully to the embers. In time he created a bright little fire, but the smoke was heavy.

"The smoke is getting in my eyes," Heather said.

"Well, I can't stop it." Where did she get off complaining? "Do you want me to take the fire outside again?"

He thought he would be damned if he would, even if she asked him. Sure it was smoky in the shelter, but wasn't fire man's first and best friend? "Did you know that?" he asked.

"Know what?"

Why did he have to be stuck on a mountain with a dumb little girl who could not even carry on an intelligent conversation? Well, that was the story of his life all right. You did things for people and they barely bothered to thank you. "I asked you if you knew that fire was man's first and best friend."

"You never asked me that."

"I didn't? Well, let's not make a federal case out of it."

"Federal case? What are you talking about?"

"That's just a phrase people use when they want to call a halt to a disagreement. It means let's not make so much of this thing that a high federal court has to decide who was right."

"Please don't talk down to me, Jerry. *Please.*"

Criminee! What was happening here? "Okay, okay, okay," he heard himself saying. And for the life of me, he thought, I cannot get that note of annoyance out of my voice. "I apologize."

"You don't have to apologize for anything, Jerry."

"Yes, I do. And let's get back on the original track. Is there anything I can do for you before it gets dark?"

"You could tell me some more about your life so I could concentrate on that instead of my back."

"There's nothing more to tell you." There was a lot more, he thought, but who could make sense of it to a dumb little girl?

Suddenly he was inspired. The notion spun down out of the smoke. Why not? At last here was something that might be a distraction.

He reached for the mail sack he had been using as a pillow, untied the drawstrings, and took out a handful of letters. Arranging five in his hand like cards, he offered them to Heather. "Pick any one. We'll see what the writer has to say."

She hesitated. "Won't that be prying?"

"In this situation I would say it's permissible." And very necessary, he thought. "Go ahead. Pick one," he urged.

She closed her eyes a moment as if to guarantee her selection would be chance, then pulled one letter from his hand. He took out his knife and slit it open for her.

"You want me to read it to you?" she asked.

He nodded and waited for her to commence. He did not care what the letter said if it kept Heather's—no, *the girl's*—mind on something besides her back and his mind off their troubles. She remained silent, and in the gloom he could see she was reading the letter, but she seemed reluctant to share it with him.

"Well, are you going to read it?" he said impatiently.

"It's sort of a funny letter, not really funny like the Katzenjammer Kids or something like that. It's really sad and I'm not sure I understand what the person is trying to say."

"In about five minutes it will be darker in here and you won't be able to read anything. So you'd better hurry up." He placed a twig on the fire and tried to ignore the ache of hunger in his belly.

Maybe he could make a trap from parts of the wreckage and set it outside. Then breakfast would be waiting in the morning.

"This letter is from a lawyer, and this is what it says: 'Dear Mr. Antonivich. We are pleased to report that we have finally made a settlement out of court with the Nevada Mining Corporation with respect to your injuries sustained in March of 1926. The settlement is for a sum of one thousand dollars, and in accordance with our previous agreement the check was made out in our name. . . .'" She paused and said, "There is a word here I don't understand. Co-in-cidental-ly?"

"Coincidentally, maybe?"

Satisfied, she read on. "'We have retained these monies for our own account, since *coincidentally* the amount happens to match our fee for attorneys' services rendered in this matter. May we take this opportunity to wish you continued recovery. Kindest regards,' and it's signed by a Mr. J. K. Monroe."

She handed the letter to the pilot and puckered her nose. "I don't think I like Mr. Monroe."

He put the letter in the envelope and stuffed it back in the sack. He wanted to say that he liked Mr. Monroe because he had obviously caused the girl to think about something other than her own troubles. He slit open another letter. "Try this one."

"It's pretty hard to read, but I'll try. The handwriting is not Palmer method like we learn in school. It says, 'Dear Mom. I guess you have not heard from me since Pop died and maybe it was before that. So I'm saying I'll spend the extra money and write you a letter airmail. I guess I'm sorry Pop did die even if he never sent me no money. Now I wonder if the old man had a change of heart and left me some dollars in his will. Even though we never got along too good blood is thicker than water. Ha! Ha! So if there is any money just send it to this address below. If you and Sister swallowed *all* the loot I hope it rots in your pockets because that is not fair. I guess everything is all right with you two because I hear no different. Your son, Carl.'"

The pilot tried to smile. And for this sort of thing, he thought, I sometimes risk the only life I have.

Heather asked him to explain the letters to her, but he could find no logical way to explain cunning to a young girl, and he had even less success with greed. By the time he had tried, the only light in the shelter was a dim glow from the fire. "We had better try to sleep now," he said grumpily, because he was dissatisfied with his inability to define the baser urgings of human behavior. "Do you want to go to the bathroom first?"

There was no response, and soon he suspected that he had said the wrong thing, for the girl was crying again. Was he going to have to watch every word he said?

"Cut it out, Heather," he said before he could stop himself. Then to his amazement he heard himself adding, "Please knock off the bawling, will you?"

If I bite my tongue off, he thought, our little world may spin more slowly. But holy simoleons, how could anyone be expected to keep a civil tongue in his head when he was locked up in a cave about six feet long and four feet wide and three feet high? Right here was a grave occupied by a whining kid and a broken-down aviator who could not think of a way to save his passenger, not to mention himself— Some hero.

"I'm sorry, Heather," he said. "I guess I'm tired. Cry all you want. I don't mind."

He crawled out the entrance, then stood up and looked at the sky. A few snowflakes touched his face, and he thought, Somehow I've got to find a way to get us out of this. As if the night might give him comfort, he stared into the black void below. The only sound was the soft rustle of the parachute silk in the breeze. He considered his few options, but he was light-headed from hunger and he had difficulty separating wish from reality.

He could wait for someone to come, yet that could be forever. He could leave the girl here and try to make his way down the mountain by himself. That was what he would have done if he had been alone, even though it was a violation of the old rule to stay with a downed aircraft. A piece of wreckage was much easier to see from aloft than a human being.

He dismissed the idea instantly. He could not even consider

leaving the girl for more than a few hours. He raked his thoughts for other ways to escape and found only a familiar one. They must go down the mountain together.

He looked out into the darkness again and tried to imagine how many days it would take for a descent. Early in the day he had consulted the road map which served all mail pilots. Spreading his fingers, he had measured the approximate distance, about twenty miles, from where he thought he was to the little town of McDermitt, Nevada. Most of the distance was downhill. The last ten miles looked easier because they would be in a relatively flat valley. Still, the snow might be deeper there.

Time was wasting along with his strength. If he could find a way to carry Heather, then how long could he expect his strength to meet the demands of twenty-plus miles through snow? She was little, but she would become very heavy after a few hours.

Another unknown. What were the odds on leaving the protection of a shelter that might keep them alive for another week and taking a gamble on an open mountain? If the weather worsened or if he fell, it would probably be death for both of them.

Suddenly he heard a scream that became a hysterical wail. He ran to the shelter and found Heather trembling and almost incoherent. "Please . . . *please* . . . Jerry . . . help me!" As he took her in his arms he heard her say something about a gun and then a long series of unintelligible mewings. Finally, very clearly, she said, "Please, Jerry, kill me now. I can't stand it!"

He covered her mouth with his hand and tried to calm her flailing arms. Then he took the bottle from his pocket, shook out a pill, and put it on her tongue with some snow from outside.

He had no idea how long it was before she was quiet again because he tried desperately to steer his thoughts away from the shelter. Hoping to soothe her, he maintained a continuous monologue, telling her more of his youth in Nebraska, of his flying, and even of Sally. He told her that he knew what it was like to be in pain and how the worst of all pain was loneliness. He caressed her cheeks and, without realizing what he was saying, told her how he yearned for love of any kind. "We do not last very long on this earth, and I don't know whether that is good or bad. But I can tell you that a person who is not loved is near dead."

When at last her breathing became regular he bent down and kissed her forehead. She was asleep.

CHAPTER SIX

THIS night Moravia went home early because his sense of frustration had become overwhelming, and he believed an obsessed man was not a clear thinker. He needed a shave and a bath and his spare pair of glasses. And the comfort of his wife, Marsha, although he wondered how he was going to tell her that her husband, whom she often claimed was unflappable, had so lost control of himself that he had whipped off his glasses and slammed them down on the desk. The result of his pique was a broken lens—plus some release of dangerous steam.

His surrender to passion had occurred as a culmination of minor defeats beginning with the pussyfoot Stiller, who he thought should be selling neckties, and the later discovery that Stiller was the last pilot who might have stood a chance of locating Fourteen. Then, as if Stiller's arrival had triggered some malicious intent in nature, the whole area weather had gone to hell.

Reports had come in from everywhere within conceivable range of Fourteen's plane. "I want the whole picture," Moravia demanded. "All reports from within a four-hundred-mile circle."

Now he thought bitterly that he could as well have asked for a single report, since they were all nearly identical. Snow. Low ceilings. Poor visibility. No aircraft had landed. Everything west of the Rockies was locked up tight by the snow. Moravia hated the silence surrounding him. It savored too much of death.

By late afternoon he had managed to assemble what should have been an efficient search force. Two Ryan M-1 aircraft had been offered by Pacific Air Transport, and every pilot they had volunteered for the search. Also standing by were two private planes based in Boise, a Waco Taperwing and a Curtiss Oriole. There were three of Moravia's own Stearmans waiting in the hangar, and their pilots were eager to go. The Air National Guard DH-4s from Spokane had been forced to turn back because of the weather. Moravia now considered them as an ultimate reserve.

Yet it had all been useless. Not a propeller was turning, and as night came it was obvious that nothing could be done presently. If the forecasts were correct, only a limited effort could be mounted on the morrow.

Within the warmth of his home, Moravia took off his artificial leg and allowed it to thump against the bathroom floor with a satisfying note of defiance. He lowered himself gently into the tub Marsha had prepared for him, and he thought that of all the aviators he had known in the war and afterward, Fourteen was the most appealing. Was it because they were both handicapped? A sharing of perpetual misery? Moravia thought not. Physical impediments were too personal to be easily shared. You simply learned to tolerate them or face disaster.

Floating comfortably in the warm tub, Moravia regarded his stump and thought that it was much easier for people to accept a one-legged man than a two-sided face. Only the very brave would dare imagine an event tragic enough to leave them with a face like Fourteen's. A face was the owner's mirror of himself displayed before the outside world, and the mask Fourteen was obliged to wear reflected nothing except a ruin. And yet, Moravia thought, although ruins were always sad, they usually held an aura of mystery. You wanted to know more about a ruin than was normally exposed.

Moravia regretted that he knew so little about Fourteen and decided that if Fourteen survived, he would try to know him better. He doubted if he would continue to identify him as simply a number. In the future, if there was any future for the man, he would make a conscious effort to think of him as Jerry. He would invite him to the house for one of Marsha's special dinners, but he would not sentimentalize over his most recent misfortune, because that was not the way of aviators. He would say, Jerry, I never gave you a moment's thought. In fact, while you were freezing your butt off, I was basking in a nice hot tub.

The Aviator

During the night the pilot slept fitfully. Once he heard someone screaming, but when he rolled over he realized the girl was asleep. Then he knew he had been dreaming, and afterward he was almost afraid to try to sleep. I just cannot stand one more scream, he thought, real or imagined. I have to tell the girl never to scream again while we are together. I have to explain to her that any kind of screaming just does me in, because it was the last sound my student made just after we crashed.

Lying in the darkness, he turned his head and felt something hard beneath the mail sack and he knew it was the gun. He resolved to try hunting again. Maybe there was something out there that would make a meal. Then he thought about the pills and remembered there were six left. That might be barely enough for another day and a night. Then what? Would she scream again?

He forced himself to count his resources. Despite his trouble starting fires, the box of matches was still half full. There were three chunks of chocolate left. Small. There was an unlimited amount of pine needles for tea, but their bitter, rancid taste made him wonder if they might not better enjoy pure snow water. If there were berries or nuts or other food in the vicinity, he had not seen any. Incredible, he thought, that two nice people could starve to death on an American mountain in this day and age. But it was happening.

The only solution was as obvious as it was frightening to think about. During one of his attempts to get away from Heather's whimperings he had made an excursion across the plateau to the steep side of the mountain. He had floundered down through the snow for ten minutes to test his endurance and found himself in poor condition. As he waited for his heart to stop pounding he almost convinced himself that it would be impossible to descend the mountain while carrying a girl who could not tolerate movement.

By the time he had made his way back to the shelter he was exhausted. He told himself, Look, walking in deep snow is tough labor even if you're going downhill. You have to organize your thinking and be realistic. And while you're at it, he thought, you might apologize to the girl. What kind of man are you to cut her short when she had asked again what would happen if no one came today? And then capping that by saying that by now her mother would be very worried.

He had said, "Anyone who would send their daughter away in an airplane ought to expect some worrying. There was a perfectly good train you could have taken. Now shut up!"

What kind of man said things like that to a little girl who hurt? If anything, he thought, her mother should be censured for sending her precious daughter away in an airplane piloted by an incompetent fathead.

When the first hint of light filtered through the parachute silk, the pilot crawled outside the shelter and saw that it might be a fine day. Venus was still visible, as were a few stars to the west, and there was not a cloud in the sky. There was no wind where he stood, but a plume of snow trailed south from the top of the mountain. A north wind usually brought clear weather. He thought, If they are going to come, this will be the day, but he decided against sharing his hopes with the girl. If they did *not* come, then there would be no recovery from her disappointment.

He had removed the magnetic compass from the Stearman on the previous afternoon. Now he poured a little of its alcohol content on his kindling and soon had a snapping fire. The ease of starting it cheered him. He was beginning to make do. In spite of the fine fire, it took him almost an hour to make enough snow water for tea, and he was reminded of the altitude while he waited interminably for the water to boil. If anyone came for them today, they were in for a long climb. The altimeter on the Stearman read four thousand five hundred feet, but he mistrusted it. The impact of the landing could have made it inaccurate.

He sprinkled pine needles in the water and mashed them against the bottom of the landing-light receptacle with a stick. He crawled inside the shelter and presented the girl with hot tea along with a chunk of chocolate. He took a piece for himself, the first food he had eaten since he left Elko. He wondered if he could explain to Heather that unless he had something to eat, his remaining strength would not last through the day. He decided against it. I must be her knight on a white charger, he thought, even though my horse is dead.

"Mind if I join you for breakfast?" he asked, smiling.

He saw her try to return his smile and his hopes were renewed. She had not uttered a sound since last night. Maybe everything was going to be all right. He held her head up so she could sip the tea more easily, and her helplessness nearly unnerved him. "What's the matter? Cat got your tongue again? The least you could do is make some comment on my cooking. Just remember, all chefs are sensitive and our feelings are easily hurt."

She swallowed a gulp of tea and took a bite from the chocolate he held in his hand. At last she said, "Don't you think it would be better if you left me here and went to get help?"

"I couldn't do that. Absolutely couldn't even consider it." At least he was as quick in that response as he had been with some of his previous snide remarks.

"Why not? Probably I would be all right."

"It's the probably part I don't like. It's a long way to the nearest town. It might take me two days just to get there."

"Could you take me with you?"

"I thought about that, but I don't see how it could work."

She was silent for a long time, and as she sipped her tea, her eyes were aimed directly at him and unflinching. And he thought they looked very old. He took a bite of the chocolate, relishing the taste, but he soon became uncomfortable when he realized she was watching his every move. Finally he asked, "Why are you looking at me like that? If you have something to say, say it."

There he was being snappish again. Fathead. Why not just tell her it seemed like it might be a nice day outside?

"I am looking at your face. You are a very handsome man."

He knew now that instinct had caused him to keep the bad side of his face turned away from her. At the airport his helmet had covered some of his affliction, and since then, when her pain and the dim light in the shelter allowed her to see anything at all, she could only have seen flashes of his misfortune.

He deliberately turned his full face toward her. The chocolate had given him a huge jolt of strength. For an instant he thought he could conquer the world. "Look at me now." He could not believe his daring. "Still think so?"

He watched her eyes, seeking the revulsion he was certain would be there, but he found only the same determined and peculiarly ancient stare.

"Yes, I think so, Jerry. You are beautiful because you are. I know all the things you have done for me. I want to ask you to do something else."

"Okay. Whatever it is, I'll do it."

"Don't leave me here to die by myself."

He caught his breath. He must be hallucinating. "What in the sam hill are you talking about, girl? The way I have it figured, you aren't going to die for eighty, maybe ninety or more years. You'll be an old lady with a hundred great-grandchildren. Besides, they're bound to come for us today, or if not today, maybe tomorrow. All we have to do is sit right here and wait."

"And slowly starve, Jerry? You haven't had anything at all to eat since we came here."

"I just had a big chunk of chocolate. I feel like a tiger."

"You had two bites. That isn't enough for a grown-up."

"What makes you so sure? Are you a nutritionist or something? Why, in the big war some prisoners didn't eat for a week. As long as we can make water from snow we'll be fine."

"Did you fly in the big war?"

"No. That is, I didn't get overseas where the shooting was. I trained in Texas, and when I was through, so was the war."

"Then you have never killed any person?"

"No." If I were being completely honest, he thought, I might qualify that. There was always, and would forever be, that student he had failed to save from himself.

"If they don't come today, I want you to go by yourself."

"I thought you said never to leave you."

"I won't be here." She paused, but her eyes remained fixed on his. "You have that gun," she said softly.

He took her face in his hands and looked at her for a long time without saying anything. Finally he pinched her cheeks very gently and said, "Listen to me, my little friend. I don't know what kind of fairy tales you were brought up on, but you have no right to even think that way. If your back wasn't hurt, believe me, I would spank your bottom so you would never forget it. I never want to hear another word on the subject. We are in this together. Is that perfectly clear?"

What kind of world was this when an eleven-going-on-twelve little girl asked a guy to put her out of her misery with a gun? He saw that she was weeping, and he took the sleeve of the teddy bear and dabbed at her tears. "And don't bawl."

He looked about the shelter, frantic for something to divert her thoughts. "Heather, listen!" He scrambled across to the mailbag. "Let's read some more letters. We'll hear about other people's troubles and ours won't look like anything. We'll think we're on vacation."

He took a handful of letters and held them out to her. She hesitated, yet he saw that she was making an effort to recapture her spirit. She selected one and he opened it without taking his eyes from hers. Distraction . . . anything to get things rolling again. She absolutely must be forced to realize the real world was still there. So must I, he thought. This shelter is only a long nightmare. I am going to keep her reading letters all day if I have to. Maybe her back will improve and maybe her mind won't go off the trolley. Maybe we can wait this thing out in style.

She studied the letter a moment. "Gee, this is nice handwriting, and it isn't even big loopish stuff like in the Palmer method." She flipped a page at him so he could see it. Then she held it to her nose and sniffed. "It smells good. That's what I'm going to have someday, Jerry. Really smelly stationery."

Good, good, the pilot thought. She is planning. Now she has something to hold on to. He wished he could feel the same.

"Here we go," Heather said with new brightness. "It starts out, 'My dear Mrs. Tracy. This is the most difficult letter I have ever written in my twenty-five years of life, yet I feel it imperative to share our mutual sorrow. I suppose there was nothing really so different about your Jim and my Jim except his capacity for love, but I shall never be sure. Certainly he was a most extraordinary man. Forgive me now that he is gone if I feel the need to write to you. Please be tolerant of this stranger you may despise because I was for such a short time another Mrs. Tracy.

" 'It seems to me no one can teach anyone how to love. We learn of love's existence very early, but where and how do we learn to give it? I must confess confusion now that I have been able to take out my love for Jim, hold it tenderly in my hand, and look at it. I don't know why Jim was killed and I survived. I've tried to think why and only become further confused. In time I guess the physical Jim will fade from my memory and perhaps I will meet another man with whom I'll want to share this precious life. Yet even if that happens, Jim will always be with me in the gift of love he left, and I will be eternally grateful for his legacy.

" 'Is it not so that every person creates his own version of love? Some allow it to wilt and others nurture it to full strength. And usually they build a fortress that cannot be destroyed. Now I realize that love is available to anyone who will open his arms to receive it. Jim taught me that, and he was dealing with a shy and rather wary apprentice.' "

Heather took a deep breath and whispered that on this page there were some words she had never seen before—even in English class, for heaven's sake. He urged her to read on.

"Okay then, here goes.... 'After the two years I had with Jim, I think the love between a man and a woman is like one of those old-fashioned ka-lei-do-scopes ... the kind of cardboard tube you look in one end and turn and find you can create different patterns. Some cause you to actually cry out in such delight, you never stop to think they are all created out of the same crystals. Our love was like that—as I suppose yours was—sometimes joyful, all red and yellow dancing across each other, and other times soft and serene, with mauve and deep blue-green. It just depended on how we turned the crystals that day, or hour, or minute.

" 'Just before that awful night, Jim asked me if I would mind

living in Ireland if his job took him there, and I said, "Well I don't care where we live . . . on the moon or Manitoba." As long as we were a unit, my happiness would remain unbounded. At that time I could not imagine living without Jim and certainly never thought I might have to. Then so suddenly there was no choice.

" 'Don't worry, Mrs. Tracy. I'm not going to show up at your front door just so we can have a good cry together. From what Jim told me I gather you must be a very private person, and it is very difficult for relative strangers to share grief. Also, at this time you would not need my tears, which are stubborn about drying. But I will stop crying—I *will*. I think people who know how to love are able to conquer anything they desire.

" 'Also, Mrs. Tracy, I hardly think you need a sermon on love, as so recently discovered by a twenty-five-year-old late bloomer. This little epistle is intended as just a reaching out to touch the woman I never knew, but who shared Jim. Sincerely, Janet.' "

CHAPTER SEVEN

MORAVIA was elated.

This morning, the kind of morning to reinforce a man's faith in some kind of supreme manager, proved the weather people were worse than economists at their predictions. Marvelous, he thought, as he surveyed the cloudless, pale blue winter sky through his office window. Now, by God, there could be a proper search for number Fourteen. All along the line to Elko the weather was reported clear, and Moravia knew from the rising barometer that it was almost certain to remain so for a few days.

"All right, my friends, let us proceed," he muttered. He was watching the flashing propeller blades of two Stearmans warming up on the ramp in front of the hangar. The pilots were already in their cockpits, bundled to the eyes against the cold. They were good men and not encumbered with aeronautical doubts like Stiller. If they saw anything worthwhile in the area where Stiller had thought he might have seen "something," Moravia knew nothing would prevent them from further investigation.

The Aviator

Two additional Stearmans would be searching out of Elko to the south, east, and west just to cover the chance that Fourteen might, for reasons unknown, have chosen to fly in one of those directions. The two remaining Stearmans would handle the mail.

Now that the weather was clear, four National Guard De Havillands were due in Pasco by noon. Moravia planned to dispatch them southward from Pasco. A ranger who lived east of Pendleton, Oregon, had called to say he had seen something flashing on one of the summits. A rock reflecting the wear of a glacier fifty thousand years ago? A bird with a white wing? Who knew? Even the most improbable must be investigated.

They must all hurry, he thought. The days were too short in these latitudes, and clear weather brought its own curse. Tonight would bring the stars and, just as surely for the homeless, agonizing cold.

THE pilot was silent for a long time after Heather had finished reading the letter. It was as if he were waiting for her answers to all the questions now confusing his thoughts. He glanced at his watch. How did it get to be ten o'clock? Another day already well worn and still he had not accomplished anything.

Now where were all his brave projects? Where were the necessities to keep them alive, and most of all, where were his guts to keep this awkward situation from calamity?

Heather also remained silent, fingering the letter.

"What did you think of the letter?" he asked finally. He wanted to hear her say it was the most intriguing one she had ever read, because it most certainly had been written by a woman he longed to know better.

"I think she must be the opposite of you," Heather said. "She doesn't squirm around when she talks about stuff like love. She just opens herself and lets it go. I like that."

"What was her name again?"

"Janet. What I want to know is, who is the other Mrs. Tracy?"

"I gather she must be the mother-in-law."

Heather studied the letter a moment, then she said, "No . . .

maybe not, because she says it is very difficult for relative strangers to share grief."

"She called her Mrs. Tracy, didn't she?"

"Okay, but she says right in the beginning that they have never met. Doesn't a wife have to meet her husband's mother?"

"Not necessarily."

"Well, that's a funny way to be married. When I get my husband I want to know his mother. She might be a witch."

"And I say your wisdom is beyond your years. When are you going to tell me the story of your life?"

"All eleven years and eight months of it? You want me to tell you how I got an A on my geography exam and I didn't even know where Bolivia was?"

Sunlight flowed through the parachute silk, and the pilot took this as a signal of overall improvement. The weather was clearing, and more important, the girl was beginning to think of the future. If she could be locked on to this letter, or anything else tangible, then that niggling notion that she was telling him what she thought he wanted to hear would go away.

"Do you suppose," Heather asked, "that Mr. Tracy could have had two wives?"

"I doubt it. Didn't she say they were going to live in Ireland? She wouldn't write that to another wife, and besides, the husband doesn't sound like a bigamist."

"What's a bigamist?"

"You might say it is a man or woman who can't count."

"Listen to this, Jerry. She says she is just reaching out her hand to touch the woman she never knew, but who shared Jim." She stared at him over the top of the letter and asked him what he thought of that.

He said, "Maybe she was a former wife."

"You mean the husband was divorced from the first Mrs. Tracy?"

"Could be." He was becoming bored with Heather's curiosity and her preoccupation with only one of the letter's revelations. He tried to remember what the woman had written about love.

"I've got it!" Heather's voice rose triumphantly. "Right here it says, 'Please be patient and tolerant with this stranger who was for such a short time *another* Mrs. Tracy.' She has to be his second wife writing to his first!"

Heather held out the envelope. "The person's name is Mrs. James Tracy, and she lives in Portland." She then slipped the letter back in the envelope and said, "You're not paying attention. It's no fun if you don't care what the letter says."

It was true. He had not been listening. Instead his ears were tuned to a sound he thought might be a trick of the wind. It was almost inaudible against the soft whirring of the pine boughs, but it was there. He sat with his head cocked, his whole body tense, his eyes roving as if he were examining every seam in the parachute overhead.

"What are you looking at?" Heather asked.

"I'm not looking at anything. Do you hear what I hear?"

"I don't hear anything."

He began a very slow crawl toward the entrance, pausing often, listening, his head tilted toward the silk above him.

Heather called out to him. "Where are you going?"

"Shut up!" he said harshly. "Don't make a sound."

As he continued toward the entrance he heard a stifled whimper behind him. He ignored it, he had to, because another sound had absorbed his entire being. "I think," he whispered, "it's very far away, but I *think* I hear an airplane."

MORAVIA was on the telephone with Elko, and he was reasonably satisfied with what he heard. "We had trouble starting one of the Stearmans. A magneto. So we dragged out an old Swallow. By the time we got everything squared away it was eight o'clock."

"Are they all in the air now?" Moravia asked.

"Yes. But Montgomery, who is flying the Swallow, has never flown one before."

"Is he nervous?" Moravia was mindful of the Curtiss K-6 engines powering the Swallows. Their record for reliability was dismal.

"He says he'll fly a manure shovel if he can just find Jerry."

"All right. How long have the planes been off the ground?"

"About an hour. They should return for fuel about noon. I'll call if they've seen anything."

"Call me anyway. Get them back in the air as soon as their tanks are full."

"They'll need some rest. They'll be cold."

"Not as cold as Jerry." Moravia was pleased that he had hesitated only briefly in referring to the pilot as Jerry rather than Fourteen. He was making progress toward a new portrait in his mind. He saw now the erasure of a mere number, and in the man he had just called Jerry he viewed the refreshing arrival of a human being who also knew what it was to suffer personal defeat.

"Keep searching until dark," Moravia said into the phone.

BY THE time he had emerged from the shelter the pilot knew that he was not just imagining a sound he longed to hear. His every instinct concentrated on what he thought would probably be inaudible if he had not been listening for it. For two nights and almost two days he had literally dreamed of this moment.

The sound faded and again there was silence except in the pine trees. He thought the wind must be fighting the sound waves and destroying normal echoes. Sweet music swept away from an audience of one. He ran a few steps through the snow. What for? Was the music any clearer here—ten paces from the shelter? He paused and listened again, craving to hear the rhythmic beat of an aircraft engine. He could hear it in his mind, the lazy reverberations as the propeller slapped at the air, yet he knew he was not really hearing anything except the squeaking of his leather jacket as he turned his head slowly back and forth.

The girl would be upset, because he would have to tell her it was a false alarm. And she would probably whimper worse than ever, and he would begin to think seriously about jumping off the mountain now—before rather than after he went crazy.

The fire signal was ready to go, but it had to be a one-time event. It would take him more than half a day to gather enough good wood for a second one. He had piled his best wood in a pyramid below the shelter. The oil to pour on it was in a crude container he had made out of a piece of exhaust stack. It was ready near the pyramid and should make fine black smoke that a blind man could see for miles. That is, if the oil was not too congealed to burn, and if the gasoline he had salvaged would make the green wood burst into flame. There were a lot of ifs.

Yes! There . . . over there! It was. It absolutely was. And the sound was approaching. No question.

He reached in his pocket for the box of matches, then remembered he had left them in the shelter. In his glove. To keep them dry. *Now* was when the matches should have been handy.

WHENEVER she was alone like this the idea kept returning. Miss Phipps, who taught world history, would understand. Once she told the class about Joan of Arc and how she chose to be burned at the stake rather than keep on fighting.

Heather tried to remember who Joan was fighting, but failed. She did know that this pain was what it must have been like for people who were burned at the stake. Heather of Arc. No one in the entire world could ever, *ever* say she was a crybaby.

Every time the idea came back it was stronger than before. Heather stared at the place where Jerry had been sleeping. The fabric from the airplane was still rumpled where his body had pressed against it. The mail sack he used as a pillow was at the far corner, and protruding just a little from beneath it was a piece of leather.

No one in the whole world, no matter how much they wanted to be brave, could stand this pain. Like Joan of Arc some people were better off dead. She reached out and pulled the fabric toward her. It slid easily over the packed snow, and the mail sack with the leather underneath it moved with the fabric. When it came within reach, her fingers closed on the holster. She brought it up slowly and held it in front of her. Then she took the gun out of the holster and shivered because it was so cold to her touch.

She thought about Jerry. No one would ever believe what an extra, extra special man he was. Like the Prince of Wales, or one of the great men Miss Phipps talked about. He should go down the mountain while he still had time. Of all the people in the whole entire world that anyone could possibly think of, he should know that someone loved him. Like one of those kaleidoscopes? It just depended on how the crystals fell into place. People who knew how to love could accomplish anything—just like Mrs. Janet Tracy said in her letter.

She experimented by poking the muzzle of the gun at her heart. Then she tried it against her forehead and flinched at its coldness. A different kind of pain.

Now the engine sound was unmistakable and it was approaching rapidly. In his haste the pilot fell down twice as he struggled up the rise toward the shelter. He knew he had a minute, maybe two, to fetch the matches. Then it might be too late. His anxious mind suddenly seized upon the fact that he was hearing an in-line engine. It sounded like a Curtiss K-6, which meant that it would be on a Swallow. What difference did that make when seconds were wasting? Get the matches and forget everything else!

He scrambled quickly into the shelter. Once inside, he raised his head and looked into the muzzle of his gun.

"Go away," Heather said quietly. "Go back outside, Jerry."

He hesitated, unbelieving. His body remained motionless. "What do you think you're doing?"

"Go away, I said. I mean it, Jerry."

He watched her eyes and saw that she was totally serious. "Heather. That thing is dangerous. Put it down."

He started to reach for the gun, but he saw that her finger was on the trigger. "Heather. There's an airplane coming. I've got to build a fire right this minute. It may be our only chance." He tried to keep his voice even, but he heard the fear in it.

"I love you, Jerry. I want you to live. Please go away. . . ."

He knew then exactly what he had to do, and he forced a smile. "Okay. If that's the way you want it." He moved as if to back out of the shelter, then halted. "Can I get the matches?"

She nodded slightly. He reached for the glove and took out the box of matches. Momentarily he turned away from Heather. Then he spun around, whipped the glove hard, and knocked the gun from her hand. He grabbed it instantly, tucked it in his belt, and started for the entrance. Panting from his exertions, he glanced back once. He was going to say, "You are a naughty girl." Then he saw she was weeping.

He scurried out of the shelter and ran down the slope to the pyramid of wood. He tried to force himself to think only of a fire, but his thoughts tore at his concentration. Was there anything else in the shelter she could use to harm herself?

The engine sound was getting louder. As he took a match from the box, he stole a glance at the sky. Bare, blue. There was still time for a fine fire.

He struck the match. It fizzed, but failed to ignite. He repeated his action and was appalled to see the same result. What kind of matches did they make these days? He saw that his hand was trembling. Calm down and stop panting. There is still time. He forced himself to breathe slowly as he struck a third match and cupped his hands around the feeble flame. All right, this was it. Here now was man's first and best friend, ready to start a fire that would signal a true friend aloft. He would have to be stone-blind not to see the black smoke that was about to be.

The sound of the engine echoed against the side of the mountain and seemed to fill the entire area with its resonance, yet he dared not look up from his task. All his attention was on the match, and he held it protectively until a few wood chips took fire. He reached for the oil container, determined not to pour the oil on too soon. That would be the dunce act of all time, he told himself—build a fine fire and then douse it at just the wrong time.

He stole a glance at the sky. It *was* a Swallow. Coming right on target. It could not miss. Hallelujah.

He poured the oil on the fire and threw the container aside. He rose to his feet and jumped up and down in the snow, waving his arms and shouting as if the Swallow's pilot could hear him.

The airplane passed across the sun and he was blinded momentarily. Then he was able to see it again, so close he could see the

oil stains along the belly of the fuselage. He yelled until he became giddy, clasping his hands together and raising them over his head in a victory salute. Finally he waited impatiently for the first hint of the airplane's banking, but the Swallow continued in a straight line, directly toward the summit of the mountain.

The pilot glanced at the fire. There was a good column of brown smoke rising from the pyramid, even though there was little flame. He looked up, his hands still poised above his head. The Swallow will turn now, he thought. He is just checking for possible downdrafts before he commits himself. He saw in his mind how the Swallow would bank and then descend in a graceful dive, and whoever was flying it would give him an unforgettable buzz job. Then he would fly back to Elko and give the Stearman's position on the mountainside, and a rescue party would be on the way. It was going to be that simple.

He found that he was holding his breath. The Swallow dipped a wing to the left, and he thought it was the start of a bank. But then the right wing went down and came back up. He thought it must be rough up there. Okay, my friend. I've got plenty of time.

"Hey, wait a minute!" The pilot began a frantic waving. For the Swallow continued on a straight-line course to the north. "Come on . . . !" The pilot's mouth fell open and a strange cry escaped him as he watched the airplane continue toward the summit, glisten for an instant in the sun, and then disappear.

Suddenly there was no sound of an engine. Suddenly there was only the immaculate sky, the sun, and the mountain. He stared at the peak for a long time, hoping the Swallow would reappear, although he knew that it would not. How could anyone fail to see a man standing in the snow on the bare side of a mountain? How could anyone miss seeing that great brown pillar of smoke?

He dropped his hands and bowed his head. I must be very, very small down here, he thought . . . an invisible runt. He stared at the smoke and knew that he had been too late in starting the fire. By two or three precious minutes. He looked at the summit again and down into the valley below. And he began to laugh, softly at first and then more forcefully. His eyes filled with tears as he shook his fist at the sky. And he yelled with all the power left to him. "Right! I *know!* I am a nothing, a for damn sure nothing."

He continued to laugh as he shuffled up through the snow toward the shelter. And he noticed that his merriment sounded almost exactly like Heather's whimpering.

CHAPTER EIGHT

He lay on his back, using the mail sack for a pillow. His eyes were wide open and he was staring at the fading pattern of light on the parachute silk above him, forcing himself to visualize the present activities of the Swallow's pilot. He would probably be having coffee in Elko or Boise or even Pasco, and he would be explaining to Moravia, or someone who would relay the fact, that he had not seen anything of special interest.

Who could have foreseen that a two- or three-minute delay in starting a fire might be so crucial? Who would ever imagine that a little girl would even think about killing herself? And how could any pilot miss seeing so much smoke against snow? Easy. Pilots were not equipped with eyes in the back of their heads. And the Swallow might not even belong to the line. It might have been a private aircraft or someone flying for the Forest Service. And its pilot would not necessarily have known anyone was lost. Why should he have bothered to look down?

If the Swallow had been sent out by Moravia, its pilot might now be saying, "I've been over that area, and I did not see a thing. It was a perfectly clear day, so I could see for a couple of miles on each side."

Would Moravia then ask the pilot if he had been able to see directly underneath him? Because of the location of the lower wing on the Swallow and the forward angle of view from the cockpit, visibility straight down was poor. Moravia had never flown Swallows. They came along after his flying days were over. Would he have asked if the pilot zigzagged so he would not miss anything, or just assume he would not fly in a straight line? Would a new man, say like Montgomery, who had never flown a Swal-

The Aviator

low, be so preoccupied he would not realize how much he was missing below until it was too late?

After the pilot of the Swallow made his report, it would be logical for Moravia to abandon this area and move on to another. He would be pressed for time, men, and airplanes, and he would say, "All right, let's get on with the search, because we have a whole lot of real estate to cover."

The pilot whispered to himself, "Blaming a little girl is not going to get you out of this fix."

Just then Heather called out to him. "What did you say, Jerry?"

"I didn't say anything."

"Jerry, I want that horse over there."

"You want what?" She was mumbling and still whimpering, and he thought he had certainly misunderstood her.

"I want that black horse. I've always wanted a black horse."

He crawled to her side and looked into her eyes. They were vacant of expression. "What's this about a horse?" he asked.

Heather pointed and screamed. "The one coming at us! It is going to run over us. Stop the horse, Jerry. Stop him before—"

She screamed again, and he covered her mouth with his hand. She bit his finger. He jerked his hand away.

"The horse, the big black horse," she repeated over and over again as he sucked at his bloody finger.

"You sure have sharp teeth," he said. He was so shocked at her behavior he barely felt the pain in his hand. How do you bring delirious people back to real life? Quick now, Doctor.

Her voice rose in another scream. Instinctively he clapped his hands over his ears. "Will you please stop screaming?" he asked as evenly as he could manage.

Heather shook her head violently and made a choking sound. He reached out to raise her head, but she pushed him away. Then she started to claw at her face and she mumbled, "Keep my horse from hurting me," over and over again.

As he pulled her hands away from her face, she tried to strike out at him, but she could only slap at his leather jacket. They struggled in silence, and he was astonished at her strength. When at last she subsided he pulled off his belt and tied her arms to her sides. When she realized her confinement, she began to sob violently, and for a long time she seemed not to hear his attempts to soothe her.

Finally she lay cradled in his arms, and he thought his reassurances sounded more like the mumblings of a madman. "Quiet down or the neighbors will complain. Sure we are in trouble, but haven't you ever heard about people who were shipwrecked and just sang until they were rescued? Sing, don't yell. Let's make that our motto."

He debated giving her another pain pill. But maybe they triggered her delirium. He felt her moist brow and decided that if she'd had a fever, it had now left her. He caressed her hair and could hardly believe the sound of his own voice as he told her, "I need you, Heather. I need you more than you could ever imagine."

She finally quieted, and soon he knew she was herself again. He removed his belt from her arms, and she smiled.

"Show me your dimples, but don't look so wise," he said.

Heather said, "I'm sorry to be such a troublemaker." She brightened slightly. "I've been thinking about Mrs. Tracy, and I think the second Mrs. Tracy wrote that letter about love to the first Mrs. Tracy because they both loved the same man. She was trying to share her trouble with her because she must need a friend."

"What are you, a psychiatrist or a fortune-teller?"

"Mrs. Gooch says I'm forthright. My mother told her I have powers of deduction because it runs in the family."

"Who is Mrs. Gooch?"

"My math teacher. May I please see the letter again?"

He knew exactly where the letter was because he had placed it carefully in the pocket of his jacket. His intention had been to read it again. He thought it odd that now it had become *the* letter, while all the others were of little interest.

He held it out to her, and after studying it a moment she said, "This is the part I like best—where she is telling about how she is going to stop crying. Right here she says people who know how to love are able to conquer anything they desire."

"Maybe she's right."

"Okay. How about if I pretend to be in love with you, then maybe I can stop being such a nuisance?"

"You're not a nuisance. What would I do without you?"

"If Mrs. Tracy can stop bawling, so can I. And if I can stop, maybe we can go down the mountain together."

"There are a lot of reasons why it's too risky."

She held out the letter. "Read it again, Jerry. I bet when she was in school Mrs. Tracy got *forthright* on her report card."

SOME hours later he estimated his physical strength and found it wanting. He reckoned he might have one more day at the most before he would be too weak to do anything but wait. And to wait, he thought, was to die.

Even now he rose only slowly from his fabric bed, and signals of his general lethargy were everywhere about him. When the pyramid fire had burned itself out he had not rebuilt it. Available wood seemed much too far away. The fire in the shelter had gone out twice, and each time he had been a long time reviving it. Soon he would find excuses not to leave the shelter.

He crawled outside, taking the letter with him. The sun had gone, and the snow squeaked beneath his boots as he walked. He noticed a new chill in the air, or was it hunger that so lowered his resistance? How he longed to be alone for a time, alone with the letter, which had somehow become the voice of a third party on the mountain. Camp Tracy, he thought. Will the second Mrs. Tracy please join us for dinner? We can offer you superb pine-needle tea, and I will split half my piece of chocolate with you.

He halted in the twilight and stood looking down at the distant valley below. There was no wind, and from the look of the sky he supposed there would be little chance of wind in the morning. Still, he must remember the snow would have a hard crust, and if he broke through that crust with his burden, then that might be the final calamity. Twenty miles to McDermitt at, say, half a mile per hour . . . say forty hours. That was almost two full days of plowing through heavy snow, if they were lucky.

He took the letter from his jacket pocket and began reading. Now he was sure he could visualize Janet Tracy. She would be small and spunky and dark-haired. Her words gave away her enthusiasm for all things. She would know humility because she obviously had the courage to censor herself for self-pity.

"These are the things," he said, "that I understand." He decided that Mrs. Tracy must also know what it was like to barely escape being killed, and he thought that people who knew what that was like were never the same again. After what he thought must be his tenth rereading, he found he particularly liked what she said about holding her love for her husband in her hand.

He folded the letter carefully, reinserted it in the envelope, and placed it in his jacket pocket. Suddenly he knew what he must do. There was a way to take Heather down the mountain—maybe. All of the risk was still there, but at least they could die trying.

He made his way back to the fuselage as quickly as he could. He would use the last of the twilight to see all of the things he had to conquer in the morning.

FAR to the west of the mountain, beyond the Quinn River and Desert Valley, a spur of warm, humid air had separated from a major low-pressure ridge flowing eastward over the Sierras. The spur developed into a small front and brought rain to regions that had only recently been buried in heavy snows.

The warm air seeped in during the night, enveloping the higher altitudes first and then flowing down into the valleys. The antelope and other wilderness creatures found the rain beneficial, since it quickly reduced the snow pack and made movement easier for grazing. But by dawn those animals, who were hungry and alert to every feeding opportunity, became wary. For now they heard familiar sounds, the hiss of small snowslides slithering down from the higher peaks and the occasional roar of big avalanches thundering down the mountains. The animals moved gingerly, heedful of the slightest uncommon alarm, for experience warned them of the new hazards. Their well-developed instincts urged them to avoid the southern sides of the mountain.

Long before the first light came through the parachute silk the pilot awakened. The girl was still asleep and he was grateful. There were three pills remaining, just enough, he hoped, to last her down the mountain. He rose to his knees and shivered uncontrollably. Had they really been on the mountain only three nights and two full days? It seemed like months since he had flown.

He crawled to the fire, and when he saw that the ashes were cold he debated starting another. It took such a long time, and every minute of this day would be precious.

He glanced at his watch and decided he had no choice. They would need water, and they might as well start with hot tea. Six o'clock. Now there would be no more waiting, and he thought, If what I am about to do is a mistake, then it will be my final mistake. But I am strong this morning, stronger than I have been since the landing. I am hungry as an animal, but I am still strong.

He started a little fire with the handful of chips he had saved from the previous afternoon. It smoked heavily, and he thought he might hear the girl complain, but she made no sound.

He crawled back to her, listened to her breathing for a moment, then kissed her gently on the cheek. A moment later he crawled outside and was disappointed in what there was of a dawn. All of the sky was covered with dark cloud. Yet it was warm, so very warm the snowflakes that struck his face melted instantly. Again he was grateful. Now he could work without gloves and his task could go much faster.

He returned to the fire with the landing-light receptacle full of snow. He piled several broken ribs from the Stearman's wing on the fire to make a fine blaze. There was no longer any need to keep them as an emergency supply. Then he awakened the girl. He asked her if she were going to lie in bed all day, and he called her lazybones. "Do you hurt too much to sit up?"

"Yes."

"But you have to be in a sitting position when I take you down the mountain."

She hesitated and after a moment pressed his hand with her fingers. "Then I will sit up."

"Are you ready for a test flight?"

She smiled and nodded, but he saw the fear in her eyes, and he thought, If she screams just once, then we are not going to be able to do it. "Do you want to try a pain pill first?"

She shook her head in refusal. He saw her lips were compressed in anticipation, her little jaw was thrust forward, and her hands were doubled into fists.

"All right, we'll take it very easy," he said as he slipped his hand beneath her shoulders. "Now, if you can't stand it, we'll have to think of something else." What else, he wondered? There was barely time and energy for what he had so carefully planned.

He watched her face as he lifted her shoulders very slowly. As the teddy bear fell from her he was reminded how small she really was. "All right, so far?" he asked.

She nodded affirmatively, but her lips were quivering and he knew she must be hurting. "Not much farther to go," he said, and he marveled that, at a moment like this, he instinctively kept the good side of his face toward her.

He paused. "You're almost there," he said. "Do you want to go for all the way?"

"Yes. I'm okay," she said, and her voice was so faint he could barely hear her.

He eased her forward another fraction of an inch. "Can you stand it? This is the approximate position you'll be in. If you can't hack it, we have to know now."

She swallowed, and he looked away from the distress in her eyes. He eased her slightly forward again and waited. "Well?"

"I can do it. I *will*."

"Congratulations." He eased her back to a prone position. "We'll have a big breakfast and then I have about an hour's work to do. Soon, my friend, we'll go down the mountain."

Her eyes filled with tears and he very much wanted to wipe them away. But he also thought, I must not weaken all through the hours to come. We can't win bawling together.

When the water was hot he made some pine-needle tea. Then he crawled back to Heather and asked her to hold the tea receptacle while he served the main course. He broke the last piece of chocolate in half and advised her to chew slowly since the portion was so small. They sipped alternately at the liquid, passing it back and forth between them with solemn formality. They said nothing to each other except with their eyes, and that, he thought, was quite enough. For he knew people who were about to put their lives on the line were rarely given to conversation.

When they had finished he told her to be patient and started his usual crawl for the entrance. He had just turned away from her when he halted. He listened to a rumbling sound outside the shelter. It grew in volume, then ceased abruptly.

"What was that?" Heather asked.

"I don't know."

"It sounded like a train going by. Every day at three o'clock the Union Pacific goes through Elko, and it sounds just like that."

"I hardly think that's what we heard."

He continued toward the entrance. He had never before heard such a sound and he did not like it.

His spirits rose as he emerged into the full light of the morning. How warm it was! And altogether it did not appear to be a bad day for their expedition. The peak of the mountain was obscured in cloud, yet the visibility in the lower slopes was good. He could see a hump of bare granite far below which previously had been covered with snow, and the dark configurations of the many streams were now clearly defined.

He crossed his fingers as he approached the Stearman's aft cockpit. Now, he thought, I will need a sackful of pure luck to accomplish phase one of my plan. He brushed the drifted snow away from the seat and the fastenings that secured it to the fuselage. And he thought, God Almighty, why did they have to build this airplane and everything in it so strong? Then, as he fingered the double retaining nuts and the six bolts that held the back of the seat to the airframe, he chided himself for being unreasonable as well as ungrateful. No, he decided, I would not vote for a less sturdy aircraft even if I never suspected I would have to put one down on the side of a mountain.

Thanks to Moravia's foresight he was not without resources. Yet the strength of the seat fastenings was going to make removing the seat difficult when the only tools available were a screwdriver, pliers, and crescent wrench. He had given himself one hour to accomplish the task. Almost two hours later, with bloodied knuckles, he removed the final nut, knocked away the last bolt, and heaved the seat out of the cockpit. He put it down in the snow and sat on it. He licked at his hands and remembered the actual weight of the seat was a factor he had neglected to include in his plans. Good God, it was heavy.

His scheme had been to fix the parachute straps to the seat, then slip his arms into them in the normal way. The rear side of the seat would rest against his back, with the seat facing away from him. Heather might be at least tolerably comfortable, and her weight would be evenly distributed. When he felt the need to ease the burden on his back, he would find something of equal height to the seat and back up to it. If Heather wanted to lie down, the harness could be slipped off his shoulders. Still, the weight of the seat, even without Heather in it, was shocking.

He sat in the snow trying to think of some way he could carry the girl without the seat, but everything he imagined was even less practical. He decided to dispense with the seat belt, which would save weight. Heather would have to hang on if the going got rough. Securing the parachute straps went more easily than he had expected, yet it was midmorning before he carried his creation to the shelter. Just outside, he prepared a waist-high mound of snow and placed the seat on top of it.

Weary from his exertions, he promised himself he would sit down and rest for five full minutes before he brought Heather out of the shelter. He had caught himself staggering occasionally, and he had experienced moments of vertigo which infuriated him. If he could only lie down and close his eyes for a short time, then maybe the dizziness would go away.

Suddenly he changed his mind about even a short delay. For at the opposite end of the plateau, where a gigantic jaw of granite projected from the mountain, he saw an ugly mass of snow and rock tumbling out of the upper cloud. It moved swiftly downward, topped like an ocean comber with a crown of froth, and vomited into the valley below. Moments later he heard the roar of its passing.

He went at once for Heather.

CHAPTER NINE

SOMETIMES Moravia thought his little operation might be a sort of leftover casualty station from the Great War to save the world for democracy. He was at his window again, brooding on the disappointments of the search for aircraft number Fourteen and the luckless man who had been its pilot.

Had been? Perhaps if he had been killed instantly, the kind of death every aviator preferred if it must come, then he was not so unlucky after all. Ever since Moravia's own first time aloft, the creed had always been, "If it's going to happen, I don't want any fire and I don't want things coming to pieces bit by bit with a long ride down while I watch it happen. Just let me go straight into a mountain or something, then one minute I will be and the next minute I will not be." It was not a prayer, Moravia mused, but it echoed the philosophy of every pilot he had ever known from his days in France to the present ominous-looking morning.

There was number Fourteen's face, of course, which had hardly been decorative to the establishment. Now beyond the window was the mechanic Rohrbach, missing one hand, thanks to the propeller of a Jenny. Long ago some fool student who was sitting in the cockpit became confused, although he claimed afterward to have misunderstood Rohrbach's command to make sure the magneto switch was off. Instead the student left it on while Rohrbach backed the propeller, and the damned OX-5 engine fired. The propeller removed Rohrbach's left hand, and he was very lucky his head did not follow the same route.

Moravia now saw Carson, known as "Kit," come into view. He was wearing his teddy bear and would be flying the regular morning mail, hopefully through to Elko. Carson was an old-timer. He had flown with Pershing in Mexico when the army was not at all certain what to do with airplanes, much less how to classify aviators. When he had finished his chore south of the border he had gone north to Canada, joined the Royal Flying Corps, and flown against the Germans with the likes of Billy Bishop and Quigley and McCall. He had been shot down, crashed between the lines, and spent the night in a shell crater. Sometime during the night he had gotten a whiff of mustard gas with no mask to protect him, and because of a long wait before he was hospitalized he had eventually lost one lung.

At least, Moravia thought, Carson's missing anatomy did not show, and visitors to the line, including those post-office inspectors, who stuck their noses into everything, would not be further convinced that the business of flying was no business at all.

Moravia returned to his desk and stared at the map that covered it. There were now large areas which he had crosshatched in pencil. These were the squares his pilots had flown over and presumably seen everything below. And reported nothing of interest. There were still some considerable areas where number Fourteen might have gone down—the Strawberry Mountains to the southwest of Baker, Oregon, for example, although it seemed incredible that he would have strayed so far off course.

Presently the National Guard De Havillands were searching around Pendleton, Oregon, and would work south during the day. Two of the locally based Stearmans were already over the Blue Mountains and should be returning soon for refueling and further assignment—unless, of course, they spotted Fourteen.

Moravia heard a discreet knock on his door. He turned to see Stiller standing in the doorway, his teddy bear draped over his arm and his helmet and goggles in hand.

"Good morning," Stiller said in his guarded way, and Moravia thought that of all his charges this man, who bore not a scratch from his profession, was probably the most severely wounded.

"I didn't know you were scheduled to fly today," Moravia said.

"I'm not, but I will if you want." Stiller moved into the room warily, as Moravia remembered he did everything.

"I've been thinking," Stiller said, "and I talked it over with the wife and she suggested I see you about it if I really feel that way."

What way? Moravia mused. Now, in the midst of what may be a tragedy, my life is going to be illuminated by whatever Stiller's wife thinks ought to be done. Remarkable that she has loosed her silken chains long enough for her precious mate to come to the airport on his day off. "What's on your mind?" Moravia asked.

"Well, I've been up most of the last couple of nights worrying. I told the wife about that flight I had when I *thought* I really might have seen a piece of an airplane north of Capitol Peak. Well, the more I discussed it with her, the more certain I became that I did see something. Then last night when the lights were out I found I could visualize things better, and now I am ninety per cent sure I did see something down through that hole."

For a long moment Moravia managed to remain silent. He resisted the temptation to describe in a series of colorful phrases exactly what he thought of Stiller's character. Instead he bent over the map and beckoned Stiller to join him. "Show me again where you think you were."

Stiller made a circle on the map with his finger. "I was somewhere in here. I am sure of that."

"Okay. I'll train the morning's mail. You take the last airplane we have and get yourself back there. By afternoon you should have a lot of company, because as they become available I'm going to send every airplane we've got to join you."

And just in case you become wishy-washy about having a good look this time, Moravia thought, I will put a bird dog right on your tail. For that job I will send Carson, who has already used up most of his lives and does not baby those he has left.

NEAR the end of the plateau the pilot halted momentarily and looked back at the shelter he had created. From even this little distance it was not nearly as imposing a structure as he had assumed. Now it appeared to be only a small scratching on the snow-covered mountainside. He could see the folds of the parachute draped over the fuselage and a piece of the Stearman's tail sticking

up, but the wings were so concealed by the trees, he had to reassure himself they were not just two irregularities in the snow.

"Say good-by to your happy home," he said over his shoulder.

"Aloha," Heather said.

"Where in the world did you get that?"

"My uncle lives in Hawaii and when he came to see us last summer he was always saying it. That's good-by in Hawaii."

"Do you ever forget anything you're told?"

"No. Especially not if I like it."

"How are you doing back there otherwise?"

"I'm still here. Am I too heavy?"

"I'm glad you've been on a diet."

They were able to talk lightly throughout the first hour, and then the silences between them became increasingly longer. In time he knew the effects of the pain pill he had given the girl just before he hefted her to his back were wearing off. It had always been the same, first the silence, then the little whimperings, and finally the agonized screams. There was one pill left.

While the sun was at its zenith their descent remained surprisingly easy. The pilot found a gully leading off the plateau, and the footing was good until it steepened and joined a streambed. Here there were countless huge rocks and boulders interlaced with brush and broken trees all swept together. He realized nervously that the debris must have been left by a recent avalanche.

He looked back at the hulking mountain. It appeared more sinister than ever. Turning again, he saw that the jumble of rock and forest he must now negotiate was strewn across the bottom of a natural chute. He had not rested since they left the plateau, but this was no place to linger. Across the chute was what seemed from a distance to be easier going. Less than two hundred yards away was a long slope, clear of trees and angling gently downward. Now the afternoon sun polished the virgin snow of the slope, and it appeared to be no more than a few minutes trudging around the hodgepodge of obstacles. Once there, he would rest.

Two hours passed and they were still in the chute. It seemed that every time he thought he had found a way across, some insurmountable object stood in his way and forced him to retreat. The stream flowing in the chute was the principal villain. He was afraid to cross where it was deep, and where it was shallow it ran so fast he thought it might knock him off his feet. With the weight of Heather and the chair he doubted if he could rise again.

He checked his watch. Two o'clock. They were already three hours behind his hoped-for schedule, and he estimated they had made less than two miles of progress. He listened to the rumble of another avalanche; so many had shaken the silence that he had almost ceased to notice them. He knew his strength was ebbing fast, but he was committed now, and unless he continued, this ugly ravine could become their tomb.

"Heather," he said quietly, "we are not doing very well."

"Are you very tired?" she asked.

"No. I'm fine." He knew nothing would be gained by telling her the truth.

"I've been thinking about the letter," she said. "I especially like that part where she says every person creates his own version of love. When I think about that I forget my back, because . . . well, if a person uses a little imagination, which Miss Livingstone says I have plenty of, that just might describe you and me."

"I take it Miss Livingstone is one of your teachers?"

"No. She's our next-door neighbor, and I don't think she knows much about love, because she's an old maid."

"Aren't you being sort of rough on Miss Livingstone?"

"Yes. I know I shouldn't be, because she's very nice, even if love has not been her specialty."

He joggled the seat badly as he worked his way along a rock ledge that promised to provide a new exit from the chute. He heard her cry out, and then she stifled the sound.

Hoping to distract her, he asked, "Does Miss Livingstone discuss her personal life with you?" There was no reply, and he thought, I must ignore whatever is happening behind me. The only thing that counts is to get out of this ravine before dark.

Later he heard her voice. "Jerry, are there people who specialize in love?"

"You sure are a question box. I don't know how to answer that." And, he thought, I don't have the strength left even if I did know.

"I don't want to be like Miss Livingstone."

"No chance. You won't be."

"According to that letter from the second Mrs. Tracy, I guess there are different kinds of love and you can take your pick."

"I'll have to think about that for a while." He would not, he knew. He must not permit himself to think about anything whatsoever except getting down this damned mountain.

As he worked his way cautiously from boulder to boulder and around the ravaged trees, he sensed that he was no longer entirely himself. While he seemed to have command of his body, his mind wandered out of control; he was no longer able to consider the distance they had to go as real.

He moved automatically. The dull aches caused by the parachute straps digging into his shoulders became almost intolerable. I cannot go on like this forever, he thought. At last he found a way across the stream, and Heather asked if she could have a drink of water, so he backed up to the end of a fallen tree until it took the weight of the seat. He eased off the shoulder straps and moved around the tree until he could see her face. And for a moment her blue-green eyes held him spellbound. She said, "You're so tired. I am so sorry for you...."

He reached down impulsively and took her hands in his. And he could not help himself, although he knew he must be hallucinating, when he brought them to his lips. "You are a beautiful woman," he heard himself saying, "and I love you very much."

He saw her attempt to smile and heard her say, "I love you, Jerry, and I hope we will always be together."

He moved quickly to the stream and caught up some water in his cupped hands. He brought it back and tipped his hands slowly as she drank.

He returned to ease his own thirst, and as he bent over the stream he saw his face reflected in the water. He pulled back. He had forgotten his face. He had thought he was like other men—momentarily.

He closed his eyes, bent his head for a gulp of water, and stood up. He returned to Heather and found that she had been transformed. Now she was only an unhappy-looking little girl bundled in an overlarge flying suit. "Are you ready for some more walking?" he asked flatly. He did not welcome the irritation in his voice, but it was there.

"Can I have a pill?"

"No. You're turning into a junkie."

He squatted until he could slip into the shoulder straps. He rose slowly until he felt her weight, then stood up.

He heard her ask, "What's a junkie?"

Still irritated, he answered gruffly, "None of your business."

He started down the open slope as rapidly as he dared. Between the creaking of his leather jacket and his own labored breathing he thought he heard the girl weeping. He did not pause but continued downward, his shadow long on the snow.

Never again, he thought, never again will I allow myself such pipe dreams.

CHAPTER TEN

CARSON was the last pilot to leave Moravia's office. The others had reported in or telephoned after they had landed, with almost identical findings. They had all spied the wreckage, but it was Carson who best described what he had seen.

He had stood before Moravia's desk, pulling at his cold, purple nose, still in his teddy bear and boots, while he said, "I must have circled the wreckage twenty times, and I buzzed what was left close enough to wake the dead—pardon me, wake anybody in the world. I knocked the place up at about fifty feet, and I'm damned sure if anybody was half listening, they woulda heard me. I saw the wings. They were smashed up between two trees. Then there was the fuselage with his chute hung over it, and it was all smashed. It would be a miracle if anybody got out of that one."

"But weren't there tracks in the snow?"

"The light was very flat when I finally got there, so it was hard to tell. But I did see a place where it looked like he might have built a fire. But one thing is for sure. There is no sign of life anywhere around there now."

"It seems to me that if he was strong enough to rig his parachute over the fuselage, he must have been mobile."

"Maybe. But the chute could have opened on impact and spread itself around. I damned near caught a wing tip trying to get an angle where I could check to see if he was still in there, but the fuselage was on its side, so it was hopeless."

"But it did look like he built a fire?"

"It sure looked like it, but everything is so covered with snow that even when I slowed down to sixty miles an hour it was impossible to confirm anything except that it was Jerry's airplane. I could see the fourteen on the tail. No question."

Moravia lit a Caporal, sucked the smoke into his lungs, and coughed gently. It would now be his unhappy duty to call the passenger's grandparents, and her parents in Elko, and inform them the airplane had been found. What else? That both occupants were undoubtedly dead? They would have died without pain, of course. Whenever Moravia had anything to do with notification of next of kin, the relatives were never told the truth about the manner in which their beloved had actually departed. In this case he supposed he would follow custom. The pilot and his passenger had died instantly and painlessly.

As for Jerry, the man without a home, there would not even be the need for that. Moravia thought that he had best stop by his room and see if there were any clues to people who might be slightly interested that Jerry, whose last name Moravia was ashamed to discover had been forgotten until now—it was Amity, what a name for a man so out of harmony with the rest of humanity—the man who was flying number Fourteen, has, you may be relieved to know, perished without suffering. Not good enough. Without *excessive* suffering.

"There are times," Moravia said, snorting smoke through his nostrils, "when I truly hate this business."

"I understand," Carson said, and Moravia knew that he did.

Carson had left then, saying he was going down to Fred's Place, the local speakeasy, and take on some whiskey.

Moravia sat alone and in silence until it was dark in his office. Finally he sighed and switched on his desk light, because he knew he would soon be required to answer certain questions, and he wanted to be prepared. He made a series of phone calls and finally located a Maxwell Foster at his home in Reno, Nevada, and told him of finding the wreckage. "Since you're chief of the forest district, I would like to know how soon you can bring down the bodies . . . that's assuming there are any."

"Wait a minute. I'm not even sure that's in my territory."

"And if it is not, are you telling me that you would ignore the situation?"

"You don't have to be so testy. I wouldn't consider sending a party up into that country until late spring anyways."

"Why not?"

"It's too dangerous. Avalanches, for one thing."

"The Forest Service is financed by the taxpayers and that includes your salary, Mr. Foster. We cannot leave those people up in the mountains until it is convenient and comfortable to bring them down. They have relatives. . . ." At least, one of them has, Moravia thought sourly.

"I would have to get authorization from Washington and that takes two weeks, maybe a month."

Moravia wiggled the Caporal between his lips so violently he spilled ashes on his sweater vest. Someday, he thought, the world will be populated entirely by bureaucrats, because all the real people will do away with themselves in frustration.

"Very well, Mr. Foster," he said slowly. "We will send our own party to the wreckage. And be advised that any assistance you might be inclined to offer will be considered a hindrance."

Moravia hung up the phone and decided he felt much better. Now, he thought, it will do no harm to procrastinate. Bad news is easier to receive in the morning than at night. Furthermore, the bearer should be composed himself, lest his private sorrow multiply the grief of those entitled to it. They have lost a daughter, he thought, and I have lost a son, and the combination is volatile.

I will wait, Moravia thought, at least until morning.

He turned out the light, but did not move from his desk chair. He sat in the darkness for a long time, wiping at his eyes frequently and wondering why after so many years his missing leg still felt like it was there, and why it even hurt when anger or sadness took him over.

ALTHOUGH the twilight lingered, the pilot knew at last that he was lost. He paused at the mouth of a narrow canyon because he realized that to continue on he must climb. How could this be? It was now obvious that for the past several minutes he *had* been climbing. . . .

From a distance it had appeared that the floor of the canyon sloped downward and offered easy access to the valleys below. That had obviously been an illusion. The canyon was blind, terminating in a vertical rock face that rose at least a thousand feet. Not even a mountain goat, he thought, could find an exit from where he now hesitated.

"What's the matter, Jerry?" Heather asked.

Now he recognized a sensation he had not known for a long time. All airmen experienced it at least a few times in their careers, and once their feet were planted firmly on the ground they were given to smiling sheepishly and admitting they had been "surrounded by lostness."

"We are in deep trouble," he thought he was saying in a whisper, but instead heard his voice booming across the snow.

"Why? What's wrong?"

He was glad he could not see her face. It was easier to think of her as just a weight on his back, something he could not get rid of, no matter what. "You tell me how things are in the caboose," he said, hoping to divert her long enough to figure out how they had wound up surrounded by impossible obstacles. If he turned right and avoided the canyon, there was the edge of the slope and a straight drop of several hundred feet. If he turned left, he would hike right smack into the mountain itself.

"Things are fine back here, but it's getting dark."

"I can see that." He wondered how he was going to tell her they had no alternative but to turn back and retrace their route, which meant a long up-slope climb. But to where? Where had the wrong switch been turned? Even if he found it, he could not possibly climb all the way back to the shelter and start over again.

He turned around slowly and blinked at the trail his long descent had made in the snow. And he saw that he had not walked at all in an orderly fashion; the trail curved and recurved, snaking gracefully back up the mountain and finally disappearing over a rise. A drunk could walk a straighter line, he thought.

He was stunned at the prospect of reclimbing the mountain. It just could not be done by *anyone,* with or without wobbly legs. Maybe he should sit down and think things over.

He canceled the notion. Somewhere he had read something about men lying down in the snow and never getting up again.

"Jerry? What's the matter? Why don't you rest for a while?"

"I'm afraid we would go to sleep and never wake up."

As the vapor from his breathing formed clouds in front of his face, he supposed he must have said the wrong thing. But damn it, he needed to share his troubles with someone close to him, and this was a world populated by only two people.

"Do you still have the letter?" he heard her ask. "We could read it to each other and that would keep us awake . . . especially if we read the part about how every person has his own idea of love, sort of. . . ."

"My friend," he said, keeping his voice as casual as he could manage, "I'm not only sleepy, I'm lost. I guess we have to go back to the stream and find another way down."

She seemed not to have understood him. "When you were in school did you ever play that game where you canceled out the letters in another person's name that were the same as in your own name . . . and then you try to figure out if the other person happens to be the right person for you? A while ago I did it in my mind with your name and it came out perfectly, so I guess somebody here in the caboose loves you."

I must not slip away into another dreamland, he thought, or I will never come back. "You understand what I said about going back up where we came from?"

"Yes. Maybe it will help if you think of the letter."

He reached instinctively for his pocket, then dropped his hand. Somehow it was enough to know the letter was there.

He leaned toward the mountain and took a step forward, then another and another, bending far over to ease the strain on his shoulders. His heart was pounding alarmingly, he gasped for every breath, and clusters of tiny lights swam across his eyes. Darkness came while he was trudging upward, and he was grateful for what little illumination the stars offered.

They came to a forest, as he had anticipated, and still climbing, he listened carefully for the gurgling of the stream where he had given Heather a drink. There was no sound other than his own labored breathing and, God Almighty, there it was again, the stifled whimpering from behind. If she starts screaming, he thought, I'll just have to slap my ears until I'm deaf.

Deeper in the forest there was almost no light, and he nearly collided with trees only a few feet away. He heard her say, "Jerry? I think you're going wrong. We should be more over that way."

"What way? I told you we had to go back to the stream and start over."

"That's just it. The stream is over that way."

He paused. Holy simoleons, all I need right now, he thought, is advice from the peanut gallery. "Hey, you in the caboose. Why don't you just go to sleep and not confuse things—"

"The snow is much deeper here and it hasn't snowed. And besides, I saw the old trail turn off that way a while ago and I just thought, well, you knew a better way to get where you wanted to go. You don't have to get owly with me, Jerry."

"I'm not owly. I'm just tired. And I apologize."

He focused on the snow ahead of him and was shocked to see there were no tracks. He *had* wandered off. "All right, my friend," he said slowly, "you win. Which way were you pointing?"

"If you turn around and go back down not very far . . . I know where there's a big hump of something under the snow, and that's where you left the trail. The stream is off to your right."

When he found his original tracks again he resolved to follow the stream, no matter how his instincts argued. "I'm going to give you a medal," he said. "You are one smart little cookie."

"Remember my mother said I have a logical mind."

Slipping and stumbling in the darkness, he made his way around boulders and through the chill tributaries that fed the main stream. Each time he slipped he heard Heather cry out in pain, and when he said he was sorry that he could not help his clumsiness, Heather said she could not keep from bawling sometimes because her back hurt her so. "But I promise, crisscross my heart, that when we get out of this I will never never bawl again."

At last they left the forest behind and continued downward along a more open slope. They came to a flat area where the snow was deeper, and he decided it might be a road. Now, his mind drowsy, he heard Heather call to him as if from a great distance.

"Jerry! I see something. Back where we just came from. It looks as big as an elephant. Or something."

He turned around and saw a dark shape against the snow. After only a few steps he saw that it was a truck, a lumber truck, he thought, and momentarily allowed his spirits to soar.

Heather said, "If it's a truck, we must be on a road. And the road must lead to *someplace*."

"Okay, okay...." As he trudged toward the truck he found that he had a tendency to hold his breath. Just suppose he blew the horn and someone did appear to find out what was going on with his property? Just suppose he did live in a dry, warm cabin and they would be led to it and this awful endless night would end?

His hopes sank as he approached the truck and saw that the driver's window was broken and the cab was filled with snow. Yet still hoping, he reached through the window and pressed on the horn. The only sound was a whisper of wind through the cab.

As he leaned against the door he heard Heather say, "Well, I don't care if it is old and fallen to pieces. If it got up here somehow ... we can get down. That's logical."

CHAPTER ELEVEN

THE pilot knew they had been in a valley for a long time, a month, a year, possibly forever. As night came, the terrain had less slope to it, and in the easier going his strength was renewed. Yet there was no horizon, and he had ever more trouble keeping his equilibrium when he lost the stars. They were only occasionally visible through breaks in the overcast, and he thought that if he knew them better, he would be more confident he was proceeding in the right direction. He tried to keep the belt of Orion over his left shoulder, which should steer him in a westerly direction, but as the hours passed, it climbed directly over his head and looked approximately the same from any angle. He was grateful for the few bright stars and planets that sailed through holes in the cloud cover and provided enough light to distinguish rocks and major depressions in the snow. Each time he became unbalanced he fell almost to his knees before he recovered, and each time he had less will to rise.

"How goes it back there?" he asked Heather.

"I'm still here. Are we lost?"

"No. And I don't think we have much farther to go. Why don't you try going to sleep?"

"I hurt too much."

"Do you want a pain pill?" There was only one left.

"No. I don't want to be a junkie."

When Heather grows up, he thought, let us pray her husband never tells her anything he wants her to forget.

Now in his fatigue he was bent nearly double under his load. There were times when he was convinced he had fallen asleep and then awakened to find himself still slogging through the snow. To keep alert, he tried various mental excursions, like repeating the Lord's Prayer. He calculated the distance they had gone and the distance remaining to the town of McDermitt, but the numbers were based on his inexact knowledge of the crash site, and the reckoning proved more discouraging than helpful.

When there seemed to be no conceivable end to his exertions he found distraction in trying to recall parts of the letter. He could remember certain lines verbatim and they seemed to prod his almost total exhaustion. Yet gradually he became aware that his thoughts about the letter were growing more confused. The face he so often visualized in the snow was not the face of the letter writer he had pictured originally. Now she had become a woman he knew well. She spoke to him in phrases apparently set to a metronome, and her voice was sonorous and familiar. Later he discovered that the cadence of his stride had become a slave to her voice.

There came a time in the middle of the night when he could not force his legs to obey his commands for one more step. He stood wavering in the feeble starlight, regretting his weakness all the more because they had come to a barbed-wire fence, and he knew it must lead to somewhere. Now there was something to follow, but he could not follow anything. He knew he must relieve himself of his burden immediately or he would fall face down and that would be the end of things.

At last he dropped to his knees and leaned to one side until the weight of the seat was eased. He slipped off the shoulder straps and told Heather they would rest until morning.

"Why are you whispering, Jerry?"

"I don't know. I just can't talk—"

Still on his knees, he made a shallow place in the snow, and when it was done he pulled the seat away from Heather and eased her into the depression as gently as he could.

She reached out to touch his cheek and said, "You must be very tired, Jerry."

He realized suddenly that she had caressed the disfigured side of his face, the sunken area where the tortured skin stretched drum-tight over the twisted bones and looked so much like half a skull that he had never dared to suppose anyone would touch it.

He started to speak. "I—" But that was as far as he could manage. A new peace took him over; he was serene as he had never been before, but he could not find the words to tell Heather what magic she had performed. My legs are gone, he thought, and I don't care. At least this is the end of loneliness. This is the true life and everything else has been a nightmare. . . .

He adjusted the teddy bear protectively about Heather until only her nose and eyes were visible. He could see in the starlight that her eyes were smiling. Finally he lay down beside her and drew her to him for warmth, and he thought, We love each other. We will not die here.

MORAVIA had fixed noon as the time he would abandon all hope for the occupants of number Fourteen. Once noon had passed he would force himself through the gloomy business of telephoning the girl's relatives. He had already rehearsed his opening lines. "I am extremely sorry to inform you . . . if there is anything the line can do to make things easier . . ." et cetera.

As for Jerry, the man without home or family, what to do? Write a letter to General Delivery, Anywhere, U.S.A.?

The pilot's application lay on the desk before Moravia and now he found it hard to forgive the number of blank spaces he observed. At the time of hiring, of course, no one paid attention to application forms. The applicant's experience was reviewed orally, a far more reliable gauge than mere hours recorded on paper. If a pilot could fly, he could fly, and if he could not, he should not be allowed to kill himself or anyone else.

Yet at times like this, Moravia mused, lack of paperwork was inconvenient. And damn the flying business anyway. The war was long over. People should not die trying to earn a living.

Moravia glanced at the wall clock. Then he checked it against his wristwatch and found they agreed it was thirty-three minutes past eleven. Twenty-seven minutes to sorrow time. Damn! It had been a long morning and it was becoming interminable.

SOMEWHERE in the distance the pilot heard Heather's voice. At first it was almost inaudible, then it grew in volume, and he thought, She has gone cuckoo again and I don't know what to do for delirium. She was back on the same old track about a horse.

"A horse, Jerry! A horse is right over there! Look!"

He rose slowly from the depths of his slumber and opened his eyes to the gray morning. He was confused until he raised his head and realized Heather was shaking him.

She was still shouting. "The horse. Make him come, Jerry!"

He reached out to cover her mouth, his dull wits asking if perhaps this time he would have to seize and hold her tongue to keep her from choking. Somewhere he had read about people strangling in delirium.

Then by chance he looked beyond her and was momentarily convinced he was still asleep. For there was a horse moving across a nearby rise in the terrain and there was a man on the horse.

The pilot pushed himself quickly to his feet and waved his arms and yelled incoherently. The horse stopped and the pilot saw the man turn his head. After a moment the rider took off his wide-brimmed hat and waved it. He seemed to hesitate a long time before he turned the horse.

The pilot continued his own waving and shouting until the horse was kicking up fountains of snow as it sped toward them.

AT NOON Moravia decided to procrastinate one more hour. He was chewing on a peanut butter sandwich at his desk and noted that his already questionable digestion was not improved by the hands on the wall clock. They were stiff reminders of the sixteen remaining minutes before one o'clock.

When his telephone jingled he picked it up and gave his name. Still chewing, he listened; then he stopped chewing as he heard a rancher who identified himself as "Moose" Taylor explain that he was calling at the request of one of Moravia's pilots. He was presently "asleep in my own bed. He is pretty tuckered. I put the little girl on the couch in the front room and the doc is on his way. Her back ain't so good, but our doc is."

After Moravia had determined the exact location of the Taylor ranch and asked what he could do immediately, he was told, "There ain't nothing you can do right now, I guess, except maybe give this fella a couple of days off. He said for me to tell you he would like that, because there is one letter he wants returned to the sender, and he would like to deliver it personally. I dunno what he means by that, but he said it was very important."

"I don't know what it means either," Moravia said. "And I don't care. Just tell him . . . welcome home."

An *"Individualistic Swashbuckler"*

Prodigious energy and enthusiasm for life characterize everything that Ernest Gann does. "I'm about to turn seventy," he says, "but I feel like forty-two." Home for Gann and his wife, Dodie, is Red Mill Farm, a working ranch on San Juan Island off the coast of Washington. Here he raises cattle and grain hay and writes his best-selling novels. But his other activities are legion. He is an accomplished artist, horseback rider, tennis player, and sailor. And he pilots his own plane—a twin-engine Cessna 310.

"I've been flying for forty-four years and I can't imagine *not* being able to fly," the author declares. "I'm most content in the sky, where I feel an eerie sense of peace." He has covered millions of air miles—as a barnstormer, as a commercial pilot, and as a member of Air Transport Command during World War II—and his experiences aloft have inspired much of his writing, notably *The High and the Mighty* and *Fate Is the Hunter*, both Condensed Books selections.

Recently Gann was invited to Beale Air Force Base in California, headquarters of the 99th Strategic Reconnaissance, America's only U-2 squadron. Accompanied by an air force pilot, Gann was permitted to fly a U-2, a thrill he calls "the ultimate consummation of a flying lifetime." So awesome are these high-altitude superspy planes with their sophisticated camera equipment that they are known to the men who fly them as Dragon Ladies. Yet their basic design is simple, almost primitive. Says Gann, "The flight controls are activated by wire cables, just as in a conventional airplane, and there is a bare minimum of black boxes. The pilot 'feels' the airplane rather than senses the simulated inputs of a computer, and he makes judgments and important decisions without help from ground control." In this respect, U-2 pilots—garbed in their orange flight suits and checked scarves—are the contemporary equivalents of the valiant aviators of yesteryear who donned teddy bears and white scarves to fly the mails in open-cockpit planes.

At one point when Gann was at the controls, he took his U-2 to a height of seventy-one thousand feet—"as close," he says wryly, "as I will ever get to paradise. Mountains," he recollects, "were tiny dots, but what held me spellbound was that the curvature of the earth was vaguely apparent." On his return from this adventure, members of the 99th squadron presented him with the coveted black wings worn by U-2 pilots—a rare honor for a civilian.

According to Ernest Gann, the men who fly the Dragon Ladies are "among the last of the individualistic swashbucklers." The same could be said for Gann himself.

PHOTO BY R. SCOTT HOOPER